THE GARDEN OF EMPIRE

Also By J.T. Greathouse

Pact & Pattern
The Hand of the Sun King
The Garden of Empire

To Carisa

THE GARDEN OF EMPIRE

PACT AND PATTERN

BOOK II

J.T. GREATHOUSE

JABberwocky Literary Agency, Inc.

The Garden of Empire

Published in 2022 by JABberwocky Literary Agency, Inc.

Originally published in the UK by Gollancz,
an imprint of the Orion Publishing Group, Ltd.

Cover Art © 2022 Ashley Ruggirello // www.cardboardmonet.com

ISBN 978-1-625675-72-9

JABberwocky Literary Agency, Inc.
49 W. 45th Street, 12th Floor
New York, NY 10036
http://awfulagent.com

Introduction

We should pause, here at the place where the tale begins to be more than mine, and speak of what has transpired, and what is yet to come.

Though there is much of my story yet to tell, it becomes the story of an empire, and a world, and its breaking. Of choices made in ages past and their rippling through the centuries, each choice like a series of sharp notes embrittling a pane of glass until it shatters in resonance with a final, shrieking tone.

Recall, then, the notes played by my own short life.

First, my divided education, given by day to lessons in imperial doctrine and by night to secrets hidden from imperial eyes. The most potent secret of all, my grandmother's magic—forbidden by the conquerors, granted by her people's pact with their gods—kindled in me a thirst for mastery and a chance at freedom. A thirst that led me into the service of the empire, who alone in all the world wielded magic without fear, sanctioned by the will of the emperor.

Second—a bright note decaying into melancholy—my apprenticeship with Hand Usher, who taught me to read the wakes of magic through the world. My disappointment when the canon of imperial sorcery led only to a parcelling-out of power—magic not mine to command but granted to me by the emperor as the lord of a house might grant his steward some small measure of authority—with all the rest hidden behind impenetrable walls. Such walls denied me the power to save the life of Oriole, the governor's son and my first true friend, while he died choking on his own blood, his throat opened by a rebel's knife.

A third note, then, dark in the aftermath of loss, which led me to the oasis city of An-Zabat, where the secrets and struggle of the windcallers eroded the last of my loyalty to the empire. Where the winddancer Atar taught me my first lessons in love and sacrifice, and in heartbreak. My ignorance and arrogance betrayed the secret of her magic to the empire and, in a thundering of grenades, a shriek of tearing silver, and the roar of sandstone crumbling to earth, cost her people their city.

Would that I had stayed with her, upon the deck of her windship, to fight by her side and repay the debt I owed her people. But dreams of fire and the Nayeni wolf-god Okara called me back to my island home, promising a true teacher—a woman of the bones—who might at last part the veil that had been woven between me and the magic I longed to master.

Finding her proved no simple feat. I travelled the length and breadth of Nayen, guided first by the wandering Doctor Sho, who had restored me in childhood from my first foolish brush with magic, and then by a wounded dog wearing the scars of the wolf-god. At last, I found that true teacher in Hissing Cat, who told me of the ancient war between gods and witches, and of the pacts, sealed in flesh, which ended that war by structuring, separating and apportioning magic to the peoples of the world.

Such pacts I wore on my hands and my arms, sealing me with the magic of Nayen and An-Zabat—and Sien, until I cut away the mark of my office, and their magic with it. Each pact granted power, but also constrained it—the price paid by those ancient witches for peace with the gods and a world free from their interference.

That peace had endured for millennia. And that peace—if the wolf-god could be believed—the emperor intended to break. His empire was but a tool to unite the disparate magics of the world under the Sienese canon of sorcery, his Hands and Voices but weapons. His aim, through a clever subversion of his canon, was to empower them with old magics forbidden by the pact with the gods, and in a single breath scour his ancient enemy from the world.

Of course, the gods were not blind and did not long tolerate the threat the empire posed. Another choice, then, in the fourth and final note of my adolescence: to stay with Hissing Cat, seeking understanding for its own sake as I had longed to all my life, or to join with the Nayeni rebellion, led by my uncle and grandmother, to liberate my homeland and strike a blow against the emperor's apocalyptic design.

My decision led me to Greyfrost Keep, to serve as an agent of the rebellion's salvation from a siege led by my old tutor, Usher, now a Voice of the emperor. At the cost of my pact marks and my right hand, I grasped at last powers beyond any ancient pact or imperial canon and severed him from the emperor's gift. In terror and desperation, he shattered himself against a prison of light. Seeing this, his apprentice, Hand Pinion—brother to my lost friend Oriole—led the remnant of their army in retreat and left me to tend to my wounds. And my grandmother's.

While I cradled her and reached deep into the well of healing magic, the gods held council. As the first true witch—a witch of the old sort—in millennia, I threatened them, but as an enemy to the emperor, I might serve their ends. They let me live but forbade me to teach the powers I had discovered.

Their decision sounded a grace note, heralding the next movement in this fraught composition—a movement that would shake the world, perhaps ultimately rending the pane of glass, though I was blind to its consequences then.

I was, after all, new to my power and young in my understanding, but had found at last a cause in which I could believe. One that would carry me first to the heights of mastery and thence to the depths of despair.

But this is no longer only my story. Others played a part in the aftermath of that shattered peace. It is past time their voices joined the song.

Part One
Kindling

Prelude
The Stormfather's Gift

She lies bound in light, her cheek pressed to wood that rasps over sand. She plunges forwards into the blinding chaos the light has made of her mind, grasping for thoughts, for memories, for a way out.

She is Ral Ans Urrera. A child of the Girzan steppe. Born beneath the Belt of the Stars into a thunderstorm that flattens the prairie grasses, into air thick with the screams of storm-frightened horses. Yet she does not cry out. Or so the elders say, when she is young, after the lightning calls her from her mother's tent to dance to the percussion of the rain and thunder, the dizzying thrum of lightning.

She remembers feeling it, more clearly than anything. Like the pulse of a muscle rippling through the air and then through her. Telling her she will be safe from the lightning even as it blasts the earth to glass not half a morning's ride from camp.

As the elders take notice, her mother becomes afraid—first of her, and then for her, once the notion settles in her mind that her daughter might represent a rebirth of old powers thought lost to the grasp of empire.

Ral Ans Urrera remembers nights tied on her back to the saddle, face exposed to the gaze of the Skyfather, to the howl of the wind, the ferocity of the sun, the mercy of clouds and rain. Old traditions, passed down through the generations, though the empire has killed the Stormriders to whom those traditions belonged.

One secret has been kept too closely. The marks that would give her the Stormfather's gift of light and lightning have been lost with the last Stormrider. Yet the elders have hope and train her anyway.

She remembers, with a clarity no blinding light of empire can blot out, the months spent enduring every storm cross-legged upon a sacred flake of shale while lightning burns the air around her. How it makes her hair rise and flutter, her eyes shut and mind open to the threads in the divine tapestry that will one day—if the elders' hopes prove true—be hers to weave. Until at last, with thunder still rumbling in her joints and the jagged light still bright against her eyelids, she reaches out and weaves lightning of her own.

Years pass. She grows into her power, refines herself into a leader as respected as the elders, known beyond the small circle of her tribe, visited by raid leaders, by hunting parties, by horse lords and plains queens.

This, she knows, was her undoing.

Her secret survives as long as it does because Sien takes little interest in the doings of the steppe folk. Since stealing their magic, the empire touches their lives only once a year, when even the farthest flung of the wandering bands sends a drive to the Skyfather's Hall. Tribute in fur and hides and meat, in the bodies of livestock herded into imperial pens. Ral Ans Urrera attends once, after her awakening but before her first success with magic.

She remembers the jagged ridge of the crater wall, the natural fortification forged by the Skyfather himself in an age recalled only in legend. A wall that protects the Stormriders until the empire shatters it and its armies pour through the gap. A wound yet unrepaired. The Voice of the emperor stands on the battlement, surveying the Girzan herds driven through that wide reminder of imperial power, written in cracked and crumbling stone. Ral Ans Urrera remembers most clearly of all—for the memory is recalled by the light that blinds her now—the ribbon of silver that reaches from the Voice's brow and towards the south, heavy as iron, terrifying as the cry of a starving lion.

She carries that terror with her back into the reaches of the steppe, far from the edge of the empire. Her fear strengthens her resolve to find other children like herself who feel the muscles and tendons of the world, to rebuild the Stormriders quietly and beyond the gaze of imperial eyes. That, she believes, will be her people's hope: to one day break the shackle that binds them to the empire.

But word trickles out, rumour flowing through the tribes like rain through runnels, and reaches the empire at last.

They answer with the pounding of hooves, the cut-short cries of children, choking plumes of smoke, the blaze of fires, bolts of lightning—her own and her enemies'—which melt armour and char flesh, the chains of light—the blinding that makes her clumsy when she reaches for her power—and, at last, the hull of the ship. The rasp of sand.

The death of hope.

Why they have not killed her, she cannot begin to guess, nor does she intend to learn. When they arrive at their destination, she will strike back and pray the smouldering flesh of her enemies might be a worthy incense, that the Skyfather might grant her a swift and brilliant death. She paws through the blinding aurora that baffles her mind, reaching for the threads of power, and knows she has found them by the searing pain that pulses through her. She grits her teeth and holds firm. The chains of light are like anything else in the world—only the flexing of a muscle, the bending of the world's sinew. She will break them, as any limb might be broken, and when she is free she will call a thunder to tear the empire from the world.

The deck lurches beneath her. Her eyes flutter open. Her chains cast a ghostly light in the darkness of the hull. Panic grips her throat. For uncountable days the ship has sailed in a straight line. Now it turns, which means they have arrived at their destination. She is out of time.

Her eyes ache as she reaches again into the aurora. The memories that guide her paths to power are muddled, but she finds them, wraps her will around the threads, and swallows a scream.

The light begins to flutter, to soften. She can feel it breaking. The pain rises and falls through her, again and again, flowing down the ridges of her spine, piercing her joints. It cannot stop her. She pulls, and feels the first link in the chain begin to snap.

The world shifts beneath her. Thunder bursts through the bulkhead. Splinters of shattered wood needle her bare arms and legs. Momentum bleeds into rasping sand as the ship eases to a stop.

She blinks against the desert sun glaring off the slopes of dunes. The aft of the ship that bore her lies on its side, dozens of paces away, visible through a gaping hole in the hull framed by planks like shattered teeth.

Yet the chains of light remain.

Clanging steel and the screams of the dying sound from the upper decks, and then are silent. She lies against the bulkhead, breathing softly, as muted words drift down in a language she does not know.

Another shout of pain, and the aurora within her mind is gone as though it had never been. The chains of light fall apart like brittle grass. For a moment she is, in her surprise, too numb to react. She pushes herself upright and stares at the nearby ladder that rises from amid the empty spaces where other cargo should be.

Footsteps. A squealing hinge. The flash of steel in the sunlight, hanging from a silver-threaded sash. The man on the ladder is strange to her. Sun coppered, bright eyed. One of the people of the Waste. He hangs from the ladder by one hand, the other on the handle of his glinting sword, and watches her.

'No need for that,' he says in the trade tongue of her people, though at first his accent confuses his meaning. He points with his chin to her hand, and she realises with a start that she holds a crackling arc of lightning ready to throw.

'You are no Hand.' It is not only an accent; his voice trembles. 'What are you?'

She closes her fist and releases the spell, though holds near to it, ready to destroy herself before she can be made powerless again. Her knees ache but she stands and speaks through the grit in her mouth, the want of water, the exhilaration of freedom and the fear of the unknown, and begins to tell her tale.

1

Harrow Fox
Foolish Cur

I had met my uncle only twice before.

First, as a child. Young enough that time had long since filled the memory with fog. Yet through the mist, his wild eyes glinted sharp, as did the spears of the soldiers who followed after him to search my father's house.

Our second meeting had been only a week ago, in the midst of a siege he had fled and I had broken, casting back the army that would have put an end to his rebellion.

Our third meeting would not be so brief. For the first time in my life, I would sit across from him and we would speak—the severed Hand of the emperor and the notorious rebel Harrow Fox, whose name and legacy had haunted me throughout my imperial career.

The stump of my right wrist cramped and seized as my uncle and his cadre approached Greyfrost Keep. The muted scrape of shovels rang in the crisp winter air. A remnant of the Nayeni army—a bare twenty-seven souls—had spent the last week digging pits in the ash for the blackened bones of the countless Sienese dead felled by the storm of fire, wind, and lightning I had conjured.

A flock of mismatched birds descended upon the courtyard. Ten in total, led by an eagle hawk that burst into a cloud of cinnamon scent, then resolved into my uncle. Harrow Fox rolled back his shoulders, working cramps from the thick muscles of his chest.

I approached as his cadre veered from the shapes of ravens, vultures, owls, and hawks into their natural forms, filling the air with the smell of magic. They stretched battle-hardened limbs beneath patchwork armour stitched with feathers, bones, and shards of stone—fetishes to mark them in a language of identity I might have understood, had I grown up learning Nayeni ways of thought rather than the doctrines of the empire.

'Well met, Sun King.' I bowed deeply at the waist. 'Greyfrost Keep is yours.'

'What remains of it, at least.' Harrow Fox's flint-sharp gaze lingered on me as I stood, marking my obeisance. 'What honours the Sienese is an insult to the Nayeni, Nephew. You would do well to remember that. Where is my mother?'

'In the main hall,' I answered, flushing with embarrassment. 'She awaits us there. Our contest with the imperial sorcerers left her weakened but alive.'

'And cost you a hand.' He nodded towards the stump at the end of my arm.

I wondered if, in giving evidence of my vulnerability, that wound reassured him. He knew little of me, save that I had overcome an imperial legion with powers beyond any ordinary witch—and, in turn, defeated a Voice and two Hands of the emperor. And, of course, that I had served the empire before coming to serve him.

The urge to restore my missing hand swept through me. I could envision the magic, not so different from the healing I had wielded to restore my grandmother from the brink of death and reknit her arm, torn apart when Voice Usher had tortured her with the three powers the empire had stolen from Toa Alon—dowsing, to find a cluster of nerves; cultivation, to force a vine of carrion creeper to grow rapidly through her flesh; and healing, to keep her on this side of death's edge.

I massaged the stump. Memories of Oriole's open throat and the crumbling obelisks of An-Zabat drifted behind my eyes. Arrogance had dealt me many wounds and, through me, shattered the lives of those I held dearest. I could ill afford to let it rule me now. My purpose was to serve my uncle and to see his vision of a free Nayen brought to fruition. I needed to assuage his doubts and fears, not inflame them, no matter what bruises my pride must suffer.

'A small sacrifice compared to your decades of privation and struggle,' I said, resisting the deep-trained urge to bow again. Instead, I gestured towards the doors to the main hall. 'Shall we? Grandmother would like to speak with you, and we have a great deal to discuss ourselves.'

Harrow Fox stroked the grey streak in his beard, then issued swift orders to his cadre. While they called the remnant of the rebel army to muster before the broken gates of Greyfrost, my uncle followed me into the hall.

The bite of winter gave way to the languid warmth of braziers. Hissing Cat loomed over one of them. The glowing coals cast orange light and shadow across the ravens' skulls threaded in her hair. A pile of bovine shoulder blades lay close to one hand, already carved with her questions in the ancient runes that none alive save her could read. The other held a long iron needle, its tip white hot in the coals. My grandmother sat at the table in the centre of the hall, transfixed by the other woman. She started at the bang of the door behind us.

'It is good to see you hale, Son.' My grandmother pushed herself to her feet, bracing herself on the table with her good arm. The other, withered by Usher's torture, hung loose at her side, the fingers flexing one by one. Though I had saved her life and done what I could to restore her health, she seemed reduced, weaker than the warrior witch she had been, who had bested Hand Cinder with veering and flame.

'And you, Mother.' Harrow Fox wrapped her in an embrace, his eyes never leaving Hissing Cat. 'Who is your guest?'

'Just another batty old crone,' Hissing Cat said. She waved the glowing tip of her needle. 'We're starting a knitting circle.'

'This is Hissing Cat, my teacher,' I interjected.

'Ah.' Harrow Fox nodded slowly. 'She taught you to call that storm, I take it.'

'No.' Hissing Cat stabbed her needle back into the coals. 'He collected that bag of tricks on his own. What came after, though, I'm willing to take credit for.'

'We're getting ahead of ourselves.' I pulled out a chair. 'Please, Uncle. Sit.'

Harrow Fox leaned on the table, drumming his fingers. 'You say there are things we should discuss, Nephew. I agree. First, explain what you are doing here.'

My knuckles went white, and I feared the wood of the chair would crack. 'I owe you—and all who would fight the empire—not an explanation but a debt. I have found the power I sought. My hunger for it led me, fool that I was, into imperial service. Now, I would use that power to repay what I owe. To see Nayen free, and an end to the empire and all its cruelty.'

'You said he was ambitious, Mother,' Harrow Fox said. 'I see that has not changed.'

'Ambition is only a failing if one cannot live up to it,' my grandmother answered. 'I have seen what he can do. Sit down, Son, and listen.'

Harrow Fox's lip twitched, but he took the seat I offered. 'No matter how powerful, you are only one man. The emperor has a legion of Hands and Voices, and the Fist that guards him day and night. Perhaps you have uncovered some secret that makes you more than a match for his sorcerers, but can you do battle with them in their thousands? More, are you a match for the emperor himself?'

A sharp crack echoed through the hall, followed by the acrid smell of burning bone. 'He isn't.' Hissing Cat scrutinised the shoulder blade in her lap. 'At least, not yet.'

'There is more at stake than freedom, Uncle. You know that the emperor has reigned for a thousand years, yes? Slowly expanding his reach, swallowing the magics of the conquered and adding them to his canon. Have you ever questioned why he does this?'

'The thousand-year reign is but a Sienese story meant to cow us,' Harrow Fox snarled.

Hissing Cat threw back her head and laughed, a sound like grinding stone rolling up from the roots of a mountain.

'Boy, I count my days from before your first Sun King conceived of a nation called Nayen,' she said. Her eyes caught the glow of the coals. 'I remember when the emperor called himself Tenet and fancied himself a poet. I watched him melt the better half of a continent down into a single language and a single way of life. Your little rebellion is hilarious to me, like a pin scratching at the flank of a lion serpent. Be grateful you have yet to rouse his ire. Tell the Toa Aloni, or the Sienese petty kings, or the gods themselves that the thousand-year reign is *but a story* and see how they laugh in your face.'

Harrow Fox's hands curled into fists, his hackles high. 'Nephew, are you certain this crone is on our side?'

'I'm on my own side,' Hissing Cat smiled. 'For the moment, our interests align. I'd rather the world not end. How about you?'

At last, he turned his attention back to me. Though a duel between us could only end in my victory, I felt cowed by those hard eyes, so comfortable with violence. 'That is what the emperor plans? To end the world?'

'He means to avenge himself against the gods.' I gestured to Harrow Fox's right hand and the subtle scars that were the mark of his power. 'Those represent an agreement to save the world from the chaos of war between witches and gods. The emperor was there when the agreement was made, as was Hissing Cat.'

At this, Hissing Cat waved and grinned, then reached for a fresh shoulder blade.

'In exchange for the gods' retreat from the world, the witches agreed to weaken themselves. The pact marks carved as a result grant a limited ability with magic—fire and veering, or mastery of wind and water, or the power to heal the body and speed the growth of vegetation—but more important than the power granted is the *limit*. A witch bearing a mark is dulled to magics beyond their own pact, even if their natural sensitivity and talent might allow far more. Thus the gods would no longer rend the world with their war, and the witches would pose no threat to them.

'But Tenet conceived of a way around this limitation. He chose for the magic of his pact the power to transmit thoughts from one mind to another. This he used not only to unite his empire but to grant his servants the powers of other pacts. So long as his empire has conquered the people to whom those magics belong, he might add them to his canon of sorcery, conveying the knowledge of how to wield them to his servants without violating the agreement with the gods.'

Harrow Fox stared at me, fingering his beard, absorbing all that I had said. Deciding, perhaps, whether to believe my story.

'And you think the emperor will fail?' he asked at last.

'The gods will not stand idly by,' I answered. 'Some would strike now, but others believe his reach exceeds his grasp, that the project of his empire will fail before it reaches completion. The wolf god Okara is among the former. He would have us disrupt the emperor's plans before the gods agree to resume their war.'

My uncle leaned back in his seat and folded his hands across the broad plane of his chest. 'And you know this because they speak to you, as they spoke to the first Sun King.'

I opened my mouth to protest, but he pressed on.

'An eagle hawk's eyes and ears are sharp.' He planted his palms on the table and leaned towards me. 'I heard whispers from those soldiers you've set to burying the bones of our enemies. They speak of you as a miracle worker, as one sent by the gods to liberate this island. In the few days of my absence, they have stitched charred scraps of that shattered forest to their jerkins—fetishes not to reflect their own histories, but to show their loyalty. Not to the rebellion, but to you, as though you were a god made flesh.

'Do you know what I think, Nephew?' His finger rose and stabbed at me. 'I think the hierarchy of the empire corralled your ambition, and so you have come here to pursue it to the hilt. How better to wrest control of an army than by swooping in and saving it from certain doom? How better to consolidate that control than with a tale that lends your leadership divine purpose and the weight of the world's salvation?'

'Is his power not testament to the truth of what he says?' My grandmother's voice hardened in my defence. She raised her withered arm, grunting when it seized. 'Do you see this? He has no marks of any pact, yet he brought me back from the edge of death.'

'The best lies are built upon a cornerstone of truth.' The muscles of my uncle's arms were taut as cables, as though he might at any moment reach for his swords. 'He has some secret knowledge, I am sure, but he twists it to his own purposes.'

His words struck like knives. How often in my short life had I armoured myself in half-truths? Yet now I came to him honestly, and to be accused of past sins when I had resolved to put them behind me wounded my heart.

A silence held between us, broken by the rattling of the skulls in Hissing Cat's hair and her slow, rumbling chuckle. We all turned towards her. She looked up from the brazier.

'Don't mind me,' she said. 'I was just thinking about how much I miss my cave. Lovely paintings. The quiet. You know.'

I took a deep breath. 'What can I do to convince you?'

He held his palms upright, like the bowls of a scale. 'This is Nayen, Nephew. There is no hierarchy of empire to dictate who should stand above whom, only the scales of power and prestige.' He lowered his right hand and raised the left. 'You hold knowledge I lack. Your strength in magic is greater. There is an imbalance between us. One which dictates that you, and not I, should lead, though I, and not you, have dedicated my life to this struggle. Shift the balance in my favour.'

'Gladly,' I said. 'How?'

He closed his hands and lowered them to the table. 'Teach me to wield the old magic as you do. Let us fight side by side as equals, at the least.'

Hissing Cat's bark of laughter echoed with the parting words of Tollu, the wolf-daughter, Nayen's goddess of wisdom, as the gods held council to decide my fate. *If he teaches the old magic, his life will be forfeit.*

'I am not jesting.' Harrow Fox pointed to his witch marks, heat rising in his face. 'If all you have said is true, I need only carve away these scars and I, too, will be free to call down storms of wind and lightning, no?'

'It is not as simple as that,' I began. The muscles in his jaw rippled with mounting fury.

'You ask for the one thing he cannot offer,' Hissing Cat said, still smiling cruelly in the aftermath of laughter. 'And there's no telling whether or not you would even have the capacity. The old magic is not like the new. It is fickle and bound by no rite of initiation.'

'But I *could* do as the emperor has done,' I blurted. 'Create a canon and transmit my power to others. I have no desire to hoard it, Uncle, but offer it freely in service of the rebellion.'

'Bah!' Hissing Cat rose to her feet, her voice stripped of mirth, casting a long shadow across the hall. 'Pure idiocy! If you could even manage it!'

'For the first time, the crone and I agree.' My uncle crossed his arms and studied me, as though searching for thorns around a piece of tempting fruit. 'You have said yourself that the emperor wields his sorcerers as weapons. Doing likewise will only weigh the scale more heavily in your favour.'

'What if I could make a canon outside of myself?' The words leapt from my mouth before I had truly considered them, my subconscious mind—that constant traitor—piecing ideas together in desperation. If my uncle rejected me, as the empire had rejected me, to where else in the world could I turn? 'The pacts rely on no transmission. I could make something like them, a means to grant the power to call the wind or heal wounds. To create witches to match Sienese sorcerers, but free from my interference.'

My arrogance and my hunger for magic had shattered countless lives. I could never trust myself to rule, nor to command a canon of sorcery. But I could make one and pass it on, giving the Nayeni the magic they needed to free their homeland. And perhaps, if I could win their trust, they might aid me in subverting the emperor's plan to wage war against the gods. More, I could earn a place beside them, as one of them. The place I might have found if I had followed my grandmother into the mountains rather than chasing the treacherous golden path of imperial service.

If I had only hesitated, given this wild plan another moment's thought before offering it to my uncle, how much might I have lessened the suffering to come?

Harrow Fox tilted his head. 'Crone, you know his capacity. Is this a thing he can truly do?'

'Not without my help,' Hissing Cat fumed. 'That, or fumbling like a babe in the dark for a few dozen years, grasping for layers of magic he hasn't yet brushed with his fingertips.'

'Will you help him?'

A line of tension held between Harrow Fox, Hissing Cat, and I. She looked at the shoulder blade in her lap, sneered, and tossed it back onto the pile.

'We may well need something like this to challenge Tenet,' she muttered, 'but giving power is a far more fraught business than seeking it.'

'Very well, then.' Harrow Fox's chair scraped the stone floor as he stood. 'I will leave you to your work and tend to mine. This army—such as it is—must be made ready to march. The empire is on the back foot. We will not waste this opportunity.'

My grandmother brought her good arm to her collarbone in salute. I mimicked her, while Hissing Cat snorted and stirred the coals with her needle. Harrow Fox lingered a moment longer, his fingers still touching the tabletop as he examined me.

'Mark me, Foolish Cur,' he said. 'As long as you serve the cause of Nayeni liberation, I will count you an ally. The moment I have reason to fear your betrayal, I will not hesitate. You may be stronger than me, but I would sooner die than give way to another tyrant like the emperor, no matter his blood.'

'I have no intent to become a tyrant,' I said, taken aback.

He rapped his knuckles on the table, narrowed his eyes, and swept from the room with no further word. The echoes of his footsteps and the slamming of the door hung heavy in the hall. Words of protest swirled within me, unspoken, leaving me unsettled.

He had accepted my help. That was a first step. Now I needed to deliver what I had promised. Perhaps then he would learn to trust me.

'Come along, Cur.' Hissing Cat had abandoned her brazier and now walked towards a shadowed door in the far corner of the room. 'We should have a conversation of our own.' She inclined her head towards my grandmother. 'In private.'

'Oh, don't mind me,' my grandmother muttered, flexing her withered arm. 'I understand the need to teach secret lessons far from prying ears.'

I followed Hissing Cat down a dark hallway and a crumbling stairwell into a wide room with low ceilings. A fire smouldered in a circle of stones, waging a pitiful battle against the damp chill in the air. Marks and stains on the floor and walls spoke of a history of barrels and crates, some reduced by time and decay to smears of blackened dust. The shards of some dozen shattered shoulder blades littered one corner of the room.

'You idiot!' Hissing Cat snarled. She held out a finger, and the iron spike of her will drove into the pattern of the world. A tongue of flame danced in her hand, casting off cinnamon scent and filling my bones with phantom warmth. 'Extinguish the flame, if you can.'

The old test, which I had failed dozens of times until finally overcoming it in battle with Voice Usher. Now, as then, I descended into the pattern of the world, becoming as a sphere of jade in the heart of the eternal interchange of birth and death, light and shadow, the rising and setting of the sun. One with the pattern, I reached out towards the weight of the flame she had created, a violent intrusion upon the natural flow. The walls of the emperor's canon had crumbled at my touch, swallowed up and scattered, leaving Usher without his sorcery. The fire in Hissing Cat's hand would crumble just the same.

My will splashed against hers, a single drop of rain upon a towering mountain.

Frustration echoed from afar, disturbing the tranquillity of mind that came from wielding the old magic. I had mastered this, hadn't I? And with it the power I would need to overcome the emperor and his sorcerers. I shut my eyes and hurled myself at her will. She would *not* unmake all my hope so easily.

For the briefest moment I felt the spike shift, like a splinter slowly pushed out by healing flesh. Hissing Cat grunted, and then power descended like nothing I had felt since kneeling before the emperor and his Thousand-Armed Throne.

The spike became a blade as hard as imperial steel, driving for the heart of the pattern. Feverish heat swept through me. I opened my eyes, gasping, expecting to see the flame in her hand raging like a forest fire. It flickered, gentle as a candle flame, unchanged but for the weight of will behind it.

'Tenet's attention is always scattered to the far corners of his empire,' Hissing Cat said, her wrinkles deepened by flickering shadows. 'You disrupted his transmission before he noticed what you were doing. Don't think that trick will work again.'

She closed her fist, extinguishing the flame. As the flush and weight in the wake of her magic faded, weakness gripped my knees.

'You look sick, Foolish Cur,' she said. 'And you should. You've just promised to help your uncle fight a war he hasn't a hope of winning, and to give him a gift that, if given poorly, will shackle him with a curse. Do you have any notion of how to begin crafting a canon? Even I have little notion of how it might be done. Tenet alone in all the world's history has made such a thing. And you yourself rejected it for the prison it truly is.'

I rolled my shoulders back, trying to project confidence I did not truly feel. She was right. I had no idea how to make good on my promise to Harrow Fox, but I had no choice but to try. The rebellion—and any hope I had to earn my uncle's acceptance—depended upon my success. 'I know I am no match for the emperor, but you are. You must be. With your help and guidance, I will find a way. And my canon will be no prison. I mean to give magic freely, not bind it to my will.'

Hissing Cat snorted. 'As though that were possible. You speak with such certainty of things you do not understand. Five hundred years ago, maybe, I might have matched my strength to Tenet's, but I've been lurking in a cave all that time while he's been building an empire. If we took him by surprise, or you held his attention, I might stand a chance of overpowering him. But even that is no sure thing.'

I swallowed bile. 'You said you would help.'

'In time, when you are strong enough and I have regained more than a fragment of what I once was, we will make an army of our own and do what me must. But there is a great deal of the world left for Tenet to conquer. We have time, Cur, before he begins his war.'

'Then why are you here, if not to fight?' I demanded.

'You're the first witch of the old sort in a thousand years,' she snapped back. 'I don't know *why* the pattern saw fit to spit you out, but I'm not going to let you get yourself killed fighting in a doomed rebellion.'

I seethed, terror and frustration mingling, becoming a potent fuel for my anger. 'If you intend to keep me alive, you will need to fight beside me.'

The grey cloud of her hair seemed to crackle, as though ready to hurl lightning. Her mouth twitched and her eyes narrowed to pinpricks.

'I could go back to my cave, Cur,' she said, her voice a whisper like the first distant crash of thunder. 'You'll bash yourself to death against Tenet's will, and I will laugh at your foolishness.'

'We all die.' I summoned all of my courage in the face of her fury. 'At least my death will mean something while you wither away to dust and bones in your pitiful buried temple.'

Her body twitched, her face rippling in the wake of some hidden battle. I thought she might raise a hand and scour me from the world. Instead, a low rumble of laughter built in her chest till it echoed in that small stone-walled room.

'You fought the gods once,' I said. 'Where is that courage now, Hissing Cat?'

She scowled. 'Lost to the depths of regret and time. And that was a war fought with weapons we can no longer wield. We are trying to *stop* a war with the gods, Cur, not spur them into one.'

'The gods are on my side!' I held the momentum of the conversation now, and seized upon it, as though I were back in my father's garden bandying questions of doctrine with my tutor, Koro Ha, not debating the fate of the world with a witch who could snap me in half with a thought. 'We fight their enemy. They will surely forgive the use of any power to that end.'

She took a slow, deep breath and shook her head. 'You leap ahead into dangers you hardly understand, trusting in beings you *cannot* comprehend. Come back to the cave with me. Caution is not the opposite of courage but its ally.'

Arrogance buries its roots deep. No matter how we think it is weeded from us, it springs back anew, masking itself with the flower of benevolent purpose.

'I abandoned my people once to serve the empire. I will not abandon them again. We will stay and fight beside them. Nayen's liberation will be the foothold we use to break the empire and all of Tenet's plans.'

'Will it now?' The ravens' skulls in her hair rattled as she shook her head. 'I suppose I can either help you, abandon you, or kill you where you stand.' A shiver rippled through me. She grinned at my discomfort and shrugged. 'Only one choice might put a wrinkle in Tenet's plans.'

The tension in my shoulders began to loosen. 'You will stay, then, and fight with us?'

She harrumphed and slumped down beside her fireplace, her furs pooling around her crossed legs. 'Oh, I'll stay. At least until you butt up against the walls of your own idiocy and are ready to listen to wisdom.' She stirred the coals back to life. 'But know this, Cur—no mere imperial career or glimpse of magic is at stake, now. We contend with powers that once birthed mountains and boiled seas.'

My next word might have been the breath of wind that sent her willingness to support me—so precariously balanced on the edge of a cliff—tumbling to its destruction. But I had the good sense to leave her there, with her fire and her bones, and her promise, however reluctant, of co-operation.

Unsettled by a pair of fraught conversations, I went in search of the one place I thought to find comfort.

During our week-long stay at Greyfrost, Doctor Sho had converted one of the few rooms in decent repair into a makeshift infirmary. Bedrolls and blankets left behind by those who had died defending the keep now kept their wounded comrades warm. In the aftermath of the battle, I had healed dozens of wounds with magic, though most of our patients had needed only rest and rejuvenating herbs to restore them. There were three, however, who had lain unconscious while I knit their bones and sealed their weeping flesh, and had yet to wake.

Doctor Sho knelt over one such young woman when I arrived, supporting her head while he tipped a cup of warm tea to her slack lips. At his heel, the dog we had saved from the brutality of an imperial patrol—and who had, for a time, played host to Okara, his divine namesake—perked up at my approach. Okara rubbed against my leg, tongue lolling, while I scratched his ears.

'I didn't hear any explosions, so I'm assuming things went fairly well with your uncle,' Doctor Sho said by way of greeting, not looking up from his task.

'Well enough,' I muttered. 'We're to march tomorrow.'

Doctor Sho dabbed tea and spittle from his patient's mouth, then sighed and ran a hand through the wispy cloud of his hair. 'I thought I had seen my last of war a lifetime ago.'

Guilt twisted in my chest. For the better part of the last year, Doctor Sho had been my constant companion while we traversed the length of Nayen—a rare ray of friendship to pierce the dark cloud of my lonely life. To drag such a peaceful man into violence felt like a profound betrayal, but the thought of leaving him behind made me ache with regret.

Before I could muddle through these feelings, let alone give them voice, he began stowing sacks of herbs, his mortar and pestle, and a few small metallic tools of uncertain purpose into the drawers of his medicine chest. 'We'll need to craft some stretchers for our patients. I'm not monstrous enough to leave them behind. Go find some spear shafts. They'll do once you break the blades off.'

Gratitude welled in me, drowning my guilt. 'Of course,' I said, ashamed by the hitch in my voice. 'And thank you.'

Doctor Sho looked up, his brow furrowing above dark, timeless eyes that had watched the advance of the empire from its founding.

Once, in childhood, he had warned me away from my hunger for magic, painfully aware of what it would cost me. I had been too arrogant then, and ignorant, to heed it. Perhaps a second warning, delivered at Greyfrost, potent with the mystery that swirled around him, might have turned me from my ruinous course.

Instead, he opened his mouth, closed it, and nodded sharply. And so I went in search of spear shafts, believing in my ignorance that I might lead this little army to victory, liberation, and the empire's end.

2

Impossibility
Hand Pinion

Certain things were supposed to be impossible. The sun could not rise from the west, nor could it set in the east. The dead could not rise from their graves. No magic could overcome the will of the emperor.

And yet Wen Alder, the severed Hand, had torn apart the canon of sorcery as though it were wet paper.

Pinion felt his soldiers' eyes as he led them in humiliation down switchbacks they had ascended only days ago. Then, their banners had fluttered bright. Marching songs had risen from a forest of spears. Though they had traversed fields of snow to do battle in the dead of winter, there had been a sense of purpose and a certainty of victory behind every step they took.

Riding at the head of that column, beside Voice Usher and Hand Cinder, Pinion had understood, if only for a moment, his brother Oriole's love for the gallantry of warfare. A fascination that had allowed Wen Alder—the traitor—to lure Oriole to Iron Town, where he had died.

The clop of hooves rose above the shuffling march of soldiers. Captain Huo, Pinion's second in command, reined in beside him and brought his fist to his chest in salute.

'Hand, it grows dark.' Huo's voice carried wisps of frosty vapour. 'Might it be time to find a level place to camp?'

Pinion took in the deepening twilight with surprise. He had left Alder standing over the corpse of Voice Usher only moments ago, yet the better half of a day had passed since. The company had been marching without food or rest. Yet when he attended to his own stomach, he felt no hunger, only a churning nausea and long-simmering fear beneath the cold seeping through the fur of his coat.

'No, Captain. We will press on to Burrow.'

Huo straightened in his saddle. A slight twitch in his brow betrayed disagreement, yet an ordinary man, no matter his rank, did not question a Hand of the emperor. Not even a Hand who, in an act of pure cowardice, had abandoned certain victory.

'Your Excellency,' Huo said, a strain in his voice, 'the men need to eat and sleep. We are fortunate that there is no snowfall, but the night is cold. We need time to prepare a proper camp—build fires, get something warm into their bellies. Burrow is half a day's march yet.'

Pinion straightened in his saddle. Huo was no more than five or six years his senior, but that time showed on his hard, weather-beaten features. Beside him, Pinion felt childish, as though he were still learning to sit a horse in his father's garden, not commanding a legion.

'I did not ask for your advice, Captain.' Pinion made his voice flat and hard, mimicking the tone his father used when some minor official had bungled his duties. 'We press on to Burrow.'

A long, steadying breath curled from the captain's crooked, oft-broken nose before he spoke again. 'We are not pursued, Your Excellency. And if we were, the survivors of Greyfrost—'

'I do not care,' Pinion snapped. Anger made his shoulders tight. He glared at Huo for a moment longer, getting himself under control. 'I have given an order, Captain. It will be followed.'

'Of course, Your Excellency.' Huo's salute was no less sharp, despite the frustration creasing his face. He wheeled his horse and trotted back down the line, announcing the order to press the march to Burrow.

A few hushed groans rose from the column, each one stabbing Pinion with shame. The few survivors of Greyfrost were no threat to his soldiers, and they knew it. And while they had seen the fire and wind that had left so many of their fellows dead and scattered before the walls of the fortress, they had seen, too, Wen Alder and his witch grandmother brought low.

But *they* had not felt the wake of that fire and wind, nor felt the canon of sorcery stripped away, nor seen Voice Usher's blackened corpse.

Pinion had gone to Greyfrost seeking an answer. The answer Oriole deserved. Alder had offered him comfort at his brother's grave and asked for comfort in return. Kindness like the petals of a rose, drawing the eye from wicked thorns.

Does this seem right to you? Pinion had planned to ask when Alder lay broken and chained. *Did it seem right to betray first my brother and then the empire that gave you everything?* Now, another question would need to be added: *Did it seem right to kill Usher, your mentor?*

But in order to pry that explanation from the severed Hand, Pinion would need power. Magic, yes, and the whole might of the empire behind him.

The sharp cry of an eagle hawk sounded from the forest. Pinion scanned the skies and reached for magic, flailing in the emptiness, shrinking back from the unbridled power his mind brushed against. Those depthless pools promised only chaos. Without the canon of sorcery and its guidance, he was as likely to burn himself to ash as conjure any defence. Soon, he told himself, the column would be near enough to Setting Sun Fortress for him receive the canon from Voice Age-of-Plenty, who governed there. And so they would press on.

Before anything else, he had to survive.

A s Pinion's exhausted company came upon the town of Burrow, the first light of dawn cast the snowy ground in sharp, glittering blue. Most of the soldiers collapsed half a dozen paces from the side of the road, hacking away bits of underbrush to make space for their bedrolls while their sergeants barked perfunctory orders to clear away the snow and build fires.

Pinion followed Captain Huo and an honour guard to the magistrate's house. They dismounted in the courtyard beside glowing braziers that stood in circles of melted snow. Pinion handed his reins to a sleepy groomsman and fought the urge to join his guardsmen as they warmed their frigid knuckles over the coals. A Hand could no more indulge in so open a display of discomfort than accept the dishonour of sleeping on the ground.

Voice Usher had never put much weight on such notions of propriety. But he was a Voice, renowned for his skill and wit. Pinion yet needed to prove himself, and so he stood away from the fire, shivering at the edge of the circle of warmth.

He had to endure only a handful of moments before Magistrate Lu Clear-River appeared in the doorway of the main house, flanked by three members of the town garrison. Pinion remembered him from the journey north, a short man with the dark colour and reddish hair that marked his Nayeni heritage in unsettling contrast to his silk robes and scholar's cap. His sleeves rippled as he chafed his hands together against the cold, but he otherwise presented the polished posture expected of a Sienese magistrate, even if one of barbarian provenance.

'Your Excellency.' Clear-River bowed, then straightened after Pinion acknowledged the obeisance with a short nod. 'We did not expect you to return so swiftly. Are Voice Usher and Hand Cinder still at Greyfrost?'

Pinion suppressed a sudden flare of hatred towards the man. He walked stiffly past Clear-River and folded his hands into the sleeves of his coat, lest their shaking give away either his rage or the cold that gripped him. 'My men are bivouacking outside your walls. Have them fed and resupplied by noon.'

'Of course, Hand Pinion,' Clear-River said, dipping his head again, holding a dozen unspoken questions behind his shrewd gaze. The same shape and shade of eye that had once studied him over Oriole's grave.

Pinion wanted nothing more than to collapse beneath warm blankets and sleep as long as caution allowed, but the very danger Pinion fled would fall upon Burrow soon enough. These people deserved the chance to escape. 'Voice Usher and Hand Cinder are dead.'

Captain Huo coughed deep in his throat, not expecting the tragedy at Greyfrost to be presented so bluntly. Clear-River blinked back surprise.

Pinion continued. 'Wen Alder, the severed Hand whom you allowed to pass through Burrow, overcame them. And before you protest, I do not fault you. Had you attempted to stop him, I suspect this town would be but a smear of ash and old blood. Voice Usher underestimated his strength. Wen Alder leads the remnant of the rebel force at Greyfrost. We will need reinforcements to face him.'

'Are you pursued?' Clear-River asked nervously. 'Do you intend to make a stand here?'

Pinion bristled at the questions. Clear-River would not have dared ask them of Voice Usher or Hand Cinder. 'We are of an age, Magistrate Lu, but in the great family of empire I am your elder brother.'

'Of course.' Clear-River dipped his head again. A few curls of hair came loose from beneath his cap. 'I apologise for any impudence, Your Excellency. My surprise at your arrival briefly overtook my good sense. It will not happen again.'

'How many in the garrison?' Pinion snapped.

'Sixty-five men, Your Excellency, including my household guard.'

Not nearly enough. He had known that would be the case, hadn't he? His head felt full of fog—a consequence of the bitter cold and the long march. 'They will withdraw with us when my company moves on.'

'What—?' Clear-River swallowed the rest of that question. 'There are still bandits in the highlands, Your Excellency.'

'Who will be joining forces with the rebellion before long,' Pinion said. 'We thought to grind them to paste at Greyfrost, but we no longer have the advantage in magic. Better to withdraw and survive to fight when it will matter.'

'To Setting Sun Fortress,' Clear-River said, careful not to inflect the words as a question.

'Where are your guest rooms?' Pinion cast about the strange interior of the magistrate's house. It was built in the Nayeni style, like a great box surrounding an inner courtyard. 'The captain and I should sleep for a few hours.'

'Of course, Your Excellency.' Clear-River gestured to one of his guardsmen. 'Lieutenant Pa will show you the way.'

Huo snapped a quick salute. 'If it's all the same, Your Excellency, I would bivouac with the men.'

Seeing their captain enduring those same conditions would hearten the men after the forced march in winter, or at the very least ease their resentment. Yet Pinion bristled. Every one of Huo's suggestions, no matter how reasonable, felt like a bid to undermine him.

'Very well,' Pinion said at last. 'Post a minimal watch. I do not expect the rebels to pursue us yet, and the men will need their sleep.'

Huo saluted again and left. Pinion followed Clear-River's guard up the stairwell, his leaden calves burning with each step. A brazier had already been lit and filled the guest room with a steady warmth. He stripped off his coat and armour and left it piled by the door. When a servant appeared with a tray of food and a silver basin of steaming water, Pinion peeled out of his travelling robe and washed his chest and arms. The warm water had been scented with citrus peel—an extravagance in winter, obviously meant to honour him, but which left Pinion all the more incensed by Clear-River's impudent questioning. Washing eased the chill in his muscles but did nothing for the fear coiled in his stomach. He ate only a few bites of the rich-smelling fare—bean curd in a thick pork sauce over rice—before collapsing onto the bed.

Reaching for sleep proved as futile as reaching for the canon of sorcery. He lay awake, listening to servants' feet on the floorboards beyond his room, voices echoing up from the courtyard, and the crackling of fires in hearths. At last, the exhaustion gripping his limbs began to drag him down to sleep. His thoughts swam. His fear uncoiled.

He managed perhaps a dozen heartbeats of rest before a wake of sorcery fell upon him, heavy and solid as the roots of a mountain.

<Hand Pinion,> a voice said, speaking into his mind as thunder echoes through the sky.

The fear returned, coiled tighter than before, till Pinion felt he would vomit. He sat bolt upright, casting aside blankets and gasping in the sudden cold. The emperor had spoken into his mind, as though he were a Voice.

'Your Majesty,' he said to the empty room, then rose from the bed and fell prostrate, shivering in the cotton robe he had worn to sleep. He had been in the emperor's presence only once before, when he and Oriole had accompanied their father to an audience in Centre Fortress. Now, as then, he pressed his forehead to the floor. 'What have I done to deserve this honour?'

<There is no need to speak. Your very thoughts are mine to hear.>

The emperor's attention passed through Pinion's mind as a wave of pressure, pulling memories into focus. In flashes as quick as the flutter of a moth's wings, he recalled the battle at Greyfrost. The storm of fire, lightning, and wind. The witches' escape. Cinder's throat torn open. Alder, bound and then—impossibly—free. Usher's blackened, smoking flesh. Pinion fought down nausea at the horror of those moments, as real as when he had lived him.

The weight of the emperor's attention lessened. <A debacle. But a salvageable one. You will fortify this township. Reinforcements will come from Setting Sun Fortress.>

Horror boiled into panic. 'Your Majesty,' Pinion said, then remembered the emperor's instruction not to speak. He conjured the thoughts as though to give them voice but let them die in his throat. <Far be it from me to question your wisdom.>

<Yet you do,> the emperor said. <I see the objection even now. I do not fault you your fear. Even I did not expect the severed Hand to reach such depths of power so quickly, but I will be ready for his tricks this time.>

<You surely will be, Your Majesty,> Pinion replied. <Sadly, as Traveller-on-the-Narrow-Way wrote, the greatest craftsman can never achieve his aim with imperfect tools.>

There was silence, for a time. The great heaviness of the emperor's transmission gripped every nerve of Pinion's body, holding him to the floor, all but naked, shivering, his palms going numb against the floorboards. Then a ripple moved through him, like a breath of wind on a hanging silk.

<Amusing. Your point is well taken, Hand Pinion. Nevertheless, I will not allow this threat to the empire to stand. You will await reinforcements in Burrow.>

The weight began to lessen as the emperor withdrew, leaving Pinion with orders that would surely see him and all his men to their deaths.

Guilt stabbed at him. Did he lack faith in the emperor's power? No. Only in his own. Even aided by the emperor himself, there was a chance that Pinion would not survive to pry his answers from Alder.

'This is an opportunity,' he blurted, the words leaving his mouth at the speed of thought.

The weight of the emperor's attention returned. Clear-River's questioning of a Hand had been an insult; to question the emperor shattered all notions of propriety. It bordered on treason. Yet Pinion pressed on, his heart thundering.

He had the presence of mind, at least, to convey the words without speaking. <Ever since the conquest, rebellion has plagued this country. When one fire is extinguished, another springs up in its place. But Wen Alder has given us a chance to stamp out every ember in a single blow. After Greyfrost, the rebels will rally behind the severed Hand. Not only those who already wage war against us, but those who sympathise with their fight.>

The plan began to build in his mind. A way to survive long enough to see Alder brought low, and a way to justify actions that would seem like cowardice at best and madness at worst.

<Is that all?>

<No, Your Majesty.> Pinion told himself that the texture of the emperor's attention had changed, that there was a vein of curiosity somewhere in that mountainous weight. An absurd thought, for the emperor—who knew all—to feel curiosity. Yet he felt the weight of the emperor's mind scrutinising his thoughts, leafing through them like the pages of a book, reading not only the half-conceived plan he had been about to propose but the cowardice that motivated it. He shuddered and tried to tamp down his revulsion. Already he had questioned the emperor; to contest the imperial right to peruse a subject's mind would surely invite his death.

Pinion braced himself against the floor, his hands and forehead numb. His breath came in shallow, frigid gasps while he waited for the emperor to condemn him for his impudence or kill him with a burst of magic delivered from halfway across the world.

<By your father's account, your brother was the one interested in strategy and tactics, yet it seems you have some talent for it as well,> the emperor said at last. His attention began to recede. <Very well. Lead your withdrawal. Should this scheme of yours succeed, I will commend you personally when we meet face to face at Eastern Fortress.>

The weight of transmission fell from Pinion's body, leaving him at once exhausted and light of limb. His thoughts were ajumble, like the smeared lines of a child's first practice at calligraphy. He had challenged the emperor, and he had won.

That, too, should have been an impossibility.

His astonishment had no time to settle before an equally stunning realisation struck. The emperor had implied that he would personally lead the punitive army to Nayen.

To Pinion's knowledge, the emperor had not left Centre Fortress since crushing the stonespeakers of Toa Alon. He had levelled their sacred city of Sor Cala and buried it beneath a mountain. What doom had Pinion, in his plotting, summoned to Nayen?

It did not matter as long as he survived and Alder was left broken and defeated, forced to answer for all the pain he had caused.

Alder would learn the cost of betrayal, and in the end it would all, at last, feel right.

3
An Offer
Koro Ha

'Once more,' Koro Ha said, tapping the side of his head with the handle of a writing brush. 'What are the three pillars of the empire?'

Bo Spring-Happiness, his student of the past two years, stared back at him wearing a familiar mask of bold, blank gormlessness.

'I just finished reading the passage from Traveller-on-the-Narrow-Way aloud.' Koro Ha took a breath to steady his voice. Anger never motivated any pupil to the heights of success. 'If you would be so kind, young Master Spring-Happiness, to cast your mind five minutes into the past, you might find there the answer you seek.'

The boy blinked at him. 'I can't remember.'

Koro Ha shut his eyes. Teaching the boy was like teaching a stone. No wonder the boy's father had been willing to pay so well. He had even promised a pension and retirement house should Spring-Happiness pass the imperial examinations.

Thrice in his life, Koro Ha had completed a ten-year tutorship and begun again with a fresh pupil. The transition from dredging the depths of the finer points of Sienese doctrine with a bright, well-read youth back to the company of a seven-year-old in need of the most basic instruction had always been difficult. The transition from teaching Wen Alder to Bo Spring-Happiness was like drinking nothing but the finest tea for a decade, only to find one's cup then refilled from a pig trough.

He wondered how Alder was doing, now two years into his apprenticeship with Hand Usher. Koro Ha paid close attention to any news out of Nayen and had heard rumblings of rebellion in the north—the notorious bandit Frothing Wolf, still skulking about the highlands—but nothing of the first Nayeni Hand. A good thing, he supposed. It ought to be another half-decade yet before Alder was sent off on his own to administer some colony or serve the emperor in the heartland.

He felt a twang of self-pity and a lingering resentment, one he thought he'd long put to rest after decades but now stirred again by his pupil's unprecedented success. First Hand of the emperor from Nayen. Where was the first Hand from Toa Alon, then, so much older a colony?

Ah, well. Old regrets and old injustices would do nothing to make his immediate situation any easier to bear. He opened his eyes to find Bo Spring-Happiness digging deep in his sinuses. The boy's eyebrows shot up. Koro Ha watched, revolted and astonished, as the offending finger eased its way out of the boy's nostril, trailing a ribbon of slime, and towards his upper lip.

'Master Koro Ha!' A blessed voice echoed through the stand of bamboo that isolated the Pavilion of Grace and Harmony from the myriad distractions that readily stole Spring-Happiness's attention from his studies—such as servants doing laundry, or sparrows pecking on the paths, or any noise or visible motion whatsoever. This once, Koro Ha was grateful for the distraction.

'Go wash your hand in the pond, young Master Spring-Happiness,' Koro Ha said.

The boy stared up at him, eyes widening with a glimmer of hope. 'Do I have to come back for more lessons?'

Koro Ha sighed and shook his head. Spring-Happiness shot to his feet and dashed down the pavilion steps towards the main house, nearly tripping over his robe. On his way he passed Steward Rin, who watched the boy with concern as he continued shuffling down the path.

'Done for today, Master Koro Ha?' Rin asked. 'Did you not begin only an hour ago?'

'Done for now.' Koro Ha stood to greet the steward. 'The boy needs a rest, as do I. One can only try to carve stone with a writing brush for so long before one becomes exhausted.'

'Harsh words for your pupil. Was that a quote from the sage?'

'No. You called. Does Master Winter-Starkness need me?'

Rin dipped his balding head. 'A guest has arrived. A merchant from Toa Alon. He is dining with the magistrate as we speak, and in their conversation the topic of the young master's education arose. Master Winter-Starkness mentioned your name, and our guest reacted with pleased surprise. It seems the two of you were friendly in youth.'

'Is that so?' Koro Ha had not set foot in Toa Alon in twenty years. Not since his mother's death. Another decade separated his first departure from Sor Cala and that brief return. The only ties he maintained to Toa Alon were with his father and sister, and those maintained only by the occasional letter and a handful of silver sent each autumn for the Festival of Reaping.

Even as a child, he had been fully aware that the keenness of his mind would be his means of escape from the poverty and desperation that had gripped his people since the destruction of Sor Cala. There had been fellow students—neighbourhood children whose parents pooled their resources to hire a single tutor for a dozen pupils—but no one that stood out in memory as a *friend*. Certainly no one he could imagine welcomed as a guest in a magistrate's home.

'Come, come,' Rin said, beckoning Koro Ha to follow him. 'You must eat and drink with them. Our guest is most insistent.'

'What is our guest's name?' Koro Ha said, falling into step behind the steward.

'Mr Orna Sin. A merchant specialising in gemstones and rare minerals, brought north from Toa Alon.'

An unfamiliar name, though Koro Ha had to admit that he might not recall every one of his childhood acquaintances. 'And what is a Toa Aloni merchant doing here, so far inland?'

Rin shrugged. Like many stewards Koro Ha had known, the man had a talent for incuriosity. 'Mountainsfoot Fortress may be on the southern edge of the heartland, but it is an important town,' Rin said. 'Perhaps he is exploring new opportunities?'

'Perhaps,' Koro Ha allowed, and gestured for Rin to lead on.

Rin led Koro Ha over to a delicately arched footbridge connecting the private estate to the middle partition, thence to the Centre of Prosperity Reception Hall, which stood out as something of an anomaly. The other buildings of the Bo family garden favoured the dark shades and delicate latticework popular in the south rather than the ostentatious colours and weighty, imposing construction of the north.

But the northern heartland was *true* Sien, whereas the south had once been independent, generations upon generations ago. Koro Ha had travelled far and wide in his career, and no matter how the winds of fashion blew, every magistrate from Toa Alon to the Girzan Highlands designed his reception hall in the northern fashion.

Magistrate Bo was the fourth undermagistrate of Mountainsfoot Fortress. Not a Voice, nor even a Hand, but a skilled politician and a man of some means and influence. Thus his reception hall was vast, imposing, and decidedly northern in style, complete with such flourishes as lion-serpent scrollwork and drifting clouds engraved on the doors, all of which stood wide, opening the hall to the fresh air. A round table had been laid in the centre of the hall, where Magistrate Bo and a Toa Aloni man lounged in high-backed chairs. They conversed over plates of candied lychees and peanuts seasoned with flaked salt, a steaming pot of mossy-smelling tea between them.

'Ah, here he is!' Magistrate Bo swept one arm towards Koro Ha. 'The tutor I mentioned. Koro Ha, this is Orna Sin, a merchant from your homeland. He says the two of you knew one another when you were boys.'

Koro Ha bowed to the merchant and, at a gesture from the magistrate, eased into the chair left empty for him. Steward Rin filled his teacup before bobbing his head and retreating from the reception hall, leaving them with the servants who lingered in the corners of the room, waiting to refill the teapot or the dishes on the table.

'Koro Ha is an auspicious addition to my household,' Magistrate Bo went on. 'He had offers from a dozen other families after his success in Nayen, but after months of correspondence—and, I'm sure, something of a bidding war—he accepted the position as tutor to my heir. A good boy, if a bit stone-headed. But if anyone can crack that stone, it is the great Master Koro Ha!'

Koro Ha smiled, sipped his tea, and lowered his head. 'You give me too much credit. As the sage Traveller-on-the-Narrow-Way writes, a sculptor is only as good as the jade in his hands. And there were five offers, not twelve.'

Magistrate Bo dismissed Koro Ha's humility with a wave, which sparked a somewhat embarrassing rush of gratification.

'What is this success he speaks of?' Orna Sin said.

'Why, I'd have thought Koro Ha would be famous among you Toa Aloni by now!' Magistrate Bo said. 'He was single-handedly responsible for the education of Wen Alder, the first Nayeni Hand of the emperor. Imagine that! A Hand forged from that barbaric, unruly province. Only a true genius of instruction could have managed such a feat.'

'Magistrate Bo, again, is overly generous,' Koro Ha said. 'Hand Usher meant to choose an apprentice from among the successful examinees.'

'Ah, but he chose *your* pupil!' Magistrate Bo pointed out. 'You are fond of Traveller-on-the-Narrow-Way and the aphorism of the sculptor, but you neglect its second half: the finest jade, in the hands of an amateur, is wasted.'

'And now he works for you.' Orna Sin raised his cup in a toast. 'Well hired, Magistrate Bo. And well done, Koro Ha. If only Teacher Zhen could have lived to see his star student rise so high.'

Surprise darted through Koro Ha. He raised his cup in return, sipped, and considered the warming, mild flavour of the tea while he collected his thoughts. 'That is how you know me?' he asked, placing his empty teacup softly on the table.

Orna Sin showed heavy teeth, stained by tea and tobacco. 'Everyone in that classroom, even those of us who snuck in and lurked in the back of that dusty schoolhouse, tolerated but never called on, out of some...' he trailed off, gestured dismissively. 'I don't know, some frantic hope...we all knew you, Koro Ha, if not in those days then later, after the examinations.'

There was nothing dismissive in Orna Sin's eyes, which searched Koro Ha as a prospector studies a vein of gold. Koro Ha was not unaccustomed to being thought of as an investment, but the naked scrutiny in the merchant's gaze, as though he were a prize horse meant for breeding, unsettled him.

'Yours was always the first hand to rise when Teacher Zhen asked a question,' Orna Sin went on, 'and you were the subject of his only praise. Then later, we all knew you as the only one to make anything worthwhile of all that time and all the neighbourhood's money.' A smile carved deep dimples in his white-stubbled cheeks but did not touch his searching eyes. 'And now he works for you, Magistrate Bo.'

'Only the benevolence of the emperor and the generosity of the examinations could make such a thing possible,' Koro Ha said, not so subtly hinting at how far he outranked the merchant, and at how impudent and improper it was for the man to stare at him like some mercantile good to be evaluated, bought, and sold.

'As it has created the means for me, a child of poverty born in the ruins of Sor Cala, to rise to wealth and travel the world.' Orna Sin at last broke eye contact as he leaned back in his chair, spreading his hands wide. 'Leaving so many others, less fortunate than me, behind.'

'Indeed.' Magistrate Bo refilled all their teacups and raised his again, in what seemed an attempt to cut the line of tension between the two Toa Aloni at his table. 'A toast! To the benevolence of the empire!'

Koro Ha drank, then set his cup down with a click. 'How long will you be staying in Mountainsfoot, Orna Sin?'

'Only as long as I must to complete my business,' Orna Sin answered. 'Perhaps a day…perhaps longer.'

'Well.' Magistrate Bo plucked one last candied lychee from the platter. 'It has been delightful to meet you, but I am sure you are itching to attend to that business, and I have, alas, more tedious matters to attend to. Besides, we have kept Koro Ha too long from *his* duties with my son.'

They stood, exchanged a few final pleasantries, and left the table for the servants to clean and stow away. Steward Rin intercepted Magistrate Bo outside the hall and began reciting a list of meetings, documents, and legal matters in need of his immediate attention. They soon disappeared behind the boulders on the far side of the stream. Koro Ha began to follow them, wondering whether he could stand another few hours of hammering away at Spring-Happiness's skull, when Orna Sin touched him on the elbow.

Koro Ha frowned at yet another violation of propriety. This one he would not let pass so easily. 'I realise we are countrymen, Mr Orna Sin, but we do not know each other well enough for physical contact.'

Orna Sin produced a slip of yellowed paper from his sleeve and offered it. 'Teacher Zhen was himself a failed examinee. I think you surprised, perhaps even humiliated him, when you passed.' He stepped forwards and pressed the paper into Koro Ha's hand. 'Imagine what a school such as his, but taught by someone of your quality, might achieve for Toa Alon. Far more than what you are achieving here, I think.'

Koro Ha's fingers crinkled the paper. Words of protest rose within him. Who was Orna Sin to suggest that he, who had brought more honour to Toa Alon with his success as a tutor than had any of its countless merchants, owed something more to his people?

'What is this?' Koro Ha demanded.

'*You* are the business I have come to conduct in Mountainsfoot Fortress,' Orna Sin answered, showing his stained teeth. 'That is the address of the house where I am staying. If you wish to discuss the future of Toa Alon and your place in it, meet me there tonight.'

He bobbed his head. Without so much as waiting for a servant to escort him, he left the magistrate's garden. Koro Ha watched him go, twisting the rough paper between his fingers.

It was not every day one met a man of Toa Alon elsewhere in the empire. Rarer still to meet one who spoke his mind, even couched in euphemism and performed humility.

The future of Toa Alon, he mused. Not the future of the empire.

Too many years had passed since he had last set foot in the city built around the ruins of Sor Cala. Closing his eyes, he could hardly recall the southern slopes of the Pillars of the Gods or the cold stone of a sacred cave beneath his feet.

When last had he thought such things?

He nearly crumpled the paper, tossed it into the stream, and forgot Orna Sin. The man had insulted him in front of his employer, trampling on propriety, showing Koro Ha none of the deference his accomplishments warranted. Yet rather than finding these things repulsive, infuriating though they might be, they stirred Koro Ha's curiosity. A brute Orna Sin might be, but what sort of brute would spend his money to build a *school?*

Koro Ha tucked the paper into his sleeve and went to a quiet part of the garden to listen to the birds, smoke his pipe, and think.

4

A Robe of Thorns
Hand Pinion

Twenty-six members of the Burrow garrison stood at attention, armed and armoured. The cast of their eyes alone betrayed the rebellion in their hearts. At the front of the loose formation stood the company commander, his eyes hard as slate above a sharp-cut beard. A scar seamed the bridge of his nose. The muscles in his jaw bunched as he watched Pinion, Huo, and Clear-River approach.

He had disobeyed orders and knew what he deserved as a result. Yet he did not throw himself to the ground and beg for mercy.

Pinion had never wanted control, or authority, or any of the other burdens of his station. Oriole might have won these reluctant soldiers over with his smile and quick wit. How many times had he convinced a gaggle of reluctant cousins or the children of his father's friends to indulge in wild games of his own design? Or, at the very least, Oriole might have taken some grim satisfaction in carrying out the brutal punishments their crimes demanded.

Pinion, meanwhile, should have been at home, taking satisfaction in a comfortable chair, a pot of warm tea, and a book of poetry, burdened with nothing more than a few thousand taels of his father's silver to manage and a handful of guests to entertain. That had been his destiny as second son, unless Oriole were to fail or—the emperor forfend—die.

But the paths laid out for them had contorted, delivering Oriole into the treacherous company of Wen Alder and Pinion to this moment, standing in the snow in Burrow's garrison yard.

Pinion puzzled over such strange behaviour. They must all have known that this protest would accomplish nothing and end only in their deaths. If he could understand why the man was willing to throw his life away in a stupid, hopeless act of disobedience, he might find a way to convince them all without the need for any bloodshed.

But they had already whiled away the morning. Captain Huo had been infuriatingly slow to comprehend Pinion's orders—orders endorsed by the emperor himself! Now these garrison men refused to ready themselves to march. If Pinion let this offense stand, word would spread among his soldiers, already sceptical of his leadership. Leniency would only shred what little authority he had, and with it any hope of reaching safety before Wen Alder's rebellion swept southwards on wings of wind and fire.

Knowing this made the words no easier to say.

'Commander, would you like to explain yourself before Captain Huo takes your head from your shoulders?'

The commander straightened his back. 'Your Excellency,' he said, 'this is our home. We cannot abandon it.'

'You are soldiers of the empire,' Pinion said sharply. 'As the emperor's Hand and the agent of his will, I have ordered you to join my army in retreat. You have no home but in that column.'

The commander stared at him but did not answer. Pinion wondered how Oriole might have addressed such defiance in his place. Easier to imagine, and to emulate, how Hand Cinder would have dealt with the situation: swiftly, callously, with all brutal efficiency.

It was necessary, wasn't it? Though that made it no easier to swallow. Pinion imagined the commander's head rolling from the stump of his neck. The spray of blood.

'Captain Huo.' Bile burned the back of his throat, but he gestured to the garrison commander. 'Execute this man for insubordination.'

Huo hesitated—only for a moment, enough to make his distaste

for the order clear, to put his toe right up to the line of mutiny—
before his sword rasped free of its scabbard. The blade flashed in the
noon sun as he turned to take his swing.

'Your Excellency,' Clear-River blurted, bowing his head to his chest.
A flush had turned his reddish skin a darker shade, making his splash
of freckles stick out like flecks of paint. Shame, perhaps, or anger?
'Please. You must forgive me. A private word, if I may.'

Pinion scowled at the magistrate. Clear-River deepened his bow,
his expression drawing taut with worry. He surely knew he had over-
stepped, especially after his slip into impudence the night before, yet
his eyes were hard and determined. Was his willingness to risk himself
on behalf of his men a noble act, itself a fulfilment of the magistrate's
duty as elder brother to his commander?

The garrison commander stared straight ahead, jaw tense and
eyes set, a tremor in his lip the only betrayal of the terror that surely
gripped him. Yet he held firm, even at the sight of a naked blade. Huo
held his sword ready but waited, though Pinion had neither said nor
done anything to indicate he should. Had this all been a question on
the imperial examinations, the answer would have been simple: four
words to Huo, issued firmly—*Do as I command*—and then, perhaps,
a second execution to follow the first, to reward a local magistrate for
repeatedly violating hierarchy and propriety. At the very least, a public
humiliation—perhaps a flogging—and the stripping of Clear-River's
imperial commission.

This was no essay, however, but living, breathing reality, and the
words—so quick to flow from his brush—caught in his throat.

'One moment, Captain,' Pinion said and followed Clear-River to a
far corner of the yard.

'If I may be so bold, Your Excellency, though I know I have no
right…' Clear-River bowed again. 'Please. Commander Wei is a good
man. He has two young sons. He would sooner die than leave them
behind, as you have seen.'

Pinion shook his head. 'Your man has undermined my authority—
as you so nearly do, now. The cost of that is death. As the sage Rush-
es-in-Water wrote, "The weed of chaos must be pulled out by the root.
Wherever it is found, destroy disorder and eradicate disharmony."'

'So he did, Your Excellency.' Clear-River winced, only briefly, at mention of his own violation, but pressed on. 'I do not challenge the fact that the commander has disrespected you, nor what doctrine would demand for his punishment. I only wonder what the empire stands to gain by killing him. The men here love him well. If you take his head, it will give them cause to resist you further. They may walk in your column from Burrow on pain of death, but at the first opportunity they will desert, or slit your throat in your sleep.'

'I am Hand of the emperor.' Pinion felt a quaver in his voice and flattened it, though he could do nothing to ease his nausea. 'I am bound to abide by the will of the emperor as codified in doctrine.'

Clear-River nodded deeply. 'Of course, Your Excellency. But what serves the empire better, to kill a well-loved commander who has disobeyed a strange and unexpected order, or to place him where his talents are useful? Is it not a recurrent theme in the writings of the sages that things must be put to their proper use, in their proper place? Perhaps there is value in leaving a small force here to delay the rebellion.'

Pinion's heart lurched to clutch at that reasoning and let it carry him away from brutality and horror. But there was still the threat to his bloody, unwanted authority. 'If I had been presented with this notion before the commander disobeyed me, I might have accepted it.'

'To spare a life for the good of the empire is not weakness, Your Excellency.' Clear-River's voice carried a note of desperation. 'It is mercy.'

Was it indeed? Pinion could not help but feel that, whether by his hand or Wen Alder's, the commander would be slain soon enough.

Earlier that morning, he had offered Clear-River a chance to come with the column when it left, but the magistrate had refused, saying that he and his household, including his guard, would remain at their post. 'What use, after all, would you have for a common magistrate?' he had joked, his smile dimpling his freckled cheeks. 'I've no martial training, nor any sorcery. Better to leave me behind. I doubt the rebels will bother attacking so small and insignificant a place as this, anyway.'

If Clear-River wished to die in his home, who was Pinion to drag him to safety? He didn't have time to convince every sceptic of the emperor's will, to enforce his authority by argument *or* by the sword.

Why should the same not be true for the commander of Burrow's garrison and the fools who would stand with him?

'Very well.' Pinion folded his hands into his sleeves and turned back to Huo. 'Captain, you may sheathe your sword. These twenty-six will stay and guard the walls, to delay the rebels if my friend the magistrate is wrong and they do indeed mean to ransack this place on their way south.'

Despite his military bearing, the commander's face sagged in relief. Huo's posture, too, relaxed as he put his weapon away.

There was a benefit in showing mercy, Pinion supposed. He had not forced his captain to do something distasteful. On the other hand, he had allowed his captain to watch him change his mind based upon arguments offered by someone far below his station.

Which would prove the worse mistake?

'We should be on our way, Captain,' Pinion said, casting aside such circular, dismal thoughts. 'Have the men ready to march. I will be there shortly.'

'Thank you, Hand Pinion,' Clear-River said when the captain had saluted and gone to follow orders. 'You will not regret this.'

Pinion smiled, thanked Clear-River for his hospitality, and sent the men of his honour guard to fetch his belongings from the magistrate's house. While he waited, he wondered whether it mattered at all if he regretted the decision to leave those men behind. They, after all, would certainly regret it, and Clear-River with them, before long.

5

The Tools of Canon
Foolish Cur

After half a day of marching, my body found the familiar rhythm that had carried it the length of Nayen after my flight from An-Zabat. Ahead of us, my uncle's army left an ankle-deep furrow through the snow. His scouts had returned the day before, telling that Pinion had already led his forces onwards, towards Iron Town. Harrow Fox would seize the opportunity to follow one victory with another—though none of us were certain why Pinion had not fortified Burrow to await us, given that he led several hundred men, at least, and we were a scant thirty.

I hoped that my appeal to Pinion's better nature after Usher's death had succeeded, and that his retreat was a sign of his own disillusionment with the empire. It was more likely that he had fled for want of the canon of sorcery. Without Voice Usher, Pinion's connection to the emperor would have been severed, and without magic he had little hope of defeating my uncle's cadre, let alone a witch of the old sort.

No one can truly know another person's mind, of course, especially not from leagues away—save the emperor, whose sorcery of transmission gave him access to the minds of his Voices. But I was not the emperor, and I could not hope to unravel the knot of Pinion's motivations, so I turned my mind back to the problem at hand.

'The gods are bound by the pact, are they not?'

'No more bound than you were by the oaths you swore to the empire.' Hissing Cat, who trudged along beside me bearing no luggage but her sack of shoulder blades, grimaced and tapped one of her teeth. 'Maybe a *bit* more. But the pact isn't *real*. Not like the world is real, or the canon. It is only an agreement, albeit one bound by magic that restricts what pact-marked witches can do.

'But, like any agreement, it stands only as long as the parties who forged it believe that it serves them. The moment Tenet thinks his empire and its little army of sorcerers can defeat the gods, he may well break the pact in a bid to destroy them once and for all, no matter the damage he would deal to the world in the process. And if the gods think they could defeat him—or if they become convinced that *he* means to rekindle the old war—they may well break the pact themselves.'

It was like one of the old logic problems my tutor and I had puzzled over in my father's garden. A dozen factors to consider, interests balanced against one another, such that any action might cause the whole arrangement to tumble apart. Only, rather than a crisis of local governance or trade, this puzzle concerned ancient forces beyond my understanding, and failure to solve it would mean apocalyptic war.

I shifted the weight of my pack from one shoulder to the other and watched Okara snuffle through the undergrowth at Doctor Sho's heels. A wistful nostalgia for the year I had spent travelling with them swept through me. 'I thought I was through with these sorts of headaches,' I muttered.

'Why do you think I spent the last five hundred years living in a cave?' Hissing Cat asked, amused.

'What of Naphena, then?' My mind had turned to her tale since my conversation with my uncle. She had worked magic that endured without her, long after her death. A model, perhaps, for the canon I would build, able to function independent of my own power. 'The gods killed her for building the oasis at An-Zabat. Why didn't that lead to a rekindling of the old war?'

Hissing Cat inhaled sharply. The muscles in her face pulsed once, as though she swallowed a spike of rage. 'It could have,' she said simply. 'But it didn't.'

Here was another hook for my curiosity—every conversation with Hissing Cat was littered with them—but I chose to ignore it. There would be time, I hoped, to dredge the story of her long life for all its fascinating detail after Nayen had been freed and the emperor dealt with.

'All magic is permitted to me,' I went on. 'The goddess Tollu said so herself. And I was not at the signing of the pact. Perhaps I *could* build this canon without sparking a war. The emperor has managed it.'

Hissing Cat bit back a retort. Like a breath upon embers, her hesitation stoked my own anxieties. I was deep in unfamiliar territory, navigating around unmapped dangers. If she insisted that I abstain from some magic, that should have been enough to dissuade me.

'I will help you,' she said at last, then put up a gnarled finger. '*If*—and *only* if—the dog agrees that you'll not go barrelling past a line the gods would rather you not cross.'

As though he knew we spoke of him, Okara paused in his exploration of the underbrush and peered over his shoulder. I searched his scars for the glimmer of light that told of the god's presence—or so I had surmised—but saw only pale, wealed flesh. He yipped at us, then flattened his ears and turned back to whatever scent had occupied him.

'A ringing endorsement if I ever heard one,' I said.

Hissing Cat snorted a laugh, then shook her head, jangling the skulls in her hair.

We made camp that night on an outcropping above the gentle, snow-swept valley where the town of Burrow lay. Once the fires had been built and the watches set, music rose from among the tents—the spike fiddle, hand drum, and flute, playing a looping melody into which listeners injected snatches of folk songs. Tales of bravery, mostly, recounting episodes from the legends of Brittle Owl and Iron Claw, from the time of the first Sun King.

From the edge of the ridge, where I sat and listened, I could see distant flickering lights, like bright jewels stitched onto a sash of dark cloth—the campfires of Pinion's army.

Though we had lived in the same household for three years, Pinion and I had never been close. We had exchanged pleasantries a few times and eaten the occasional meal together when his father gathered the household and its guests for special occasions, but until Oriole's funeral we had never conversed in any depth. Yet I had left that brief meeting at Oriole's grave, beneath the flowering plum tree, feeling close to him. We had expressed our shared grief and our parallel anxieties, and come away each accepting the paths before us.

Without warning, a wake of magic roiled through the world. Heavy, like the emperor's transmission, but with a swell of heat behind it.

<Hissing Cat says you have a question for me.>

Okara circled me, then sat at the edge of the ridge. Lines of fire flickered up and down his scars as the god's voice echoed in my mind.

'I intend to make a canon of witchcraft,' I said, and explained the plan I had proposed to my uncle. Okara's expression shifted while I spoke. It was tempting to read surprise, or worry, or even anger in those quirks around his eyes and the twitching of his nose. 'If I do this, will the gods punish me as they punished Naphena?'

The light in his scars burned bright; the weight of his presence in my mind hung heavy on the pattern.

<No, I do not think so,> Okara said at last. <I certainly would not.>

'What of Tollu and Ateri?' I pressed. 'Or the Skyfather?'

<I can no more speak for them than you can speak for Tenet.> Okara's tail twitched in what I took for annoyance. <But the emperor and his canon are a threat to us *because* he can change what magic he conveys. At any moment, his Hands and Voices might wield the old magic. You intend to make a canon *separate* from yourself and fixed in nature.>

'But will I violate the pact by doing so?' I asked. 'Naphena was punished for far less than I intend.'

<Does what you have described test the boundary of what my kin will tolerate? Yes. But if this is the weapon you need to fight the emperor, they would be fools to throw you away for building it.>

'And are they fools?'

The dog barked and lolled his tongue, as though laughing. <An excellent question. Nothing is certain in life, Foolish Cur. But I can promise you this: as long as you work against Tenet's aims, I will support you. That might be enough to restrain my kin, regardless of what old rule you violate or threat they think you pose.> The dog shut its mouth and tilted its head. <Then again, it might not. Regardless, I will tell Hissing Cat that I endorse your plan.>

The weight of his magic receded from me, then carved a new furrow through the pattern of the world, towards where Doctor Sho, Hissing Cat, and I had built our campfire. A moment later, the light in Okara's scars went out. The dog bolted to his feet, yipped in distress, and rubbed up against my legs.

I shuddered. I shudder still. What agony gripped the mind of that poor mountain dog when the wolf of guile used him as a vessel?

The dog stuck close to my heel while I returned to the campsite, the sound of music and song receding. Hissing Cat sat with a shoulder blade spread across her knees and the tip of her iron needle glowing in the fire. Doctor Sho's chest of medicines lay propped against a stone nearby. The doctor himself had gone to check on his patients, I assumed.

Hissing Cat pressed the glowing tip of her needle to the shoulder blade. It split with a sharp crack and a waft of bitter smoke. Something in the pattern of fissures made her grimace and hurl the bone away. It whistled through the air and clattered against the ground somewhere beyond the light of our campfire.

Her hard gaze met mine. I felt a heavy dragging through the pattern of the world.

<All right, then.> Her voice echoed in the back of my mind and I gawped. Only Okara had ever spoken to me that way before. <First, you will need to master the magic of transmission, both the tool and material Tenet used to make his canon of sorcery. Sit down and open yourself to the pattern.>

Astonished—and wondering, for the first time since An-Zabat, about those old rumours that the emperor could read the minds of his Hands—I sat, breathed deeply, and became that sphere of jade submerged in the eternal interchange of energies.

<As other magic reshapes the external world—wind, fire, water, and growing things—compelling them to appear and behave out of their natural turn, so transmission reshapes the mind, filling it with thoughts, sensations, even movements of the will that are not its own.>

A subtle modulation followed in the aftermath of her magic, like the wake of a fish darting just below the surface of the water.

'You make it sound terrifying,' I muttered.

<It is. Now be silent and focus. If you are to build a canon of your own, you will need to become *very* adept with the magic of transmission. I'd rather you not burn out the minds of these witches you would make the moment they reach for power.>

'I have some familiarity with it,' I protested. 'I spent years as Hand of the emperor, and—'

<What did I just say?>

The words carried an echo of her frustration, twisting in my gut.

<To convey a thought from one mind to another—worse, to a *specific* mind in a crowded world full of them—is like reaching out with a brush in the dark, intending to write on a blank sheet of paper somewhere on the floor. It can be done, though you must have enough familiarity with the mind you would reach, like a memory of where the sheet of paper lies. When you reach for me, recall and focus on a familiar sensation. Perhaps the clatter of ravens' skulls or the crack of a shoulder blade.>

A glimpse of matted hair and a whiff of a dank, dark cave, I very nearly said.

<I hope that is not how you think of me,> she chided.

I flinched.

<Focus, boy! The key to finding some minds might not be so tactile. Perhaps only a feeling. Many of us, when we remember our mothers, feel a warmth in the chest. Others, a stab of terror.>

Pressure eased from the base of my skull and my shoulders, leaving me feeling strangely empty, as though my mind had expanded to fit her presence and had yet to return to its natural shape.

'Now,' she said. Her voice seemed far away and strange, yet carried only a few paces through the air. 'Whatever you feel or see or hear when you think of me will be the key to making contact with my mind. It is a name of sorts, but written in a deeper, older language than words. Seek that name in the pattern and write your thoughts upon it.'

I reached through the pattern, brushing against the motion of our campfire's flame, drawing energy out of the wood as it burned and casting it into the wider world, where it struggled against the chill of the wind. Then deeper, into the slower, oft-unnoticed changes, marching to the rhythm of aeons as soil compacted into stone, then into iron. But nowhere could I find Hissing Cat, focus as I might upon every memory of her that I could conjure, as though my consciousness shied away from other minds.

'You are afraid of me,' Hissing Cat said, snapping me out of frustrated introspection.

'Are you suggesting that he *shouldn't* be?' Doctor Sho's voice rose over the swish and crackle of his footsteps through the undergrowth.

Hissing Cat ignored him. 'In the same way it's bloody hard to ride a horse when it knows you're scared of it, it's bloody hard to reach out and touch a mind you fear. We should start with someone you're less afraid of. Someone you know well, who won't think themselves mad when they hear your voice in their head.'

The only name that came to mind was Oriole, long dead. Perhaps Atar, though I rejected the notion immediately. Though we had grown close, we had been together for only a year, and another year had passed since our parting. How well did I *truly* know her?

I opened my eyes to find Doctor Sho warming his hands over the fire. He met my gaze. A moment later, he balked in surprise. 'Am I the closest thing to a friend you've got?'

Heat rose in my face. 'I've had little opportunity to build real friendships,' I said softly, staring into the flames. Even my grandmother, who once had known me better than anyone, had become little more than a stranger.

'I don't have time to muddle through this,' I said finally. 'You need to show me how to do it.'

Hissing Cat barked a laugh. 'You don't think I've been trying?'

'Make a canon,' I said. 'A simple one, with only one channel. Let me feel what it is like to wield this magic successfully.'

She leaned towards me, shadows filling the skulls in her hair.

'That won't solve your problem, Cur. Not in the way you think. It's a shortcut.'

'I can wield battle and healing sorcery well enough,' I protested. 'I used them through the canon, learned their textures, and made them my own. I can do the same with transmission. Show me how to reach your mind. Or would you rather go on watching me fumble in the dark?'

She curled her lip and stabbed her iron needle into the fire. A moment later, the familiar weight of her transmission burrowed into my skull. Waves of pressure washed out from her, building up walls within my sense of the pattern—heavy, unyielding, like the canon of sorcery.

A groan slipped between my teeth. Doctor Sho muttered something under his breath, then turned away from us and began pulling open the drawers of his medicine chest and slamming them shut.

At last, the pressure subsided, though the walls she had built remained.

I moved the phantom limb by which all magic is worked, pawing my way through the structure Hissing Cat had made. Once, little more than a year ago, I had wielded all magic like this, reshaping the pattern of the world, not by an exercise of my own design but according to the designs of the emperor, drawing upon the structure of his canon.

That thought kindled guilt and anxiety. What was I doing? I had moved beyond the need for others to tell me how to think, how to feel, how to make my way through the world—hadn't I? Or had I only substituted the emperor for Hissing Cat and my uncle, the empire for the Nayeni rebellion?

I swallowed regret. My philosophical misgivings would do little to aid the liberation of Nayen, nor the defeat of the empire. I needed to prove my loyalty to my uncle, to show him that I belonged with the rebellion and to balance out the harm I had done as Hand of the emperor. There would be time for guilt and rumination later.

As my will reached the end of the channel, sensations washed through me. The crack of scorched bone. A vision of shadowed eyes on the far side of a fire. And beneath these sensations, a well of power. I drew from it, and the wake of my own magic became as heavy as Hissing Cat's as I redoubled the knitting of our minds.

<There.> Her thoughts washed through me, bubbling up from some deep, unseen corner of my mind. <You've done it. But could you do it again? On your own? Could you find Doctor Sho's mind, or your uncle's?>

<No,> I thought, and knew that she heard. <That is the knowledge I needed you to give.>

<Could you have brought your grandmother back from the brink of death with the power Tenet gave you? To truly learn—such that you can make something *new*—requires struggle and the hard-won realisations that lead to understanding.>

Words that stirred another pang of guilt, quickly stifled. Once, I had hungered for mastery, and that hunger had led me astray. Perhaps accepting my own limitation was, in a way, a more genuine acceptance of my place in the pattern of the world.

<What does it matter to you?> I replied.

At once, the weight of her magic vanished, and with it the guiding structures she had built within my mind. I flailed in the pattern, trying to maintain our connection, to capture what it felt like to wield that magic before I lost the chance.

Too late. I was alone once more in my own mind.

'You want me to fight this war with you?' Hissing Cat said flatly, reaching for another shoulder blade. 'Show the strength needed to win it.'

I glowered at her. Doctor Sho shifted uncomfortably, visibly confused after missing so much of our conversation.

'Fine,' I said, putting an edge of anger into my voice. In truth, I felt relieved. Perhaps she had glimpsed my misgivings. Or perhaps she nursed doubts of her own. What questions, I wondered, did she carve into those bones she so often cast away?

I reached back into the pattern, seeking the sensation of her mind, dredging blindly through the depths long after she and Doctor Sho had gone to sleep, long after our fire had burned down to ash and embers, until, shivering in the cold winter night, I wrapped myself in my bedroll and collapsed into a few hours of agitated rest, my filmy dreams full of scenes of violence written in vanishing smoke and vapour.

* * *

T he clatter of pots being stowed and campfires scattered woke me. I spent the day heavy lidded, my head full of fog, walking at the back of the column. Tired enough to swear off any attempt to work transmission that night—I needed to actually *sleep* if I was to have any chance of success. So tired was I, in fact, that I did not realise we had reached the outskirts of Burrow until my uncle summoned me to his tent and explained my role in his plan of attack.

Scouts had counted eight soldiers patrolling the walls. Assuming the garrison worked in three shifts, that meant there were approximately twenty-four soldiers left in Burrow.

'A town that size should have more than that,' I pointed out.

Harrow Fox looked up from his map table. Tawny Owl, the witch who led his scouts, had sketched out the borders of the town and its key structures—the garrison house, the magistrate's hall—with coal on a scrap of birch bark.

Tawny Owl crossed her arms, thin as tree branches but corded with vines of muscle. 'You would know, wouldn't you?' she sneered. 'Not so long ago, you'd have planned the defence here rather than the attack.'

The other witches of the cadre had joined us, along with four newly appointed captains chosen from the twenty-seven able-bodied soldiers left after Greyfrost. All four captains wore a scrap of burnt wood on their jerkins, pinned below the arrowhead that marked their office in the Army of the Fox.

'They might be hiding in reserve.' I fixed my attention on Tawny Owl's map, ignoring her and avoiding my uncle's gaze. 'Burrow might be too far from the Voice at Setting Sun Fortress for the canon to reach Pinion here, but it might not. He could be playing on that uncertainty to lure us into an ambush.'

A part of me knew I ought to show deference to my uncle, particularly in this company, but another, larger part of me was too exhausted to care, particularly with battle looming.

I remembered the last time I had visited Burrow, and the blood and terror I had left in my wake. The thought of encountering Clear-River again, returning to his home now with the *intent* of doing violence, weighed heavy.

'Or the bulk of the garrison might have retreated with Hand Pinion's army,' Tawny Owl said, glowering. 'Even if they didn't, what difference does it make? We have six witches, plus you and that matted hag.'

'Pinion could turn and trap us against the walls if the garrison is able to hold,' I said, and thought without saying that it was the sort of stratagem Pinion's brother would certainly have tried. 'One Hand of the emperor is worth a dozen witches, and a bit of fire or the ability to veer are little defence against chemical grenades.'

'This will not be a siege, Nephew,' Harrow Fox said. 'We will strike at dusk and take the town in a single night.'

He went on, explaining the roles he had envisioned for each of us, even my grandmother—though he showed enough restraint, at least, not to suggest that Hissing Cat would fight on his behalf. I felt some relief that I would not be at the forefront of the fighting. I knew that the liberation of Nayen would come at a cost in bloodshed, but that did not make it any easier to accept.

At least, not yet. It *would* become easier to embrace such moral flexibility, and swiftly, just as it had been no great challenge to my integrity when I had led imperial soldiers against the rebels at Iron Town.

As dusk approached, Harrow Fox dismissed us to our work. Doctor Sho met me as I left the camp and set off with Okara at my heel for the low ridge overlooking the town.

'Do you know when last I willingly walked towards a battle?' he muttered.

I shrugged. 'I'm guessing long before anyone else here but Hissing Cat was born, except perhaps my grandmother.' Though in fact, I suspected he was older than her by decades, if not centuries. In Hissing Cat's cave, when he had spoken of the war between the gods and the witches of the old sort, his words had seemed less like those of a historian than those of one who had witnessed them.

He fidgeted with the straps of his medicine chest, more agitated than I had seen him even in the aftermath of the bloodshed when last we had visited Burrow. 'This isn't a thing I do lightly, boy. I'm a doctor now, whatever else I have been. Killing's not my way.'

'No one is asking you to kill.'

'No,' he said with a heavy sigh. 'Only clean up the mess afterwards.'

I clapped him on the shoulder, thinking of no other easy way to offer comfort. He furrowed his brow at me, but he did not shrug away. Such casual physical contact broached Sienese propriety, but neither one of us was properly Sienese. Not anymore.

'Stay safe,' I said.

'I'd say the same to you, but I don't think there's much here that could hurt you in a way that matters. So I'll say instead, keep your wits. We all have a moral compass, boy, though not every needle points to true north. This is where your own will start to drift, if you let it.'

Again, he seemed to speak my own worries back to me, and I wondered—not for the first time—what magics he kept hidden away. Something to prolong his life, I was sure. Why not something like transmission, also? How else to explain how he seemed to read me like a logogram?

One of the four squads that made up our pitiful band loped past, their makeshift battle harnesses clattering. Their captain, a young freckled woman with close-shorn hair beneath an ill-fitting helm, paused. Her hand drifted to the burnt wood she wore at her collar. She broke from her company and approached me, dipping her head in simplified imitation of a Sienese bow, apparently having decided that this was the special deference I was owed.

'Foolish Cur,' she said, her voice thin with nerves but quiet and secretive. 'Is there a blessing you could offer? A charm against arrows and blades? As the first Sun King gave in the ancient days?'

I looked towards my uncle's tent, terrified that he or one of his cadre were close enough to hear. I ought to have answered firmly and finally that I was not the Sun King, that she owed me no special deference nor loyalty, but I saw the terror in her wide eyes and rigid shoulders. Her captain's badge could little hide the young woman just on the far side of adulthood, who had in all likelihood never carried a blade until she left her home to join the Army of the Fox.

Her faith threatened my uncle, and therefore endangered me, but I could not crush it in the moment before she stared death in the face for the second time in as many weeks.

'What is your name?' I asked.

'Running Doe,' she answered.

'I will be on the ridge there.' I pointed to the position Harrow Fox had picked out for me. 'You have no need to fear, Running Doe. We witches will do most of the fighting. The battle will be over before you come near enough to feel a sword.'

It wasn't what she had asked for, but it was all I could give. Again, she dipped her head.

'Thank you,' she said, then returned to her soldiers, still tense but bolstered—or at least I hoped so.

'You need to be careful with that,' Doctor Sho said softly.

'I know,' I muttered, 'but what else was I to do?'

Doctor Sho shrugged, then shifted the weight of his pack to settle it better on his shoulders and set off after Running Doe's party. They should have asked for *his* charm, I thought wryly. He might actually have something in that great wooden hulk on his back that could help them fight.

As the first blush of sunset lit the sky, I reached my place on the ridge. Burrow lay below me, a cluster of houses encircled by a wooden wall. Terraced farms and rice paddies ringed the hillsides of the valley. A peaceful place. While I waited for dark, I imagined a life for myself on one of those terraces, raising livestock, keeping fields. A path that might have left me happier, I thought. Until, of course, the fires of rebellion kindled to turn that happiness to ash, or the fist of empire closed tight around Nayen.

I sighed and reached out into the pattern of the world. A chill swept through my lungs as I bent the wind, tracing the line of the town wall, building up a dome of swirling wind, much as I had done in defence of Greyfrost Keep. Now, as then, I would shield Harrow Fox and his cadre from the grenades and crossbow bolts of the enemy while they led the assault.

At such a distance, I did not hear the shouts of alarm, nor the snap of bowstrings or thunder of chemical grenades. But the pattern carried the ripples of arrows caught and cast aside by my spell, of clay shattered against walls of wind and flames splashing harmlessly in the air. Cramps lanced up and down my limbs as my uncle and his cadre veered and took to the sky. I bent my windcalling to open a path through the dome, and they fell upon the town in a flurry of talons and fire.

I watched the town, waiting for the gates to open, wondering if I should release the dome of wind, veer, and join in whatever fighting still raged within. Harrow Fox had predicted a swift victory and given me no orders beyond his initial plan. The crescent moon had risen, casting silvery light through the billowing smoke before, at last, the gates swung open. I swallowed worry, let the churning winds over Burrow fade, and started down the slope, hoping the Sienese garrison had surrendered, that the violence had ended quickly and with minimal bloodshed.

A hope, like so many, that would go unfulfilled.

6

A Chest, a Cask, and a Question

Koro Ha

'If he has offered you more money, at least allow me to match the bid,' Magistrate Bo said, brows knit in frustration, when Koro Ha announced his decision to return to Toa Alon with Orna Sin. 'I will be happy to surpass it. The time it will take us to find another tutor of your calibre will deal irreparable damage to Spring-Happiness's education.'

Koro Ha swallowed the urge to suggest that the family's wealth would be better melted down and sold off as raw silver than paid to a tutor, and said only that it was no matter of money but a matter of the heart. 'As an elder brother ought to pass on hard-won lessons to the younger, I have a duty to accept his offer, Magistrate Bo. Orna Sin has presented an opportunity to create opportunities for the children of my country such as those that formed the foundation of my own success.'

Now, beneath the latticed gate of Magistrate Bo's garden, with the palanquin Orna Sin had sent to bear Koro Ha to the merchant ship *Swiftness of the South Wind* waiting in the street just outside, the magistrate dipped his head to Koro Ha, the barest fraction of the respect a tutor was owed, and his thin smile below flint-sharp eyes did little to mask his indignation. 'I suppose it was inevitable that, as old age approaches, you would long for your homeland. Rare is the provincial mind that can overcome the urges of provincial blood. It seems I have given you more credit for overcoming such urges than you deserve.'

Koro Ha chose to ignore the insult.

'I wish you and your son success to match your ability and ambition.' He smiled and bowed deeply. 'It is a shame our working relationship has ended in this way, but I hope you see it—as I do—as an opportunity to find a tutor better suited to your son's particular educational needs.'

Before the magistrate had a chance to feel the prick of the thorn hidden in those flowery words, Koro Ha mounted the palanquin and shut the windows. He listened to the muted sounds of Mountainsfoot Fortress's streets while the palanquin gradually became warmer and warmer as day filled the town with early summer heat. Memories of Toa Alon, its fierce sun and humid summer air, gripped him.

Memories that called to mind the terrible, constant question of whether there would be enough money to pay his tuition, or enough food to fill his belly each day.

The *Swiftness of the South Wind* was true to her name, even laden down with iron from Nayen and spices brought across the Batir Waste. At the command of Yin Ila, a stocky Toa Aloni woman who served Orna Sin as captain of the ship—a shock, at first, to Koro Ha, who had long grown accustomed to the separation of men and women demanded by Sienese doctrine—oarsmen pulled the *Swiftness* down the silty southern arm of the Two Forks River and into open water. There, three ribbed sails unfurled and carried them along the coast. Koro Ha had never been fond of sailing, particularly upon the sea, where the constant dance up and down the swells turned his stomach, but the *Swiftness* carved waves like a knife through butter and to his surprise he began to enjoy the journey, watching the horizon from the deck, sipping wine with Orna Sin and discussing the school they would build together.

They went back and forth over the number of students to be taught at once. Koro Ha wished for no more than ten, the better to give an adequate measure of his attention to each. Orna Sin had envisioned more—as many as thirty.

'You will bastardise the educations of all,' Koro Ha said firmly. 'No. Our goal should be to cultivate ten successful examinees, not thirty hastily moulded students with half a chance at passing.'

In the end, they settled on seventeen, with Orna Sin's assurance that, if the number proved too high, Koro Ha might expel one or two of the least promising students.

This business settled, the two fell into more companionable conversation. They discovered a shared appreciation for tobacco—a common vice in Toa Alon, but also a locus of culture and camaraderie. Orna Sin kept dozens of varieties aboard the *Swiftness of the South Wind*, which they sampled together, making a game of describing the subtleties of flavour in ever more unlikely ways. A slight sweetness in one dark, richly aromatic variety became *honeysuckle*, then *vanilla*, then *the lips of a young bride*.

'My sister has long insisted I give up this habit,' Koro Ha said one evening, as the ship glided southwards in still waters, the coast to starboard showing the faintest purple outlines of the Pillars of the Gods. 'My mother died of weakened lungs, and she blames overconsumption of tobacco. Every letter ends with *and I hope you've thrown that pipe down a well, Brother.*'

'She learned to write?' Orna Sin said, surprised. 'I don't remember any girls in the school room. I think we all would have noticed and doubt Teacher Zhen would have tolerated it.'

Koro Ha shook his head. 'I shared some lessons with her, when we were children. She reads and writes like a ten-year-old, without any elegance, yet it is enough for us to communicate.' He took a slow drag on his pipe, a thought occurring to him. 'Do any of the boys you have in mind have sisters?'

Orna Sin cocked his head. 'They may.'

'Few things keep a young boy in line better than the presence of an elder sister,' Koro Ha mused, smiling. 'There is no reason why our school, which is already doomed to waste time on students unlikely to pass the examinations, should not include a few girls as well. Three or four, perhaps.'

Orna Sin laughed, then took a long pull and blew a series of smoke rings, filling the air with a scent they had described progressively as *oaken*, and then *like twilight in a mountain forest*, and finally *like the breath of an elk fed only on the leaves of mighty trees*. He gazed towards the shore and said, in unfamiliar syllables that at first struck Koro Ha's ears as gibberish until, like water bubbling up from a deep spring, their meaning returned to him, 'It is a shame we cannot write in our own tongue, no?'

It had been a decade and a half since he had heard the speech of Toa Alon. Orna Sin kept his gaze fixed, his expression flat and veiled.

'Who could have taught us Toa Aloni letters?' Koro Ha brushed rust from a language engraved deep into him in his childhood but rarely used. 'The library of Sor Cala was buried with the city. The stonespeakers were hunted down and slaughtered.'

'That they were,' Orna Sin said, before reverting to Sienese. 'Your first task will no doubt be imposing strict use of the Sienese tongue upon your students. Toa Aloni is still spoken in most homes, and it does not translate well into logograms. They must begin to think in the empire's language if they are to master its poetry and doctrine, no?'

His words kindled a strange guilt. 'For a man who will spend a great deal of money and effort to build this school, you seem to doubt its value.'

'I have lived my life in Sor Cala, when I was not abroad pursuing business.' The sea breeze made the oiled curls of Orna Sin's beard dance around his throat. 'With your success in the examinations, you might have pursued a career in imperial service. Yet you chose instead the transient life of a tutor. Why?'

A question many prospective employers asked. Koro Ha's usual response was to claim a selfish motivation. Pure philosophy, he liked to pretend, was his passion, and the vagaries of practical governance could only sully it.

He studied Orna Sin. The tight curls of his white hair. The dark cast of his skin, so strange to see in another man's flesh after so many years among people unlike himself. The lines around his eyes that hinted at unspoken hardships and a complexity of perception Koro Ha had never encountered among the Sienese, and only rarely in Nayen.

Wen Alder's grandmother had looked at him with eyes like that, on the rare occasions when they had encountered one another. Seeing through his mask of respectability, of scholarly distance and calm.

'I imagined myself sitting upon a magistrate's dais,' Koro Ha said, shifting their conversation back to Toa Aloni, and speaking plainly, for inexperience with his own tongue stole away the vocabulary he might have used to phrase the truth in anything but the bluntest of terms. 'I imagined Sienese merchants, military captains, and landowners bowing to me. Imagined myself speaking to them with authority. And even in my own imagination, those things seemed impossible.'

'Ah.' Orna Sin's smile split the veil of his expression. 'And that is why you were so quick to come with me.'

Koro Ha inclined his head. 'Oh?'

Orna Sin laughed and tapped out his pipe over the gunwale, letting the still-smouldering tobacco drift into the sea.

'Indeed, my friend,' he said, returning to Sienese. 'Now, let us talk of simpler things. It is still a long way to Sor Cala.'

Some days later, while the rising sun glittered on gentle waves, the *Swiftness* angled towards the shore. Soon they sailed between jutting sandbars and boulders, with the emerald hills of Toa Alon filling the whole of the western horizon. Koro Ha sat near the bow of the ship with a favourite passage from the Classic of Poetry, trying to distract himself from the notion that the *Swiftness*, laden down as it was with cargo, ought not to be sailing such shallow waters.

A sudden thump behind him made him spit out his tea, thankfully onto his lap rather than his book.

'Morning, Teacher,' Yin Ila said. She held a strange staff, thrice her height, tipped with a broad-barbed hook. 'Sorry for the bother.'

'It's quite all right,' Koro Ha assured her, wiping droplets from his robe with the back of his hand. He returned to his reading but kept one eye on the stocky woman.

She watched the shallows, and then, with a muted 'Aha!', plunged the hooked end of her staff overboard.

'There we are,' she whispered, drawing the hook back over the gunwale. A tangle of half-rotted vegetation trailed from its barbs, along with a large empty bottle tied to one end of a thick rope. Yin Ila pulled the rope hand over hand, then, with a grunt, heaved whatever lay at the far end of it onto the deck. Her prize proved to be a wooden box banded in copper. Yin Ila drew a knife and cut it free, then dropped the rope and bottle back into the sea.

Yin Ila tucked the box under her arm and set off towards the cabin, glancing at Koro Ha. He made a show of turning the page.

'Have a good day, Teacher,' she said, bobbing her head, and disappeared belowdecks.

At almost the same time, a chorus of shouts went up from the aftcastle of the ship and the steersman turned back towards the open sea.

Koro Ha puzzled over this curious sequence until his customary noon meal with Orna Sin. While they ate, Koro Ha resisted the urge to ask after Yin Ila's odd behaviour and the strange copper-banded chest. Surely Orna Sin must know what his ship's captain was up to, and it would not be Koro Ha's place as a guest to pry. Yet if Orna Sin did *not* know, surely he would want to be informed.

'By the way, we'll be making a slight detour before Sor Cala,' Orna Sin said, breaking Koro Ha out of the spiralling conflict between his curiosity and sense of propriety. 'A delay of no more than a few days. I trust you won't mind.'

'Of course not.' Koro Ha hesitated for a moment. 'Why the sudden change of plans, if I might ask?'

Orna Sin shrugged his heavy shoulders and showed his single golden tooth. 'Something came up. Nothing you need worry about.'

What, Koro Ha wanted to ask but restrained himself, could come up in the span of days since their departure from Mountainsfoot Fortress, isolated as they had been on the open sea? The only explanation was the chest. Its contents, and what Orna Sin's new errand might be, Koro Ha could not begin to guess.

In the following days, as Koro Ha mulled over these strange events, the sour demeanour and many scars common to the crew took on a more sinister cast. Trade throughout the empire had long been dominated by Sienese adventurers and speculators with access to financial capital, whether borrowed or inherited, not by ascended street children from conquered, ruined cities. Yet Orna Sin had risen from poverty to command significant wealth.

The only sensible explanations were impossible good fortune or criminal enterprise.

Koro Ha should have been afraid, but part of him—the part that had won out so many years ago, when he had turned away from the golden path of imperial service—was intrigued by the idea of working with a man who had clawed his way to success despite the constraints of empire, even if by nefarious means.

All these questions mounted to a climax three days later, when the crew struck the sails and let the *Swiftness of the South Wind* drift in what seemed to Koro Ha the middle of the open sea. The only means of marking their position, beyond sextants and star charts, was the distant silhouette of a dark island, jutting like a mountain above the haze of the horizon. As the ship slowed to a near halt, Yin Ila flew a brilliant red kite from the aftcastle, then tied it off and let it flutter in the afternoon breeze.

One of the sailors scurried up the mainmast and, clinging to the yard arm, peered at the distant silhouette through a spyglass. She watched the sea for a while, then shouted something down in the clipped sailor's cant commonly spoken aboard, which Koro Ha understood well enough only to gather that another ship was approaching.

'You ever see the Black Maw before, Teacher?' Yin Ila asked, startling Koro Ha. She'd joined him at the gunwale. 'It's quite the sight. Closer up, of course.'

'You mean that island there?' Koro Ha asked.

She nodded. 'Doubt you'll ever have the pleasure of getting any nearer. Strange to me that Orna Sin decided to let you stay abovedecks for even this little glimpse.'

'Strange that he would conduct secretive business with a passenger aboard to begin with,' Koro Ha said. 'Perhaps he trusts me more than you believe.'

'Ha!' Yin Ila tapped the side of her nose knowingly. 'Or perhaps he wants to see what you'll do.' She fixed Koro Ha with a long stare.

He matched it, despite the shudder working through him, until she smiled and turned away, then breathed a sigh of relief and sagged against the guard rail.

A new shape came into focus between the *Swiftness* and the Black Maw. A pair of white rectangular sails carried an outrigger canoe at incredible speed, leaping and bounding over the waves. Koro Ha watched it, mesmerised, until it struck its sails and came coasting a stone's throw from the *Swiftness*, which in turn lowered one of its two longboats with Orna Sin aboard.

Longboat and outrigger met, rising and falling on the waves. The lone pilot of the outrigger tossed first one small cask and then another, which Orna Sin fished aboard the longboat with a hooked pole. Their business concluded, the outrigger unfurled its sails, eased itself about, and then returned to the dark spot on the horizon at a much more leisurely pace.

The next day, after the *Swiftness* had reoriented itself and returned to its southwesterly course, Orna Sin invited Koro Ha to join him in enjoying a dark, complex tobacco. They sat out on the foredeck, as they had many times before, though Koro Ha's mind wandered away from their usual game, instead pondering the chest, the casks, and the mysterious island.

'Well, Teacher, you've heard my first proposal. What name would you give this fine blend?' Orna Sin asked, gesturing with his pipe.

Koro Ha blinked. The game had begun while he wasn't paying attention. He took a hasty pull.

'Well?' Orna Sin pressed.

'There are…ah…layers to it,' Koro Ha said. 'Something secretive and sensual. Why not *forbidden midnight kiss?* The title of an old morality tale.'

Orna Sin guffawed. 'Hackneyed bullshit! I've gone to a great deal of trouble to hire you, Teacher. Don't you want to impress me? Or does something distract you?'

'Simply nerves at our impending arrival.' Koro Ha said, enduring a flush of embarrassment. 'It has been, as I said before, a great deal of time since I set foot in Toa Alon, and I wonder how it has changed.'

A shout went up from the watch post atop the mainmast. 'Red sails to port! Yellow kite!'

'Couldn't make just *one* trip without interference,' Orna Sin muttered. He rolled his shoulders back, tapped out his pipe, and tucked it into his pocket. 'Apologies, Teacher. It seems our game will have to wait.' He bounded off towards the ladder that led belowdecks, shouting clipped orders. 'Draw in the sails! Fly the green kite! Be sure whatever you lot don't want the Sienese getting their noses into is tucked away and hidden well!'

Koro Ha watched, bewildered, as sailors dashed to their tasks. Soon the *Swiftness* had slowed to a crawl. He shaded his eyes from the noon sun and peered to the port horizon, where a triangular kite trailing a long yellow tail darted on the breeze. Soon a trio of red ribbed sails appeared, carrying a narrow-hulled cutter at a sprint towards the *Swiftness*.

'No need to piss yourself, Teacher,' Yin Ila shouted down from atop the forecastle. 'It's only a patrol out keeping watch for pirates and the like.'

Koro Ha thought of the Black Maw and the strange casks retrieved by stranger means, which did little to calm his mounting nervousness. Surely Orna Sin and Yin Ila were crafty enough to evade detection.

'What interest do they have in us, then?' Koro Ha shouted back. 'You're flying merchant's flags.'

'Flags bearing the port sigil of Sor Cala.' Orna Sin emerged from belowdecks. He had switched his usual rumpled coat for a more dignified robe in the Sienese style—green silk stitched with a simple geometric pattern. 'Their captain will have a quota to fill. So many ships searched per month, so many crates of smuggled goods seized, and so on.' He rolled his shoulders again, as though expecting a brawl, and offered Koro Ha a reassuring smile, his gaze piercing and unflappable. 'Taking seasick are we, Teacher? We'll be on our way before long.'

Before Koro Ha could decide whether or not to raise the issue of the strange, surely contraband cargo from the Black Maw, the Sienese cutter angled in beside the *Swiftness*. Men wearing bandoleers heavy with grenades manned a pair of swivel-mounted ballistae atop the fore- and aftcastles. While they threatened the *Swiftness*, the cutter's longboat crossed the narrow gap between the ships. On Yin Ila's order, the crew lowered a rope ladder and a detachment of six Sienese soldiers bearing crossbows and wearing swords climbed aboard, led by a young lieutenant.

'Welcome, welcome, honoured guests.' Orna Sin bobbed his head like a caricature of the merchants often featured in Sienese didactic tales. 'I am Orna Sin, owner and proprietor of this vessel. How might my crew and I serve the empire?'

The young lieutenant swept his gaze over the deck. 'We will need a copy of this vessel's charter and a complete manifest of crew and cargo.' His gaze narrowed on Koro Ha, who hoped the trembling of his hands would be hidden by his sleeves. He suppressed a sigh of relief as the lieutenant turned back to Orna Sin. 'Smugglers and pirates frequent these waters and are well known to berth in Sor Cala.'

'Loathsome ingrates.' Orna Sin gave a disappointed shake of his head, then gestured to Yin Ila, who stepped forwards with an armful of scrolls bearing seals in the bright red ink favoured by the imperial bureaucracy. 'I assure you, my people and I appreciate the empire's protection. My captain has prepared our charter and manifests.'

The lieutenant accepted the scrolls from Yin Ila, though he wrinkled his nose and refused to look at her, making no effort to hide his disdain for the notion that a woman might serve as captain of a trading ship. 'My men will need full access to your hold, as well.'

'Of course.' Orna Sin gestured to the ladder belowdecks. 'I will personally ensure their search is unobstructed. Allow me.'

The lieutenant and three of his detachment followed Orna Sin while the others remained on deck, eyeing the crew, who in turn did their best to look anywhere but at the soldiers and their crossbows. Koro Ha stood awkwardly by the gunwale for what felt like hours, though the sun tracked less than a hand's span across the sky.

'You there.' One of the soldiers stepped towards him. 'You're a passenger?'

Koro Ha swallowed against a lump in his throat. 'I am. Koro Ha. A tutor. On my way to a new position in Sor Cala.'

'A barbarian tutor...' The soldier narrowed his eyes. 'Where are your papers?'

'Below, in my cabin.' Koro Ha cringed at the eagerness in his own voice. How was a person *supposed* to act while aboard a ship under search? 'I will go and fetch them, if I must.'

The soldier sneered. 'You must. Luo, Yan, keep your wits about you while I check on this *tutor's* story.'

The scrape and clatter of crates being dragged out of place and pried open resounded through the middle decks of the ship. Koro Ha fought the urge to peer over his shoulder at the ongoing search as he led the way to the small passenger's cabin below the aftcastle. Orna Sin had hidden the casks well, surely. He would not have so easily let the Sienese aboard otherwise.

'Here we are.' Koro Ha eased into the cramped cabin. The soldier lingered at the hatch, his crossbow at his side and his hand on the hilt of his sword, as though he expected Koro Ha to produce a brace of daggers from beneath his blankets. Slowly, Koro Ha shuffled through the papers in his footlocker and produced his records of employment and residence, as well as the lacquered case that bore the essays he had written for the imperial examinations and a certificate identifying him as a successful candidate.

Raised voices sounded from the corridor behind the soldier while he scrutinised the papers. Koro Ha peered past him. Sweat crept down his back, dampening his robe.

'What's a scholar of the first degree doing working as a tutor?' the soldier sneered. 'Couldn't hack it as a bureaucrat, eh, Toa Aloni?'

'And this, then?' the young lieutenant's voice resounded, followed by the thump of boards falling to the deck. The soldier turned towards the raised voices, shoving the papers and the lacquered case back into Koro Ha's arms. Koro Ha stumbled backwards, managing to deposit his burden on his cot before following the soldier out into the corridor, then down another ladder into the hold. His blood thundered in his ears. He was desperate to flee yet was running *towards* danger, with nowhere else to go, his mind blank with fear. At the bottom of the ladder, the lieutenant stood over an open crate, waving a torn sheet of paper in Orna Sin's face.

'This manifest says silk of the third rating, while this has the texture of second rating at best, if not first!' The lieutenant ran a thumb along the bundled silk carefully packed into the crate. 'Do you take me for a fool? My father dealt in silks. What sort of merchant makes that mistake, eh?'

Orna Sin cringed, putting on a performance to make any operatic actor proud. 'Please, sir, I submitted all of my goods to inspection in Centre Fortress. The customs agent himself recorded the rating for the silks. You can see his seal, there.'

'After you passed him a tael or two, I'm sure,' the lieutenant barked.

'Take the crate, sir, all of it,' Orna Sin insisted. 'Consider it payment for the difference between the duty I owe and what I paid in Centre Fortress.'

The lieutenant's scowl might have curdled milk, but he made a sharp gesture to the soldiers with him, who began awkwardly hauling the open crate up the ladder.

'You barbarian scum are always looking for an angle, aren't you?' The lieutenant cast one more glance at the open crates and broken boards that littered the hold. 'Too lazy to succeed honestly even in so lowly a role as mercantilism. You're lucky I don't seize this entire ship and drag the lot of you before the magistrate the moment we dock in Sor Cala.'

'Of course, sir,' Orna Sin bowed deeply. 'I can only apologise for my lack of care, though I swear I did not intend to deprive the empire of any taxes owed.'

The lieutenant grunted. 'Don't let it happen again.' At last, he started up the ladder. Orna Sin followed, but not before gesturing for Koro Ha to remain in his cabin.

'You did well,' Orna Sin whispered, planting his foot on the first rung. 'Now go and have a drink. You look like you need it.'

A few cups of rice wine later, after the *Swiftness* once again surged over the water, Orna Sin reappeared in the hatch of Koro Ha's cabin, his silk robe exchanged for his usual rumpled coat, which hung about his shoulders far more naturally. With a thousand questions competing in his mind, Koro Ha offered him a cup, which he rejected.

'You asked before how Toa Alon has changed.' Orna Sin shrugged dismissively and retrieved his pipe from his coat pocket. 'The streets have been repaved, but the rest is all the same. The empire still rules.

The poor still suffer. A few of our people have risen through the cracks and a few others have fallen.'

Koro Ha had worked for odious men and taught obnoxious students when there had been a promise of security in exchange. The school in Sor Cala would not offer a gentle retirement, as Bo Winter-Starkness might have done. Quite the opposite, in fact, if the empire learned of Orna Sin's secret dealings—the sort that necessitated dead drops, signals written with kites, and exchanges of goods upon the open sea.

He took a deep breath, stifling Yin Ila's warning even as it echoed in his skull.

'You are one of those who have risen through the cracks, of course,' he said. 'I wonder how, and whether I might learn the answer to that question if I were to investigate those casks you brought aboard the other day. I wonder, too, what might have happened if the Sienese had found them.'

Orna Sin showed his golden tooth. The wrinkles around his dark eyes deepened, blending with the thin lines of old, faded scars. 'I want things for my people, Koro Ha, to make their lives better. To do that, I need money, but how is a man to make money in a world where the best trading rights—even to our own forests and mountains, cedar and marble—are never given to any but the Sienese? Where, as you saw yourself, they construct any pretence to harass us and seize our property? You found a way to live in their world in comfort, on the fringes, but there was no way to make my dreams come true while shackled by their law.'

He leaned back and struck a match, then pulled the flame into the shadowed bowl of his pipe, filling the air with a rich, woody aroma. Koro Ha considered that aroma. It was the same tobacco they had been smoking before the Sienese had interrupted their game, and it held scents and flavours he found difficult to name—a complexity much like that which he saw in Orna Sin's eyes.

'*A righteous crime,*' he murmured.

Orna Sin raised his eyebrows. Koro Ha gestured to his pipe.

'A name for that blend. Appropriate, I think.'

The merchant laughed.

'Perhaps, Teacher,' Orna Sin said. 'Time will tell.'

7
Return to Burrow
Foolish Cur

Furrows of blood and ash ran through Burrow's central street. Sienese garrison troops lay in the snow, blackened by conjured fire, savaged by the claws and fangs of beasts. War is a horror—even the Sienese sages admit as much. That horror gnawed at the base of my skull, though I could only walk forwards, numb to my own nausea.

What other path was left to me?

A door banged open, making the wainwright's slate hanging from the lintel sway on creaking hinges. An old man toppled out of the doorway, landing hard in the mud. Two young men in the mismatched armour of the Nayeni rebellion followed, one with a sickle to hand, the other levelling a spear.

'A whole tael to fix my father's broken axle, and now you say you've no money but a few strings of cash?' the boy with the spear snarled. 'Do you think we're stupid? Where are you hiding it?'

The wainwright put up his hands. 'Please! Take whatever else you want, but don't hurt us!'

A woman stepped into the light of the doorway, trembling and clutching a young boy who pulled against her grip, desperate to come to the wainwright's aid. The young soldier prodded the wainwright with the tip of his spear, drawing a trickle of blood from his shoulder.

I had accepted the reality of war, the tragedy inherent to any effort to answer violence in kind, but this was no act of rebellion against the empire, only a settling of old grudges. I reached for magic, sure that a burst of flame or lightning out of the dark of night would be enough to frighten off these fools.

'Weevil! Singing Thrush!' Running Doe, the young captain who had asked for my benediction, appeared from an alleyway, a lantern in one hand and her sheathed sword in the other. 'What the hell do you think you're doing?'

The young soldiers snapped to attention. 'Captain, this bastard bilked my da for all our savings just to fix the cart,' the one with the spear said. 'He knew we needed it to bring our crops to market. Knew we couldn't afford to haggle—'

'Do I give a shit?' Running Doe's breath curled around her in the cold. 'This isn't what we do, Weevil, you stupid bastard. Now get to the magistrate's hall. The fighting isn't done yet.'

The boys were bigger than her, and their weapons were drawn. For a moment they hesitated, and I wondered if petty vengeance would take precedent over loyalty to the rebellion.

I made to step out of the shadows, to lend the weight of my power and strange authority to Running Doe's command, but the boys brought fist to collarbone in reluctant salutes and jogged off down the central road. Running Doe sagged, heaved a sigh, and bent to help the wainwright. Only then did she spot me. Her eyes went wide and bright as coins.

'That was well done.' I moved to lend her a hand. We soon had the man on his feet, thanking us both profusely—then shuddering and taking a sharp breath as I wove healing sorcery to knit the wounds in his brow and shoulder. Which prompted another round of thanks and the promise that if either of us ever had a wheel, an axle, or an entire cart that needed fixing, we needed only bring it by.

'I should tell you, there's business at the magistrate's hall,' Running Doe said when the wainwright had shut and locked his door. 'I'm to send anyone I can find that way. You...ah...especially, I'd guess.'

It seemed to dawn on her just then that she had been speaking rather casually to me. Her face reddened and she touched the fetish of charred wood at her collar, then saluted again before darting off in search of any more young fools in need of stern orders.

When she had gone, worry crept back in. Signs of a fighting retreat marked my way: bundles of arrows dropped and scattered, bodies felled in flight, their backs torn by swords and talons. No Nayeni corpses, thankfully, though the memory of the Burrow common house haunted me.

Smoke billowed over the walls of the magistrate's hall in thick clouds, catching the glow of an unseen fire in the courtyard beyond the gates. My grandmother, my uncle, his cadre, and half a dozen rebel soldiers maintained a loose siege, bearing torches and tongues of conjured flame for light. Cramps trickled down my limbs. Tawny Owl, veered into her namesake, appeared in the light that rose from the courtyard, swooping over the roof. A volley of arrows herded her away. She wheeled and dived, drawing out another volley, before landing beside my uncle and, with a gust of cinnamon, returned to human form.

'Ah, Foolish Cur—good,' Harrow Fox said as I approached. 'We have need of you.'

I saluted while he explained that the magistrate had barricaded himself inside the hall with his servants and what remained of the garrison. I felt a pulse of relief to hear that Clear-River was still alive, then a clenching in my chest while my uncle told that he had refused to surrender.

'Unfortunate,' I said, 'but no great difficulty. They likely have a well but will run out of food before long.'

My uncle stroked the stripe of white in his beard. 'I declared that Burrow would fall in a single night, and it will. At dawn, word of our victory will spread to the nearby villages and we will begin to rebuild our army.'

Greyfrost, and the ensuing retreat of Pinion's legion, should have been a sufficient foundation for rebuilding our forces. But of course, Greyfrost was *my* victory, and this would be his.

'End this paltry siege,' Harrow Fox went on. 'With your command of the wind, you should have no trouble shielding yourself while you assault the hall.'

'If they attack me with grenades, the hall will catch flame,' I said.

Harrow Fox frowned. 'Well then, they will burn themselves out.'

'And half the town as well.'

'Would they be so foolish?' he asked.

'Who can say what the desperate will do when faced with death? Let me try to convince the magistrate to surrender.'

'You might appeal to his Sienese thinking, I suppose.' At last, Harrow Fox shrugged his heavy shoulders. 'Very well. But when dawn touches the horizon, this hall will be ours, even if we must claim it as a smouldering pile.'

I swallowed a dozen more arguments, reminding myself again that I had returned to Nayen to support my uncle. I had abandoned both my imperial career and what happiness I had found with the An-Zabati to join him and my grandmother, to earn a place at his side, a place among my family and my people. Already he had accused me of intending to usurp him, and to challenge him overmuch would only set him against me. There might be greater need to blunt the thrust of his brutality later. Instead I cast my voice at the window of the magistrate's hall.

'Clear-River! It is Foolish C…' I began, before correcting myself to use the name he would know. 'Wen Alder, that is. Please, you must surrender. You'll not win this fight.'

There was no reply at first, and I thought back to the Sienese morality tales I once had studied for the examinations. How many ended in suicide when the upstanding protagonist found himself cornered, unable to escape some profound violation of doctrine?

'Pinion warned that you would come,' Clear-River called back, speaking Sienese, his voice strained by terror. 'You were the one who made that wind, weren't you? I watched the arrows thrown back. The grenades spilling their fire in the air.' Another pause. When he spoke again, a vein of wild rage ran through the tremble of his fear. 'I didn't want to believe it. Wanted to think you would lead your army past this place. This is no great city, not even a fortress. What strategic value does it have?' His voice broke into a short burst of laughter. 'We were peaceful here. You saw that much yourself. Was it to destroy the symbol of what could be if not for this constant push and pull between the empire and the rebellion?'

My uncle's brow furrowed. He understood enough Sienese, I was sure, to follow our conversation.

'This isn't my army, Clear-River.' I followed him into Sienese. 'I am only my uncle's Hand, as once I was the emperor's. And he offers you mercy. Surrender. Have your guards throw down their weapons. Keep your lives.'

'You have destroyed our lives! And for what? Tell me, Alder, what was the point of this?'

I had no answer that could satisfy him. Nor one that satisfied myself, in truth.

'This does not seem to be going your way, Nephew,' Harrow Fox said flatly.

'Would you rather die than live?' I called back. 'Does it matter that much to you whether you serve the emperor or the Sun King?'

'One let me build something good here.' There was a new, mournful note in his voice. An indication, I hoped, that I was beginning to crack the armour of his anger. 'The other destroyed it.'

'It can be built again. And do not pretend Burrow was perfect under the empire. I remember the intrusion of that Sienese patrol. You may have built an island of peace, but it was ever dashed by the waves of conquest. There could be real peace, Clear-River. You need only surrender and lend your skill to the cause of Nayeni freedom.'

For a time, only the crackle of the torches and conjured flames answered, which stoked my hope. He was considering. Struggling through his fear and anger to the truth.

'I remember that patrol, too,' he answered, at last. 'And their bodies, carved apart and scattered on the ground. And now you ask me to trust you? To put my life in your hands? You must think me a fool.'

My heart sank. He would never believe me, not with the memory of the blood I had shed at the forefront of his mind. Since our first meeting, when we'd sat for the imperial examinations together so many years ago, there had never been trust between us. Why should that change now? If only I could show him my sincerity in a way more profound than words.

Realisation was slow to dawn. I remembered Hissing Cat's presence in my mind. How I had felt her frustration with me as my own, twisting in my gut. If I could reach Clear-River with transmission, I could make him understand my regret and my genuine hope to save his life in a way he could never dispute.

'You've stopped talking, Nephew,' Harrow Fox said, crossing his arms. 'Should I take that for an admission of defeat?'

'I've one more trick,' I said and shut my eyes.

It was not so different from other magics, I told myself, and my memories of Clear-River were sharp. His freckled cheeks, dimpled with a smile of feigned sincerity when, after witnessing me conjure fire in self-defence, he had promised to keep my forbidden magic secret, then twisting into a sneer as he threatened to expose me. His gaze, shadowed by envy, as he watched me on the dais, then full of disgust and horror at the sight of the violence I had visited upon his home.

Heavy weight in the wake of my magic descended as I reached through the pattern towards him, seeking the echo of those memories. There were no channels to guide me now. It was like dredging my mind for a half-remembered thought or a forgotten word on the tip of my tongue.

'What are you doing?' Harrow Fox demanded, but his voice was distant, muted by the depth of my focus as I reached into the pattern of the world, seeking Clear-River's mind.

There. The mirror-image of my memory. A huddled, road-worn figure, hands curled around swords of whirling air, rough clothes spattered with blood. I cast myself towards it, and felt Clear-River recoil in terror as my mind pierced and expanded into his. I enjoyed a rush of victory before I felt the echo of Clear-River's fear and confusion. His thoughts swirled and churned like a violent rapid, wordless in their panic.

<Clear-River, it's me,> I assured him, trying to project calm, hoping it would quiet his mind. <It's Alder.>

In response, he managed a single coherent thought. <What is this? Have I gone mad?>

<I am speaking to you with the same magic the emperor uses to speak to his Voices.>

Fragmented questions broke through the turmoil of his mind, like waves cresting in a storm-tossed sea. They washed over me, leaving me to make sense of them where Clear-River himself could not.

<Our minds are joined, yes,> I admitted, <but I've no desire to compel you. Words leave room for deception and disbelief. I would show you the truth of my intentions.>

I tried to project calmness and compassion, and with it my guilt over the violence I had brought to Burrow, both in this visit and the last. His mind began to still gradually, like a storm slowly spending itself against the shore.

<You will let us live? Truly?> he thought at last, and I felt a swell of triumph.

<Yes,> I told him, and believed. <There is no need for you to die today. Throw down your arms and walk out, and you will be spared.>

I felt his hesitation like a rip tide, pulling away from me, but with it a fatal certainty that to go on resisting would mean death. Finally, the placidity of a sheltered cove as he gave in. <I will need time to convince my men.>

'They're coming out,' I blurted in Nayeni and opened my eyes. Murmurs of surprise rose from my uncle's cadre.

'I know that magic,' Tawny Owl said, her eyes full of accusation. 'I've felt its wake from Voices of the emperor.'

I ignored her and turned to my uncle. 'I assured the magistrate that you would spare their lives.'

His face hardened. 'You are not my Voice, Nephew. You do not speak for me.'

I blinked. Surely I had mistaken his meaning. 'They will surrender. You—'

'Which of us leads this army?' he demanded. Behind him, my grandmother flinched, flexing her withered arm. Fear rippled through her expression. But of me, or of Harrow Fox?

The frustration of his suspicion—so easily overcome if I merely reached into his mind, as I had reached into Clear-River's—rankled. Yet I felt Tawny Owl's accusing gaze and knew that if I turned any magic on my uncle, no matter the benevolence of my purpose, our fragile alliance would shatter. 'You do, Uncle. Would you lead it as a tyrant who murders those who bend the knee, or as one who would liberate *all* of Nayen, even those who once served the empire? Clear-River has skills that we could use. An army survives not only by the sword but by bread and medicine, by supply trains and wagons. Logistics is the life and death of any campaign. Why kill a man—Nayeni by blood, even—who could help you?'

'So a traitor twice over, then?' Tawny Owl cut in with barely restrained fury.

'As am I,' I shot back, 'yet I have my uses.'

She stepped towards me, snarling, but before she could respond, the door to the magistrate's hall opened. Clear-River, dressed in plain robes, stepped out, his hands spread wide. His gaze lingered on me for a moment, then swept to my uncle. Six men in Sienese armour followed him. They showed their empty hands and wore empty scabbards. Clear-River fell to his knees and touched his forehead to the snowy ground.

'We surrender,' he said, 'and beg your mercy.'

'On your knees,' Harrow Fox barked. 'All of you.'

One of the guards, his face crossed by a horizontal scar, scowled in disgust, but they all did as commanded. Harrow Fox placed his hands on the hilts of his swords and stepped forwards.

'My nephew begs for your life, Magistrate,' he said in accented Sienese, as though Clear-River did not have the same reddish curls and tanned skin as Harrow Fox—darker, more Nayeni than mine. 'He says you might serve me well, as he has come to serve me. There is wisdom in this. I mean to rule Nayen for all Nayeni, even those who were once led astray by the allure of the empire.'

Clear-River's eyes peered up at me from where he lay prostrate. Cords of tension ran up and down my back. I had often been toyed with by men in power, and I recognised the posture and tone in Harrow Fox's words. Arrogance and cruelty carried their own accent.

'I will spare you.' Harrow Fox nodded as though he had only that moment come to a decision. He swept his gaze over the six Sienese soldiers kneeling behind Clear-River. 'You are Nayeni, after all. But we lack the manpower to keep prisoners, least of all these Sienese dogs.'

Tawny Owl's swords rasped from their sheaths. A shout of protest broke against my teeth. She swung once. Bright blood spattered the half-open door and the snowy ground. The first of the Sienese guards fell, his head drooping on a broken neck and strands of flesh.

Howls of disbelief rose from the other five, who began scrambling to their feet. Tawny Owl and my uncle's witches went among them, slashing and burning. The man with the horizontal scar made his feet, gripping a stone, blood running from a sword's gash in his shoulder. He yelled and lunged for Harrow Fox. A flush swept through me as Harrow Fox raised his hand and conjured fire. The scarred soldier collapsed, pawing at the flames that engulfed his face. His yell became a guttural scream, fading only as he died.

Clear-River, still kneeling, his robe speckled with blood, lifted his head just far enough to stare at me with accusing eyes.

'You promised,' he said, his voice a hoarse whisper.

'He has no power to make promises,' Harrow Fox said flatly. He loomed over Clear-River, his hands once more on the hilts of his swords. 'Now swear fealty, Magistrate, or die in the snow and mud with your soldiers.'

Clear-River's face twisted into a snarl, his teeth flashing in the light of torches and burning bodies. His hands curled into fists, ready to lunge for Harrow Fox, to die swinging as his men had died—or to lunge for me, I thought, as I became the target of his hateful glare.

He slammed his forehead to the earth. Hard enough to draw a trickle of blood.

'I swear fealty, Sun King.' His voice cracked. Then again, his words quiet and fading like the wisps of his breath. 'I swear fealty.'

Harrow Fox nodded once, then strode past Clear-River and into the hall. One by one his cadre followed him, stepping over the corpses of Clear-River's guards. The Nayeni soldiers who had been present for the spectacle left the scene, whispering among themselves, glancing at me over their shoulders.

Before long, only my grandmother, Clear-River, and I remained, standing in the flickering light and stagnant air filled with the stench of blood and charred flesh.

'Clear-River, I'm—'

'Leave me,' he snarled into the earth.

I swallowed. My grandmother shifted her weight, flexed her arm, muttered something about the cold, and followed my uncle's party into the hall. A pressure as profound as Hissing Cat's presence in my mind filled me, desperate to find words that might deflect my guilt and shame for what Harrow Fox had done—what I had enabled. Twice now I had ushered brutality and violence into Clear-River's home.

'It is war, Clear-River,' I said, as though that justified anything. Absurd words, maybe, but *honest* words. Weren't they? I hardened the part of me that ached with guilt and turned it into a shield. If Nayen was to be free, far more blood than this would need to be spilled. I left him there and went in search of Hissing Cat, or Doctor Sho, or anyone else who was neither my victim nor my rival. As I left, I muttered, in a moment of weakness, 'Be thankful that you are still alive.'

Clear-River began to laugh, a sharp, cracked sound in the brittle air that followed me through the streets of Burrow long after its last echo had fallen away.

8

What Remains in Sor Cala

Koro Ha

S or Cala was not as he remembered it.

The mound of upturned earth and jagged stone at the city's heart still cast its long shadow. This was the burial plot for the erstwhile capital city of Toa Alon, its great domes, hanging gardens, and masterful carvings preserved only in artists' renditions and old stories passed down by families who still felt the sting of its loss. Families like Koro Ha's own, whom he now went to visit, riding in a palanquin hired on his behalf by Orna Sin.

The climate, at least, had not changed. Though much of Toa Alon sprawled through the muggy, rain-thick jungles in the lowlands south of the Pillars of the Gods, Sor Cala had been built in their temperate foothills. Koro Ha had known the humid river lands of the Sienese heartland and the heat, rain, and snow that swept through Nayen, but home would always feel like the crisp breeze carried down from the Pillars, cool as marble even in summer.

Nevertheless, Sor Cala had been transformed by time, money, and Sienese influence. Gone were the dusty streets of broken tile, shattered by the magic that had called a mountain down fifty years before Koro Ha's birth. In their place, his bearers walked streets paved with brick in the Sienese style. Estates now dotted the surrounding hillsides, housing those Sienese landowners granted imperial writ to pull marble and gold from the mountains or reduce the dense jungles that filled the valleys and foothills to lumber. Walls had carved the sprawl that spiderwebbed around the burial mound of the ancient city into districts, and those districts into courtyard houses and tenements.

The piss-stink of tanneries and the acrid smoke pouring from kilns and chimneys told Koro Ha that his palanquin had reached the trade district, where he had lived the first and most difficult years of his life. The smell conjured old memories, and with them the urge to tell his bearers to turn around and return to Orna Sin's garden, leaving old scars undisturbed. Part of him longed for this reunion. Another dreaded it. When last he had visited his father and sister, shared grief had been enough to bridge the rift between them rent by time and the divergence of their lives—a rift that had only widened in the intervening twenty years. Too wide now, he feared, for already strained familial bonds to bridge.

Stone slates hung from lintels marked with simple illustrations to advertise various trades and services. They came to a stop before one such gateway bearing two slates, one marked with a needle and thread, the other with a chisel. He stepped down from the palanquin and told its bearers that he would be a while and that they should set their burden down. They exchanged glances. When most passengers spoke to them, Koro Ha knew, it was either to name a destination or to express annoyance at the slowness of the traffic. Koro Ha had risen high enough to ride in palanquins, but not high enough to forget that he had once imagined the men who bore them lucky.

A craftsman such as his father had a certain dignity, but people in a broken colony had little need for fine sculpture. The wealthy always needed conveyance, however, lest they scuff their slippers in the streets. An able-bodied man with a share in a palanquin never went hungry, nor put his son's future at risk for failure to pay his share of the teacher's fees.

A heavy wooden knocker hung from a hook on the door. He thumped it and waited. Shuffling feet and muttered curses in the Toa Aloni tongue sounded from within.

'Too busy to open the door, is she?' a gravelled voice said. 'Forces her father, after seventy years of eating dust and swallowing shit for her, to get up and open the door, does she? With rust in my joints and granite caked in my bones, eh?'

There was a grunt, the *clunk* of a bolt sliding open, and the squeak of hinges.

'Who's there?' the voice said, louder, the added effort and volume raising a rattle in the speaker's throat. The door swung open a crack. Two pinprick eyes in a face like a wrinkled prune peered out. Then widened.

'Hello, Father,' Koro Ha said. 'Might I come in?'

E ln Se, as it turned out, was not too busy to greet her long-absent brother, home suddenly and without a letter to announce his visit. She and her daughter, Rea Ab—who had been but a chubby, toddling child when Koro Ha had last seen her, and now stood taller than he and thin as a willow—cleared bolts of cloth and spools of thread from the broad table in the house's small central courtyard. The awning overhead had been unrolled to let in the bright summer sun and the cool mountain breeze. Koro Ha's father tried to join in the bustle, poking around in the kitchen in the back of the courtyard for cups and, as he put it, *something drinkable*, until Eln Se forced him onto one of the low-backed wooden chairs at the table.

'It is so good to see you, Brother!' Eln Se gushed, returning with a bottle and four pewter cups. Rea Ab sat beside her, studying her uncle with dark, curious eyes. Had Eln Se read his letters to her? Told stories of her brilliant uncle and his keen mind? Or had the silver he sent home been the only balance against her father's slow-burning hatred for him? 'Why didn't you write to say you were visiting?'

'It was a sudden decision,' Koro Ha said. 'In fact, my ship sailed the day after I decided. Had I sent word—short of convincing a Voice of the emperor to convey my tidings by sorcery—I would have arrived but a footstep behind the messenger. And this is not a visit. I intend to stay.'

Not the whole truth, he thought with a twinge of shame. The messenger would have arrived a few days ahead of him, thanks to Orna Sin's detour into nefarious, secret business and the brief, harrowing encounter with the imperial patrol. But the less said about that, the better.

'Oh?' His father filled cups with rice beer as white as milk. 'Hired to teach the son of some merchant, I hope, or one of the ministers. Our magistrate is a right bastard. And word is his son's even worse.'

'Magistrate Tan's children are already grown.' Eln Se narrowed her eyes at their father, either annoyed or concerned by his lapse in memory.

'I will be opening a school,' Koro Ha said, 'like the one Teacher Zhen held in the market square. The merchant Orna Sin has hired me to do so.'

His father nearly dropped the bottle. 'A school!' he blurted, then glared daggers at Eln Se. 'You said he was doing well! Taught up a Hand of the emperor, even!'

'Is he paying you well?' Eln Se asked. 'More than you made tutoring one student at a time?'

'About the same, actually.' A slightly embarrassing admission. 'And yes, I realise that it will be more work, having more students.'

She smiled, puzzling over him.

'What?' Koro Ha said. 'Does this surprise you?'

'I never thought you would believe in something enough to give up comfort,' she said.

He shifted in his seat. Her words, though pleasant enough, felt oddly like an insult. 'Do not the children of Toa Alon deserve the same opportunities as the sons of wealthy and powerful Sienese?'

'*You* had such an opportunity!' his father snapped. 'And what did you make of it? Nothing! A few fistfuls of silver sent home. Did your mother sew until her hands went crooked and her lungs gave out so that you could become a *tutor?*'

'I am making something of it *now*,' Koro Ha said. 'Something for Toa Alon.'

'Pfa! We *had* a school, and all it produced was *you!*'

Anger flared in Koro Ha's chest. He stifled it with a long sip of the rice beer his father had served. It left a bitter, burning taste in his mouth.

What had his father accomplished, for all his vanity, for all his unwillingness to bend in his principles? Koro Ha remembered nights when their home—smaller than this one, and older, built hastily by his grandfather in the aftermath of Sor Cala's destruction—had echoed with his mother's frustration, given vent in darkness under the false belief that her children slept. There were Sienese building estates in the hills. Mansions in the city. Sienese who needed sculptors. Did he not hear their children's groaning stomachs? Did he not see the other men, working under the same slate and symbol, bringing back silver from those mansions and estates and building better homes of their own?

But the Sienese wanted their own forms. Carvings of lion serpents and clouds, of trees and leaves and songbirds. Forms Koro Ha's father could have made but which he refused to.

If they wish to pay a Toa Aloni craftsman to do Toa Aloni work, I will gladly take their silver, but they have taken everything else and made it their own. They will not have the skill of my hands, too.

So he had gone to the quarries and carved blocks from the mountain's flesh, earning a bare fraction of his capacity but with his dignity intact. And Koro Ha's mother had worked her fingers into gnarled claws to feed their family.

There were so many cruel words swirling in Koro Ha's mouth, ready to spill forth, but at that point the door of the house swung open, interrupting him before he had a chance to plunge this reunion into deep hostility.

'Yan Hra!' Eln Se rose to greet her husband.

Yan Hra shrugged out of his light outer coat, shook it free of quarry dust, and hung it on a peg by the door. 'Your brother is here, I see,' he said sharply, lingering at the edge of the courtyard. 'That explains the carriage-bearers lounging in the alley.'

Koro Ha stood and bobbed his head, which made the other man's already wary expression sour.

'Did you know he was coming?' Yan Hra pointed the question at his wife.

'She did not,' Koro Ha said. 'As I explained earlier, my decision—'

'You talk like them now,' Yan Hra said. 'All lilting. Been north of the mountains too long. Now your mother tongue's infected.'

Koro Ha closed his mouth. How many times had he listened to an employer, or the friends of one, or even one of his *students*—

always after clarifying that they did not mean to lump Koro Ha in with the rest of his kind—speak of the untrustworthy Toa Aloni and their inherent deceitfulness, inextricable from their wild, uncivilised blood? If his father had possessed even a fraction of that strength and restraint, their family might have lived in relative ease rather than suffering years of privation.

Such restraint he exercised now, in the face of his brother-in-law.

'Uncle Koro Ha has come to open a school.' Rea Ab tried to add a bright note to her shaky voice. A lump filled Koro Ha's throat and warmth swelled in his chest. It was no easy thing, he knew, to stand up to one's father, and he felt an immediate fondness for this young woman whose childhood and youth he had witnessed only through the clouded lens of the occasional letter. 'He's going to help the children of Sor Cala now.'

'Help them?' Yan Hra shook his head. 'Steal them away, you mean. Make them Sienese, as he was made Sienese. That's what they do, Rea. They take for their own whatever they can use—our bodies, our skills, our minds—and hurl mountains down to bury the rest.' He fixed Koro Ha with a long glare before mounting the staircase to the upper floor of the house.

'I'm sorry about him,' Eln Se said softly. 'Please. He's tired after a long day. Let's pick up where we left off.'

But where they'd left off was the tearing open of old scars. Koro Ha shook his head.

'Thank you, but I should go.' He offered Rea Ab a grateful, apologetic smile and resolved to visit again soon. They had already lost too much time. More, he feared, than they could ever make up. 'We plan to begin classes next week. There is much to be done before then.'

He bade his father, niece, and sister goodbye. Next time, perhaps he would invite them to Orna Sin's home, where Koro Ha had been offered an apartment in the guest house. They would enjoy a tour of the merchant's modest gardens. His father, though he would balk at the Sienese style of the house—but weren't all rich men's houses built in that style, all throughout the empire?—might forgive a great deal when he saw the old-fashioned knotwork on the stone railings of the garden's pavilions. Perhaps then they would understand.

He was a few strides from his palanquin when footsteps sounded on the street behind him.

'Wait.' Eln Se stood in the street, her brow knit. 'I'm sorry. It is good to have you home, Brother.'

Koro Ha turned back towards her. 'Your love for your brother must run deep, to not have been spoiled by the hate that surrounds you.'

A ripple of anger tightened her face. 'They have suffered, Koro Ha. You have not been here. Is it so difficult to understand their feelings?'

'Yes!' She flinched, and Koro Ha took a deep breath, lowering his voice. 'How do they fail to understand, Eln Se? The emperor rules the world, by his Hands and his Voices. The Sienese are here to stay. But that does not mean Toa Alon must be ground beneath their heel. I raised a boy up from the island of Nayen, a land where rebellion *still* rages, to be the emperor's Hand. He has *proven* the capacity of his people. Because of him, in a matter of a generation, perhaps two, the Nayeni will become like the people of those scattered kingdoms in the Sienese heartland—once independent, once despised by their conquerors as we are, now welcomed, unquestioned, as citizens of the empire.

'Toa Alon will never be what it was. Always, the ancient city will lie crushed and buried beneath that cast-down peak. But *we* need not. I will raise up a generation of Toa Aloni scholars. Ministers. Magistrates. Even—yes! I have done it; I can do it again!—a Hand of the emperor. Your husband and our father nurse the wounds of the past and hate me for trying to build a future.'

The last words fell from his lips and silence rushed in to fill the space between them. Regret tugged at the back of his mind—but what had he to regret? What had he said but the truth? And more of it than he had offered to anyone but Orna Sin, on the *Swiftness of the South Wind*, while they had discussed their shared vision. Yet she looked at him like she had never understood him less.

'Then I wish you luck, Brother,' Eln Se said finally and left him there with his palanquin bearers, who kept their gaze low and away from him as he mounted and bade them carry him to his new home.

* * *

The challenge of teaching a classroom of students proved no mere product of multiplication. Koro Ha had expected the additional workload when the time came to answer his students' questions, or provide feedback on their essays, or drill them in the proper format of an oral examination, but difficulty struck from unexpected angles.

In the three weeks since his arrival in Sor Cala, Koro Ha had met the fathers of his pupils at a series of small gatherings hosted by Orna Sin, where Koro Ha impressed upon them all the value of the opportunity being provided to their children. Meetings which left Koro Ha wondering how much these men knew about their merchant benefactor and the source of his wealth.

When they first arrived, his students seemed awed by seriousness and weight of purpose. They sat quietly and listened respectfully, the five girls—whose presence Orna Sin had grudgingly approved only after Koro Ha agreed to a total of twenty students—clustered together to one side, any fidgeting quickly stifled with a hard glance. Or perhaps they were merely unsettled by being in a rich man's garden, sitting in rows beneath the eaves of a vast pavilion with nineteen comrades. Or discomfited by Koro Ha himself. He imagined himself from their point of view—a tall, serious man who spoke to them half the time in simple Sienese before repeating himself in Toa Aloni, explaining the arc of the next decade of their lives, culminating in the imperial examinations, the gateway to better futures for themselves, their families, and all Toa Alon. A speech which Tul Elna, the oldest of the five girls, sat through with a knowing, ironic detachment. *Say what you will, Master Koro Ha*, her sharp gaze challenged, *but some of us will never reach such heights.*

Weighty, momentous days for his students. But also, Koro Ha came to realise, they had simply been uncomfortable with one another. That discomfort gradually eroded, and as it did the scaffold upon which his instruction relied began to collapse.

The first crack showed on the seventh day. He was teaching them the proper method for holding a writing brush, moving from student to student, arranging their small fingers on the thick bamboo of the practice brushes.

'No, Kan In, the fingers must be spaced out, like so.' Koro Ha bent down to rearrange the digits of Kan In's pudgy fist while the boy stared, eyes bulging in quiet, frustrated concentration.

A shrill scream nearly split Koro Ha's eardrums. His hands clamped down. Kan In yelped, jerked back, and opened his mouth in shock and hurt.

'My ear!' the voice shrieked.

Koro Ha stood and swept his gaze across his pupils, most of whom were facing away from him, towards the other side of the pavilion, where the shriek had come from and from where hushed giggles now bubbled up.

'I could never have *imagined* such disrespect.' Koro Ha made his voice flat and hard as a blade. He crossed the pavilion in two long strides. All the children quailed, save two. One, his ear still dripping ink, had tackled the other. They rolled in the space between their writing desks, atop broken brushes and a toppled ink-pot, smearing both of their clothes with black while Tul Elna watched their antics with open contempt.

'Lon Sa!' Koro Ha roared. 'Quon Lo!'

The boys froze, then peeled apart and scrambled to their knees, whereupon they immediately began talking over one another, as though the truth of history were decided by who created the first record.

'Be silent.' The boys' mouths clicked shut. He studied their faces, offence and embarrassment mixing in his gut.

Lon Sa was one of the brightest of his students, already able to write some basic logograms in a steady enough hand for a seven-year-old, and with an attentive glint to his eye. Of all the boys, Koro Ha had imagined he would sit patiently, waiting for the next step in the lesson.

The other, Quon Lo, had been of average promise among the several dozen prospective students Orna Sin had presented. Koro Ha had been convinced to give him the last of the twenty seats only after a meeting with the boy's father—a sculptor who had done the stone-work for Orna Sin's gardens—and hearing the man's emphatic assur-ances that his son was a hard worker, from a family of hard workers. He had seen something of himself in the boy: a better retelling of the childhood he might have lived.

The smear of ink on Quon Lo's ear dripped onto his shoulder. Anger bristled on his young face. Lon Sa sat quietly, alert, face flattened by a poor attempt at hiding guilt.

'There are buckets behind the pavilion,' Koro Ha said. 'We will need water to clean our brushes when we are done, and to refresh ourselves. Fill the buckets from the well for us.'

'But Master!' Quon Lo protested. 'It's not fair! Lon Sa started it! He jabbed my ear with his brush, you see?'

'I do see,' Koro Ha said. 'And you attacked him. Is it the son's role to punish his brother, or the father's?'

The boys blinked up at him. Not their fault. He sometimes forgot that even the most basic precepts of doctrine needed to be taught.

'You should have informed me and let me mete out Lon Sa's punishment,' Koro Ha said. 'One must never strike a fellow scholar, nor take justice into one's own hand. That was your wrongdoing. Now do as I have said.'

Quon Lo grumbled but got to his feet and trundled off towards the buckets. Lon Sa stared up at Koro Ha.

'Doesn't Master Orna Sin have servants for fetching water?' the boy said. 'We're not servants. That's not our job.'

'How rude!' Tul Elna blurted. Koro Ha quieted her with a hard glance of his own, which she answered by tucking her hands into her armpits and hugging herself tight—a visible effort to constrain her fury that almost shattered Koro Ha's severe expression into laughter. He cleared his throat to regain composure and turned his attention to Lon Sa.

'That is true,' Koro Ha said. 'And if you attend to your lessons and succeed in the imperial examinations, a day may come when you fetch water for the last time and then have servants of your own. But if you continue behaving as you did today, you will be *lucky* to find work in a fine house such as this, carrying water for the rest of your days. Which future do you prefer, Lon Sa?'

The boy considered this for a long moment—too long, almost rebelliously so—before he finally did as he had been told.

Koro Ha stuffed down his lingering aggravation, adopted a placid, teacherly affect, and knelt back down beside Kan In, whose pudgy cheeks were wet with tears. Gently, he opened the boy's fist and set his fingers to the writing brush, while out of the corner of his eye he watched the other seventeen children at their desks, where they sat as unmoving as stones.

'It is absurd.' Koro Ha thumbed tobacco into his pipe, stuffing the bowl tight. Orna Sin sat beside him in the Pavilion of Contemplation, which overlooked the small pond in his garden. It was a simple structure, ornamented by only a few stone tiles bearing Toa Aloni knotwork. Unpainted paper screens hung between the support columns, thrown open now to let the mountain breeze circulate lest the warmth of late spring settle into muggy heat. Koro Ha took a taper from the lantern hanging in the centre of the pavilion and lit his pipe.

Orna Sin lit his own pipe, took a slow draw, and let the smoke trickle from his mouth. It formed a cloud above them, obscuring the rafters overhead.

'Do you want to remove them?' Orna Sin asked. 'There are other candidates.'

'No. Quon Lo certainly not. I considered Lon Sa, but…' Koro Ha watched the swirling complexity of the smoke. 'It is my fault, in truth. How can I blame him for being bored and frustrated when I spend all day teaching things he already knows?'

'That is very fair of you,' Orna Sin said.

Koro Ha gestured sharply with his pipe. 'It is not a problem I have dealt with before. With a single student, I tailor instruction to ability and make steady progress, whether that student be brilliant or a stone wall. This…I am not sure how to deal with.'

'You could do as Teacher Zhen did,' Orna Sin suggested. 'Put the brilliant ones at the front and teach them, and hope something reaches the stone walls in the back.'

'A strategy that produced exactly one successful examinee.' Koro Ha shook his head. 'Our goal is to raise up a generation of Toa Aloni ministers, magistrates—even a Hand, if we can manage it. They must all be taught as best as I can teach them. But I have only so much time. To build a plan of instruction to cultivate a single mind is challenging enough. To do so for twenty students at once…I would need twenty of myself to do the work justice.'

'If I am honest, I anticipated this challenge, and I have a thought.' Orna Sin tapped out the spent ashes from his pipe on the rim of the brazier and sat, staring into the flames. 'Something I planned to propose later on. In a year, perhaps two, when the inevitable differences between your pupils made themselves more keenly felt. But perhaps it is worth trying now, from the beginning.'

The hairs on the back of Koro Ha's neck began to itch. Orna Sin kept far too many secrets, and this one in particular rankled. He wanted to make some sharp reply, to question why Orna Sin had not proposed this idea when they first discussed the school. Instead, he said only, 'I would be grateful for any help you might offer.'

Orna Sin smiled. 'You mean beyond the use of my garden, food and board, and an ample salary?'

Koro Ha returned the smile. He was accustomed to this kind of jesting, this gentle mockery of his dependence on the money and power of others. He wondered sometimes if it were possible to make one's way in the world without tolerating such humiliation. Or at least possible without risking one's life and career at every turn.

'Any *further* help,' he said genially.

'What would you say to sending Lon Sa—and perhaps Quon Lo, and any other students who are quicker to master your lessons—to a separate class…perhaps once a week? That way, they could be engaged in learning while you are free to devote your attentions to those students who need more direct instruction.'

Koro Ha felt his smile falter. 'What will be taught in these separate classes?'

Orna Sin began to repack his pipe and did not meet Koro Ha's gaze. 'If I were to propose that the students spend time with, say, one of the scribes I employ in my business to practise their calligraphy, you would counter that this would only make the problem worse. They will suspect that their time is being wasted on unnecessary repetition, and they would be right. You and I are both intelligent men who know that intelligence hates nothing more than being wasted on a pointless task.'

'Indeed,' Koro Ha said. 'Then you must be proposing something else.'

Orna Sin put the pipe stem in his mouth and placed the taper back in the lantern flame.

'Tell me, Koro Ha,' he said, 'is our goal only to create ministers, magistrates, and—yes—even a Hand of the emperor of Toa Aloni descent? To more fully integrate ourselves into the empire? Or is it to create *Toa Aloni* ministers, magistrates, and even a Hand of the emperor?'

Koro Ha frowned. 'I'm not sure I understand.'

Orna Sin lit his pipe, took a few long puffs, and levelled his gaze at Koro Ha, whose heart began to pound for reasons he could either not identify or not admit to himself.

'You're suggesting…what?' Koro Ha pressed. 'A day learning about stone masonry and carving scrollwork? Or old stories of silent gods? What good will that do them?'

'If they are to advocate for their people, they must know who their people are,' Orna Sin said.

'And who will teach them?' Koro Ha went on.

Orna Sin gestured at the carvings decorating the pavilion. 'There are people in Sor Cala who keep our ways alive. Old folk who remember older stories. Craftsmen who kept up their art, even when there was no money to be made from it. Leave the question of *who* to me, Koro Ha.'

Orna Sin spoke with an uncommon gravity, selecting words carefully as though talking around some larger truth. Here, Koro Ha was certain, dwelt a hint at the merchant's true motive for creating his school. A motive he might have explained outright from the beginning, but which, whether due to a smuggler's trained caginess or a fear that Koro Ha might bolt, he continued to obfuscate, revealing it only in hints and implications.

'You have put a great deal of thought into this, from long before I accepted your proposal, I suspect.' Koro Ha's humiliation had condensed into a coal of smouldering anger. He had allowed himself to believe that the school was *his* project, that for once he was his own master. 'Do you even need my approval in this?'

Orna Sin paused, took a deep breath, and leaned towards him. 'I told you that they were your students, Koro Ha. That you would decide their course of study. Do you doubt me?'

'It sounds to me that you have decided a course of study for my best students without consulting me.' Koro Ha felt his pulse quickening and knew he might say something he would regret later, but he forged ahead anyway. Better to air grievances now while the project could be abandoned with minimal consequence. 'It is bad enough that I now teach in a school rather than as a tutor—a school funded by a merchant who seems to be on poor terms with the empire, no less. If it is discovered that this school served as a front to promulgate Toa Aloni culture, considered barbarous by the empire, I will never teach again, no matter my past successes.'

'I am making a suggestion,' Orna Sin said gently, as though soothing a frightened child. 'That seems to lie within the bounds of our agreement.'

Koro Ha puffed on his pipe, stared off into the garden, watched the birds of evening dart after insects, listened to the repeating chorus of their songs, and willed his anger to cool.

Whatever his deeper motives might be, Orna Sin's suggestion had merit on its surface. In fact, Koro Ha had long suspected that Wen Alder's grandmother had provided something similar, at least until she had mysteriously disappeared from the estate. Perhaps such an education—a view of the canon and doctrine from outside—had its benefits, the better to make the unexpected, cutting insights that had been key to Alder's success—once they had been refined in dialogue with Koro Ha to make them more palatable to conventional minds.

There was risk of confusion, and the method was certainly unorthodox—to put it mildly!—but worth trying. More importantly, it did seem likely to solve the immediate problem of Lon Sa and Quon Lo's distractibility. And, whatever Orna Sin's true motives, Koro Ha had agreed to this project for reasons of his own. This school and these students would prove, as Wen Alder had proved for Nayen, that Toa Alon was no longer the colonial backwater of his childhood but a province able to produce scholars of value to the empire.

'Very well,' Koro Ha muttered. 'We will try it, so long as you agree that any students who fall behind will return immediately to the regular course of study, with me.'

Orna Sin lifted his pipe in salute. 'Naturally.'

9
The Makings of a Pact
Foolish Cur

'I knew you would figure it out,' Hissing Cat said, lurking against the wall of the makeshift infirmary, which had once been Burrow's garrison house. The Nayeni wounded—ten of our forces, among them the three who had been catatonic since Greyfrost, and a dozen villagers who had been hurt in the fighting—lay convalescing in what had been cots belonging to Sienese soldiers. After the debacle at the magistrate's hall, I had sought out Doctor Sho. Now, I slouched on an empty cot, exhausted by a night spent mending wounds while he prepared medicines to bolster our patients after my healing magic drained them of strength. Okara lay nearby, dozing in the warmth of the brazier.

'I wish I hadn't.' My thoughts had been a swirling chaos since I had left Clear-River cackling in the snow.

'You don't mean that,' Doctor Sho chided. He had heard rumours whispered by soldiers who came to deliver the wounded. Soldiers who had only suspicious eyes for me now, and who no longer wore the blackened remains of Greyfrost's forest. 'From what I've heard, you saved a life.'

'And lured half a dozen to brutal deaths,' I said wryly.

The scraping of Doctor Sho's mortar and pestle paused. 'More brutal than being trapped in a burning house, choked on smoke and cooked alive?'

I thought of the scar-faced guard, his head wreathed in flames.

'At any rate, you've learned transmission now,' Hissing Cat cut in. 'You'll be wanting to learn about how the pacts were made next, I expect.'

I looked to one of the children in our care. Her arm now ended at the wrist, like mine. How could I, after this, give Harrow Fox *another* weapon, and so powerful a one as a canon of sorcery? He intended to remain in Burrow for a few days—long enough to bolster our forces with reinforcements from the surrounding countryside—but we would march before long, pressing on to the next battle, the next opportunity to wound the empire in the wake of Pinion's unexpected retreat, each wound another rallying cry for the rebellion.

Was Hissing Cat blind to the suffering around her? How many more children would bleed if I gave Harrow Fox what I had promised?

But no, Hissing Cat was not unfeeling. She stared at the floor, her eyes misted, as though veiled by a wilfulness not to see the pain around her. Not quite as effective as isolation in a cave.

'Why can't we stop this?' I demanded of her, something within me giving way like a breaking dam. 'You and I can reshape the pattern of the world to our whim, yet it is still so full of suffering. I thought...' Thought what? That I might find peace in the midst of rebellion? Pure foolishness. There might be peace when Nayen was free and the empire destroyed, but the road to that future would be paved in blood and bone. 'Why is it that, for all your power, for all you wrested away from the gods, you witches of the old sort left the world so broken?'

'This isn't a thing of the pattern, Cur,' Hissing Cat said, her voice sharp. 'This is a thing of human will.'

Silence stretched between us. I stood and moved on to my next patient, an old woman, the side of her head broken, breathing shallowly but still alive. I shut my eyes, reached for the canon of healing, felt the cooling calm in its wake, and began to knit her wounds.

Whatever I felt about my uncle and the power I had offered him, this at least was an unquestionable good.

'What you describe,' Doctor Sho said softly, his hands still gripping the mortar and pestle in his lap, 'that's what Tenet is trying to do. To drag the world howling and biting to his vision of peace and harmony. And how well has that been going, would you say?'

'Not well,' I said, thankful that the wake of healing sorcery had helped to calm the tenor of my voice.

'If you choose not to fight him, you accept that his vision of the world should endure.' Doctor Sho tipped the contents of his mortar out into a paper sack, then began riffling through the drawers of his medicine chest. 'That was the choice I made for many years.'

'And do you regret that choice?' I said, fusing plates of shattered bone, mending burst veins, doing my best to rebuild bruised and broken nerves. The woman in my care winced. Even healing magic caused some pain, though I did my best to dull it.

Doctor Sho shook his head. 'It was either fight back and die in futility or go on living and do what I could to ease suffering where I found it. You aren't as powerless as I am. The choice is more real for you. Can you accept the world as Tenet would have it—and the war with the gods he means to wage, which will cost far more blood than this rebellion—or will you drag yourself and a great many other people through fire and pain in your effort to stop him?'

'Well, I *do* regret it.' Hissing Cat shifted against the wall, clattering the ravens' skulls in her hair. 'Sitting by, I mean. Doing nothing. Enough that I've taken to disobeying the bones once in a while.'

'Then why bother consulting them?' I said.

Hissing Cat grumbled and crossed her arms but otherwise ignored my jab. The woman in my care took a steady breath. A bruise still mottled her face, but beneath it the bones and flesh were whole again.

This was what it came down to, then. A willingness to hurt the world, and those within it, in order to make it whole. The strength to reckon with the brokenness and the pain, and accept what had to be done to fix it. A strength my uncle possessed but I lacked.

A good thing, then, that he should be Sun King.

But perhaps it was a strength I could learn.

'Well then, Hissing Cat.' I stood from my patient and curled my hand into a fist. 'Tell me how the pacts were formed.'

It was one thing to hear an explanation, but without an example her words were only wind, and she would not take the risk of creating another pact herself.

'All magic might be permitted to *you*,' Hissing Cat said when I asked for a demonstration, 'but *I* made certain promises that I intend to keep.'

Okara was little more helpful. Reaching him with transmission proved a challenge—my every memory of him was a confused blending of stone statue, mortal vessel, and divine voice, and I doubted very much any of the three was more than a facet of the whole— but whether because I succeeded at last or he detected my attempt to reach him, we spoke.

<We did not make the pacts,> he said plainly. <We only accepted them as a compromise. The witches bound themselves.>

<But you have said—many times—that you were bound by pact,> I protested.

<Our half of the compromise,> he explained. <All that binds us is the agreement the pacts represent, and the threat of war should we break it. A consequence I would like to *prevent*.>

So it was that, in need of an example, I sought my uncle in what had been Clear-River's home and hall, now the Palace-in-Exile of the Sun King. Morning light glittered on the snow and stung my eyes—a reminder of my exhaustion after two days without sleep.

A raised voice echoed down the central street. One of my uncle's cadre—the Vulture, I thought of him, for the form he took when veering—stood on an overturned crate. Townsfolk peered from their doorways or huddled nearby, hoping his words would help them to understand the shifting of the world beneath them and the character of their newly arrived king.

'...atonement for your complacency beneath the yoke of empire!' the Vulture declared. 'Spread word! One able-bodied member of each household will march from here under the banner of the Fox! The liberation of Nayen has begun!'

Whispers of outrage drifted in answer, but I did not linger to hear them. As I approached the magistrate's hall, I found Running Doe and two others sorting through a collection of armour. Running Doe lifted a shirt of bloodstained Sienese mail, considered the broken links where an arrow had pierced it, and added it to one of several piles. As I approached the door, she snapped a salute. The others with her did likewise. All three still wore scraps of burnt wood on their collars. I answered with a nod.

The smell of burning dogwood in the brazier was pleasant after the cloying reek of sickness and injury in Doctor Sho's hospital. The high windows stood open, filling the space with the cold light of winter. Between them, a few painted scrolls still hung on the walls. Landscapes, mostly. Those that depicted heroes of Sienese legend or calligraphy had been slashed. The remains of a quote from Traveller-on-the-Narrow-Way fluttered on a torn strip of silken backing. I recognised it, even in fragments.

The elder brother's first duty is to the father,
then to the younger brother.
By serving the former, he serves the latter.
So, too, the magistrate serves those who rule on the emperor's behalf.

Voices drifted from the far end of the hall, where my uncle held court at a broad table flanked by Tawny Owl and my grandmother. Clear-River stood across from him, his shoulders stooped, dressed in the same plain silk he had worn the night before, mottled with the rust brown of bloodstains. His hair hung in loose, unkempt curls.

'...forced withdrawal to Eastern Fortress.' Even his voice had changed. Flattened, as though crushed beneath a heavy stone. 'The garrison would have been empty if he'd had his way. I suspect he will do likewise in Iron Town and Setting Sun Fortress, though doubt he will bother with other small towns and villages such as this.'

'He has some six hundred men, you say?' my uncle asked.

Clear-River nodded. 'Though he will lose a few to fatigue, sickness, and desertion. He pushed them hard from Greyfrost and gave no indication that he would slacken his pace.'

'Madness.' My grandmother thumped her cane on the floor. 'He pushes his men to their deaths, and for what? To flee our little army?'

'It is not your army he flees,' Clear-River said.

Harrow Fox ran his fingers through his beard and looked up from the table, spotting me where I lingered in the entryway.

'That will be all, *Magistrate*,' Harrow Fox said, speaking Clear-River's title like a curse. Clear-River bowed deeply and backed away in Sienese fashion. As he turned to leave, his gaze found mine and flashed with hatred, like fading coals stoked by a bellows. He strode stiffly past me, then down a corridor towards the servants' wing of the hall.

Harrow Fox beckoned me towards him. I approached with a salute. He planted his palms on a Sienese map of Nayen that had been laid out on the table. Tawny Owl leaned against the wall and regarded me coldly. Disgust swirled at the sight of my uncle and the memory of Tawny Owl's sword falling, the spray of blood, the howls of shock and betrayal.

The pain of setting a broken bone, I told myself, tamping down my doubts. The rebellion needed the canon of witchcraft, and would need it before its first true battle. Better my uncle's brutality than the empire's.

'Do you grow tired of tending the wounded, Nephew?' Harrow Fox asked.

'I left them in Doctor Sho's care,' I said. 'I have come to tell you of my progress in making the canon of witchcraft, and to ask for aid to that end.'

He continued studying the map. 'Well? What do you need?'

'The canon I will craft will mimic the magic that binds pact marks. As you can see…' I trailed off, gesturing with the stump of my right wrist. 'I no longer have one of my own.'

Harrow Fox looked up from the table. 'You want the use of one of my cadre?'

'I thought that Grandmother might be willing—' I began, but Harrow Fox cut me off.

'Tawny Owl,' he said. 'Go with him.'

Tawny Owl balked, her surprise mirroring my own, though she likewise mastered it before it became an insult to Harrow Fox.

'I'd be more than happy to help him,' my grandmother said. 'There's no need for the girl to do what she doesn't want.'

'I still have need of you.' Harrow Fox nodded sharply to Tawny Owl. 'You have orders. See to them.'

Her mouth twitched, but she saluted and turned to me.

'I will need quiet. To concentrate,' I said.

Wordlessly, Tawny Owl set off towards what must once have been the guest wing of the hall. Before leaving, I saluted my uncle. 'Thank you, Sun King.'

He did not answer, only went back to studying the map. My grandmother flexed her withered arm, meeting my gaze with an unspoken warning before I left the room. A warning I appreciated but did not need. I trusted my uncle very little, and the cadre that served him not at all. Not yet. Perhaps never, after what they had done the night before.

Tawny Owl led me to a guest room. The bookshelf was empty, though a few wooden spines still bearing silken bindings stamped with the titles of Sienese classics survived among the coals of the brazier. A half-empty bottle of fine rice wine, likely looted from Clear-River's cellar, stood on the table. Tawny Owl slumped into one of the two chairs and grabbed the bottle.

She sipped, thumped the bottle back down, and gestured to the other seat. I lowered myself into it.

'Well?' she said. 'What now?'

'I need to see your witch marks,' I explained.

Tawny Owl took another sip, then put the back of her right hand on the table between us and opened her fist.

'May I?' I said, reaching towards her scars.

She grimaced but nodded sharply. As I reached for her hand, she flinched back. Then, with a deep, steeling breath, she opened her hand again. I traced the lines of her witch marks with the tips of my fingers, feeling a pang of nostalgia for those I had once worn on my missing hand.

Tawny Owl's palm tensed beneath my touch. 'How long is this going to take?'

'Some time,' I said flatly and shut my eyes.

Unlike the canon of sorcery, I had never felt the structure of the pacts when I had worn them—neither my Nayeni witch marks, nor my wind-caller's tattoos, now nothing but puckered scars on the underside of my forearms. My witch marks had first manifested as a limiting of my sense of the pattern of the world, a veil I had lived behind—despite many attempts to pierce it—from the moment my grandmother marked me until Voice Usher had cut my right hand away. My windcaller's tattoos had achieved the opposite effect: an opening up of possibilities that had been hidden, a new well of power to shape the wind and summon water.

'Tell me, Cur,' Tawny Owl said suddenly, 'why do you pretend to serve a man you hate?'

The complexity of her question, and the challenge it carried, jerked my attention out of the pattern.

'I don't hate him,' I said firmly. 'And I am not pretending.'

She scoffed. 'I know a few things about hate. There's been tension between you two since you first landed at Greyfrost, but when you looked at him just then I saw it in your eyes.'

I stared her down. Who was she, after all, to demand proof of my loyalty? I was no longer a pawn of the empire, threatened from all sides by Hands and Voices powerful enough to kill me with a flick of the wrist and a thought. She was only a witch, whereas I was one of the old sort.

'My work requires silence,' I said and returned my attention to the pattern.

'With one breath, you burn away a Sienese legion,' she said, ignoring me. 'With the next, you demand we spare a Sienese magistrate and go pale when Sienese heads roll. You make no sense.'

'The first was necessary to save the rebellion,' I said. 'The second was not.'

'And you have the right to decide this?' Her voice had turned bitter. 'You salute Harrow Fox and call him Sun King, but you hate him.'

'I do not hate him,' I repeated, 'but I do question him. Is Nayen like the empire, demanding not only loyalty but unquestioning obedience?'

'We obey him because he knows what it takes to survive as the wolf in the woods, surrounded by hunters. He taught us how to fight them, and how to win, even at great cost. Even if only to have our revenge.'

I felt my pulse like a hot thread in my neck. 'You feel no guilt, after such brutality?'

'Does a wolf feel guilt for tearing out a hunter's throat?'

'But you are not a wolf, and those men were not hunting you.' I would not convince her. She would not convince me. What, then, was the point of this conversation? Yet I plunged onwards, full of righteous anger, no longer restrained by the fear that had stilled my tongue for so many years. 'I agree that the empire must be stopped, and when necessary we may have to fight and kill those who serve it. But those men had surrendered. They were no more threat to you.'

She stared at me, her face flat, and did not answer.

'Just let me finish my work,' I muttered and descended again into the pattern.

I reached towards the subtle walls of her pact, and a wave of sensations washed over me. Flashes of memory not my own. Cold streets on snowy winter nights. Alleys I vaguely recognised from Iron Town, though now I saw them from a child's perspective. A ceaseless rumbling in my stomach. A tangy smell I did not know but which the memory told me was the scent of a brothel too poor to refine itself with incense. Leering Sienese eyes, dark and hungry. A boot thudding into my back. A hand helping me up, and Harrow Fox's face.

A sharp cry split the air. A wave of revulsion washed through me, as though I had reached into a dark pool and brushed my hand against the mouldering flesh of a corpse. I gasped and retreated back to myself. Tawny Owl stood against the wall, her chair overturned, her teeth bared. She clutched her right hand, massaging her witch marks.

'Bastard! You could have warned me,' she snarled. Her eyes were red and wide, her body hunched like a cornered dog. 'It burned and ached liked I'd grabbed a coal from the brazier.'

My pulse slowed as the flashes of her memories faded, not enough to string together a narrative but enough to understand her a little better. More importantly, in the moment before I touched her mind through her pact, I had felt the structure of the spell that bound it to her. Hissing Cat had tried to describe it—the magic of the pacts was *like* transmission, yet it dealt not in the conscious layers of the mind but in the deeper reaches of the subconscious and the soul. Her explanation had meant little to me at the time but now felt profound and coherent, as though her words had been a poem full of strange allusions I had only now come to understand.

There were *layers* to the pattern of the world that I had, until now, failed to grasp. Conjuring fire, calling the wind, and even healing wounds all dealt with the surface layer, manipulating forces of the physical world. When I delved into Clear-River's thoughts, I had passed through the first and into a second layer, full of its own complexities, comprising countless overlapping patterns, each corresponding to a single mind. Deeper still was a layer in the soul buried within the mind where dwelt the most heartfelt feelings, the most sacred beliefs, the most powerful fears, like veins of diamond condensed from earth by vast expanses of time and pressure.

Tenet had built his canon within the mind, wielding transmission. But it was here, in the soul, where the gods and witches of the old sort had forged their pacts.

More vitally, I now understood how to forge one of my own. A realisation which did little to dull the echo of Tawny Owl's horror, still reverberating within my mind.

'I'm sorry for any discomfort,' I said, slowly standing, forcing my voice into an even register. 'I have what I need now.'

Looking at her, I felt a flush of shame. I had taken truths from her that she had not shared, some that had been deeply buried. But I had not touched her conscious mind. Perhaps, unlike Clear-River, she did not know what I had done. I turned to leave.

'I saw something,' she blurted. 'A...a woman standing against the moon, wreathed in fire. A boy with his throat cut open. And a dog with eyes like a wolf, drenched in blood.'

My hand slipped on the latch of the door. I stared at her, certain that she was lying, but her face was open and afraid. I was not the only one who had glimpsed the buried pain at the heart of another mind.

'The old magic leaves a strange wake in the world,' I said. 'To you, it may have manifested in these hallucinations. Think nothing of them. And thank you. The help you offered will be the cornerstone of the canon of witchcraft.'

I was careful to keep my pace steady as I left her and made my way out of the magistrate's hall, though my feet longed to flee as though a Sienese legion were at my heels. She had glimpsed Atar and Oriole, certainly, and the grief I carried. The third image…I cast it back into the depths of my mind. It was meaningless to me, but it made my blood thunder and my knees stiffen. I had kept enough secrets in my life, but never secrets from myself. At least, so I believed. What, then, had Tawny Owl seen?

The winter air shocked me back to myself. I breathed deeply, trying to find some ember of pleasure in having accomplished my goal. Here was another secret mystery of magic, now mine. Yet there was only horror, and with it the burden of the next step required of me in service to my uncle's rebellion.

How many such steps yet stood between me and a line I would not cross? Twice in two days, I had invaded another person's mind, as old wives' tales warned the emperor invaded the minds of his servants. I had brought a storm of blood and death down on Burrow—again. And here I was, in the midst of building a weapon to rival the canon of sorcery.

Another breath. I focused on the cold air in my lungs and the strength it carried to my limbs. Remembered the cost of healing: a burning fever, the agony of setting a bone.

The thought did little to quell the churn in my stomach, a revulsion all my own. The rebellion needed me, true enough, but was a place at my uncle's side worth becoming what I hated, a sorcerer who tore into people's minds, unearthing secrets and old agonies? A tyrant who contorted magic into a tool of war?

No. Tenet and I were nothing alike. We were opposites, as the rebellion and the empire were opposites. I was not making a weapon, I told myself as I went in search of Hissing Cat and the next tool I would need to make my canon. I would not make a sword but a scalpel. Not a means of conquest but a tool for lancing the boil of empire, which had infected hearts like Tawny Owl's and mine with such unspeakable pain.

Part Two
Cadre

Interlude
Stormrider

There is a woman called Atar upon the *Spear of Naphena*, the ship that rescues Ral. A dancer and a storyteller who speaks Ral's language well. Something of an elder, in her way. Though she is younger than Ral, she carries the history of her people. They exchange stories, Atar listening with a glint of starlight in her eye while Ral tells of her childhood, of her power, of the blessing of the gods. At this last, Atar scoffs.

'The gods are cruel,' she says. 'What you possess is not their gift but a weapon against them.'

It is hard to understand at first, but the longer Ral spends with the An-Zabati, the more she comes to see their world. The Skyfather gives them no rain, only the scorching sun upon the sands. Everything they have, they take, whether drawing water from deep beneath the earth or the wind down from the sky, and these gifts they received from their high priestess, Naphena. They call her a goddess, but Atar explains that she was a woman first, a powerful windcaller who built the city of An-Zabat and filled its oasis in defiance of the Skyfather's cruelty. A mercy that cost her life.

The city, too, has been lost. Atar is reluctant to explain, but Ral needs no explanation. She understands the brutality of empire. Remembers flashing steel and screaming horses. Smoke and fire.

Ral hopes that some of her people survive. She wishes to go in search of them and says as much, but her existence presents a question to the An-Zabati, one they wish to discuss.

They are fond of discussion. The captain, a man called Katiz, decides little without the commentary of his crew. And, Atar explains while Ral swallows a swell of fresh and too-familiar fear, the question Ral poses will require a gathering of captains and a longer discussion.

Katiz flies a kite tailed with flags of brilliant orange and yellow. Soon their cousins flutter on the horizon, and in days a dozen An-Zabati ships gather. Ral watches their convergence with a deepening nausea. They freed her, but they will not let her leave. With a horse and the north star, she could find the sheltered valley where her people have for generations gone to ground in dangerous times. If any survive, they will be there, and she should be with them.

'What is the question they seek to answer?' she asks Atar.

The dancer studies her, perhaps finding the words in the Girzan tongue, perhaps hesitating while she crafts a convincing lie. 'You have no mark of power, Ral, yet you were seen to conjure lightning. This should not be. It signals a great change in the world. Something to be feared, perhaps, but perhaps also an opportunity.'

Ral's stomach turns. Another question—*An opportunity for what?*— dies on her tongue.

The An-Zabati are not as cruel as the Sienese, but neither do they take her to the edge of the steppe and set her free. Instead, they take her to a gathering of ships, to the top of a dune where Katiz buries a silver bowl and works a magic—cool, refreshing—not unlike the magic that drives their sails. They drink the water he conjures and they talk, and go on talking, speaking about her in a tongue she does not understand.

She thinks of her people. The smile of her sister. The keen eyes of the elders. Her father's pride and concern. Of the screams at night. The blinding light, and then the darkness. Waking in the hold of a ship that sails across the earth.

Do any of them live? Her heart aches as one of the An-Zabati captains jabs a finger at her. Atar meets Ral's gaze, and for a moment she hopes the dancer will speak on her behalf, but the others go on arguing and her sadness turns sour, and then begins to burn.

Three strides bring her to the centre of the circle beside the silver bowl. Their babbling falls silent. Her gaze finds each pair of eyes, holds, accuses, and moves on. Finally, she finds the words, though stiff with her underuse of the trading tongue.

'It is not yours to decide my fate,' she declares, and welcomes their challenge. 'I am Ral Ans Urrera, Stormrider of the Girzan steppe. My place is with my people. I will not be held captive, neither by the empire nor by those who would claim friendship.'

They exchange glances, whispering to one another while she makes her face iron. Katiz steps forward, all concern, palms offered in submission. It is a gesture he learned in trade with her people, she is sure, and it only hardens her heart.

'You are not our captive,' Katiz says. 'We rescued you. If you rush back to the steppe, there can be no guarantee that the empire will not simply capture you again. This is what we fear, and what we cannot allow. You are too important. What you represent...Magic without a mark should be impossible.'

She grinds her teeth. They are no different from the empire. She is not theirs to protect, nor to control, nor to use.

'I am Ral Ans Urrera!' she shouts again, hand reaching for the sky. 'I am no wind to fill your sails, An-Zabati. I am the storm!'

Magic comes easily after so long in the blinding light. A single forking pulse turns sacred water to steam, silver and sand to shimmering glass. Shouts rise but she strides through them, puts her left side to the afternoon sun, and walks north.

Let them pursue her. She will kill them if she has to.

Footsteps stir the sand. She turns, sees the dancer, Atar, her hands outstretched as Katiz's were, but her face is full not of fear, nor of pity, but of understanding.

'You are right, Ral,' Atar says and steps forward. 'But you will never make it on foot. Wait for nightfall and I will help you find your people.'

Ral considers this, and the rolling dunes stretching to the horizon, and her want of water skins.

The steppe is there, just beyond the thin band of shimmering haze that marks the reach of her vision. She does not trust Atar, but neither does Ral wish for death, only for the freedom to do right by what remains of her people.

'I will wait,' Ral says. 'But only once.'

To Ral's mild but pleased surprise, Atar proves true to her word. That night, the dancer comes to Ral, motions for silence, and leads her past sleeping An-Zabati in their hammocks to the deck. The night watch fix their attention outwards, on the horizon, seeking the plumes of roiling sand that would mark a sandstorm or the approach of an imperial ship. Atar and Ral creep towards one of the two skiffs that hang from the ship's flanks. They are strange vessels, like offspring of the ship, only with long arms reaching upwards to meet above their decks rather like a mast. The one they approach has been nearly freed of its intricate web of knots and cords, and a shrivelled, dark-skinned man lurks between its benches.

'This is Jhin,' Atar whispers. 'He is helping us.'

Ral lets this strange, skinny person help her onto the boat, then furrows her brow with a question for Atar. Jhin answers instead.

'I would like to see something of your homeland,' he whispers in studied Girzan, stilted but comprehensible, his eyes bright with excitement. 'And Atar felt the need for a translator. Trade tongue can only carry so much nuance.'

Ral accepts this with a nod. It does not matter to her, beyond a thin gratitude that this man, seemingly a guest of the An-Zabati, would put himself at risk to lend her aid.

'Brace yourself,' Atar says, nodding to one of the benches. Ral sits and grips the gunwale tightly while Atar and Jhin untie a final knot. They pass the lines hand over hand through freshly oiled pulleys and the ship falls almost silently to the sand, settling with a gentle thump.

Ral knows little of ships, but she knows that they require a sail. Before she can ask after the absence of a mast, Atar opens a hatch at the front end of the vessel to reveal a billowing kite, bound to the deck by three long, thick cords. Atar casts it upwards and calls her thin, lung-chilling magic to fill it with a wind. The skiff lurches, then begins to scrape across the sand.

'They will realise we are gone and come after us,' Ral observes, 'and we seem to be far slower than the ships.'

Atar laughs brightly. 'I left a note for Katiz. He may not seem it, but he will be understanding. And by the time the other captains argue their way through him, we will be halfway to the steppe.'

With this declaration, she unveils the skiff's final, most vital secret. She unties one last cord and lets the twin arms swing down, bringing their long pontoons to the sand on either side of the hull. The scraping fades, and the ship feels suddenly lighter. It picks up speed, soon darting towards that blurred horizon, where Ral must believe some remnant of her people waits.

10

A Moment of Fatal Uncertainty

Hand Pinion

A thin column of smoke stood against the northern sky, visible from the walls of Iron Town. Wen Alder had come to Burrow and put it to the flame, as Pinion had known he would.

A sentimental part of him hoped that the foolish magistrate and his scar-faced captain had escaped. But then, perhaps their deaths would be the just outcome of their disobedience. The question of whether or not they should be pitied was not unlike the puzzles posed during the imperial examinations. A bitter laugh crawled out from the back of Pinion's throat.

A cough sounded behind him. He clicked his teeth shut and turned to find Captain Huo on the battlement. The captain dipped his head in salute.

'Your Excellency,' he said, 'our rear-guard scouts tell of movement in the mountains. Unusual birds—eagle hawks, vultures, falcons—flying to and from the villages. Groups of peasants making their way towards Burrow. The rebels appear to be mustering.'

'The witches spread word of Greyfrost,' Pinion muttered. 'The power we must evade draws rebel sympathisers like a lodestone.'

'That is not all, Your Excellency,' Captain Huo went on, his head still dipped in deference. 'There are other reports of skirmishes to the west of here. Rebels beneath a different banner. Witches who stalk the forest in the bodies of wolves and ambush our patrols from the undergrowth.'

A complication, but not one he had failed to anticipate. It was not Harrow Fox, after all, that Alder, Oriole, and Usher had ridden out to fight so many years ago.

'Frothing Wolf's faction, thinking we are on the back foot and taking advantage.' He turned his gaze on the thick forests of the island's western slopes, protected by topography from the brunt of the typhoons as they swept in from the east. More populated but wilder, a breeding ground for insurgency. A thread pulled at his pulse. Frothing Wolf. Other than Wen Alder, she wore the darkest stain of Oriole's blood.

'Their numbers are small, Your Excellency,' Captain Huo said. 'We might not be able to corner and destroy them, but it would be no challenge to beat them back into hiding. It would do the morale of our men some good to taste victory.'

More, it would do *Pinion's* morale some good. Frothing Wolf's death would be no small balm for his soul. Not a complete revenge but a vital part of it.

But this was not what he had promised the emperor, no part of the case he had made for retreat—or, at least, the case he had *intended* to make but had never given voice, not even within the confines of his mind. He suppressed a shudder at the memory of the emperor leafing through his consciousness, treating his innermost thoughts and fears, his secret desires and resentments, like the pages of a book...

'No,' he said, masking his regret and revulsion. 'We have orders. It is time we moved on. Muster our men in Iron Town's garrison yard.'

Captain Huo's shoulders tensed. 'Your Excellency, I recognise the wisdom in retreating from Harrow Fox and the severed Hand, but this Frothing Wolf and her forces have no such powerful magic. If we continue to flee the rebellion without so much as crossing swords—'

'I did not ask for your counsel, Captain,' Pinion snapped, 'and you overstep propriety with this questioning. I speak for the emperor here. Now go and do as I have commanded or risk a charge of insubordination.'

The Captain rocked back on his heels, his eyes narrowing. Pinion met his gaze, hoping the man would cow, uncertain of what he would do if he persisted. He could not afford to let himself be undermined—not for youth, not for inexperience, not for the madness he was sure the men whispered must have gripped their Hand. Why else the forced march in retreat, the unwillingness to meet so much as a rebel patrol in the field?

'Of course, Your Excellency.' Captain Huo's bow was sharp and far too short, bordering on an insult, before he left Pinion alone atop the wall.

The moment the grand hierarchy of the empire had to contend with anything beyond the explicit dictates of doctrine, it began to crumble like the walls of a sandstone canyon. Pinion flexed his right hand, feeling the pull of the tetragram branded there in silver lines. They were near enough to Setting Sun Fortress, and Voice Age-of-Plenty, for the heavy walls of the canon to reach him. All it would take was a single bolt of lightning. It need not even strike Captain Huo, only scorch the earth at his feet, and all the man's questioning would be done with.

Where hierarchy failed, brutality might take its place.

Of course, Captain Huo was far from the only person he needed to convince, and not all would be so easily cowed by a sorcerous demonstration.

Pinion braced himself and sought out the magistrate of Iron Town. He had met Hand Beneficence on the way north when their legion camped outside the walls and resupplied. The elderly Hand had invited Voice Usher, Hand Cinder, and Pinion to a single meal, which he'd spent wrapped in furs with his knobby hands around a steaming teapot, grumbling about the cold when he was not sharing tales of his youthful glories fighting in the conquest of Toa Alon. Now, Pinion found the magistrate in his study, sitting no more than a hand's span away from a radiant brazier. The heat of the room pulled beads of sweat from Pinion's brow.

'Ah, young Pinion.' Hand Beneficence shifted slightly in his wide-backed chair and nodded towards its twin, inviting Pinion to sit. 'Have you reconsidered your mad dash to Eastern Fortress, then? As you have seen, Iron Town's walls are strong. We have collapsed and filled those mining shafts the rebels used to sneak up from beneath and seize the city years go. And between the two of us we are more than powerful enough to rebuff a dozen witches. Better to stay here, is it not? At least while we wait for orders from Voice Age-of-Plenty.'

'I have not reconsidered,' Pinion said, not taking the offered seat. 'I already have my orders from the emperor himself. We will press on to Setting Sun Fortress, and then to Eastern Fortress. And you and your garrison will be coming with us.'

The old Hand looked up at him, his yellowed eyes glistening in the light of the brazier. 'I have lived a long time, young Pinion, and never heard of a Hand receiving the words of the emperor.'

The subtle accusation gnawed at Pinion, but he tried to ignore it. 'We live in strange times,' he said flatly.

'Indeed.' Hand Beneficence bobbed his head slowly, as though to nod with too much vigour might snap his brittle neck. 'The obelisks of An-Zabat have fallen. Rumours circle the Girzan steppe of a Stormrider born again, if the little news that reaches me here can be believed. And a few hundred rebels and a severed Hand threw back one of our mighty legions. Strange and stressful times, Hand Pinion.'

A servant appeared bearing a folding table and tea set, which he set between the two wide-backed chairs. Hand Beneficence removed the lid from the teapot, breathed in the curls of steam, and sighed. 'A delightful jasmine,' he murmured. 'I find it soothing on a bone-chilling day such as this. Would you care for some?'

Though they were both Hands, age and experience weighted the scales of propriety in Beneficence's favour and demanded that Pinion accept such an invitation from an elder brother in the great hierarchy of empire. If he meant to hold Captain Huo to the requirements of doctrine, he could hardly violate them himself. He took the offered seat and waited while Hand Beneficence filled two cups with shimmering amber.

'No one will blame you for collapsing beneath your fear,' Hand Beneficence said gently. 'Not after you watched two of your superiors brutally killed and faced such powerful magic. I felt it through the pattern even here. There is no shame in admitting to fear, or to its lingering effects.'

Pinion's hand paused, hovering beside his teacup. He searched Hand Beneficence's face, but the old man kept his eyes downcast, sipping his tea.

'The emperor does not speak to his Hands,' Hand Beneficence went on. 'You claim to have heard his voice only the once, and after a long and terrified march, while lying in wait of sleep. Might it have been a dream, or a conjuring of your addled mind to justify your flight in the face of terror?'

Of course not. Pinion had felt the weight of the emperor's transmission. The pressure filling his skull. A presence sifting through his every thought and memory. The words in a voice he had heard only once before, while kneeling at the foot of the Thousand-Armed Throne.

Pressure that might be explained by exhaustion, the voice by the madness of a half-waking nightmare.

What *had* his orders been? He could recall conceiving of the plan, and then his terror at the emperor's attention, and then the emperor's agreement...but to what? Neither he nor the emperor had ever laid out the entire plan directly.

'No one will blame you.' Hand Beneficence's words hung thin in the air. Muted, as though spoken through glass, or from far away. 'You are safe here, Hand Pinion. There is no more need to run.'

The emperor would not so casually shatter the structures of his hierarchy, would he? It had seemed absurd that Pinion—a mere Hand, little more than an apprentice—should change the emperor's mind, and with a plan only half thought through. Had he only dreamed it and latched onto the dream as justification for his cowardice?

His pulse thrummed to the rhythm of his racing heart.

'No,' Pinion said firmly. 'It was no dream. It was real. And I will not disobey an order given by the emperor, no matter how unusual. The emperor built these hierarchies, did he not? Why should he not break them to meet the challenge of what are, as you admit, strange and dangerous times?'

'You are still afraid.' Hand Beneficence shifted in his seat, rearranging the fur that covered his shoulders and arms. The corner of his mouth quirked in a frustrated frown. The expression vanished quickly but lingered long enough to signal his frustration. 'But you must see reason, young Pinion. I am your elder brother in the empire. Heed my advice. Stay here. Give your terror a chance to ease. Or go out into the forest and hunt the bandits who raid the nearby villages. Prove to yourself again the might of the empire and the weakness of these Nayeni rebels. There is no need to run from them.'

A decade of training in doctrine and propriety needled Pinion, urging him to acquiesce to his elder. Of course, a few Nayeni witches were no threat to Pinion's army, nor to an Iron Town reinforced and defended by two Hands. But his fear of Alder was justified, his solution rational. *That* was why the emperor had agreed to his plan. He too understood the danger Alder posed.

'Much as it grieves me to say this, Hand Beneficence, and to continue to argue with one who should be a guide and mentor to me—whose patience I am surely straining—you were not there.' Pinion shook his head. 'Neither at Greyfrost, nor in Burrow when the emperor conveyed his orders to me. Iron Town will fall, as Burrow fell and as Setting Sun Fortress will fall. As this island will fall if we do not lead the severed Hand into the trap the emperor himself will spring. To that end, you and your garrison and those people of Iron Town who are willing and able will follow me in retreat.'

The words left him in a rush, as though by speaking quickly he might assuage the elder Hand's frustrations. Hand Beneficence took a deep breath and shifted once more in his seat.

'I had hoped that you might still be reached by reason.' There was a mournful note in his voice. A ripple ran through the fur that covered him. 'I can only hope, now, that healing sorcery might repair your damaged mind.'

Pinion's lungs seized. Weight settled on his shoulders in a wake of sorcery he knew well from Greyfrost Keep.

Hand Beneficence's arm lanced out from beneath the fur, trailing ribbons of light. Panic darted through Pinion. He raised his own hand in response and raced through the channels of the canon to answer binding sorcery with a bolt of lightning.

The smell of burnt cinnamon faded to the smell of scorched flesh. With a wordless grunt, Hand Beneficence collapsed back into his chair. A blackened weal showed through the charred ruin of his furs and robe.

A numb shock held Pinion in his seat while Hand Beneficence's lungs rose and fell with wet, rattling breaths.

'No,' Pinion murmured. He pulled himself from his chair but weakness gripped his knees. He leaned on the folding table, which collapsed beneath his weight. Amber tea flowed through the cracks in the tiled floor. He scrambled to the old Hand's side and reached for healing sorcery, touched burnt flesh with trembling hands. Calming wakes of magic carried his mind further and further away from the reality of what he had done.

The flesh knit, returning to a hale colour and texture, if made sallow by age. But somewhere in the hand-span of time while Pinion knelt and worked magic, the old Hand's chest had ceased to rise and fall, and the last flicker of light had gone out of his eyes.

Pinion jerked backwards, rising to his feet, opening and closing his hands, trying to deepen his breathing, to quiet the storm raging in his mind. No. The wounds had healed. He stared at Hand Beneficence, willing the old man's eyelids to flutter, his whiskers to stir with a sudden intake of breath.

It had been a reflex. A lashing out in fear and shock. And now a man—a Hand of the emperor, no less—lay dead.

Thoughts began breaking through the chaos. No one could find this body. Captain Huo already questioned him, likely thought him mad. Here was all the confirmation he would need—and crime enough to haul Pinion in chains before Voice Age-of-Plenty, to be executed the moment they reached Setting Sun Fortress.

He took a breath to calm himself. They had been alone—were still alone. Not even a servant had seen what had happened. Some of their conversation might have been overheard. The crack of lightning most certainly would have been. And before long the body would be found.

The wound itself had been healed, though, and singed clothes could be explained. If he set the stage well enough, whoever found the body would arrive at that explanation on their own. Old men, after all, often died without violence. He returned to Hand Beneficence's side and carefully arranged his body in its seat, then righted the folding table. Thankfully, the teapot had not shattered, though one of the cups had cracked. This Pinion placed on the floor at the old Hand's feet, as though he had dropped it. There. As the old man's life had slipped away, his fingers had lost their strength and the cup had fallen, *crack*, just so. The brazier still blazed like a furnace; a servant who found the corpse might plausibly believe that the old man had succumbed to age at last and, after he had collapsed forwards, the front of his robe had been singed by its heat. Not *might plausibly*—some leap of logic would be required to draw any other conclusion. By the sages, it was the conclusion *he* would have drawn himself had he stumbled on the scene.

Never mind the argument with Hand Pinion. Never mind the thunderclap out of a clear sky. Was it any servant's business what transpired between Hands of the emperor? Captain Huo was at the garrison yard. The nearest sorcerers were days away, though Voice Age-of-Plenty would have felt the wake of their duel. He had conveyed those sorceries, after all. But he would also be in contact with the emperor, who would come to Pinion's defence.

Assuming, of course, that Hand Beneficence was wrong and that Pinion had indeed conversed with the emperor during that sleepless night in Burrow. If this were all some waking nightmare, born from a madness conjured by exhaustion and fear, then Pinion would be captured within moments and executed within hours when he reached Setting Sun Fortress.

No. The emperor *had* spoken with him. Had, in his infinite wisdom, ordered Pinion to continue his retreat. Had, in that same infinite, unquestionable wisdom, not reached out to Hand Beneficence, to share with him the details of his plan...

Pinion's blood pulsed thick and loud with terror and his limbs twitched between the urge to collapse and the desperate need to flee. But either would only signal his guilt.

Another breath—deep and calming, at last. Everything would be fine. He was not mad. The emperor's orders had to be followed, even if they caused the death of a Hand. He rolled his shoulders, turned away from the corpse, and set out at a walk—brisk, but carefully unhurried—towards the garrison yard.

* * *

Captain Huo, though bull-headed and sceptical, was at least a
man who followed orders. Between the remnant of their retreating legion and the three hundred men of Iron Town's garrison, fully
a thousand soldiers stood mustered in tight formation beneath a slow
and drifting snowfall. Pinion mounted the low dais built into the
garrison wall, where Captain Huo and Garrison Commander Zhu
greeted him with a bow.

'Your Excellency.' Commander Zhu lifted his eyes to peer over Pinion's shoulder. 'Where, if I might respectfully ask, is Hand Beneficence?'

Pinion dismissed the question with a gesture, though it caused his
heart to stutter. 'He is resting and preparing for the journey to come.
He sends his regards, of course, and his regrets that wearing the tetragram is no true defence against the march of time.'

'Of course.' Commander Zhu was far better at hiding his true feelings than Captain Huo, but a flicker of doubt showed in the wrin-
kling of his brow. 'Should we not wait for him, or at least for him to
send an emissary, before we begin?'

'I speak for both of us,' Pinion said.

A frown creased Commander Zhu's face at that, but Pinion ignored
it and stepped to the edge of the dais, acting as though he took for
granted the assertion that the military men ought to accept his words
as Hand of the emperor—as they *would* accept them if doctrine, propriety, and hierarchy still held.

'Soldiers of the Second Nayeni Legion, of Burrow Garrison, and
of Iron Town Garrison,' Pinion called out, his voice echoing across
the courtyard. 'These are unprecedented days. The first true threat to
imperial rule since the conquest of Nayen has risen in Greyfrost Keep.
Those of you who marched from Eastern Fortress with Voice Usher,
Hand Cinder, and I have witnessed this threat, felt the heat of the
flames, the cut of the winds, heard the rumble of thunder and witnessed the flash of lightning. A severed Hand wielding untold powers
marches south at the head of a growing rebel army. And though it
humbles me to say it, we will not be able to stop him here. Thus, in
accordance with the will of the emperor, we will continue our retreat,

first to Setting Sun Fortress and then to Eastern Fortress. We will empty Iron Town of any supplies that might aid us or provide succour to the enemy and destroy what we cannot carry with us.'

Though confusion rippled across the faces of a few officers in the front row of the assembly, there were no gasps of astonishment nor murmurs of alarm. Even Captain Huo remained standing at attention, despite his grave expression.

'It is painful to lose territory yet again, and painful for the citizens of Iron Town, who will march with us, but this is the emperor's command. The severed Hand and his forces *will* succeed here, whether we give up the town or spill a river of our blood to defend it. They *will* succeed at Setting Sun Fortress. Their successes will stir the darkness in the hearts of those Nayeni who sympathise with such barbarism, and their ranks will swell. But do not despair!'

He held his right hand aloft, letting his tetragram glimmer in the sunlight. 'The embers of rebellion have smouldered long on this island, rekindling the violence that has cost you towns and villages, sons and brothers, fathers, mothers, sisters, and daughters, again and again and again. But the emperor has foreseen the final pacification of Nayen. Ours is not a retreat but a regrouping of our forces. In time, and with the grace of the emperor, we will turn this tide and crush them upon the walls of Eastern Fortress! For they are but disgruntled farmers and vagrant bandits lurking in their shadowed forests. We are the empire, and we bring the light that will burn away those shadows, and with them the last of Nayen's rebellious spirit!'

A cheer went up from the assembly, and relief blossomed in Pinion like a sip of warm tea. In those cheers he heard the threat of mutiny waylaid, at least for a time.

Of course, it would take days to evacuate the populace and empty or burn the storehouses. And the rebels might mount some surprise attack, drawing blood and reigniting his soldiers' lust for revenge. He could only hope their loyalty would last until they reached Setting Sun Fortress, where he could finally hand over command to Voice Age-of-Plenty and be rid of the curse of command.

Not long after the cheers began, a messenger appeared at the gate to the garrison yard. He rushed to the dais, his coat flapping around his ankles.

'Hand Pinion,' he whispered, head bowed. 'I bring terrible news.'

A bolt struck Pinion between the ribs, but he stuffed the feeling away. He had set the scene well. So long as he did nothing to sow doubt, there was no reason for suspicion to fall upon him. Furrowing his brow, affecting surprise and concern, he stepped down to the ground. 'What is it?'

The messenger leaned close. 'Hand Beneficence is dead.'

Pinion forced his eyebrows to dart upwards, the whites of his eyes to widen, his mouth to drop open a fraction of the width of a finger. 'W-what?' Pinion stammered, just loudly enough for Captain Huo and Commander Zhu to hear. 'How? I was just speaking with him!'

'It appears that his heart gave out,' the messenger said. 'Perhaps the stress of the growing rebellion overwhelmed him. A physician is examining him now and may be able to tell us more.'

Pinion shook his head sadly, then turned to Captain Huo and Commander Zhu. 'Another inestimable life brought to its end by the barbarism of Nayen. We must prepare his body for transport. We will bring him with us and see to it that he is buried with honour in Eastern Fortress—an honour we failed to provide Voice Usher or Hand Cinder.'

'Of course, Your Excellency.' Commander Zhu dipped his head. 'I will see to it myself.'

Pinion nodded to the commander, who gathered half a dozen men and set off.

'A true tragedy, Your Excellency,' Captain Huo said flatly. 'One that leaves you, once again, solely burdened with the weight of command.'

'Indeed, Captain,' Pinion replied. 'A burden I look forward to laying down. For now, see that our soldiers empty the granaries and strip the armoury of anything useful. Two days from now, we will burn whatever food we cannot take and continue our retreat.'

Captain Huo studied him. Searching for evidence of the lie, or of madness, Pinion was sure. But he was not mad. *Not. Mad.* And he felt, truly, the tragedy of Hand Beneficence's death, and so the lie was superficial. At last, Captain Huo bowed.

'As you command, Your Excellency,' he said.

The physician, in the end, declared that Hand Beneficence had died of old age—or at least no poison or wound. The singed clothes were explained away as Pinion had anticipated. Those servants who must have overheard their harsh conversation and the clap of thunder following the fateful lightning he'd called said nothing—at least, not where Pinion could hear. And if Captain Huo heard of such things, he made no move in Iron Town, though Pinion could easily imagine the captain stockpiling such rumours, subtly planting them among the soldiery, waiting for an opportune moment to strike...

He made a mental note to keep an eye on the captain. The threat of mutiny had only been postponed, he was sure.

That night and all the next day, while the sky filled with smoke and the streets clogged with overburdened carts piled high with the hard-won possessions of desperate townsfolk, he felt like an overtightened spike fiddle, the strings and bridge competing to see which would give way and snap first.

He was doing what the emperor required of him. Doing what they, together, had deemed necessary to eradicate the Nayeni rebellion, stamping it out like so many smouldering coals. And, just as importantly, what was necessary to avenge Oriole and to destroy Wen Alder, the severed Hand, traitor to the empire, who would, at the very moment of his death by Pinion's hand, regret the absurd, indulgent mercy he had shown at Greyfrost.

He was not mad. He was a servant of the empire and vengeance was the reward for his service.

Yet Hand Beneficence's words droned on and on within his mind, and below them, like a beat of percussion, flashes of memory. Wen Alder—still a Hand then—standing at Oriole's grave. Asking a simple question that grew more and more impossible to answer.

Does this feel right?

11

A Strip of Bone
Foolish Cur

The pattern of the world in all its layers—the physical world, the mind, and the soul—stretched out before me, a lattice of infinite, unfurling complexity, its threads pliant to my touch. Here, a little turn might spark a fire. There, a simple retwisting of a braid would transform me into a mountain bear. Other manipulations no less complex could breathe a wind from nowhere, weld sheets of light as hard as steel, or call lightning down from an empty sky. Reaching deeper, I might plant a thought in another mind or pry some deep-held fear to the surface of the heart.

I attended to my own mind, to the phantom limb that worked in the pattern, and traced the path from the jade sphere at my centre to the power to conjure flame. The stump of my right wrist ached, but I pressed it more firmly against the strip I had cut from one of Hissing Cat's supply of shoulder bones. I needed to be precise now, and I had never been a deft hand at carving.

The canon I would make was simple, unlike the maze of imperial sorcery. As I carved, I laid bricks with the sorcery of transmission, building walls within the layer of the soul soon strong enough to dull my own sense of the world beyond them. Panic reached down from the back of my mind and into my throat, warning me against what I did, as though my knife cut into my own eye, or my own tongue, rather than a length of dead, dry bone. I worked the last piece of magic, condensing power to weave threads into chains, binding my canon to the marks I had carved in bone.

At last I retreated from the walls, breathing a sigh of relief. Setting the knife aside, I brushed the tips of my fingers down the rough lines I had carved—three of them, angling down to converge with each other, like flames rising from a common source.

I held the bone to the flickering lamplight. The mustiness of bone dust mixed with the herbal scents of liniments and medicines that ever hung about the garrison-turned-clinic. Doctor Sho sat nearby, spooning broth into the mouth of a catatonic patient. He had made nurses of a few of Burrow's citizens—a boy and two young women—to check bandages, administer medicines, and feed those who could not feed themselves. He squinted at my handiwork and grunted.

'It looks like one of those runes she makes for her oracles,' he said. 'Does it work?'

I offered him the strip of bone. 'See for yourself.'

Horror flashed across his face—for only an instant—and then faded to a cold disinterest. 'Magic isn't my way. You know that.'

'Why not?' Something in my heart felt loose after the dark mood that had held me in the first few days after the taking of Burrow. My old curiosity had bloomed again. 'You've lived a very long time for someone without the aid of magic.'

'If it were something you should know, I would tell you,' Doctor Sho said flatly. 'I haven't because it isn't, and asking the question isn't going to do much but annoy me.'

'Fine, fine.' I put my hand up and smiled. 'Keep your secrets.'

'I will.' He nodded at the strip of bone. 'So, does it work?'

'Let's see, shall we?' I pressed the pad of my thumb to the three intersecting lines.

At once my sense of the pattern of the world faded, becoming as a muted sound or a light covered by a heavy shroud. The structure I had made possessed neither the breadth of the canon nor the subtleties of a pact. It was a single room, lacking even a window onto the outside world. A room flowing and pulsing with power, with the scent of cinnamon and a feverish heat on my skin.

My hand spasmed open. The moment my thumb left the three intersecting marks, the canon I had made vanished from my mind. The bone clattered to the floor. I stared at it as though it were a dog that had turned wild and bitten me.

'Either it didn't work or it worked too well, I'm guessing,' Doctor Sho said.

A wake of magic pulsed through the world, sending more spasms down my arms and legs. One of my uncle's cadre, I assumed, returned from spreading word of our victory. When the cramps had subsided, I picked up the canon I had made, careful not to touch the marks again, swallowing sudden nausea. It was only a dry strip of bone, but holding it felt like handling something raw and rotten.

All my life I had tried to escape the constraints of the pact, and then the canon, as I sought to comprehend the pattern of the world in all its fullness—to master magic truly on my own terms. How absurd to have accomplished that goal only to use the power I had gained to build something to constrain the minds and magic of others.

But the rebellion needed more witches—powerful ones, and soon—if we were to have any hope of victory. The tool I had made disgusted me, and I doubted I would have time to refine it further, but it would accomplish that goal.

Assuming someone without training in magic could use it.

But whom? I had been with my uncle's army for some time now but still felt profoundly isolated. Everyone I knew, it seemed, was a witch—except Doctor Sho, who had made his position on being my test subject clear. Memories of Tawny Owl and my uncle's cadre butchering Clear-River's guards turned my already upset stomach, a reminder of the risk I would take by putting this weapon in the hands of a Nayeni rebel.

Then, as if in answer, another memory arose from that same night, of Running Doe, her hand on her sword, standing between two young soldiers and the old man they had come to rob and butcher. I could not say whether she would have acted the same way if the old man had been Sienese rather than Nayeni, but she seemed at least compassionate and just.

The infirmary door swung open—one of the nurses coming or going. I studied the strip of bone again. If I made all the marks the same size, there was enough room for four, perhaps five more. What five magics, I wondered, would be most useful to the witches I would train?

More importantly, what power was I willing to provide, given that it might be used against my wishes?

'So that's it, then?'

I looked up to find my grandmother standing over me, peering at the bone in my hand. Her withered limb flexed and a muscle in her jaw twitched. A quiet fear lurked in the corners of her eyes—an echo of the night before she had left my father's house, when she had finally carved my witch marks.

'The start of it.' I held up the bone for her to examine. 'A simplified canon of sorcery that conveys only the power to conjure flame. I'll add more to it—'

'And it works?' The words fell from her mouth, short and clipped.

'It seems to, though I will need to test it on a subject other than myself to be sure.'

'Your life may depend on your doing so quickly. A messenger came from Frothing Wolf. She's a slow one to forgive.' She heaved a sigh and shook her head. 'Not that I blame her after the loss of a daughter. But she's small minded. Always has been.'

Of all that I had done in the empire's name, leading the reconquest of Iron Town had left the deepest scars. I had led Oriole to his death there and avenged him by brutally killing Frigid Cub, his torturer, the daughter of the rebel leader Frothing Wolf. I had known, when I had decided to return to Nayen and seek a home with the rebels, that she would seek revenge.

'She is demanding my head, I assume.'

'And offers her army and her fealty as payment,' my grandmother said, 'leaving Harrow Fox the unrivalled Sun King.'

My guilt caught a low flame. I might owe Frothing Wolf some restitution, but what did I owe my uncle that he should bargain with my life and death? After what I had done—at Greyfrost, at Burrow, and now, wielding magics that turned my stomach to his ends—I deserved his gratitude and a place at his side, not to be spent as political currency. 'Do you think him likely to make that trade?'

She hesitated. 'He saw what you did at Greyfrost, though he doesn't understand it. Hell, I don't either, but he knows how things would end if open violence broke out between you both.' Her hand spasmed as her eyes drifted again to the strip of bone and the magic it contained. 'But you aren't invulnerable. You sleep. You eat. He might decide that the threat you pose, coupled with the promise of Frothing Wolf's loyalty, outweighs the power you can offer him.'

My anger burned away a dozen deeply held misgivings and clouded the rest with smoke. I stood, gripping the strip of bone in my fist. 'Then let us show him what I can offer.'

No sooner had I stormed out of the infirmary with my grandmother close at heel than Hissing Cat appeared. She had taken to lurking in the forest by day—to avoid all the damn racket, as she put it. She came striding up the main road, skulls clattering in her hair, cloak of furs fluttering behind her, like a thunderhead ready to drown the world in rain and fury.

She stopped a dozen paces from me, her shoulders rising and falling in rhythm with long, agitated breaths. 'You're treading dangerous ground, boy,' she said.

My first thought was for my uncle and the anger burning in my chest, but her eyes were fixed on the strip of bone.

'I know,' I said. 'But all magics are permitted to me, and you yourself explained—'

'I explained, but I didn't know what its wake would feel like, did I?' she snarled. 'What you've made isn't like a pact. Even at a distance, and worked upon another mind, I felt those walls.'

In the time I had known Hissing Cat, I had never seen so much as a wisp of fear in her. Now it boiled from her like steam from a kettle. It was a sight unsettling enough to give me pause.

My grandmother shifted beside me. 'I'd be fascinated by this conversation, I'm sure, but a great deal may ride on our haste.'

Hissing Cat's hard, ancient eyes swung from my grandmother to me, to the bone in my hand, then narrowed. I saw then that they held not only fear but a deep hatred, the sort a hound might feel for a master who whips and starves it.

'The gods, too, are capable of transmission,' she said. 'It is how Okara speaks, of course—and they, too, are capable of building mazes in the mind. When we rose against them, they found us able to equal them in magic. They sent an earthquake; we stilled it. We called down a mountain; they shattered it. They hurled the stars themselves; we doused them in conjured seas. But their minds are vaster than ours. Older. Richer.

'The walls they could build with the magic of transmission had foundations as deep as the roots of the earth. And when they could not best us in a contest of magic, they found ways to enclose our minds in walls. Shut us off from our power. Strip away our ability to fight. Leave us impotent, constrained by mental structures we could never hope to unravel.'

She jabbed a gnarled finger at the strip of bone. 'The wake from that was just the same.'

I took a sharp, shivering breath. This was what she had kept from me, the reason for her hesitation—an ancient horror carried in deep memories, as Tawny Owl carried the memories of her life before the rebellion. I thought of the room of mental walls I had made, windowless, full of nothing but the magic I had bound within it. A well-spring, yes, but also a prison. Was I prepared to bind students of my own within such confines, as once the emperor and his canon had bound me?

'I understand your fear,' I said, suppressing the quaver in my voice, 'but this is meant to give power, not take it away.'

'You should know as well as anyone that the two go hand in hand,' Hissing Cat shot back. 'Will one who touches that mark comprehend *anything* of the pattern of the world, or only learn to wield some magic you've deigned to give them? You're not giving them *power*, Cur. Power is the ability to understand, and weigh, and choose.'

'If I could distill all I know into these marks, I would,' I told her, casting the pain her words dealt into the fire of my anger and frustration. She was right, and I knew it, but this was a war, not an academy. 'And perhaps if I had time, and your co-operation, I could! But this canon is the best I can do. And I *must* do it if we are to defeat the empire.'

'Must you?' she snarled. 'Must you *really?*'

My grandmother stepped between us—an act of brazen absurdity; a duel between Hissing Cat and I would have levelled the entire town.

'You two can have this argument later,' she snapped. 'Grandson, do you intend to make your case to your uncle or wait and see if he poisons your tea?'

Such fury poured from Hissing Cat that I feared she might turn my grandmother to ash. Yet my grandmother had lived a life under the threat of the empire, had watched her husband burn himself alive to protect the secrets of Nayeni witchcraft, and had raised a son who rallied armies that bowed to him as the Sun King. She stood firm between us, not easily cowed, and matched Hissing Cat stare for stare.

At last, Hissing Cat's ferocity turned back on me. 'We'll speak more of this later.' She spun with a rattle of skulls and stalked back the way she had come.

My grandmother slumped and heaved a sigh, then glared at me. 'I thought that woman was your teacher.'

'She is. But so was Voice Usher. Teachers aren't always enthusiastic about the choices their students make.'

She harrumphed, rubbed her withered wrist, and stepped past me towards the magistrate's hall. 'Come, then. Your uncle may well be a few dozen heartbeats and half as many wisps of paranoia away from ordering some poor idiot to try and assassinate you.'

'Is his mind so easily swayed?' I asked, falling into step beside her.

She barked a sharp laugh. 'It wouldn't be if you didn't terrify him. Fewer of Greyfrost's survivors wear that stupid bit of burnt wood, but enough still do. He's convinced you've agents of your own infiltrating the ranks of his army, slowly prying it away from his control.'

'But I don't!' I blurted.

She cocked her eyebrow at me.

I paused mid-stride, dumbfounded by her implicit accusation.

She studied me like she had back in the Temple of the Flame, as though she were scrutinising my form in the Iron Dance. A feeling of smallness came over me. The sort of shame children feel when caught in a lie.

But there was no lie, and my shame at her suspicion was only a bellows to my anger. I worked my jaw. 'I made him his canon of witchcraft—or at least the beginnings of it. Let him question my loyalty now.'

My grandmother wrinkled her nose, shrugged, and returned to the road.

As we approached the magistrate's hall, the Vulture met us with his arms crossed and his head lowered like a brawler, as though expecting that we might trade blows.

'Broken Limb.' He saluted my grandmother before turning to me. 'Foolish Cur. The Sun King is holding a private audience. You'll have to wait.'

'And who are you to stand in my way?' I demanded.

The Vulture tensed, waiting for a blow. Or readying to make one.

'Let us through,' my grandmother said. 'Harrow Fox will want to see what his nephew has made.'

He considered us for a moment longer. At last he stepped aside, his shoulders still rolled forwards.

We found Harrow Fox where I had come to expect him, sitting in the broad chair at the map table in the reception hall. Tawny Owl, of course, stood at his side, her hands planted menacingly on the hilts of her swords as she watched Frothing Wolf's messenger, their guest.

His cheeks were high and angular, his complexion darker than most Nayeni. Hair tied with ravens' feathers hung around his shoulders. They had been speaking, but the rush of my blood and the fury in my ears deafened me to their conversation. Something about Harrow Fox's willingness to kill me, I assumed.

'I've done it,' I declared, striding into the room, not bothering to wonder how best to show Harrow Fox or Frothing Wolf's emissary proper deference. I flourished the strip of bone and set it on the table, knocking aside the wooden tokens Harrow Fox had placed across the map. 'A canon of witchcraft. The power to conjure fire. Conveyed in simple enough fashion that any child could use it. This is what I promised you, Uncle, and I have delivered.'

My uncle regarded the weapon I had made, and then the messenger. 'You have my answer.'

Gaunt eyes peered out from shadowed hollows. Considered my uncle, me, the strip of bone. Then, with a brief, jagged nod, the messenger strode from the room. My uncle did not speak until the last echoing footstep faded. A wake of cramping seized us through the pattern and shot away to the south.

My uncle regarded me from beneath his heavy brow. 'I thought you were better at keeping secrets.'

'I've carried too many. They exhaust me. Now.' I jabbed my finger again at the bone. 'Touch the mark for yourself, Uncle. See what I have done.'

Harrow Fox gestured to Tawny Owl, who stepped forwards and reached for the bone.

'No,' I said firmly. 'See for yourself.'

Tawny Owl's hand hovered, her fingers brushing the edge of the bone, her eyes blazing at me like the tips of flaming arrows. At my side, my grandmother—breathing heavily after the effort to keep pace with me—fidgeted, perhaps deciding where her allegiance would land when the rumbling tremors between my uncle and I at last erupted into violence.

My uncle leaned forwards in his seat, menacing, projecting power. 'I have heard rumours that imperial magic can twist the mind,' he said.

'This is not imperial magic but magic of my own design,' I retorted. 'Have you no faith at all in me, Uncle, after I saved you and your army at Greyfrost? After I threw back an imperial legion and sent them terrified in retreat? After I have done everything I can to prove my loyalty?'

Tawny Owl searched his face, ready to take up the bone if he gave the command—or strike at me with blade, fire, or talon, as that command might be.

Harrow Fox casually picked up the strip of bone, as though he had never been wary of it. He held it loosely in his hand, studying the mark.

'Tawny Owl,' he said, and an understanding passed between them. She touched the hilts of her swords and nodded.

Before I could protest his pointless theatrics, he pressed the pad of his thumb to the three intersecting lines. A heavy wake fell into the pattern, surrounding him: the walls of the canon I had made slotting into place.

He grunted and collapsed backwards. Tawny Owl showed her teeth and stepped towards me, her swords rasping from their scabbards.

I put up my hand, ready to defend myself, my mind spinning in search of an explanation. Had the canon of witchcraft interacted somehow with my uncle's witch marks? Or was this a ruse, a ploy to put me off balance, to strike me down and make good on his deal with Frothing Wolf?

A wake sent cramps down my spine, and in a burst of cinnamon scent my grandmother reared up beside me in the body of a mountain bear, one claw withered like a blighted sapling. Tawny Owl blanched but brought up her swords. With a feverish wake, flames began to lick down their blades.

'Enough!' my uncle roared, still slumped in his chair, taking slow breaths that made his chest rise and fall like a bellows. The bone lay on the table before him. 'Owl, put your blades away.'

The flames burned a moment longer at the tips of her swords, then went out. She sheathed them, still trailing wisps of smoke. My grandmother returned to herself, rolling her shoulders to ease her strained muscles.

'When I touched this…thing…you have made…' My uncle tapped the strip of bone. 'I felt the world close in around me. The power to veer fell away, like a severed limb. Yet you promised me a tool for *giving* magic.'

'It is.' I found it difficult to look away from Tawny Owl's clenched knuckles on the hilts of her weapons. 'Not to you or I, who already have magic of our own, but to one without the marks of a pact. For now, it conveys only the power to conjure fire, but there will be other marks before I am finished, and with them other powers.'

'A potent thing, if all of that is true. A dangerous thing.'

'A weapon to put us on equal footing with the Hands of the emperor.'

'And who will wield this weapon?' he asked, finally tearing his eyes from the strip of bone.

A question I had yet to answer myself.

'You have seen that it can be done now,' I said. 'Will you let me finish my work and cease to entertain this notion of giving my head to Frothing Wolf?'

His fingernail clicked once more against the bone, and then he slid it, scraping, across the table.

'If we can arm a detachment of our soldiers with such weapons, Eastern Fortress will fall in a day,' he said. 'Take it and return to your work.'

I snatched the bone from the tabletop and left him. The Vulture stepped aside for me, though he seemed wary after the wakes of magic that had roiled from the magistrate's hall. The anger in my chest burned and burned, and I went on walking until it faded to coals.

After a long, circuitous route back to the infirmary, I liberated a bottle of sorghum liquor that Doctor Sho had secured for medical use. The second floor of the garrison house stood empty. The rasp of a cot's legs roused no one as I dragged it over to a window. There I sat, watching the sun turn the horizon a harsh, burnt orange while I took long, burning swallows.

As night fell and I reached the bottom of the bottle, I spotted a dishevelled figure, his feet dragging furrows through the shallow snow, his hands cinching the same tattered, bloodstained robe beneath a blanket tight around his shoulders. His curled hair jutted in wild knots and the well-groomed angles of his beard had given way to a week of unkempt growth.

'Clear-River!' I called down and saluted with the bottle.

He came to a sudden halt and looked up, his eyes shadowed in the moonlight glinting off the snow. An overwhelming swell of pity seized me. Here was a man not unlike myself. Risen high in the empire, brought low, humiliated and mistrusted. Hadn't he been staying in the servants' quarters of the magistrate's hall? What was he doing in the streets, in the dark, unwashed and shivering?

'Do you have a bed for the night?' I shouted.

Even at this distance, and drunk, I could see the hesitation in him before he shook his head.

'Wait a moment!'

I manoeuvred my way, half stumbling, down the narrow stairway, through the infirmary—where Doctor Sho and his nurses administered soups one spoonful at a time to their patients—and to the door. Clear-River had surely continued on his way, I thought, but when I stepped out into the night he still stood in the street, clutching the blanket, a few flakes of snow drifting around his wild mane.

'Come in, come in.' I waved him over.

At last he took a few halting steps, emerging into the circle of lamplight. Bruises mottled one side of his face, leaving an eye swollen shut and his jaw ajar. He moved with a seizing limp.

I offered my arm. He flinched away.

'You're hurt,' I said. 'This is an infirmary. We can help you.'

'Like you helped me before?' he mumbled through a swollen jaw. 'You spared my life. Look where that has left me.'

The alcohol had not doused my anger, only numbed it. His words carved through that numbness like a scalpel.

'Who did this to you?' I demanded.

He laughed, winced, and shook his head. 'What could you do about it, Alder?' His voice rose, burning with fury. 'We both know you are not in command, here. You have seen how your uncle treats me. Do you think he will care that a few of his soldiers kicked around a Sienese dog?'

As though his anger had consumed the last of his strength, he collapsed. I caught him, bracing him with my mutilated arm, holding his shoulder with my hand, and—though unsteady myself—managed to usher him through the door.

Doctor Sho nearly dumped a bowl of broth onto one of his patients in his dash to reach us. Together, we helped Clear-River stumble into an empty cot, Doctor Sho muttering and cursing all the while.

'What the hell happened?' Doctor Sho demanded when Clear-River lay breathing more easily, wincing as I adjusted his injured leg. The bone did not seem broken to me, but through the torn fabric of his trousers I saw a long, bloody welt surrounded by a knot of bruise. A blow from the butt of a spear or a sheathed sword, most likely.

'Can you move your toes?' I asked. Clear-River grunted, then shook his head.

I shut my eyes and reached into the pattern of the world. Even while drunk, healing magic came easily after so many days of working in the infirmary. The calming wake of the magic swept through me as Clear-River's burst blood vessels knitted and the cracks in his bone re-fused. He gasped, then twitched his foot. I withdrew from the pattern, my already tired body and mind pushed a few steps closer to exhaustion, and smiled at him.

'If we'd let that go untreated, the limp might have set for good,' I said. 'Now, will you let me see to your face?'

He nodded weakly and I touched his cheek. Distantly, through the fog of alcohol, exhaustion, and magic, I heard Doctor Sho muttering and rummaging through his medicine chest. By the time I released the spell, leaving Clear-River's face still bruised but his eye able to open and his jaw no longer swollen out of shape, Doctor Sho had prepared a warm, briny-smelling tea, which he pressed to Clear-River's lips.

'Drink this,' Doctor Sho said. 'You'll need to rebuild your strength. Those tricks of his seem like a cure-all, but they take just as much out of the body as natural healing, only in a hundredth of the time.'

I sagged into another empty cot and braced my forehead against my wrist while Doctor Sho ministered to Clear-River. Exhausted, yes, but feeling better than I had in days. There had been some pleasure in problem-solving to make the canon of witchcraft, but it was nothing like the pure, uncompromising satisfaction of knitting a bone or healing a bruise.

'Here,' Doctor Sho said, thrusting a teacup in my face. 'You drink too. You've been pushing yourself too hard. Plus, you stink of liquor.'

I thanked him, took the cup, and drank the bitter medicine in a single swallow. It warmed me, then filled me with a tingling chill. Clear-River lay breathing steadily, his eyes closed.

'I'll leave him to you, then,' I said and pulled myself to my feet and up the stairs to my cot, where sleep took me quickly, uncomplicated by fears, regrets, or dreams.

12

Agreements in the Face of Fear

Foolish Cur

I woke to a burst of pain in my side.

My first thought was of my uncle—the messenger with ravens' feathers in his hair.

My eyes snapped wide to find Clear-River's face hovering over mine, flecked with blood, his eyes bulging, his mouth twisted into a snarl.

Confusion swept through me behind a wave of scraping agony.

Someone shouted, then collided with Clear-River, bearing him to the ground. Running Doe hooked her feet around his knees and her arm around his neck. Clear-River thrashed, clawing for her eyes. Her free hand pawed at the hilt of her dagger.

'Wait!' I rasped. I pulled out the scalpel lodged between my ribs and fought to keep from fainting while I reached for healing magic. Pressure filled my chest as my body reabsorbed lost blood and my punctured lung sealed itself.

'Don't kill him,' I said between gulping breaths. 'Please. Let him go.'

Running Doe hesitated a moment longer, her dagger poised over Clear-River's heart, then released her hold. Both she and Clear-River scrambled to their feet. Clear-River stood stiffly, casting about for a means of escape, while Running Doe positioned herself between him and the stairs, her dagger in one hand and the other on the hilt of a sword.

'What is this, Clear-River?' I demanded. Then, equally baffled by her presence, looked to Running Doe. 'And what are you doing here?'

Clear-River glared at me with eyes as sharp as the scalpel on the floor between us.

'One of us has guarded the infirmary every night,' Running Doe said, fidgeting and eyeing Clear-River as she spoke. 'I saw you bring him in earlier, then heard movement inside.'

I thought to ask what she meant by *one of us*—but of course, she still wore the burnt-wood fetish. And it was lucky that she *had* stood guard. I looked at the blood soaking my cot, my shirt, my hand. The pain of the wound had faded, but I knew how close to death I had come. Without her intervention, Clear-River might have injured me beyond my ability to heal.

With that question answered, I turned back to Clear-River. He stood like a cornered wolf, all raised hackles and fury. If he'd still held the scalpel, he would have thrown himself at me.

'Put your dagger away,' I instructed Running Doe. She opened her mouth to protest, then closed it slowly. The knife returned to its sheath but she kept her hands on her weapons.

'What did you think to accomplish by killing me?' I asked.

'Need it accomplish anything?' Clear-River spat in Sienese.

'Great harm has been done to you, but I did not do it.'

'But you are *why* it was done.' Clear-River stepped towards me, raising his hands. Running Doe pulled her sword halfway free before I gestured for her to stand down. Clear-River watched us both, his blood-smeared face full of fury. 'Without you, the rebellion would have ended at Greyfrost. Hand Pinion would not have pulled away half of Burrow's defences. My men would still be alive. All I had worked to build would *still exist!*' He bared his clenched teeth. 'Every-where you go, you destroy. Every time we meet, it is a curse.'

I was seized by the absurd but powerful need to defend myself. 'I was only trying to make my way in the world, Clear-River. And now I am only trying to put right what I did wrong.'

'And making new wrongs along the way,' he snarled. 'What of the rest of us, whose world is shattered in your wake? Do you spare us even a single thought?'

'Perhaps not enough,' I admitted, and with the words I felt an understanding, finally, of why I had stayed first my uncle's hand and now Running Doe's. 'I want to make the world better, Clear-River, but I don't think I know how. You tried, at least, and seemed to succeed here at Burrow. With your help, perhaps I can stop breaking things and start to build them.'

Clear-River searched my expression, his mouth agape, lost for words.

'Not yet, then,' I said at last, 'but when you are ready, I hope.' Then, to Running Doe, returning to the Nayeni tongue: 'Let him go, unless he wishes to stay.'

She looked at me in open disbelief. Slowly, Clear-River shook his head, and when he made for the stairway, Running Doe stepped aside.

'Are you…?' Running Doe began, then frowned. I wondered what she thought of all that she had witnessed. Would it add to the myth of me she carried in her mind, or would it reduce it, making me more human, more flawed, less worthy of worship and loyalty?

How could I explain letting Clear-River go free? I leaned against the wall, feeling a few distant twinges of pain deep in the muscles of my flank. 'If this rebellion is to leave anything of lasting value, we need people who can imagine better ways the world might be.'

Running Doe lowered her chin and gestured at the blood spattered on my cot. 'He seems to think the world would be better without you in it.'

'He's deeply in pain, and his hope is shattered,' I said. '*My* hope is that he finds himself again. He built a lasting peace here before we destroyed it. We will need him when the war is through.'

She frowned, still fidgeting. I sighed and reached into the pocket of my robe, below the hole made by Clear-River's scalpel. The strip of bone was still there. There were reasons not to do what I now intended—the way my uncle's suspicions would flare greatest among them—but they seemed small and petty.

'It's all right if you don't understand. Now then, I have something for *you*.' I produced the strip of bone.

Her eyes went wide and bright as stars. In them, I saw a mirror of that night when first I witnessed my grandmother conjuring flame. If there was a person I felt able to trust among the soldiers of the rebellion, she stood before me. She had just saved my life, after all.

Three days later, at dusk, Running Doe sat atop a barrel in an alleyway near the garrison yard of Burrow, her legs crossed beneath her. One hand lay open and upturned on her knee, like a sconce awaiting a flame. The other gripped the strip of bone, her thumb pressed to the mark I had carved. She squeezed her eyes tightly enough to crease her cheeks and the centre of her brow. The fierce warrior who had survived Greyfrost, stood down a pair of vengeful soldiers in the street, and wrestled Clear-River to the ground had become a slender young woman, her freckled face pinched with concentration.

It didn't help that she wore only simple clothes, as I had done when my grandmother first took me to the Temple of the Flame, rather than her armour. It reduced her bulk, made her seem her age—a mere twenty years—though she still wore the dagger on her hip and the captain's arrow and square of burnt wood on her collar.

She took a deep breath, her collarbone pushing at the wide neck of her shirt.

'I think...I felt something. Like a warm breeze,' she murmured. She wrinkled her nose. 'Is someone cooking nearby?'

'Hush. Still and silent, now.' I tried to keep my voice level and calming despite a flutter of excitement. After three days, she had finally felt a wake of magic. The first step had been teaching her to reach into the pattern, as my grandmother and Hand Usher had taught me, though the method I passed on to Running Doe was based on Hissing Cat's lessons, requiring her to envision her self as a sphere of jade hovering over the pattern—or, in her case, within the walls of the canon of witchcraft. 'That is the wake of the magic you will wield. Focus on it. Reach towards it, and draw it into yourself, as though drinking it like water or breathing it like air.'

I hadn't thought it possible for her to scrunch up her face any further, but she managed it. I stifled a laugh, worried that she would notice and lose her concentration. She took another deep, lung-filling breath, as I had taught her.

A spark, as from steel striking flint, lit up from the fingers of her open hand. Then another, till for a breath of time as brief as the beating of a moth's wings a candle flame flickered in her palm.

'I'm not sure it's working,' she murmured, sighed, and opened her eyes in the very moment the flame sputtered to life and died.

'And yet it was,' I said with a grin.

She burst out laughing, then pinwheeled her arms to keep from toppling off the barrel. I caught her wrist and helped her settle herself. She clasped my hand and stared into my face, full of astonishment and disbelief.

'You didn't think I could bloody do it, did you?' She grinned as bright as the crescent moon.

I grinned back at her. 'I didn't think *I* could do it.'

She cocked her head and her grin became a dimpled smile, almost shy. 'Well, proved you wrong twice over, then.'

Warmth spread through me. Facing that smile, the pressures, fears, and regrets of the last weeks melted away—if only for a dozen heartbeats.

'I hate to intrude upon what looks such a tender moment,' Tawny Owl said, leaning in the mouth of the alleyway, 'but Harrow Fox wants you, Cur. And you should see to your subordinates, Doe. We march at dawn.'

Running Doe sprang down from the barrel and snapped a salute. She took half a dozen steps before pausing mid-stride, jogging abashedly back and handing me the strip of bone.

'We'll continue this tomorrow night,' I said, taking it.

She fought down a smile, evidently unwilling to let her exuberance show in front of Tawny Owl, then saluted again and went on her way. Tawny Owl watched her go, still slouching against the wall, her arms crossed and expression hard.

'So she's the first little witch you plan to make,' she said. 'You shouldn't wonder, then, why Harrow Fox still doesn't trust you.'

'Why?' I feigned incredulity. 'She is a captain in his army, and a capable one. More, she is an interested and willing student. Why should I refrain from teaching her?'

Tawny Owl stared at me, rolled her eyes, and pushed off from the wall. 'Come along, then. You are wanted at council. The Sun King has decided where we will strike next.'

I t was to be Iron Town.
   I studied the map my uncle had laid out and the three sets of wooden tokens—one with the imperial tetragram, the second with the angular face of a fox, and the third with a snarling wolf—arranged according to the reports of our scouts. Pinion had already abandoned Iron Town and now marched towards Setting Sun Fortress. Frothing Wolf, meanwhile, had been striking in his wake, looting those villages she could not rally and leading her forces to recapture Iron Town.

The situation dizzied and horrified me. It was like peering into the past at the map table on which Oriole, Usher, and I had planned our assault four years ago. It was not the same, of course: the Nayeni rebellion was divided and Pinion's retreat was an absurd reversal. I wanted to laugh or weep or both, and wondered how he felt to be abandoning the territory his brother had died attempting to reclaim for the empire.

And layered atop all the rest was the madness in my uncle's words.

'I have refused Frothing Wolf's demands.' Harrow Fox leaned over the map, the knuckles of his fist pressed against the table. 'Now we will cow her, or we will destroy her, and absorb what remnant of her army is truly loyal to Nayen.'

My grandmother fought to keep a stony face, but frustration and disgust crept in at the corners of her eyes and the edges of her mouth. The thought of Nayeni going to war against Nayeni must have infuriated her. Yet she held her tongue, for Harrow Fox was Sun King, and her son, and there were answers she could not demand of him.

'There will be no attempt to negotiate, Uncle?' I asked.

His barrel chest expanded slowly, his nostrils flaring. 'There can be only one Sun King, Nephew, and you know the cost of her kneeling.'

'Neither one of you will sit the Sun Throne until the empire is chased from this island,' I protested, waving my hand over the map and its tokens. 'All of this squabbling can wait until then, can it not?'

Tawny Owl, at my uncle's side, sneered. 'You are new to this rebellion, Cur. The Army of the Wolf has spilled as much of our blood as the empire's. If they *did* bow, it would be only to creep close enough to cut Harrow Fox's throat.'

'That seems the height of foolishness,' I said flatly.

Annoyance at Tawny Owl's intrusion flashed across my uncle's face. 'We have long shared a cause, but her methods only hindered it. She has been too soft on those who collaborate with the empire. When our swords have crossed, it has been because she stands between us and vengeance upon those who take Sienese silver in exchange for the iron and soil that are the wealth of our island.'

I parsed his words as I might a Sienese didactic tale, peeling them apart in search of what went unsaid. I thought of the story my grand-mother had told me, years ago, of the Sienese conquest, begun with ships and merchants, silk and spices and silver, and ending with my grandfather's self-immolation while Sienese legions swept across the island. Events that had defined my uncle's youth.

I began to understand his hatred for those who had grasped for the lure in the jaws of the imperial trap, seized it, and thrived, which in turn stoked his hatred of Clear-River and his suspicion of me, who had once benefited most of all from the power and wealth the empire could give. But his righteous talk obfuscated a willingness—perhaps even unto pleasure—to brutalise those only trying to make what good life they could beneath the yoke of the empire. Was there a way, I wondered in despair, to fight back against cruelty without becoming cruel oneself?

It is a question I have yet to answer.

'Let me try to convince her,' I pleaded. Desperation boiled within me, and the words rushed out like steam. I still had no desire to rule—not least because it would give justification to my uncle's para-noia—but I would do everything in my power to turn the bow of the rebellion away from this self-destructive course. 'I will fly to Iron Town, show her the canon of witchcraft, and make a case for my contrition. Perhaps she will be willing to wash the old blood from your swords and forget the violence that lies between you.'

Harrow Fox's eyes narrowed as my grandmother stiffened, and I knew, in a burst of frustration, that he had misread the spaces between my words, finding there not my old hatreds and fears but a reflection of his own thirst for power.

'She will not forget the murder of a daughter,' he said. 'No. We march to Iron Town in force. But we *will* show her your canon of witchcraft, and with it cull her ranks of those who refuse to burn her banners and bend to me.'

I curled my hand into a fist and clenched my jaw.

Better that I served my uncle than the empire, I told myself. Better that the Nayeni rule Nayen. Better that Tenet's gradual devouring of the world be interrupted, and with it his plan for war against the gods.

Yet the cost in blood—and in absurdity—would never feel worth it. The pattern of the world flowed forwards, carried on by the momentum and direction of the past. Old crimes and old betrayals would define its course far more than compassion, justice, or simple *good sense* ever could.

Unless I could divert it.

'You would do the empire's work for it, carving the heart out of this rebellion in your effort to unite it,' I said, fixing my uncle with a level stare. I had contorted myself into a shape fit for the empire's use for years. I would not suborn myself yet again to a vision and a purpose not my own. 'What is the point of victory if we must mirror the empire's brutality to achieve it? Do you think your soldiers share your hunger for power? Do they shed their blood to sate your lust for a throne?

'No, Uncle. They fight because they have suffered.' I turned my gaze to Tawny Owl, recalling the flashes of memory I had seen while reaching into her pact mark. She bared her teeth and touched the hilt of her sword, but I pressed on, undaunted and unwilling to bend any longer. 'Because they know at first hand the cruelty of the world the Sienese are building here, and they would undo it and make a better one. They follow you because they believe that you will deliver them into that better world. Will you betray that trust? Will you—'

'Enough.' Harrow Fox's voice was bared steel, sharp and rasping. 'Have you dredged the depths of every mind in this rebellion with your imperial magic for such insight? Which of us, Nephew, understands our people better? I, who have led them for decades, or you, who once spilled their blood upon the streets of Iron Town?'

My jaw seized from fury and my hand curled into a fist.

'Press further, Nephew,' Harrow Fox snarled. 'See where this road leads. I am Sun King. Challenge me for that title now, if you desire it, else step back from the edge of treason and *do as I command*.'

Once, I had longed to shape the pattern of the world to my will, without, in my childishness, any sense of what that will might be. Now I had the will and the power, and the shape of a rebellion was only a small fraction of the pattern. What, then, was missing?

I knew only that I could have killed my uncle with a gesture and a thought and taken his place, yet I kept my hand—clenched but unmoving—at my side, reminding myself of the ruin I had left in my wake when last I gave in to ambition.

'Very well, Uncle.' I raised my fist to my collarbone in salute, forcing the words between clenched teeth. 'You are Sun King. We will do as you command.'

He studied me a moment longer, peeling through my words, my gestures. At last, with a nod and a wave, he dismissed us all to our duties, though he gave me no orders, nor any responsibilities.

Why summon me to council at all? Not to hear my suggestions, nor to give me any command. Only to inform me of his plans and gauge my reaction. Our every conversation was a series of moves upon a Stones board, my words and actions part of a game that existed entirely within his mind.

I might have reached out and read that mind, perceived that game, even scoured his thoughts clean of all his fear of me—and, in doing so, justified that fear.

As the others went to their tasks, I departed as well to bring word to Doctor Sho of the need to pack up the infirmary and prepare our patients for travel. I had not walked a dozen paces beyond the magistrate's hall when my grandmother fell into step beside me, her withered hand twitching and flexing in time with a poorly suppressed tic at the corner of her mouth.

'I disagree with him just as strongly.' Her eyes darted, careful to be sure we were neither being watched nor followed. 'But by standing so directly against him, you only force him to dig in.'

I shook my head. 'If I were capable of following orders without question, I would still serve the empire.'

'He is the Sun King. In his mind, there is no difference between the rebellion and himself. You need not be silent, only find a way to explain your objections in a way he can accept.'

'Perhaps the Sun King ought to perceive that distinction.'

My grandmother glared at me and snarled, 'You are either asking me to help my grandson overthrow his uncle or inviting me to usurp my own son.'

'That is not what I'm saying,' I muttered, shaking my head, but she went on, ignoring me.

'Besides, you are as blind and foolish as your name if you think Frothing Wolf will be forgiving.' She harrumphed and massaged her arm. 'I don't like this any more than you do, Cur, but I don't see another way.'

'We want the same things. We should co-operate. All the rest…' I made a dismissive gesture. 'Short-sighted foolishness. Grudges and ambition.'

'Some of the most powerful forces in the world.' She grimaced. 'Unfortunately.'

'Not more powerful than the empire,' I countered. 'If we cannot overcome our own weakness, what hope do we have of victory?'

She put up her good hand in surrender. 'I only ask that you *think* before you act in this. Your uncle may find a way to force Frothing Wolf's surrender without slaughtering her army and breaking the rebellion. Give him a chance.'

I grumbled assent. She thanked me and went on her way.

I reached into the pocket of my robe and ran my thumb along the smooth surface of the strip of bone. My only ambition was to shape the pattern of the world for the better. To liberate Nayen and make restitution for all the wrong I had done. To prevent, insofar as I was able, Tenet from waging his war against the gods. If I meant to make good on that purpose, those who followed me would need more than the power to conjure flame. More, even, than simple magic.

Someone else would bring word of our departure to Doctor Sho. I turned instead towards the town gate, and the forest beyond, where Hissing Cat would be lurking.

There were secrets she had yet to share, powers she had alluded to but refused to explain. And my patience and fear of her had thinned, and my need grown far too heavy.

'Sho told me that Sienese boy you saved stabbed you in the lung,' Hissing Cat said, smirking, by way of a greeting. 'There's a metaphor in that, I think. You'd know better than me, though. I always was a shit poet.'

I had followed the sound of shoulder blades whipping through the undergrowth to find her in a secluded clearing. I sat on the far side of her fire while she stirred the coals.

'Well, Cur?' She lifted the glowing tip of her needle from the fire. 'What now? You've made your little canon. I can't imagine you seeking me out from fondness. Out with it.'

I had been well trained to accept boundaries—doctrine, of course, but also the walls of imperial magic. Hissing Cat had set such a boundary around what she was willing to discuss and what help she was willing to give. But I had gained little of value in life when I let such barriers constrain me.

'"And that was a war fought with weapons we can no longer wield,"' I quoted, as though from the sages. 'Your words, at Greyfrost.'

Her eyes narrowed, harsh as glowing coals. I kept speaking, worried that if I stopped she would charge into the gap and cut the throat of our conversation.

'I would add those weapons to my canon. They may be forbidden to you, but Tollu declared that all magic was permitted to me, and you have admitted yourself that our chances against the emperor are slim.'

'A declaration you heard while in a fugue, gripped by a deep and dangerous wake of magic.' Her voice was short and sharp, like the scraping of a whetstone. 'Even if she *did* make such a declaration, the gods are no more unified in their purpose than Tenet and I. It was the Skyfather alone who poured his wrath out on Naphena. And even if they agreed with Tollu *at the time*, there is no telling whether they will agree with her *later*, let alone when you start throwing around magics that truly—truly!—threaten them.'

'The gods might be fickle,' I allowed. 'Fair enough. But the risk is worth it. And if there weren't a part of you that agrees, you would still be hiding in that cave.'

Hissing Cat pointed at me with the glowing tip of her needle. 'The pacts aren't hard and fast rules like the walls of Tenet's canon. No power beyond the gods binds them to abide by them. They're agreements. I believe I mentioned that *agreements can be broken* in the same breath I speculated that you *might* be able to get away with things I cannot.'

'The war will happen either way,' I argued, 'whether because the emperor gives the gods reason to begin it or I do.'

She stabbed the needle into the dirt and stared at the curl of smoke rising from its tip. With a heavy sigh she leaned forwards, the skulls in her hair clattering in a mocking chorus. Slowly, she drew a circle beside the fire.

'This is the pattern of the world,' she said and drew wavy lines crossing the circle. 'These are the ripples of power that flow through it, the interchange of energies—blah, blah, blah. You know this part.' With a turn of her wrist, she drew a smaller circle within the larger one. '*This* is the weapon we used to force the gods into a stalemate, a wall like the ones the gods built within our minds—like Tenet's canon, and yours—but built into the world itself. Do you understand? *This* is what we did. First, we surrendered to the pattern. Then, we drew a boundary within it. Finally, we asserted the pattern's natural flow against any and all magic wielded within our boundary.'

She drew more wavy lines, but when her needle came to the edge of the smaller, inner circle, she lifted it and continued drawing on its far side. The space of the larger circle gradually filled with waves while the inner circle remained unchanged.

'As the gods waged their war, the world cracked and broke and came unwoven. Monsters twisted from the fabric of reality stalked the edges of our boundaries but could not cross them. Nor could the earthquakes the gods wrought, the fires they called down, the winds they threw against us. Nor, even, could the gods themselves.'

'And they were not able to overwhelm you?' I asked, thinking of her conjured flame in the courtyard of Greyfrost and the strength of her will, unyielding as iron—also of Tenet's canon, and how easily it had broken when I asserted the pattern against it.

She tapped the inner circle with the tip of her needle. 'This is *not* magic,' she said. 'It is the *opposite* of magic. It seals the world in its natural state rather than changing it.' The tip of her needle came up again, hovering level with my eye. 'And as iron becomes sharper and more penetrating when condensed to a point, the pattern becomes more solid when condensed, when the interchange is simplified. It is a hard thing to hold the whole of the pattern in one's mind and reassert it, as you know. Far easier to hold a *segment* of that whole and wield it as a shield.'

'And the gods fear this?' I struggled to understand how what she described could be used as a weapon.

'Of course they do!' she snarled in response. 'The gods don't exist as you or I do, all bound up in meat and bone. They are pure will exerting itself upon the world.' She stabbed the inner circle once more. 'We caught a few of them in these seals. There weren't any corpses left behind, but we never heard from those bastards again.' She began drawing more circles until they nearly filled the outer circle, leaving only narrow gaps between. 'We sealed off as much of the world as we could. There were consequences to that, too. Each seal became a bit of a world unto itself, over time. Each little pattern began to flow without the influence of anything beyond the boundary. The chaos wrought when the barriers fell and the pattern of the world was allowed to rebuild itself drowned continents and birthed mountain ranges. But it was *worth* it.'

She pointed to the small gaps between the inner circles. 'We could expand our seals no further and left the gods too little of the outside world to sustain themselves, let alone satisfy their hunger. And from that stalemate, we reached an agreement. One they will certainly consider broken should you or I—or Tenet, for that matter—reach into the pattern and start putting up walls.'

'Even if I put up those walls up to *defeat* Tenet?'

She shrugged. 'A question I can't answer. Okara might, though it would be at best only his opinion and, at worst, only whatever words might convince you to do his bidding.'

I slumped beneath a growing sense of defeat. A weapon feared by the gods ought to have been a star cast down from heaven. Something to burn the emperor from the world. Or a chasm opened to swallow him and bury him in the heart of the earth.

'Don't be disappointed.' Hissing Cat stabbed her needle back into the fire. 'Tenet would be nearly helpless if you walked up to him and sealed away a chunk of the pattern out from beneath his feet. For one thing, the magic that sustains him—that sustains *me*—would begin to erode. He might feel his age more keenly than a knife to the heart.' She cocked her head. 'But also, he might not be able to stop your knife. I don't think he can remember the last time he had to defend himself without magic.'

Her reassurance did little to uplift me. 'But then, of course, the world as we know it might end,' I pointed out.

'Though as you say, it might end either way.' She reached for a fresh shoulder blade. 'You have a choice now, Cur, to use this power or not to use it. I, thus far, have chosen not to. But I have made other choices I have come to regret.' Smoke trickled up from the bone as she began to carve the runes of her oracle. 'And it seems, at last, after so many years, that I am more tired than I am afraid.'

13

A Summons

Koro Ha

Koro Ha fidgeted with the ends of his sleeves, oddly ashamed of his own nervousness, as though the guardsman assigned to Orna Sin's gatehouse took any interest at all in his personal life. He had half expected Eln Se to decline his invitation with one of several obvious excuses—she and Rea Ab were overwhelmed with work, skilled seamstresses being in high demand these days, or perhaps their father's bad lungs made it too difficult to travel even the short distance from one district to another. But she had accepted, and now Koro Ha stood idle in the gatehouse, his classes dismissed for the day, his stomach twisting into knots.

He nearly jumped when the heavy knocker thumped against the gate. The guardsman cocked an eyebrow at him before opening the bolt. A moment later, he led Eln Se, Rea Ab, and—to Koro Ha's surprise—Yan Hra across the threshold.

'Welcome!' Koro Ha squeezed his sister's hands, and then his niece's, while they cast about themselves, wide eyed, taking in the high windows and silk-screen paintings that decorated the garden entryway. 'I'm so pleased you were able to come.'

Yan Hra answered his welcoming gesture with a glare. The burly stone-cutter rolled his shoulders within his crisp white tunic, embroidered with clouds in yellow thread and a few lines of Toa Aloni knot-work—a costume Koro Ha guessed he had last worn at his wedding.

Eln Se smiled up at him, sparing only a quick, sideways glare at her husband. 'Your invitation was a pleasant surprise, Brother. Father was unable to join us, sadly. His lungs, you see.'

'Of course,' Koro Ha said. 'Perhaps some other time.'

'Doubtful,' Yan Hra muttered. 'The old man's not interested in gawking at the plundered wealth of his own country.'

Koro Ha took a deep breath. Any answer to *that* would cast a pallor over the rest of the visit. Rea Ab spared him the indignity of stumbling to pick up the thread of conversation. 'Come along, Papa,' she said brightly, taking her father by the elbow. 'I'm sure all that plundered wealth is *lovely*.'

Yan Hra grumbled but let his daughter lead him out into the garden.

'Well, his feelings are clear,' Koro Ha said under his breath.

'He'd have his opinions either way.' Eln Se took his arm. 'At least now they'll be based on *something* rather than the grumbles of his friends down at the tavern. Now then, Brother, show me your new home, and tell me how this school of yours is working out.'

Koro Ha cupped her hand with his and followed his niece and brother-in-law. 'Better than you might expect, actually. Now that Orna Sin takes the five brightest for a few hours twice a week, I have time to ensure all are learning apace. It is not without its difficulties, of course. Conventional methods would have me lead the students in individually tailored dialogues—not something possible with twenty or fifteen at once.'

'No, I suspect they all talk over one another, or not at all.'

'More of the latter, actually,' Koro Ha smiled. 'A few of the brightest engage the most—and, you'll be pleased to hear, one of the *most* talkative is a girl, Tul Elna. The rest sit quietly. I'd like to think they're listening, but most seem more occupied by the grain of the floorboards than the conversation at hand. I've tried having them discuss in small groups of three or four while I skulk about, listening in. I'd thought to step in and correct the occasional misunderstanding…'

He shrugged. 'They need a firmer foundation in doctrine, I think, before they will be ready for that much independence in their thinking. We spend perhaps too much time practising handwriting. That, at least, they can each work on at their own pace. But I fear I will make only a dozen excellent scribes and not a single successful candidate among them.'

They emerged from the gatehouse into the garden proper, where Rea Ab stood gazing in wide-eyed wonder at the little paradise Orna Sin had built for himself.

'Oh, Uncle, it's gorgeous!' she exclaimed, then pointed excitedly at a tree branch stretching over the nearby pond. 'Papa! Look! Snowy herons!'

Yan Hra harrumphed. 'Bought from some imperial trapper, no doubt. My grandfather told of seeing them lining the lowland rivers whenever he floated marble down to Ans Alrua or Sama Ta. Now you're lucky to spot a flash of feathers.'

Rea Ab furrowed her brow. Rather than arguing with her father, she dragged him further down the path towards the sweeping gables of the Pavilion of Contemplation.

'It is lovely,' Eln Se said, squeezing Koro Ha's hand. 'I'm happy for you, Brother, that you get to live and work in such a place.'

Koro Ha felt a needle of guilt hidden in those words. 'Orna Sin has done well for himself, but he is not hoarding wealth as your husband claims. My salary is his investment in a better future for Toa Alon.'

Eln Se was quiet for a while, smiling gently while they walked alongside the pond. A carp leapt for a waterwalker lazing among the lilies, sending up a splash and drawing a delighted squeal from Rea Ab.

'A better future for some in Toa Alon, I am sure,' Eln Se said at last. 'Not everyone can live in a garden like this.'

'Of course not.' No longer a needle of guilt but a twisting knife. 'But did we all live in palaces and gardens before the Sienese?'

'Do you remember the stories Mother used to tell?' Eln Se went on, as though he had not spoken. 'Of Sor Cala, before it was destroyed? There were palaces, but built for the stone-faced gods and open to all. There were gardens, but not hidden behind walls, overflowing with food grown by the magic of the stonespeakers. We were not a powerful nation, but none went hungry and none wanted for shelter. Is that the future Orna Sin would build? Or does he only imagine that a few of those mansions they are building on the hillsides might house merchants and magistrates with Toa Aloni blood?'

'Old stories, rich with nostalgia, of a time before Mother was yet born,' Koro Ha pointed out. 'I'm sure Toa Alon saw better days before the empire, but nowhere in the world is perfect, Sister. And to answer your question, Orna Sin has seen to it that the five brightest of my students spend hours each week at study in Toa Aloni culture. He hopes that Toa Alon will one day be ruled by those who understand it, who remember what it once was, even if they must rule on behalf of the empire.'

Eln Se sighed. 'Then I suppose I must wish him luck.' She jabbed him with her elbow. 'Now, tell me more about this garden, Brother. What is your favourite place to sit and smoke that terrible pipe of yours?'

Though her words still weighed heavily, Koro Ha followed her into more light-hearted conversation as they approached the pavilion, where Rea Ab and Yan Hra leaned against the railing.

'This place is so peaceful,' Rea Ab said, watching the wading herons and the ripples of the wind on the water. Not for the first time, Koro Ha felt a twinge of regret that he had not founded his school in Toa Alon sooner, when Rea Ab might have been young enough to attend. What verses, he wondered, might she have conjured to capture the beauty she saw, clever as she was?

Eln Se went to stand beside her daughter. Koro Ha lingered behind them, feeling awkward—pleased that Rea Ab was enjoying herself, at least.

He thought back to all he knew of Toa Aloni history. A vague, uncertain mess, like an essay composed by a half-hearted student. Volumes of Sienese philosophy and doctrine filled space in Koro Ha's mind that might have been occupied by the teachings of the stonespeakers and the mysteries of the stone-faced gods. Instead, he remembered only the few stories his mother and father had told, and the tragedy that defined the geography of the city—the futile, peaceful resistance of the stonespeakers, keeping the secret of cultivation from the empire and, in doing so, inviting destruction.

His mother had led him into the mountains twice that he could remember, both times to visit old caves where faces carved in relief peered from the walls, veiled by the shadows of torchlight. They had knelt and burnt incense, and she had said a prayer, though the words of it escaped him.

What Eln Se seemed to want was impossible. Toa Alon could never be restored. No one living, save perhaps the emperor, had lived in Toa Alon as it was and truly *knew* what it should be. The empire had taken too much, burying the grand city itself, but also burying what the Toa Aloni knew of themselves beneath layers of grief before building their own doctrine and culture atop the ruin.

It was too late to restore all that had been lost. It would take a long and bloody struggle to uproot the empire from the grave of Toa Alon, and their people had never been warlike. Orna Sin's way was their only hope, a chance to seed the empire itself with what remained of Toa Alon.

'Perhaps I was wrong about this man,' Yan Hra said quietly, drawing Koro Ha from his whirlpool of introspection. The stone-cutter brushed his calloused fingers down the looping knotwork that decorated the pavilion's columns.

'I told you,' Koro Ha said. 'What we do here, we do for the good of our people.'

Yan Hra curled his hand into a fist and let his knuckles rest against the railing. 'I believe that you think so, Brother. That, at least, I will credit you.' He jerked his chin at the pond and the herons, which yet captivated his daughter. 'This, though…it is a waste.'

Before he could elaborate, or Koro Ha could offer any rebuttal, a servant arrived at the pavilion, breathing heavily.

'For you, Master Koro Ha.' The servant dipped his head and offered a scroll case sealed with the imperial tetragram.

The seal snapped cleanly. Koro Ha unrolled the crisp, heavy paper within the case. It read:

The estimable tutor Koro Ha is
hereby summoned to audience without delay.
His Excellency Tan Grazing-Stag,
District Magistrate.

Only three lines of straightforward, business-like calligraphy. 'What is it, Brother?' Eln Se searched his face.

The paper crinkled in his haste to fold it shut. He smiled. No need to let her see the storm of worries now swirling behind his eyes. 'Nothing that need concern you, but sadly something that must interrupt our visit.' He gestured to the servant. 'Sen, would you be willing to continue the tour on my behalf? I'm afraid this cannot wait.'

The servant nodded graciously, but Eln Se shook her head.

'It's fine,' she said. 'We can come back another time.' She squeezed his hand. Rea Ab did likewise, with a disappointed pout. Yan Hra lingered a moment, his hard eyes studying the broken tetragram on the scroll case, before nodding sharply and following his wife and daughter towards the gatehouse.

The moment they were out of sight, Koro Ha collapsed to a bench and scrutinised every logogram of the summons, but there was nothing to read into it, no way of knowing whether it bade well or ill.

His mind fixated on the possibility that word of the Toa Aloni lessons had reached the magistrate. What else had he done to warrant attention? If this were only about the school, surely the summons would have come more quickly after its founding.

Of course, if the magistrate had some inkling of Orna Sin's more illicit dealings, he might intend to turn Koro Ha into his spy in the merchant's household. The patrol that had inspected the *Swiftness of the South Wind* on its return voyage had recorded his presence aboard, he was sure. Thank the stone-faced gods and the sages that he had not pried overmuch into the copper-banded chest, the outrigger canoe, and the smuggled casks from the Black Maw. If the magistrate put him to the question, he could tell only of the vague silhouette of a distant island and a strange meeting on the open sea.

Did Orna Sin know of the summons? If he did not yet, he would once rumour filtered through his household from servant to servant, as it was wont to do, until it reached the ear of someone who would bring the matter to his attention.

Better for Koro Ha to inform Orna Sin himself.

He found the merchant in his offices, perusing a dusty ledger. After Koro Ha produced the invitation and explained, with sweaty palms, that he did not know what the magistrate wanted, Orna Sin said only, with a wry grin, 'You're a famous man, Koro Ha. Perhaps he wants to poach you from my school?'

What response could he make to such obfuscation? The effort of managing the school had distracted Koro Ha from his misgivings. Now he could think of nothing but the empty spaces where certain vitally important facts should have been—the precise nature of Orna Sin's illicit activities, for one, and the penalty Koro Ha might face if the magistrate concluded that he was a co-conspirator.

'I'm sure you're right, Orna Sin,' he said, swallowing his fear.

The merchant smiled wider and clapped him on the shoulder. 'I'm sure you're loyal, but if his offer is too good to turn down, you need only let me know and I might be able to scrounge a few more taels for your salary.'

K oro Ha's palanquin left him at the gatehouse of Magistrate Tan's estate, from whence a steward led him on a winding path to the reception hall. In the antechamber, he simmered in worry until the door opened. A different steward emerged, gestured for him to enter, and followed behind, announcing his arrival.

The hall itself was dizzyingly similar to its twin in Magistrate Bo's garden. The columns carved with lion serpents. The leaf patterns on the latticed windows. Koro Ha had travelled hundreds of miles to the far side of the Pillars of the Gods to arrive in exactly the place he had left.

Magistrate Tan rose from his seat on the dais and descended to meet Koro Ha. He was tall and slender, unlike the barrel-chested Magistrate Bo, and Koro Ha latched onto this difference, anchoring himself in the present moment—a moment in which a magistrate, upon summoning him, had risen to meet him.

'Master Koro Ha,' Magistrate Tan said, bowing slightly at the waist, like a paper doll gently rustled by the breeze.

Koro Ha returned the bow with thrice the depth. 'It is an honour, Magistrate Tan, to receive your summons.'

Magistrate Tan's smile, too, was thin. 'I am sure. Might I offer you tea?'

'Of course, Your Excellency.'

Magistrate Tan led him out the side door of the reception hall and onto a pathway of marble tiles that led around the edge of a shallow pond and to a pavilion, painted all in red. A figure, dressed plainly and facing away from them, sat on a bench beneath the broad eaves. A tea table had already been set with a pot and three cups of gleaming white porcelain.

At their approach, the seated figure looked up. Lines of silver traced his forehead just below his greying hairline.

Koro Ha's steps faltered.

'Master Koro Ha.' The Voice—Governor Zhou Sprouting-Elm, who ruled the province of Toa Alon—bobbed his head, smiled, and gestured at the bench across from him. 'Please. The tea should be just finished steeping.'

Magistrate Tan took a seat. Koro Ha hesitated at the table. Should he bow? Did he have permission to speak? The canon, propriety—his very imagination—had failed to prepare him for this moment.

'Thank you, Your Eminence,' he managed, and bowed, then sat, each motion precise and intentional. Perhaps overly so, but by the emperor's never-changing name, he would face whatever was to come with dignity.

Magistrate Tan poured for them. *A magistrate! Pouring for a tutor!* For a wild moment, he thought Orna Sin might be right and these men were trying to poach his services. Voice Sprouting-Elm sipped his tea, then waited for Koro Ha to do the same. It held a sharp scent of mint and earthy undernotes. Soothing, under normal circumstances.

'I can see the tension in you,' Voice Sprouting-Elm said.

Koro Ha nearly choked on a sip of tea.

'I studied some medicine, years ago, as a dalliance, so it is hard to hide such things from me.' Voice Sprouting-Elm went on, as though Koro Ha had not reacted. 'I want to assure you that, at this moment, you are in no danger.'

Not since his imperial examinations had Koro Ha scrutinised a sentence more closely.

'You wish to speak,' Voice Sprouting-Elm said. 'I see that on your face. Go ahead.'

'Your Eminence,' Koro Ha said. 'You speak as though I was in danger recently, or will be in danger soon.'

'Either is possible,' Magistrate Tan said. 'Nothing will harm you in the presence of a Voice, within an imperial citadel.'

A statement Koro Ha very much doubted. He had grown up when the streets of Sor Cala were often flecked with blood, when armed Sienese soldiers patrolled the streets against agitators. One of Koro Ha's classmates—he could not recall the boy's name—had lost a brother to such patrols before his family had fled from Sor Cala. A member of some cult, still worshipping the stone-carved gods, rumour held.

Not long after, Koro Ha had refused to accompany his mother on her pilgrimages to the caves. No more than ten years old, he had become fully aware of the danger her insistence upon the old ways represented.

'You wish to speak again?' Voice Sprouting-Elm reached for the pot, then topped off both their teacups. 'What troubles you, Koro Ha? Speak freely. This meeting is a courtesy.'

'What has prompted this courtesy?' Koro Ha said. 'Some explanation for my summons would do a great deal to set my mind at ease.'

'Are you aware of recent events in the city of An-Zabat?' Magistrate Tan said.

Koro Ha knew An-Zabat only from maps, as a speck of civilisation in the vast, empty stretch of the Batir Waste. A mercantile city, bridging the empire and the distant lands of the west, surrounded by a great oasis that the An-Zabati claimed had been created miraculously from the desert sand by their goddess. A place to which he had no connection.

Relief trickled through him, slowly easing the knots in his shoulders and slowing his racing pulse. Still, he kept alert. If anything, this meeting had only become stranger.

'I am only a simple tutor,' Koro Ha said. 'Not privy to news from far-flung corners of the empire.'

'Naturally.' Voice Sprouting-Elm tilted his head, letting his tetragram glimmer in the sunlight. 'Of course, we *are* privy to news, from *every* corner.'

'There has been an uprising,' Magistrate Tan said. 'One quickly subdued, but not before rebel forces destroyed the oasis that supplied the city.'

'Hundreds were killed in the violence,' Voice Sprouting-Elm went on. 'Thousands more were forced to flee back to the imperial heartland. There is no precise count of how many died of starvation or want of water during the long trek through the desert heat. Innocent civilians, many of them, Sienese and An-Zabati alike.'

'That is terrible to hear,' Koro Ha said. Did they suspect him of revolutionary sympathies? Perhaps this was about Orna Sin's special classes, after all. Or his illicit business. Koro Ha had assumed he smuggled narcotics or stolen valuables, but rebellions needed funding and supplying, did they not? 'Yet I fail to understand why you wish to share this news with *me*.'

'Your former student, Wen Alder, instigated the uprising,' Magistrate Tan said.

Koro Ha's head had been swimming since he had received the magistrate's summons. Now, a thirty-foot wave rose up and cast it down into the depths of the sea.

'We have this on the authority of the Voice governing there.' Voice Sprouting-Elm went on. 'Alder even attempted to murder one of his fellow Hands.'

'I-I...' Koro Ha managed to stammer. 'I'm sorry, Your Eminence?'

'It appears that Wen Alder suffered the influence of a Nayeni witch during his childhood,' Magistrate Tan continued, pouring tea, as though he and Voice Sprouting-Elm had not uttered words that shook the earth. 'He has been an agent of rebellion all along.'

'You were also a significant influence in his childhood.' Voice Sprouting-Elm scrutinised Koro Ha's face like a proctor judging a sample of handwriting. 'Perhaps the most important influence. Success in the examinations carried him to An-Zabat.'

'You speak as though the *reason* he strove for an imperial commission was to foster this rebellion in the west.' Koro Ha scrambled to orient his thoughts. 'He was only a child!'

'Who can say when thoughts of insurrection entered his mind?' Voice Sprouting-Elm said.

The memory of Alder's grandmother fluttered behind Koro Ha's eyes—a faint outline of a craggy face, marked by hardship. Her sharp eyes hiding depth, like Orna Sin's.

He fought to stabilise his expression, as though steadying a hand when practising calligraphy. Stillness. Focus. He didn't know anything. That was the key idea to communicate.

'Your Excellency, Your Eminence,' he said slowly, looking each man in the eye, 'this, frankly, comes as a shock. Under my tutelage, Alder demonstrated nothing but the keenest understanding of the imperial canon and the firmest grounding in doctrine. It upsets me immensely to hear of this betrayal, and to learn that I was blind to this weakness in his character. As were the proctors at his examination, even Voice Usher himself.'

'Indeed,' Magistrate Tan said. 'Almost as though he were taught to hide the rot that ate away at his heart.'

Voice Sprouting-Elm leaned forwards, his tetragram glinting in the dappled light that shone through the latticed pavilion walls. 'There is no need to defend yourself, Koro Ha. We are only sharing information and sharing in our grief that such a promising servant of the empire has fallen so far. It is a tragedy.'

'Of course, Your Eminence,' Koro Ha said. 'Thank you for telling—'

'A tragedy that has caused the empire to re-evaluate some priorities,' Magistrate Tan said. 'It is our understanding that you tutor children in Sor Cala?'

Ah. The thought flitted through his head. *Here it comes.*

His lungs felt heavy and full of water. They waited for him to speak. 'I do,' he said.

'You should know, then, that there will be separate examinations, going forwards,' Magistrate Tan continued. 'One examination for those of unadulterated Sienese descent, and one for those from developing provinces, such as this.'

'The provincial examination will cover the same material,' Voice Sprouting-Elm said, 'but standards will be much, much higher. As the empire expands, it becomes vital that the majority of its ministers remain Sienese. We are, after all, as elder brothers to you provincial peoples, are we not? Responsible for guiding our younger siblings in adherence to the emperor's will?'

'Of course.' The weight in his lungs grew cold, numbing him, as the Voice's words settled in his mind.

Before, by his estimation, five of his students had a chance at real success. Magisterial positions, or even a place as a Hand. Perhaps another five might have done well enough to become career ministers or scribes. The other seven, if they applied themselves and managed to pass the examinations, might have become tutors like himself.

Now…he could not begin to imagine what these *higher standards* might be. If they were designed to keep out the likes of Wen Alder, what chance did *any* of his seventeen have?

'I am glad that you understand,' Voice Sprouting-Elm said. He leaned back into his seat and blinked—and Koro Ha realised that the Voice had not done so all the while they had spoken. 'As I am sure you will understand that you must put a stop to the strange indulgence of including female students in your school. We realise there are…cultural differences…which might have led your employer to open his school to girls. He selected the students for you, of course, and so you are not to blame for this open violation of propriety, but we cannot allow the young minds of future examination candidates to be corrupted by such notions. The girls must be expelled at once.'

Koro Ha felt heat rising in his face. Indignation was a dangerous feeling in the face of imperial scrutiny, yet it welled within him. Not only on behalf of Tul Elna, who was thrice the mind of half the boys under his tutelage, but on behalf of young women like Rea Ab—like his own sister!—whose futures had been constrained by this, the most arbitrary seeming of imperial doctrines. Yet he gritted his teeth, forced the feeling to the back of his mind, and bowed.

'Of course, Your Eminence.'

'We are glad, also, that you will have no issue with one of my scribes sitting in on your lessons,' Magistrate Tan added.

Dozens of arguments against such a thing sprang at once to mind. The already distracted children could hardly be expected to ignore the sudden presence of a silent, observing stranger. His own mind would wander, scrutinising his every utterance, wondering whether he was perceived to stray from some undeclared bound of acceptability.

What would the scribe say when five of his students went off with Orna Sin once a week?

No, Koro Ha had many issues with Magistrate Tan's suggestion, but how could he voice *any* of them without drawing suspicion? He could do nothing, after all, if they imprisoned or killed him for the impudence of contesting so direct an imperial command.

'It hardly seems necessary, Your Excellency,' Koro Ha said, and bowed his head. 'But if you deem it so, who am I to question you?'

'Very good.' Magistrate Tan rose from the table. 'My steward will show you out of the garden, Master Koro Ha. Thank you for joining us, and we are sorry, again, to bear such ill news.'

Koro Ha thanked them in return, complimented the tea, and left the magistrate's palace in a fog, his mind looping endlessly through the next week of lessons he planned to teach, looking for any point of doctrine to be tightened or any question that might strike a scribe's ear as too contentious. And, again and again, to Wen Alder, standing on the dais beside Voice Golden-Finch, receiving his imperial commission and the tetragram upon his hand.

He wondered if, on that day on the dais, a seed of rebellion—some angry question or point of confusion—had already begun to germinate in the boy's heart. Pushing roots into the soil that would, in time, crack the cornerstones and collapse what had been Koro Ha's greatest success.

14

A Secret

Koro Ha

'It will be inconvenient, yes,' Orna Sin said, 'but not catastrophic.' Koro Ha stared at him, wondering how the severity of their situation had failed to strike Orna Sin with all its weight. The merchant dangled his feet in his garden pond and smoked his pipe while Koro Ha jittered on a chair nearby, his own pipe loaded but forgotten in his hand.

'I cannot possibly teach classes under such conditions,' Koro Ha said. 'The children already struggle to focus. Burn it, *I* will struggle to focus. And we will have to do away with the special lessons for Lon Sa, Quon Lo, and the others—'

'No.' Orna Sin tapped out his pipe. 'That we will not do.'

'Then we will both be imprisoned for treason, if not executed!' Koro Ha threw up his hands. 'And the children and their parents along with us. It was risky to do this before, but after what Alder has done…' He shook his head. 'You must see reason, Orna Sin.'

'You are frightened,' Orna Sin said, 'and thinking with fear, not with reason. What we are doing is a deviation from traditional Sienese methods, and therefore suspect. We knew there would be scrutiny. It has simply arrived sooner than we expected.'

'Will you have the magistrate's scribe supervise your lessons in Toa Aloni myth and stonework?' Koro Ha said. 'How is that being *careful?*'

'Those lessons will occur in the evening from now on. And we will not be informing the magistrate, nor any of his servants, about them.' Orna Sin tucked his pipe into his sleeve and stood, then began walking down the path towards the far corner of the garden.

Koro Ha stared after him, flabbergasted. 'Will those five be joining us for every day of lessons, in all their rambunctious boredom, while I review spots of difficulty with their less quick-minded peers?'

'Yes,' Orna Sin called back. 'Though I think you will find that, under the scrutiny of a strange adult, they will be far more subdued.'

Koro Ha hauled himself to his feet. 'Or they may decide to tell that stranger about the fascinating things they are learning in their secret evening lessons.'

'These are bright children, Koro Ha.'

'I have spent my life teaching children,' Koro Ha snapped, catching up to Orna Sin and falling into step. 'They are bright, yes, and capable, but no matter how much we impress upon them the need to keep these secrets, we cannot guarantee that they will do so.' *Nor*, he thought darkly, feeling the burn of his anger against Wen Alder, *can you rely upon them not to betray your trust and call suspicion down on your head.*

'Your students have always been Sienese before.' Orna Sin turned onto a stone-tiled path that led towards a small grove of teak trees. Koro Ha had long assumed the little grove to be a symbol of Orna Sin's effort to maintain his Toa Aloni identity, despite his acclimation to life beneath the empire.

'Most of them, yes,' Koro Ha admitted.

'And wealthy,' Orna Sin went on, parting the undergrowth with a sweep of his hand. A small brass staff, hooked at one end, leaned against one of the trees. 'Children of privilege who had never known a moment of true danger. The students of our school grew up in the shadow of the mountain the emperor called down to bury Sor Cala. Quon Lo's father has a small measure of wealth now, but for a long time he skipped meals to save money and food for his children, and the boy knows this. The others are much the same. If we make it known that these Sienese observers are a threat, and tell them what secrets must be kept, they will keep them.'

'But it is still a risk!' Koro Ha shook his head. 'And I do not understand your willingness to take it. Stone-carving and old stories. Is teaching them such things worth the threat of death? And what else might the Sienese discover when their suspicions are kindled to a blaze and they come and ransack this garden?'

Orna Sin hefted the bronze staff and smiled sharply. Koro Ha felt a chill down his spine. In his frustration and fear, he had spoken too directly of things better left unsaid. The merchant led him to the other side of the tallest tree in the little grove, then knelt and brushed away broad, waxy leaves and a layer of dirt to uncover a strange square stone, flush with the ground and wide as the span of Koro Ha's arms.

'Here we are,' Orna Sin murmured. He slotted the hooked staff into a crack in the stone's surface, then pulled, grunting softly. The stone swung upwards on oiled hinges—a trap door built into the ground.

Koro Ha hesitated, wondering if he was about to learn the secret of the business that had brought them to the Black Maw—dangerous knowledge he did not truly want, piled atop all the other dangers he had shouldered.

'This is where Lon Sa and the others have been receiving their lessons,' Orna Sin explained.

'In a hole in the ground?' Koro Ha blurted.

Orna Sin barked a laugh. 'Come. We've a short way to go yet.' And then, as though it were the most ordinary thing in the world, he descended a ladder carved into one wall of the hole.

Koro Ha watched him vanish into the dark, more uncertain than he had been since he was very young, listening to his mother and father argue—his mother detailing their poverty, castigating his father for his pride, while Koro Ha listened and considered whether a truly filial son would waste money and time on his own education when he might have spent his days hauling stones or laying bricks to put bread in his mother's mouth.

'Orna Sin!' Koro Ha hissed into the darkness. He swept his gaze around the garden. They were sheltered from any prying eyes by the stand of teak trees. How often, he wondered, did the servants visit this wild partition? Who knew of the hole, and did any of those people sell their master's secrets to the Sienese officials?

He muttered a curse. What else was he to do but follow?

The ladder had been carved with meticulous care, the back sides of each rung narrowed to allow fingers to curve into comfortable holds. Toa Aloni craftsmanship at its finest. Koro Ha kept his gaze on the rung in front of him, feeling his way downwards with his sandalled feet. The light from the hatch overhead became dimmer and dimmer as he descended. Just as he began to journey into dark as deep as night, the warm glow of a lantern drifted up from below.

'Not bad, eh?' Orna Sin said while Koro Ha negotiated the last few rungs. 'I had it built by a pair of old stone-carvers. Cantankerous bastards. They, and the gold miners I hired to dig this tunnel, saw every swing of their pick, hammer, or chisel as a blow against the Sienese.'

Koro Ha dismounted the ladder and rubbed at his fingers and wrists, feeling his age and the product of his inactive lifestyle. The tunnel stood a head and a half taller than Koro Ha, himself a tall man, and extended in a straight line, its gently arching roof supported by stone columns that ran down the centre of the passageway. All of it carved from the mountainside as from a single piece of rock. Intricate scrollwork looped up and down the columns and ran the lengths of the walls.

A monumental effort for a hidden smuggler's passage.

'I am glad some small achievement of mine—even if only as the financier—has stricken you dumb with awe,' Orna Sin said. 'You are wondering why I bothered with the decorations, I suspect. To lend gravity to the passage, in honour of where it leads.'

He beckoned for Koro Ha to follow once again and set off, holding his brass lantern high, its hood thrown open to fill the corridor with light and fully reveal the intricate lines of the many carvings. Koro Ha followed, mind reeling, eyes sliding from one example of the finest Toa Aloni artwork he had ever seen to the next. A generation's worth of skill, kept bottled up while craftsmen worked Sienese designs for Sienese employers, had been unleashed here. Complex, layered knots bearing old meanings—lost to Koro Ha for want of an education as thorough in his own culture as in that of Sien—all a single voice crying out, rising from beneath the feet of the empire.

Despite our buried city, despite humiliation, despite it all, we are still here and still capable of wonders.

He had never felt more humbled in all his life.

'Here we are,' Orna Sin said. He stopped before a wooden door. Beyond, the tunnel fed into a spacious cavern littered here and there with piles of rubble and broken marble. Only the darkness, the stagnant chill in the air, and the echo of their footsteps told Koro Ha that they were still underground. Orna Sin raised the lantern high so that the furthest feathers of its light brushed the ceiling overhead.

At first, Koro Ha was not certain what it was he saw. Vast walls seemed to curve inwards and upwards, like a bowl balanced impossibly on its edge at a forty-five-degree angle to the ground. And then his mind made sense of one of the piles of shattered marble: a column, toppled and broken.

He spun in a slow circle. They were in some enormous open structure—a temple, perhaps, or a palace. Everywhere the light touched, Koro Ha saw the cool sheen of marble or the glint of gold and precious jewels, dulled by a layer of stone dust.

'The excavation has more than paid for itself by now,' Orna Sin said, 'as you might surmise.'

'You knew this was here?' Koro Ha said. 'Intact?'

'I hoped.' Orna Sin lowered the lantern, plunging the stone sky overhead back into darkness. 'And my hope was rewarded, but with more than a window into our buried glory and a few bits of salvaged treasure. Come.'

'Is it safe?' Koro Ha asked Orna Sin as they crossed to what must once have been an ornate window, now resting at an oblique angle and stricken of its glass.

'I would not bring your students down here were it not.' Orna Sin ducked beneath the edge of the window. Koro Ha followed. The window led into a second, narrower tunnel, wide enough for two people to walk side by side rather than half a dozen. As they progressed, the walls showed strange patches of decoration. Older, worn scrollwork placed at odd angles. Here and there the fragment of some sculpture. The facades of buildings, Koro Ha realised. The ruins of the buried city.

'Usually, the lessons are held in the dome,' Orna Sin explained, 'but I gave no word that we would be coming.'

They passed a doorway which led to another short corridor, and then into a small open space. The entryway to a home, Koro Ha surmised, then stopped, his feet fixed to the ground in astonishment.

'Wait!' he shouted to Orna Sin. 'Come back! What is this?'

Orna Sin returned with the light, a bemused smile on his face. He held the lantern out towards the impossible thing Koro Ha had seen and thought he must be imagining. But no, there, growing in a stone trough filled with earth, was a small vegetable garden. The leaves were pale, almost translucent, but there were fat gourds and clusters of beans on the vines.

'As I understand, it took a long time and a lot of experimentation to produce a garden able to grow in darkness,' Orna Sin said, 'yet the magic of cultivation can work wonders, even here.'

Magic. Koro Ha stared at him, the gears of his mind turning at dizzying speed.

'There is a stonespeaker here,' Koro Ha said. 'That is how you excavated this place, navigating between fallen facades, keeping so many buildings intact.'

Orna Sin patted Koro Ha's shoulder, smiled, and returned to the tunnel.

'If the empire finds out—' Koro Ha began.

'The empire has suspected nothing these last twenty years.' Orna Sin's voice echoed down the corridor.

'But now they will be watching.' Koro Ha hastened to catch up. 'This is all the more reason to take care.'

'Your mind is sharp, Koro Ha.' Orna sin paused and shook his head. 'I wonder what it might accomplish if not for the dulling obstacle of so much fear.'

'And now you insult me,' Koro Ha muttered.

'I will not let them frighten us into abandoning our culture,' Orna Sin said, pressing on.

'But we can be careful,' Koro Ha argued. 'We can delay, for a while, until the moment of danger has passed.'

'There is always danger.' Orna Sin stopped at a wooden door, new and undamaged, likely made to fit the arch in which it had been set after the ruin was excavated. He rapped his knuckles against it and smiled. 'We cannot escape it, only choose how to face it when it comes.'

Koro Ha's response was cut off by the gentle creak of the door swinging inwards. An elderly man, bent backed, with a tuft of white hair like a cloud jutting from the back of his head, peered out at them. A tattoo in blue ink ran from the base of his nose, over his lips, to the tip of his chin.

'Ah, Orna Sin,' the old man said in creaking Toa Aloni. 'You've brought a guest.'

'This is Koro Ha,' Orna Sin said. 'The tutor. It is time the two of you met.'

The old man bobbed his head and extended a gnarled hand, missing one finger. 'The children have said much about you. I doubt they have mentioned me. I am Uon Elia, the keeper of these caves.'

Koro Ha took the hand and squeezed it in the old Toa Aloni greeting—a gesture between strangers which, in the context of Sienese propriety, was far too intimate. Uon Elia smiled, showing three remaining teeth stained darker than Orna Sin's. Showing, as well, that the tattoo on his mouth continued on the inside of each lip and over the gums.

'Come in, come in.' Uon Elia backed into his home and beckoned them inside. 'There are mats there. My old fingers can still weave vines well enough.' He chuckled to himself, a wheezing sound, choked with dust, which broke into a brief fit of rattling coughs.

The stonespeaker's home proved another vast domed space, smaller than the first they had encountered, though most of its columns stood strong. Lanterns burned in most of the sconces, filling the space with warm light. A vast face, impeccably crafted to seem soft and beatific, peered down from the ceiling of the dome.

'It is peaceful here,' Uon Elia said, 'beneath their watchful eyes.'

Koro Ha's knees threatened to buckle from the weight of that stone gaze. He was no longer standing in Sien but in an older world the empire had buried. 'How did you survive the purge? And how did you come to live here? How *long* have you lived here?'

'Here. Sit.' Uon Elia gestured to a collection of roughly woven mats stacked against the wall. A few of their like hung on vines tied taut between columns to divide the space. Uon Elia went behind one of these woven curtains and returned carrying a copper kettle, his cheeks puffed out and arms quivering.

'Let me get that,' Orna Sin said.

Uon Elia set down the kettle, shook his head, and waved a dismissive hand, then walked—stiffly now—back behind the curtain. While they waited for him to return, Orna Sin and Koro Ha pulled mats from the stack and sat. When they had situated themselves, Uon Elia returned with three cups of carved and smoothed stone.

'This has been stewing on a lantern flame all day.' Uon Elia set the cups down on the floor beside the kettle, then filled each one with a milky liquid that gave off curls of steam. 'Bat-ear mushroom tea. Relaxing and healthful.'

Orna Sin took a cup and Koro Ha followed suit. The tea smelled musty, with a bit of a citrus tang. It tasted much as it smelled, with a bitter, unpleasant aftertaste, but Koro Ha was not about to complain about the product of near-miraculous ingenuity and magic that most in Toa Alon believed lost.

With a dramatic groan, Uon Elia lowered himself to a mat, his knees popping. He sighed, rubbed his legs, and sipped.

'Not the same as what you get from proper leaves, of course,' he said, 'but I've had a damnable time convincing anything but vines and fungus to grow down here.'

Which prompted another question: how did he manage to grow *anything* from shattered stone in the dark of the buried city? The magic of cultivation ought only to go so far. But Koro Ha swallowed this latest burst of curiosity. He had asked enough and needed to give the old man time to circle around to answering.

Uon Elia smacked his lips and set down his half-drained cup. 'When the emperor buried Sor Cala, he trusted that dropping a mountain on the city would be enough to kill its inhabitants. It was not.'

'You've been living down here for seventy years?' Koro Ha wondered aloud.

'Healing sorcery is a powerful thing, tutor. My master—a dusty old pile of bones if ever there was one—taught me when he was three hundred years old, and he died only…oh…twenty-five, thirty years back. Can't say for sure, given how slippery time gets in the dark. He survived for quite a while though, down here with the rest of us.'

'The rest of you…?' Koro Ha reeled.

'Twenty-seven stonespeakers survived the destruction of our city,' Uon Elia said, 'and now I alone remain.'

'How?' Koro Ha said. 'Even if you survived the initial destruction and were able to knit your wounds with magic, there was no food, no water.'

'The city had several dozen wells.' Uon Elia swirled his teacup. 'Simple enough to find with dowsing magic. Digging them out again was more trouble, but doable. As for food, in the first years it was lean, yes, but there were storehouses. Market stalls. Enough dried vittles to keep a few old folks on our feet while we got the gardens up and running. Not a diverse diet, by any means, but people have always managed to survive on little. And then, when your friend here dug his way in and found us, our situation improved significantly.'

'There were five of them left then,' Orna Sin said. 'A group of us found them while we dug through the ruins for treasure, never thinking we would find something even more precious.'

Uon Elia feigned embarrassment, flapping his hand as though to bat away a fly. 'We thought they were Sienese at first, though why they would go to such effort to finish their dirty work fifty years late, we couldn't imagine. Seeing Toa Aloni faces was a pleasant surprise, even if we nearly frightened Orna Sin and his fellows out of their skin.'

'It was quite a shock,' Orna Sin said, grinning.

'I can imagine,' Koro Ha murmured.

'Not long after, I wanted them to start marking and teaching new stonespeakers,' Orna Sin went on, 'but Uon Elia insisted that his students needed to be children. Young enough, yet, for their minds to stretch and fill the new possibilities that magic would offer them.'

'Lon Sa...Quon Lo...' Koro Ha frowned. 'Have their parents consented to this?'

'They have agreed to lessons in Toa Aloni culture and tradition, as you know,' Orna Sin answered.

'The mark of power does not come until the boys are ten years old,' Uon Elia explained. 'It would be better to wait a few more years, considering I have them only one day a week, but Orna Sin fears that if we wait too long my old lungs will explode out of my chest before it is done.'

'So you will mark them. And then what? The Sienese will know that mark. They will be hunted from the moment a Sienese soldier

sets eyes on them.' Koro Ha shook his head. 'I thought we were training these boys to sit for the imperial examinations, which is not at all
compatible with this.'

Orna Sin crossed his heavy arms. 'You would prefer their sharp
minds go to serving the empire rather than their own people?'

'Of course not!' The enormity and danger of the day's revelations
had left Koro Ha like a raw nerve. 'What do you plan, Orna Sin? To
bring the marked ones down here and keep them, like a seed bank of
Toa Aloni ways, for some imagined future after the empire falls?'

'Perhaps,' Orna Sin said. 'If that is what they choose. If they prefer
to go out in the world, to serve the empire and shape it for the better
from within, that too will suit my ends.'

'Look at his face,' Koro Ha snapped, jabbing a finger at Uon
Elia, feeling embarrassed and confused and frustrated but unwilling
to back down from so obvious a flaw in Orna Sin's thinking. 'Can
you imagine a Sienese magistrate with the mark of a stonespeaker on
his lips?'

'Fortunately, this is only decoration.' Uon Elia ran a finger down
the line from the base of his nose to his chin. He peeled back his lips
in a wide grin, pointed to the marks on his gums, and spoke through
his teeth. 'These are the sign of my power.'

'And the ink need not be so noticeable,' Orna Sin said.

'You mean to seed the empire not only with Toa Aloni sympathetic
to their people's plight but with stonespeakers.' The empire would
have to be utterly careless to overlook such an infiltration, something
Koro Ha doubted it would be ever again after the debacle with Wen
Alder in An-Zabat. 'It won't work.'

'You are entitled to your opinion,' Orna Sin said. 'I show you these
things in the hope of convincing you, but ultimately the decision will
not be yours. This is the plan, Koro Ha. You are party to it now.'

'And if I refuse to teach?' Koro Ha said.

Orna Sin smiled, though it did not touch his eyes, and reached for
his teacup, as though Koro Ha's words were not a blatant threat. '*You*
are the object of imperial suspicion. Not me. And you are not the only
tutor in the world. Do not make me wonder whether you will betray
us to the magistrate.'

'I agree that it is a great risk,' Uon Elia interjected, 'but we must pass our ways on to the next generation else those ways will die and all the world will become as the empire deems it, shaped to the emperor's will. What sort of world is that, designed by a single man, with only those books he deems fit, only those magics he finds useful, and only those thoughts and beliefs he can accept?'

'A harmonious one,' Koro Ha said, 'if the sages are to be believed.'

'And why should we believe them?' Orna Sin snapped. 'The empire rules the world, does it not? Yet is there peace? Is there harmony?'

Koro Ha might have given the doctrinal answer. Told them that such conflicts were born out of the ignorance of those who had yet to accept the teachings of the Sienese canon. But he had always carried doubts, fed by every report of rebellion recast as mere banditry in the highlands.

'I for one would prefer a chaos with hope, with vibrancy, where my people are ruled by leaders of their choosing, free to worship their gods and reap the bounty of their gifts.' Orna Sin leaned forwards, his voice bright with sudden passion. 'I am willing to risk a great deal in the hope of seeing such a world. I thought we might share this dream when you ventured into the unknown with me. Or has this been only a last grasp at ambition? Do you have a scrap of bravery left in you, or has the empire stripped your mind of everything but its dogma?'

All the while Orna Sin spoke, Koro Ha felt pressure building in his skull. He thought of Wen Alder, who understood the canon better than anyone, who wove its vagaries into webs of coherence, who wrote with clarity, precision, and grace to match the sages themselves—this last, perhaps, an exaggeration, but it had not felt like much of one to Koro Ha on reading such brilliant essays delivered by the brush of a sixteen-year-old boy.

If such a mind, in command of the canon and every nuance of the sages, had arrived at some conclusion which led him from the heights of imperial esteem into rebellion, how could Koro Ha go on ignoring his own doubts, long swallowed and locked away? Doubts he had *warned* Alder of when the boy sat for the imperial examinations?

The right education...the right name...but the wrong skin, the wrong hair, the wrong maternal line. He had said these things. Understood them then, on Alder's behalf, and sent him off into the empire's upper echelons without any defence but a warning: *Sometimes, the cost of success will be humiliation or a betrayal of your own heart.*

How could success—true success that let one hold one's head up high, proud, whole, uncompromised—be born from humiliation? From self-delusion? Self-betrayal? How could he believe that any of his students, brilliant though they might be, would fare any differently than he had?

Questions Koro Ha wished, then, that he had asked himself thirty years before. Perhaps if he had better answers, he might have imparted them to Alder and the boy might not have strayed so far from the golden path set before him. Or, perhaps, Koro Ha might better understand—even approve!—Alder's refusal to accept that humiliation, instead of feeling such anger at how much damage the boy had done in rejecting it.

'If we are to do this,' he said at last, looking Orna Sin in the eye, terrified but feeling, for the first time in his memory, full of true, meaningful purpose, 'we must be careful.'

Orna Sin smiled, clapped him on the shoulder, and squeezed. And Koro Ha, despite his Sienese training, felt the warmth of that gesture and not a hint of violation.

15
Ambush
Hand Pinion

The broken wheel of an overturned cart spun lazily in the pale light of breaking dawn. The cart's splintered boards and the remnants of its cargo lay spilled across the path. Flies swam in the stink of blood and burnt flesh around the half-dozen corpses scattered with them.

Pinion tilted his head back and took a breath. A low, muted song rose from the main body of the column further down the road—Nayeni voices, singing in their inscrutable, jagged tongue, as they had sung all through the day and deep into the night ever since leaving Burrow.

One of the corpses was a soldier tasked with standing night guard here among the people who followed Pinion's army in retreat from Iron Town. Beside him, four more corpses: a pair of young men, one still clutching the bamboo staff he'd raised in pitiful self-defence; the old woman to whom the cart had belonged; and a little girl struck through the throat with an arrow. The flies, woken with the spring thaw, flitted around the eyes and open wounds of the dead.

All were Sienese. Notable, considering the majority of the townsfolk of Iron Town were Nayeni. The rebels had known where to strike to avoid spilling the blood of their countrymen. Again, Pinion's ear turned to the distant Nayeni song.

'This was the seventh attack,' Captain Huo said. 'Posting guards in the night only gives the rebels an easy chance to thin our ranks while they steal from our people.'

A few Sienese soldiers began dragging the corpses to the shallow grave they had dug in the roadside ditch. A young woman followed them, wailing, beating at her chest with her fists. One of the dead men had been a fallen brother or lover, perhaps. Pinion had no way of knowing. But he preferred not to think of the girl. The arrow. The weeping wound in her throat.

A tragedy. Terrible. Heart rending. But Pinion did not have time to dwell on pain, nor time to wait for the burying of bodies or the posting of guards, nor to lead his men out into the forest in pursuit of rebel skirmishers. Compared to the horror to come if Wen Alder swept down on eagle hawk's wings and burned the entire column to ash, the bodies and the broken cart would seem a pleasant memory.

'We must put the fight to them, Your Excellency,' Captain Huo said. 'We must protect our people.'

'I agree.' Pinion turned his horse and made ready to ride back to the front of the column. 'But the only true protection awaits us in Eastern Fortress.'

Captain Huo ground his teeth. 'We could hunt them in their forests. Keep them away from the commoners, at least.'

'In *their* forests, as you say.' Pinion spurred his horse into motion. 'These rebels have twice the woodcraft of our best scouts. It would be futile, if not suicidal. We will do what we can to guard the line and continue on, undeterred and undistracted.'

His mount had taken no more than a dozen steps before Pinion realised that Captain Huo had not ridden up beside him. He turned in his saddle. Huo's shoulders rose and fell with rage that swelled within him, barely restrained by the cage of his ribs.

'Your Excellency, morale is very low. Two dozen of your soldiers now and twice that many townsfolk have been slain since we left Iron Town.'

The bonds of imperial doctrine and hierarchy could sustain no more friction, it seemed. If they broke, Pinion would not put open mutiny past the captain, and then the whole column would fall to chaos. His own soldiers might turn their blades on the very townsfolk they had been tasked to escort—at least those townsfolk whose skin and hair carried the same colour as the rebels.

'Morale will only fall further if we send our men into the forest to be gored and burned alive by witches,' Pinion said. 'They have the advantage, both in terrain and magic.'

'It is a shame, then, that we have only one Hand of the emperor with us,' Captain Huo snapped.

'Indeed.' An ember of guilt flared in Pinion's chest, quickly snuffed. Hand Beneficence, whose funeral coffin rode upon a broad cart at the head of the column, had been the traitor, not him. 'You would not have me go out into the forest and leave the column leaderless?'

Huo's lips curled in a snarl. 'I would have you do *something*.' He gestured to the townsfolk and villagers nearby, staring wide eyed at the men in power over them now bickering like children. 'Prove to your people that you can protect them. That is our duty.'

Silence settled between them but for the rasp of soldiers' shovels. Pinion thought again of the girl. Of the arrow through her throat.

Something untwisted within his chest. He had contorted his heart since Greyfrost, hardened it against so much. It was a strange comfort to let himself feel the pain of a small tragedy, the rage of it, and let it motivate him to act, though he knew the true danger lay in wasted time.

'Very well, Captain,' he said, giving himself permission to do this, because it felt right, even if he knew it was foolish. 'But we will not go chasing the rebels into their forests. What else might you suggest?'

Pinion wondered how Oriole might have felt in his situation.

Not his literal situation, in that moment, packed into the back of an emptied cargo wagon, laying on his belly, his arms and legs coiled and ready to spring, his body pressed against the bony flanks of a dozen other men, their breath filling the space beneath the blanket that shrouded them with a musty warmth. *That* situation, he was sure, his older brother would have found thrilling rather than humiliating and uncomfortable, springing a trap on the foolish rebels, just like Su White-Knife in one of the old romances. Oriole had lived in hope of such a moment.

But Oriole had possessed a certain intolerance for ambiguity. Pinion carried a memory out of early childhood—one of his first, and shrouded in the misty haze of all such early memories, as much a story he told himself as part of his true history. He must have been able to walk for no more than a year, perhaps three or four years old. In the memory, he had come toddling out of the apartments he yet shared with his mother and into the warm sunshine and floral scents of the courtyard, seeking the source of raised voices.

'Fairness is not inherent to the world, young Oriole,' his father had said—or so Pinion recalled, though he attributed this detail to childish confusion. The conversation that ensued was the sort Voice Golden-Finch preferred to delegate to tutors. And it seemed absurd that a child of three or four should remember his father's words in such detail—much of the memory, he was sure, was the product of dozens of lectures on doctrine, which did nothing to diminish its weight. 'Any effort to balance every scale and make good on every harm would be so time consuming as to be impossible. All one individual can do is carry out the duty of their station as defined by doctrine and the three pillars of society. This is why it is *vital* that you attend to your lessons and cease this foolish obstinacy.'

Pinion had toddled towards the voices and found their source in one of the many pavilions of the garden. A tall figure in robes sat on a bench while Oriole—seven or eight years old and just beginning his education—paced back and forth, his fists balled until the skin turned a blotchy red and white.

'But it isn't *fair*,' Oriole whined. 'Little Mole didn't break the vase. I did. I should have been the one who got caned, not him.'

'Little Mole is a servant boy and two years older than you,' the tall figure said. 'He was entrusted with your care and is tasked with the care of the house. The vase broke. Your arm was cut. He failed in both of his duties. That is why he was punished.'

Oriole reached up into the sleeve of his robe and grimaced. 'It wasn't a bad cut. And anyway, he didn't do it! We were playing and I said I was Su White-Knife and I was running and swinging the stick like a sword and I knocked it off the stand.'

'And he should have stopped you. That was his duty. He failed in it.'

'But it isn't *fair!*'

'Which. Does. Not. Matter.' The figure had stood then and seized Oriole by the arm—the only detail which gave Pinion cause to think the memory might, indeed, have been wholly accurate, for no tutor would have touched a Voice's son that way. 'I will hear no more talk of *fairness*, nor of your wounded feelings on behalf of a servant, even if he is your playmate. You are the son of a Voice, who was the son of Voices and Hands. You too have your duty in this world, and it will require you to do harsher things than stand by and watch while a child you think innocent is beaten on your behalf.'

The memory ended there. Perhaps Pinion had whimpered, or begun weeping, or otherwise given himself away. Or perhaps the whole was but a construction of his mind, caricatures of his brother and father built from the fragments of a thousand moments spread across twenty years. Nevertheless, it made Pinion wonder.

Oriole would have gone into the forest after the rebels, he was sure. No—Oriole would never have fled from Burrow. At the very least, not from Iron Town. Would never have sacrificed so many lives and livelihoods without at least putting up a fight. Oriole would never have made such sacrifice even to avenge the death of a teacher, or of a brother. He would have done what was *fair*, not what was *necessary*.

Voices muted by cloth and wood interrupted his thoughts. The bodies around him shifted as the sergeant hissed an order for silence. Pinion lifted his head, peering through the narrow tented opening of the blanket. Silhouettes moved in the darkness around a pile of crates that Huo's men had positioned a few paces from the cart. Pinion counted at least a dozen Nayeni, though there were likely more beyond the narrow band of his vision. One, seemingly the leader, sent three others to the edges of the road. Two figures approached the cart, drawing near enough that Pinion could see the animal skulls, bones, and bark stitched to their leather armour.

Most of the silhouettes gathered around the crates and began digging through them, making piles of silks and bolts of cloth. Pinion raised his hand, held his breath, and waited. One of the two sent to search the cart walked around to the front side. The other, a young woman with hideously close-shorn hair, extended one finger. A warm wake of power surged through Pinion and a candle flame erupted on the young witch's finger. Pinion squinted against the sudden light. The young woman stepped forwards. The men in the cart lay still, hardly daring to breathe.

No more time to wait.

Pinion reached through the canon, first for battle sorcery. He threw off the blanket, surged to his knees, and hurled lightning. It lanced past the startled witch, who shouted and backpedalled, the fire at her fingertip erupting from candle flame to torch—a warning, but too late. Pinion shifted from the second channel to the fifth and called down sheets of shielding light. In that same moment his lightning struck the piled crates, bursting the grenades hidden within.

Pinion felt the explosion like a blow to the diaphragm. The wagon leapt backwards, its boards cracking, flames licking around the edges of Pinion's shield. Fortunately, Captain Huo's men had snapped its axles before laying this trap—key to the illusion of a broken-down wagon left behind—which kept it from rolling away. Hollering into the deafened aftermath of the explosion, the soldiers around Pinion boiled out from the beneath the blanket, drawing their short swords.

Nayeni corpses littered the road, limbs askew, bodies shattered and charred. Others stumbled about, dazed and disoriented. Only a few, who had lingered at the edge of the forest, were in anything like fighting shape. Metal rang against metal. A few arrows fell among the debris of the crates. Before long, the surviving Nayeni had fled. At Pinion's swift count, thirty of their rebel comrades lay dead.

A cheer went up, which became vindictive insults hurled into the forest after the fleeing rebels. A few went among the fallen Nayeni, burying their blades deep in the chests and skulls of the dead and those yet clinging to life.

Pinion's stomach turned. He looked away. Let the men drink deep of vengeance and satisfaction. This would be their last such opportunity until Eastern Fortress.

He looked to the edge of the road, where Huo appeared, followed by a detachment dressed in cloaks stitched with leaves and twigs. They had lain in wait, ready to reinforce the soldiers in the wagon if the fighting turned against them.

Huo watched the men vent their rage. His brows arched low and his mouth curled as though after a sip of bitter tea. Pinion approached and dipped his head.

'Well done, Captain,' he said, an edge to his voice. 'This band of raiders will not trouble us again. I only hope that, while we lingered here, the column of folk from Iron Town ahead was not attacked and looted too severely.'

Huo's expression hardened.

'Tomorrow,' Pinion went on, 'we march double time and into the night.'

'What?' Huo blurted. 'You can't mean to try and outrun them while we drag behind a train of townsfolk!'

'We may win hundreds of these little skirmishes. It matters not at all.' Pinion gestured towards a blackened corpse. 'If Wen Alder were among these raiders, we would all lie dead in their place. Morale is a currency, Captain Huo. I have earned some tonight and I intend to spend it to quicken our pace tomorrow.'

Huo's mouth hung open, his face rippling with outrage. At last, his teeth clicked together. He grunted, turned away, and walked back towards the thicket where they had hidden their horses. No bow. Not even a shadow of the deference a Hand of the emperor was due.

But Pinion did not need his respect, only his assent and co-operation, however grudging.

And yet he wondered if Oriole, with his fairness, might have earned both in his place.

16
Witches of a New Sort
Foolish Cur

Over the two weeks we lingered in Burrow, young men and women trickled into the town like streams flowing down from mountain glaciers—and even some who were not so young, grey-haired and fiery eyed, and others I would have called children and sent back to their villages rather than arming them.

The Army of the Fox now counted two hundred and thirty-two—pitiful when compared to any Sienese legion but nearly ten times what we had arrived with. Harrow Fox believed we would draw more recruits as we piled victory upon victory during our southwards march, beginning with a victory against the Army of the Wolf—who, as my uncle's scouts reported, had harried Pinion's column during its own march southwards—either by way of Frothing Wolf bending the knee or her head falling from her shoulders.

Not all our soldiers would be volunteers, however. Three days before our departure, Harrow Fox stood upon the overturned crate where the Vulture had so often announced the Sun King's will. There, with his burly arms crossed, his beard a bonfire of red, white, and grey, his eyes sweeping the assembled crowd like flights of arrows, he dealt out Burrow's punishment.

'You ate and drank with those who hunted our witches and burned our temples.' His voice was low and level yet boomed down the central street. 'You tolerated their rule. Paid their taxes. Accepted their occupation and called it protection. Spoke of your countrymen as *bandits* and said quiet blessings when we were killed in the forests, knowing that we would no longer trouble your merchants' caravans. You owe a debt to your country, men and women of Burrow. One your sons and daughters will pay.'

The Vulture had already made this declaration several times, I knew, but here was the Sun King to see his will carried out. Each family sent forwards one of their household—an eldest son, an unwed aunt, a widower father of grown children—to cut the backs of their forearms and spill blood in atonement, then swear fealty and service to the Sun King.

As a squad captain, Running Doe spent our last days in Burrow training these raw recruits to handle their weapons. 'At the very least, to do more harm to the enemy than the comrade next to them,' she said, smirking.

Without her education in magic to occupy me, I took the opportunity to expand the canon of witchcraft, and by the time we marched I had added two more magics to it. The first, marked by four curving lines in the shape of an outstretched wing, was the power to veer. This had presented a small problem when the time came to create the walls of the canon and imbue it with power. In one sense, it was no different than conveying the power to conjure fire, but as I worked a dark foreboding swept through me, punctuated by the memory of brittle limbs dragging a contorted body down an overgrown path.

The thought of Running Doe rendered into a monstrous creature halfway between beast and human left me sick to my stomach, but after some thought I found a way to narrow the walls of my canon to limit the changes that veering could work, stripping it of its danger. Anyone who used the canon of witchcraft to access that power would only be able to transform into an eagle hawk—far from ideal, but of the uses one might put veering to, flight seemed the most valuable. A wolf's claws could be mimicked by a blade; no tool in human hands could rival a bird's wing.

The third channel I added to my canon conveyed windcalling. The swirling mark—an imperfect imitation of a windcaller's tattoo—was difficult to carve, particularly with only the stump of my right wrist to hold the strip of bone steady, though the magic conveyed was far simpler than veering. With this, while my canon was not *complete*, it was at least *useful*. Conjuring fire granted a weapon, veering granted mobility, and windcalling had proved itself a better defence—and certainly a more versatile tool—than shielding sorcery, which protected only against flame and lightning.

Though I longed to bring these new powers to Running Doe and observe her ability to wield them, I held back. She had her duties to my uncle, and I was unwilling to pit her loyalty to him against her loyalty to me. So I waited until, a month after occupying the town, a fattened Army of the Fox snaked its way out onto the Sun Road, emptying Burrow of nearly a fifth of its population.

I walked at the back of the column, Okara at my heels and Doctor Sho a few paces ahead. We had left his comatose patients behind in Burrow, in the care of the town nurses who had been aiding him. Hissing Cat would follow us, I presumed, as she had followed from Greyfrost, though I had not seen or spoken with her in days. We marched beneath no banners, no cavalry preceded us, and neither supply wagons nor camp followers trailed behind. We were less an army than a host of brigands gathered together to common purpose.

That was my Sienese attitudes showing, I told myself. What was an army, truly, but a great many people armed and ready to do violence? A Sienese force might carry flags and wear matching armour, but if they alone delineated the difference between banditry and military conquest, the distinction hardly seemed to matter.

That night, Running Doe sat at my campfire, her eyes shut tight, a leaf swirling in the conjured winds that circled her palm. She had taken to windcalling within an hour. Shaping it into more complex shapes—shields, domes, blades, and the like—would take time and practice, but calling the wind and making it dance in the cup of her hand had proven easy enough.

Veering, despite my efforts to simplify it, proved far more difficult.

I felt the wake of her magic—slight cramps down my arms and legs—and the scent of cinnamon rose from beneath a blanket of char and smoke. I held my breath. Running Doe scrunched up her face, then, with a sudden exhalation, slumped her shoulders and let her hands fall into her lap.

She opened her eyes and offered an apologetic grimace. 'It should be working,' she muttered. 'I don't know what I'm doing wrong.'

I took the strip of bone back from her. Perhaps in simplifying the magic, I had rendered it impotent. I touched the mark and felt the heavy walls of the canon fall into place, then reached into the depths of power that remained. Cramps...cinnamon scent...and I shook myself, extending feathered wings, my eyes sharper, my nose full of a different, keener scent. The strip of bone had melded into my trans-formed body just as clothes or weapons were wont to, and the canon had remained in place.

'It's wonderful,' Running Doe murmured, 'but terrifying. Yet you make it seem so easy.'

Ah. So that was it. I released the spell, returned to myself, and handed back the strip of bone. 'I have a great deal more practice than you do, and I know from my own experience how intimidating this particular magic can be. With time, I'm sure you'll master it.'

She smiled sheepishly, ran her thumb down the three sets of marks, and shut her eyes. The scent of cinnamon wafted up. I returned to my seat opposite her and took up another strip of bone and my carving knife. We would reach Iron Town in a matter of days, and I intended to have at least three or four more canons of witchcraft ready. The case for co-operation I would make to Frothing Wolf would be easier if I stood beside a cadre of newly minted witches wielding my canon.

With a grunt, Doctor Sho trudged into the circle of our camp-fire, sat on a flat-topped stone, and unstrapped his medicine chest with a bone-weary sigh. 'If I never see another blister again, I'll be a happy man.'

Okara followed him into the light, snuffling in the undergrowth at the side of the road. He looked up at Running Doe, then padded over, sniffing at her face. She opened one eye, patted the dog's flank, and gently pushed him away.

'No one said happiness would be found in rebellion,' I replied, motioning Okara over to me and scratching behind his ears. His scars were dun, which meant—as far as I had been able to piece together—that he was only a simple dog for the moment. 'Have you arranged for my uncle to pay you yet, or are you taking what few coppers your patients carried from home?'

Doctor Sho harrumphed, then opened one of the deeper side drawers on his medicine chest and produced a leather bottle. He pulled the cork, took a long sip, and offered the bottle to Running Doe. Her nose wrinkled and she opened her eyes, sniffed at the vapours wafting from the bottle, and looked to me. I chuckled at her uncertainty and shrugged. She accepted Doctor Sho's offer and took a long sip, grimaced, and handed the bottle across the fire. As I took it, the tips of our fingers brushed and she gave another shy, dimpled smile—which, as it had before, sent warmth pulsing through me.

'I was hoping to invoice him when all this is through.' Doctor Sho smirked. 'After he's secured himself a proper throne and the treasury that goes with it.'

I turned away from Running Doe perhaps a breath too quickly. 'Admit it, Sho. You're not here chasing silver.' I gestured with the bottle to Okara, who had curled up at my knee. 'Like when we found this poor beast on the side of the road. You've a soft spot for patching up victims of cruelty. This army, for example.'

I took a sip of the harsh, burning, but subtly nutty sorghum liquor. It reminded me of the first bottle Oriole and I had shared, a melancholy thought that chased away whatever warmth Running Doe's fingertips had offered as I handed the bottle back to Doctor Sho. His expression matched my mood.

'Speaking of cruelty,' he said, 'have you seen what's become of Burrow's magistrate?'

'No.' I realised that I had been assuming, unthinkingly, that he had stayed behind. After my uncle had pried him for Hand Pinion's motivations, Clear-River had not been called to counsel. If we'd had a train of prisoners, I would have expected to find him there, but Harrow Fox took no prisoners. I felt a growing apprehension. 'Tell me.'

'He's been put to work as a pack mule,' Doctor Sho took another sip. 'I spent a good while rubbing liniment on his flanks and shoulders and bandaging him up where hastily made leather straps bit through his clothes.'

Guilt tumbled through me, knocking the gentle peace of the evening askew. It must have shown on my face for Running Doe frowned sharply and shook her head. 'The bastard tried to murder you,' she said.

'Tried and failed,' I replied, climbing to my feet, 'while I have destroyed his life. Where is he, Sho?'

Doctor Sho sighed, then corked the bottle and returned it to the drawer. 'Come along, then.'

'We'll need that,' I said. 'I've only once before gone out of my way to make a friend and alcohol was a vital ingredient.'

Doctor Sho frowned quizzically, shrugged, retrieved the bottle, and led me back towards the main body of the camp, where Clear-River sprawled beside a haphazard pile of sacks and crates strapped together with leather webbing. A pitiful fire nearby had burned down to dead coals. He lay wrapped only in his ragged, stained robe, arms folded tight around himself, muttering and shivering while frosted clouds of his breath curled away.

I took the bottle from Doctor Sho and knelt beside Clear-River, then gently touched his shoulder with the stump of my right wrist. His eyes snapped open, bleary and bloodshot. They narrowed on me and he recoiled, scrambling to his hands and knees, panting in terror.

'There's room by our fire.' I jostled the bottle, sloshing the liquor within. 'And a bit to drink after a long day.'

He stared at me like I had spoken nonsense.

'This is a trick,' he murmured, then looked to Doctor Sho. 'Did you bandage me up just so he could tear me apart again? What sort of game is this?'

'No game,' Doctor Sho said. 'I just agree with my friend here that you'd be better off sleeping by us. Less likely to freeze to death or get your head staved in by a village boy turned soldier who remembers when you were magistrate.'

At last he eased himself to his feet. He reached for his strange burden.

'You've carried that enough for today,' I said and heaved the bundle awkwardly over my own shoulder. It was heavier than it appeared, comprised at least in part of sacks of rice and millet that settled unevenly.

Again, I offered the bottle. Clear-River took it, still shrinking away as though he expected me to lash out at any moment. He uncorked it, took a sip, and sighed with relief. 'All I've had to drink today is melted snow,' he said.

My anger flared hot, but I swallowed it—as I had so often since my uncle's return to Greyfrost—and turned back towards our little camp. Doctor Sho soon followed, and a moment later I heard Clear-River's footsteps, slow and halting.

At our return, Running Doe straightened her back and put a hand to her dagger, but I motioned her to be calm as I set down the awkward burden. She glared sceptically but moved her hand. 'You're sure he isn't planning to knife your guts again?'

'Fairly,' I replied with a wry smile. I returned to my seat on a fallen log, took up my knife and the strip of bone I had been carving, and set to work, as though it were the most natural thing in the world that Clear-River should join us.

'Have you eaten anything yet, boy?' Doctor Sho asked.

Slowly, Clear-River shook his head.

'And I suppose no one let you in on their common pot.' Doctor Sho stowed his bottle of liquor and took a pair of half-full water skins from where he'd lashed them to the bottom of his medicine chest. 'Right, well then, how's congee with dried fish flake, a pinch of salt, and a few herbs sound? Come along then, Doe. Help me fetch more water from the stream.'

Running Doe gave me a questioning glance. I nodded for her to go with him. She frowned but stood and followed, still touching her dagger and clutching her canon of witchcraft. Okara, who had been snoozing by the fire, woke with a grunt. He studied Clear-River for a moment, then ambled over to him, sniffing at his hands. Only then did Clear-River seem to notice the dog's presence. He scratched behind Okara's ears and, once more, shook his head in disbelief.

'Now I know this is some sort of trick,' he said. 'You want me to attack you. You're goading me into it, sending your bodyguard away. Then you can kill me and go on pretending you're not a murderer. You missed your opportunity before.'

'I want you to get warm and eat something.' I braced the strip of bone against the flat rock I'd been using as a cutting surface. 'Sit down, Clear-River. Okara doesn't mean any harm.'

He looked at the dog. 'This is the same one you had that first time you came to Burrow, isn't it? The one you killed a dozen guards over. Why did you name it…? Oh.' He furrowed his brow quizzically. 'I see. I thought your uncle had already laid claim to the title of Sun King come again.'

'He did,' I said, 'and Okara is only a dog. At the moment, anyway.'

Okara lolled his tongue and tilted his head to give Clear-River a better angle on the itchy spot behind his ear. Clear-River, at last, lowered himself beside the fire, wincing as he sat with his legs stretched out and his back against a tree trunk. Okara took the newly open lap as an invitation and plopped his head down on Clear-River's thigh.

'You truly don't mean to kill me?' he said.

I shook my head and went on whittling a windcaller's mark.

'But I tried to kill you.'

'One of us must take the first step towards forgiveness.'

He grunted. 'I had very good reason. Your reasons for killing my people seem spurious at best.'

'I wish things had gone differently when I first came to Burrow. And what my uncle did to your guards was wrong.'

At those words, he finally seemed to relax, though the furrow of scepticism remained deep on his brow. We sat in silence for a time, the only sounds Okara's gentle snoring, the crackle of the fire, and the scrape of my knife on bone.

'What is that you're making?' he asked.

And here, truly, was a chance for that first step. A showing of trust and a chance to return it. I set down my knife and picked up the strip of bone. 'A weapon,' I said and tossed it to Clear-River. He caught it in his lap, startling Okara into brief, blinking wakefulness. 'A canon to rival the emperor's. Touch the first mark there, the one that looks like a flame.'

He picked up the strip of bone. 'I see a little whirlpool, some grass bending in the wind, and a chicken's footprint.'

I coughed, stifling an urge to protest. 'Fair enough, I'm not the most talented artist in the world. The third one.'

Hesitation held him a moment longer. At last he pressed the pad of his thumb to the bone. The heavy wake of my canon settled on the pattern of the world and Clear-River's eyes went wide.

'I have been teaching Running Doe how to use it,' I said. 'Would you like to be my second student?'

His hand spasmed open and the strip of bone tumbled from his hands, bouncing off of Okara's snout. The dog snuffled awake and looked about in surprise.

Clear-River scoffed. 'You can't be serious.'

'You are a better person than me,' I said, voicing a painful thought that had long needled me. 'Far better, I think. But there are reasons that your dream—of shaping the structures of empire to preserve a semblance of Nayen, as you did at Burrow—cannot come to pass. If I could pass on all of my power along with my knowledge to you, and leave you to use it, I would. But I cannot.' I gestured to the canon I had given him, now resting on the ground by the fire. 'This is the best I can do.'

He retrieved the strip of bone and turned it in his hand. 'And these reasons...they are why you killed for this dog when first you came to Burrow, and why you let your uncle's witches butcher my men?'

'No.' I took a steadying breath. 'At least, only in part. There was also fear. After what I did in service of the empire, I questioned my own moral compass. I assumed that what Harrow Fox did must have been not only acceptable but necessary.'

'You no longer think so?'

I grimaced. It was all the answer he needed. Clear-River held up the bone and, again, pressed his thumb to the first mark. He shut his eyes and breathed heavily while the canon of witchcraft filled his mind.

'How do I use it?' he murmured.

By the time Running Doe and Doctor Sho returned with the waterskins slapping against their backs, I had told Clear-River of the witches of the old sort, their war with the gods, and the emperor's desperation to rekindle it. Further, he could hold a candle flame in the cup of his hand. Doctor Sho grunted acknowledgement, then rolled a few coals out of the fire and set about boiling a pot for congee. Running Doe stood rooted to the earth, staring at the fire in Clear-River's hand.

'It's all right,' I told her. 'Have a seat.'

She did so, though she watched Clear-River like a hawk all that night and all the next, until he surpassed her on the third evening out from Burrow.

We had once again made our little camp behind the main body of the army. Okara had gone bounding into the undergrowth in search of small game for his supper while Doctor Sho once again stirred a pot of congee for ours, though flavoured with some winter nuts he had found while foraging for herbs rather than the standard fish flake. By then, Clear-River could hold a flame for a count of ten and I suggested that he move on to veering.

I did not tell him of my fear that the channel was somehow defective, not wanting to influence him towards failure. He screwed his eyes shut and pressed his thumb to the four swooping lines. The weight of the canon descended and he reached into it for power.

At once, the scent of cinnamon was overwhelming, drowning out the earthy smell of boiling congee and the smoke of the fire pit. Cramps lanced down my flanks, and in a flash of feathers Clear-River became an eagle hawk. He tilted his head quizzically, hopped about on his talons, and fluttered his wings. Then, as swiftly as he had cast it, he released the spell and sat staring at me, half amazed and half stupefied.

'What the *bloody twice-burnt shit!*' Running Doe howled, bounding to her feet. 'I've been trying to do that for *days* and this poncy piss-reeking *bastard* gets it on the first try!'

I choked on a laugh at her sudden outburst. Clear-River regarded her coolly. 'I might offer some help if you need it,' he said.

'She doesn't need help,' said Hissing Cat, emerging from the forest with Okara following close at her heel. The scars on his muzzle glinted faintly, lit by their own inner fire. Hissing Cat smirked at Running Doe. 'She's afraid, is all. Hard to blame her. You lot are toying with a hasty reconstruction of an already dubious method for wielding magic.'

Running Doe wilted at Hissing Cat's appearance. As much as she had been growing more comfortable around me, she was still terrified of my wild-seeming teacher. Clear-River, for his part, regarded her only with distant curiosity.

<We should speak.> Okara's voice echoed between my ears. <You, Hissing Cat, and I.>

An echo of worry lingered with the god's presence in my mind. 'Continue practising, Clear-River. If you've any tips to share with Running Doe, please do.' Then, to Doctor Sho: 'Keep them from killing each other, if you don't mind.'

'If they start throwing fire around, I doubt there'll be much I can do,' Doctor Sho grumbled. He watched me follow Okara into the forest, a sceptical arch to his brow, but he neither made a move to follow us nor questioned Hissing Cat's sudden appearance after days of absence.

After we had walked a few hundred paces from the fire, Hissing Cat sat down on a fallen log and motioned me to do likewise.

<It seems you're not as unique as we assumed.> Okara's scars flickered like dying embers. <There is another nascent witch of the old sort. A child of the Stormriders, born on the Girzan steppe.>

At first, his words rang meaningless to me. 'You mean another who wields magic without a pact?'

'And more competently, if the dog is to be believed,' Hissing Cat answered.

I had already considered the question of whether there were other witches of the old sort newly born into the world, but I had simply assumed that, like me, their obsession with magic would either destroy them or lure them into service to the empire.

<I would show you something.> The wake of Okara's voice became a rip tide that pulled me into darkness, as though I had been compelled to sleep. No, not to sleep—to dream, as he had shaped my dreams for years, slowly guiding me towards Hissing Cat.

An image coalesced. We stood on a gently sloping hill furred with long, grain-heavy grass. Above, a vast sky as bright and stunning as a sapphire stretched to the humped shadows of far-distant mountains. The muted sound of a waterfall rose from a nearby canyon. A circle of squat, conical tents stood at the canyon's edge. Something like a wind-ship, only smaller, with no sail that I could see and twin catamarans to either side rested against the flank of another hill. A stooped form squatted behind one of the catamarans, staring in terror at the tents.

I squinted against the harsh sunlight, trying to make sense of the figure. He was dark, with the wiry curls of the Toa Aloni. 'Koro Ha?' I wondered aloud. But no. In the context of the strange windship, I suddenly recognised my former steward. 'Jhin!'

A wake of magic settled heavy on my shoulders. I followed the line of Jhin's terrified gaze. Three more figures moved among the tents. One I marked at once for a Hand of the emperor, or a Voice, dressed in gilt imperial armour. The others were two women, both already bound in chains of light. One I would have known at a glance, from the corner of my eye, in the densest crowd in the busiest bazaar in all the world.

'Atar!'

The Hand strode forwards, his arms folded casually behind his back. Gloating.

'What is she doing here?' I demanded of Okara, who sat placidly at my side. 'What is *Jhin* doing here?'

<Watch. Focus. Don't be distracted.>

I grumbled in my throat but turned back to the terrible scene unfolding amid the tents. A powerful urge to rush down and save Atar and her ally seized me, but of course Okara had not transported us halfway across the world. This was only a vision of something that had already come to pass.

The Hand strode towards the second woman, the one I did not recognise—presumably the Stormrider of whom Okara and Hissing Cat had spoken. He said something, the words lost in the distance.

'Can't you move us closer?'

<This is only a reconstruction based upon wakes left in the pattern,> Okara said. <Such things as human speech leave little impact

until they result in action. I do not in fact know what they said, though I would *very much* like to.>

The woman twisted on the ground, struggling against the chains of binding sorcery. The Hand threw back his head and laughed, then gestured lazily towards Atar. My throat closed in on itself. Was this what Okara had wanted me to see? Her death, under these bizarre, inexplicable circumstances, in the company of a woman who should have been powerful enough to save her?

A wake like nothing I had ever felt before surged outwards from the circle of tents. It filled the world with dancing fractal colours, with shrieking notes, with the smells of cinnamon and burning hair. Then it passed and the woman stood outlined in shimmering light. The chains of binding sorcery fell from her like shredded paper. With a gesture, she speared the Hand of the emperor with brilliant lightning and hurled his body into one of the tents. Bright flames and oily smoke swirled up. Then she turned on the next tent, and the next, until she stood in the centre of a blazing ring. At her side, Atar staggered to her feet.

<You are about to ask what magic she worked,> Okara said. <You might as well ask an actual dog how to write court poetry.>

Atar and the woman—the witch of the old sort—walked to the strange windship while the circle of flames rose in fury. Glowing ashes fell upon the brittle grass, starting a dozen smouldering fires. Jhin had already begun to unfurl a strange kite from a compartment at the front of the windship by the time they arrived. Within a hundred heartbeats, Atar had filled it with wind and the ship had darted away across the steppe, leaving fire and smoke behind.

As they raced towards the horizon, the scene vanished. I blinked in the sudden darkness of the forest. Hissing Cat stared at me, deep creases of concern lining her face.

'I know.' The words fell from her like a hammer blow. 'The dog already showed me. And before you ask, I don't recognise what she did any more than you do. I doubt the woman knows herself. Which makes this all the more worrying.'

'Worrying?' I asked, breathless. 'Why? We could only hope for such a powerful ally, until now.'

<She is a witch of the old sort with a great deal of power, a great deal of apparent talent, and no guidance whatsoever.> Okara blinked, his canine eyes glinting with far too much intelligence. <How do you think my kind will react to her appearance? They are already nervous about you and scrutinising Tenet's every move. The pact is already fraying.>

'More, how do you think *Tenet* will react?' Hissing Cat snorted and shook her head, rattling the skulls in her hair. 'If he thinks the empire's about to go up in flames, why bother trying to preserve it? This might give him cause to start the war with the gods, whether he can win it or not.' She grimaced. 'Which—and I know we disagree on this point, dog—seems like the worst-case scenario, to me.'

Okara peeled back his lips. <Regardless, for the sake of preserving the peace, we must find a way to control this witch of the old sort, or at least convince her to take care.>

'And how do you suggest we do that from here?' I asked. 'They're half the world away.'

Hissing Cat's smile had a wicked cast. 'They are, but the two in her company are friends of yours, aren't they? Closer than Clear-River, whom you managed to reach.'

I felt my eyes go wide.

<Distance is no impediment to transmission,> Okara observed. <Not, at least, when properly done.>

Surprise gave way to a twisting anxiety. I had betrayed Atar's trust and destroyed her home, and Hissing Cat would have me reach out to her, to speak with her mind-to-mind.

Though I had faced death and danger, few things in my life had filled me with such gut-wrenching fear.

17
Wind and Flame
Foolish Cur

'It has to be you,' Hissing Cat snarled. 'The dog and I couldn't pick the girl out in a crowd, let alone from the other side of the world.'

'She knows the weight of transmission as the weight of Voice Rill's sorcery radiating from the citadel of An-Zabat. She will panic the moment I reach out to her.'

<Every moment you linger is a moment the Girzan might wield some unpredictable magic and frighten the gods into violence.> Okara's scars flared bright and his presence in my mind burned with urgency. <You cannot delay.>

'Fine, bleed the both of you.' I screwed my eyes shut and went searching for the keen memories of Atar that might guide me to her through the miasma of confusion and hesitancy that clouded my mind. The bounce of her ringlets as she turned to laugh at one of my foolish jokes. The scent of lavender and honey and salt. A flash of her silver-threaded scarf entwined with fire.

There, in the distance—though not distant enough, for it felt only paces away instead of leagues—I heard the echo of those memories through the deep layers of the pattern. I reached for them and felt the weight of the magic of transmission fall like chains, binding our minds.

Sensation flooded in: the earthy dried-dung smell of the steppe, the tickle of a blade of grass on my cheek, and the cool touch of a breeze. Images played against my eyelids, the colours muted, like complex shadow puppetry: the sensations Atar was feeling, the things she smelled and saw.

And then, a burst of panic. Her thoughts coalesced, less cogent words than impressions of fear mixed with memories of the empire. A single, piercing certainty that some Voice had found a way to seize her mind. My own heart thundered. A disorienting shift in perspective struck me as she sprang from her bedroll, reached for a knife, and brought it to her throat.

'Wait!' I shouted and cried out within my mind.

'What is it?' Hissing Cat asked, but I ignored her, throwing all of my attention into the path I had forged with transmission, conveying all that I could of peace and calm. A tugging on the reins of Atar's terror, however futile.

I felt cold iron against the side of her neck.

'What is this?' she demanded, the words first rising in her mind, then striking her ears and then my mind in a disorienting echo.

<It's me,> I said. <It's Alder. Firecaller!>

Her thoughts whirled in her panic—the possibility that the empire had found some way to turn me back to their cause, or that a sorcerer had dredged my voice from her memory and now wore it as a veil. She pressed the knife more firmly against her throat, on the verge of breaking skin. 'Tell me something that will convince me.'

I flailed for some secret that would bind us. A quiet moment beneath the stars, our bodies pressed together, or a whispered word and burst of laughter. I felt a trickle of blood and her quiet determination.

<A part of me wishes I had stayed with you on the *Spear of Naphena*,> I offered, hoping that this would be enough. <In dark moments, I wonder if it was a mistake to leave the place where I felt happiest.>

I waited while she bled, her mind working. And I felt, welling up within her, an echo of my own sadness and regret.

She lowered the knife. I heaved a sigh of relief.

'Bloody hell, Cur,' Hissing Cat demanded, her voice striking as though from far away. '*What is going on?*'

'It's all right,' I murmured. Then, to Atar: <Thank you. I am sorry for reaching out to you like this. I know it is an intrusion, but my need is great.>

'An intrusion, you say,' Atar scoffed. 'You nearly frightened me to *death.*'

I winced. <I know. I'm sorry. Please, just bring what you would say to the tip of your tongue. There's a terrible echo when you speak aloud.>

Another pause. I felt her brow furrowing.

<This is very, very strange,> she said at last. <I hope you did not drive me to panic for the simple pleasure of conversation.>

<I saw a vision of your escape from the Hand of the emperor among the circle of tents,> I admitted, guilt gnawing even more deeply, competing with a melancholy that seeped in at the corners. <The woman you travel with is truly powerful, Atar, and more dangerous than you know.>

I felt her surprise, and her scepticism. <How can you know more of Ral than I do when I have been in her company these weeks and you have been on the other side of the world?>

<A great deal has happened since I left An-Zabat.> I wanted nothing more than to tell her all of it and to hear how she and her people were faring without their city, waging their war of piracy against the Sienese windships that dared cross the Waste. Yet time still passed and I had only so much of it to spend with her. <I have met witches who wield magic without pact or canon and learned to wield it myself. I have acquired the patronage of a god and learned of the grand design that underlies the empire's expansion. The emperor intends to rekindle an ancient war that would end the world as we know it. I intend to stop him, but I am not yet strong enough. I must build a cadre of my own to oppose his Hands and Voices, but—>

<The world as I knew it has already ended, Firecaller,> she interrupted.

<This will be worse than the destruction of a city. When last the gods and witches fought, seas devoured continents, mountains erupted from the bedrock of the earth, stars fell from the sky, and

monsters harried those few who were able to survive. The emperor and the gods are leaning over a chasm that leads to war. Any change in the balance between them could mean the tipping point. We must tread carefully—more carefully than wielding heretofore unseen powers and breaking Hands of the emperor like twigs.>

Silence stretched between us. Her thoughts swirled deep below the surface, where I felt them only as distant shadows. One surged up, and with it a roiling, righteous anger.

<Did your vision show what lay in those tents she burned, Firecaller? The corpses of her family and teachers, the elders of her tribe, butchered like animals. Should she accept that horror and injustice? Would you have her swallow her rage?>

<No,> I answered, wondering if Atar could feel my heartbreak. Hoping that she could. <Only hold onto it. Keep it sheathed until the moment comes to strike.>

<Anger is not a sword,> Atar snapped. <It is the wind. It rises up and *must* hurl itself against the world. The only question is whether it is channelled and put to use or left to tear all in its path asunder.>

<And you are skilled in calling the wind. Do what you can to channel it.>

She fumed and I felt a strange pain in my teeth—the echo of her clenched jaw.

<You are still too Sienese. The world is not made of metaphors, Firecaller.>

<Nevertheless, I must ask this of you, else that wind might rise up and destroy all that we hold dear.>

A deep current of feeling swirled out from her and seized my chest. Grief and anger. I found myself again wondering what Atar's life had been like since the Fall of An-Zabat.

<Perhaps what is left of the world *should* be broken,> she said.

<Some of it, yes.> I tried to project comfort, though what she truly wanted, I suspected, was an echo of her rage. It roared with more fury than I could muster, and any echo I might offer would ring empty. <We will break what must be broken together, Atar—you and I, and the Nayeni rebellion, and the windcallers, and Ral—but with an eye towards the new world we would build from the ruin.>

<These words are dreams.> I felt the resistance in her thoughts give way to weary resignation. <I will present this dream to Ral. I cannot promise that she will share it, or even recognise it for a compromise. My anger burns hot, but hers is the sun itself.>

<That is all I can ask,> I said, and then, without intending to, as though the thought had leapt from some dark corner out into the full light of our conversation, I added, <I wish I could see you again, Atar.>

I wondered if the tightness at the corners of my mouth was the echo of her smile. <Perhaps someday, Firecaller, when we come together to build a new world.>

I fought down the desire to linger, to hold the spell that bound us and talk of simpler, kinder things. To share something of our lives beyond rage, grief, and war. The tides of the world so rarely bring us together with those we love and so quickly pull us apart. Every reunion is a gift, but one that bears a presentiment of the pain that will come when we must separate again.

Any further words would have been an agony.

I sat with my back to the rough bark of a tree, blinking mist from my eyes. Hissing Cat loomed over me with Okara at her side, his scars still lit like embers.

'Atar will do what she can,' I said.

Hissing Cat grunted and relaxed back into her seat. Okara tilted his head. <Will that be enough?>

'It must be,' I said when the pain and the nostalgia had ebbed away. I steadied myself, stood, and set off towards the dim glow of our campfire flickering through the trees.

One more night and then Iron Town, where the Nayeni rebellion would either be united by hunger for vengeance and liberation, or consume itself.

18

Mr Ma

Koro Ha

A few days after Koro Ha visited the buried city of Sor Cala, Magistrate Tan's scribe came for the first time to observe his class.

The scribe was a jolly-faced man with rosy cheeks and eyes that seemed to disappear behind his dimples. He introduced himself to the children as Mr Mah, told them he was there to help Koro Ha—without explaining precisely how, which prompted Quon Lo to raise a sceptical eyebrow—and positioned himself on a chair in the corner of the room. There he folded his hands across his belly, fixed his face with an unassuming smile, and waited for the lesson to commence.

After a brief lecture on the three pillars of Sienese society, which his students sat through with only occasional nervous glances towards the newcomer in their midst, Koro Ha tasked the children in pairs to come up with parallel relationships to the father–son, husband–wife, and elder–younger brother dichotomies. While they worked, he wandered the floor of the pavilion, trying not to mourn the absence of the five girls, listening over the boys' shoulders while they tucked their heads together and conversed.

'Teacher-student is like elder–younger brother, isn't it?' Quon Lo asked.

'No, more like father–son,' Lon Sa argued. 'Koro Ha is always telling us what to do, just like my father does.'

'But if your father didn't want you to be here, you wouldn't have to listen to Koro Ha at all,' Quon Lo pointed out. 'You have to do what he says because your father says so, and he has to do what your father says too.'

'What?' Lon Sa said, voice rising. 'No, he doesn't.'

Koro Ha tensed, wondering if it had been wise to let the two pair up. They had seemed to be getting along better since beginning their lessons with Uon Elia.

'Yes he does.' Quon Lo sneaked a glance towards Mr Mah and lowered his voice. 'Tell you what. When Koro Ha asks us to share, I'll give my answer and you give yours, and we'll see who's right. Fair?'

Lon Sa grudgingly agreed and Koro Ha breathed a sigh of relief before moving on to lurk just within earshot of the next pair.

When the time came for the students to give their answers, he gently corrected Lon Sa, praised Quon Lo for his incisive reasoning, and reminded the entire class that disagreement and discussion were key to the learning process.

'We can only arrive at genuine understanding by interrogating our misconceptions.' He resisted the urge to look at Mr Mah. 'There is no shame in being wrong, so long as one is able to accept correction from your teachers, your parents, and the sages.'

They finished the lesson with an hour of calligraphy practice before the children went off to await their various escorts home. Mr Mah stood and dipped his head to each of them, smiling widely. When they had all gone, he took a deep breath and turned that smile on Koro Ha.

'Your decision to allow the children to discuss doctrine with one another before correcting their misconceptions...' The scribe furrowed his brow, as though concerned. 'They are, what, eight years old? What hope do they have of understanding these concepts well enough to debate them?'

'None whatsoever,' Koro Ha said, 'yet I am not only conveying knowledge but training them to think. They must accustom themselves to grappling with these ideas on their own if they are to approach complex questions of doctrine on the imperial examinations.'

'I see.' Mr Mah nodded, touching his chin with the tip of his finger. 'Though I wonder if this method might have in some way contributed to the failure of your once most prestigious former student, now fallen in rebellion and disgraced.'

The scribe chuckled to himself. Koro Ha felt ice creep beneath his skin.

Mr Mah shrugged. 'Ah, well. It is for me to observe and report, and for Magistrate Tan to evaluate.' He bowed goodbye and shuffled off towards the garden gate. 'Have a pleasant day, Koro Ha. I will see you tomorrow.'

'It is absolutely stifling,' Koro Ha told Orna Sin that night while they waited at the gate to his garden. 'I tried very, very hard to toe the line, but my very *methodology* is apparently suspect.' He fanned his face against the lingering heat of the summer day and stared off down the road, seeking the bobbing light of a lantern. 'I don't know how long I will be able to keep it up.'

'They already think you are complicit, even if unintentionally, in what happened in An-Zabat,' Orna Sin said. 'They've always suspected me of all manner of shady business without a lick of evidence, despite my best efforts to seem the ordinary, law-abiding merchant. You saw that yourself, on the *Swiftness*.'

'All the more reason not to take unnecessary risks,' Koro Ha muttered, glaring at him.

Orna Sin sighed, lowered himself to a bench beside the gate, and folded his hands. 'I will agree that this is a risk, but it is the most necessary thing in the world, Koro Ha. It is why we are here, now, alive—to ensure that a vestige of the true Toa Alon outlives us.'

Koro Ha murmured grudging agreement, which did nothing to quiet his jittery nerves. Just because something dangerous was also right and good and meaningful did not make it any less terrifying.

At last, a warm glow lit the road. Koro Ha recognised Quon Lo's father—a wiry, severe-looking man, well dressed but with a face that spoke of hard years before reaching modest wealth and comfort. Quon Lo trotted behind him, dressed in his school clothes, face scrunched up in annoyance.

'Greetings, Master Koro Ha, Mr Orna Sin,' Quon Lo's father said.

'Greetings,' Orna Sin replied, clasping the man's outstretched hand in the Toa Aloni fashion. 'And thank you for your understanding.'

Quon Lo's father drew his mouth into a line and nodded. He looked to Koro Ha. 'I'm sorry for what happened to your student. It may not ease your worries, but know that a few of us parents feel that it only speaks better of you.'

Koro Ha tried to hide his shock. 'I suppose I am pleased to hear that, but I wonder why?'

'You placed this Wen Alder boy high in the empire's ranks,' Quon Lo's father said, 'without forcing him to give up his own beliefs about the world. That doesn't seem an easy thing to do.'

'I am not sure how much credit I can take.'

Quon Lo's father chuckled. 'You've taken on that false modesty the Sienese love so much.' He prodded Quon Lo's back with the palm of his hand. 'Go with your teacher and Mr Orna Sin now. They'll take you for your Toa Aloni lessons.'

Quon Lo muttered something under his breath and crossed his arms.

'What was that?' His father's voice hardened.

'I *said* Ola Nin and I were in the middle of game. It isn't fair that I have to have lessons *twice* in one day.'

'Who said anything about fair?' Quon Lo's father scolded.

Quon Lo huffed. 'I want to go home.'

'Hey!' His father prodded his back more firmly. 'Don't disrespect your teacher.'

'Quon Lo,' Koro Ha said. 'What is the first pillar of society?'

Quon Lo glared up at him, then took a deep breath and let his arms fall to his sides 'Sorry, Papa,' he muttered.

'Here.' Orna Sin patted the bench beside him. 'Sit with me and tell me about your game while we wait for the others.'

Quon Lo hesitated a moment, then pulled himself up onto the bench beside Orna Sin and began explaining the rules of a whimsically complicated game full of lion serpents and sea drakes and myriad other mythical beasts, riddled with inconsistent rules.

'That was impressive,' Quon Lo's father said, a smile touching his hard features. 'He's always been a stubborn boy. You're getting through to him.'

Koro Ha could only bow his head and accept the compliment.

Quon Lo's father bade his son goodbye, then left them to wait for the other students to appear. Before long, all five selected for Toa Aloni lessons had arrived, in various states of sleepiness, annoyance, and excitement—including Tul Elna, whom the boys flocked around, catching her up on things she had missed in Koro Ha's lessons and whispering about the strange man who had come to observe them. Lon Sa was the most thrilled of all, as though going to school twice in one day was less an inconvenience and more of an adventure.

The children already knew the way to the hidden door in the teak grove, though like any gaggle of eight-year-olds they chatted excitedly, pointing out the nocturnal wonders of the garden. Something skittered away as they drew near the grove—a red-furred raccoon, Orna Sin explained when the children yelped a battery of questions. There were a dozen or so living in the garden. No, he had not introduced them, as he had many of the other animals. They had simply found their way in at some point and refused to leave.

The children became more subdued upon descending the ladder into the ornately carved tunnel. Lanterns hung from the columns to fill the corridor with a comfortable level of light. Even so, the carvings held deep, mysterious shadows where one could imagine ancient gods or spirits lurking.

Finally, they emerged into the tilted dome, where Uon Elia waited. As in the hallway, lanterns hung or rested on stands throughout the room, though the space was far vaster and the upper reaches of the dome were still wreathed in shadows that clung like cobwebs. Orna Sin approached and squeezed Uon Elia's hand first, a gesture repeated by each of the children. After their greeting, the children arranged themselves on mats fanned out on the floor before the stonespeaker. Uon Elia swept a warm, inviting gaze over them all.

'Shouldn't you lot be asleep in your beds?' he said, grinning.

The children giggled and settled in while Uon Elia launched into the tale of the Gardener, the Healer, and the Stone-carver out of Toa Aloni myth. It was a gentle, romantic, and at times silly tale of three young mountain dwellers striking out on their own to build a village in the forest, each archetypical of Toa Alon's oldest and most traditional professions—a tale meant to describe, as myths are wont to do, the various layers of identity that built up what it meant to be Toa Aloni.

Koro Ha, standing behind the children, recalled hazy old memories of his mother telling the same tale when he was only a few years out of the cradle, long before Teacher Zhen opened his school and Koro Ha's sense of his own worth became wrapped up in the standards and strata of the imperial examinations and the bureaucracy they fed.

'Are your eyes wet, Koro Ha?' Orna Sin whispered.

'It is an unquestionable good that we do this,' Koro Ha said softly. 'You are right. We can't give up just because it is dangerous.'

Orna Sin smiled and patted Koro Ha's shoulder while the Stone-carver laid the foundation for what would become, by the end of the tale, the great city where they now stood, buried by the empire but far from destroyed.

For the first weeks, Koro Ha battled through a gradually mount-ing desire to shake Mr Mah until his smile fell from his face. Yet he persisted, altering his methods in response to the scribe's occa-sional commentary—always accompanied by the less than subtle implication that *this* particular failure must serve to explain Wen Alder's betrayal.

Though the eavesdropping scribe continued to annoy him as weeks stretched into months, then over half a year, Koro Ha came to enjoy the intellectual challenge his presence created. The school had become, in Koro Ha's mind, something like an illusionist's trick. Koro Ha's ordinary lessons, though of course valuable, also functioned as a form of misdirection, keeping the scribe's attention away from Uon Elia. If things seemed *too* agreeable to Mr Mah, his suspicions would be only inflamed by the belief that Koro Ha must be modifying his lessons under imperial scrutiny to hide something. Thus Koro Ha intentionally chose teaching methods he could defend as beneficial yet which he thought Mr Mah would find strange or even objection-able. To that end, as he had with Wen Alder, Koro Ha engaged his students in rigorous debates that often forced them to defend foun-dational points of doctrine—a method which, the first time he saw it, Mr Mah warned against.

'To hear arguments against the sages from the mouth of their teacher cannot help but erode their confidence in doctrine!' the scribe fumed after the first such lesson. 'You must desist from this at once.'

'To argue in defence of something is the best way to reinforce understanding. I do not mean to undermine the sages, Mr Mah, only to help my students thoroughly comprehend the brilliance of their ideas. I will gladly defend the practice to Magistrate Tan, should he desire it.'

Mr Mah glared at him balefully, making no effort whatsoever to put on his usual jovial mask, but he said no more and did not raise the issue again.

Koro Ha enjoyed far less the occasional visits paid by Orna Sin's sea captain, Yin Ila. The first time she appeared in the garden, Koro Ha did not spot her until he noticed Mr Mah squinting quizzically towards the path. Koro Ha followed the scribe's gaze to find Yin Ila leaning against a tree, watching him. She quirked a bemused smile, then returned to the path and whatever errand had brought her to the estate.

'You know that strange woman?' Mr Mah asked.

Koro Ha could have cursed her. A woman acting so brazenly—and dressed in what were, to a Sienese eye, definitively *men's* clothes— clashed with the notions of propriety Koro Ha was meant to be teaching in this garden, and which had cost Tul Elna and the other girls their places in his school.

'She is a business agent of Orna Sin's,' he said nonchalantly. 'An unusual role for a woman, of course, but Orna Sin finds her reliable and capable. He still clings to some Toa Aloni notions.'

'Of course he does,' Mr Mah mused. 'And yet he sponsors a Sienese school.'

Koro Ha tensed. 'As I did, he grew up in difficult circumstances. Do the sages not write that charity is a virtue, Mr Mah? What more reason could he need than sympathy for children who would otherwise never have a chance at an education?'

'And is that your reason for leaving Mountainsfoot Fortress, Master Koro Ha?' Mr Mah's smile, his tone of voice, and his posture all gave the impression of a relaxed, congenial conversation, but Koro Ha felt the sting of the needle prodding from within that question.

'Not only that.' He chose his next words carefully. 'There has never been a Toa Aloni Hand. I would like to raise one up, but I have only so many years left. The more students I tutor, the better chance I have of finding the perfect jade that will allow me to achieve my goal.'

'A worthy ambition.' Mr Mah nodded, touching his chin. 'Let us hope, however, that ambition does not blind you to some subtle flaw in the jade, as it so sadly seems to have done before.'

'We all learn from our mistakes, Mr Mah.'

The scribe replied with only a smile, and left Koro Ha with a week of sleepless nights.

Despite Mr Mah's scrutiny, the five children chosen for Toa Aloni lessons went on meeting one evening a week. Uon Elia eventually moved on from foundational mythology to the Toa Aloni writing system, composed of long strings of looping knots. Like Toa Aloni scribes of old, the children began with charcoal pencils and strips of paper made from tree bark. They would graduate to chisels and stone only when Uon Elia determined that they had enough skill to make such permanent marks upon the world. Lon Sa, who had always been the best at calligraphy, delighted in learning the looping forms and soon could read fragments of the scrollwork that lined the tunnel from Orna Sin's garden to the buried city.

While he watched Uon Elia teach, Koro Ha's own faded memories of learning to write from his father resurfaced with an aching nostalgia—their elbows pressed together over a strip of rough paper, his father's finger tracing the line, speaking each syllable in slow, measured rhythm. That education was later eclipsed by his lessons with Teacher Zhen, of course, which had deepened his father's resentment for Sien and begun the slow decay of their relationship into muted hostility.

Koro Ha made up for it now, as best he could, following along with Uon Elia's lessons, writing knots in a pocket notebook. Gradually, he settled into feelings of stability, though Mr Mah continued to observe his lessons by day. Apparently, Magistrate Tan was not yet satisfied with the quality of Koro Ha's instruction. Or perhaps he and Mr Mah were still waiting for the mistake that would seal his fate and put an end to his school.

Such a mistake came at last seven months after the opening of the school, striking from an unexpected angle, and it was one that Koro Ha would never forgive himself for failing to anticipate.

Children, after all, become bored. And when they develop a love for something—a game, a craft, a thrilling book—it is impossible to keep them from it. The moment they are left to their own devices, and comfortable in their environment, they will pursue their own passions.

So it was that a moment of idle, unthinking self-indulgence betrayed the secret of the Toa Aloni school.

19

Consequences
Koro Ha

One night in early spring, not long after the distant island of Nayen erupted into renewed rebellion that would lead to near defeat at Greyfrost Keep, Koro Ha and Orna Sin sat smoking their pipes and sipping refined rice spirits in the Foundation of Patience Pavilion, a small, simple structure decorated with Toa Aloni scrollwork that overlooked the grove where the secret door lay hidden.

While Orna Sin poured, Koro Ha let his gaze drift over the scrollwork around him. Mere months ago, those arrangements of interlocking loops were little more than attractive decorations to him. Now, he read the blessings and hopes for the future bound up in those knots, where any Sienese eye save the rare scholar of Toa Aloni culture would never find them. Here, a knot that read, *Let the gardens of Sor Cala be rich and green again.* There, *Let the stone-faced gods speak once more to their children.* Beside his hand, on the back of the bench, *May those who sit here know liberation in their time.*

Orna Sin's intent had been all around him from the beginning, but Koro Ha had been too removed from his own culture to see it. He recalled his family's visit to the garden and how Yan Hra's demeanour had softened while his fingers had traced these very knots.

'Thank you,' he said.

Orna Sin blew a long plume of smoke through his nose and raised his eyebrows. 'For what?'

'For what you have done here.' Koro Ha shifted in his seat, feeling awkward, but pressed on. 'And for making me a part of it.'

Orna Sin chuckled. He hefted the bottle and gestured towards Koro Ha's cup. Koro Ha extended it for a refill.

'I do not know how much thanks I deserve,' Orna Sin said while he poured. 'I have always been good at finding opportunities in places others would not think to look. The tunnel was only another invest- ment at first.' He began filling his own cup and shook his head. 'Only a mine shaft towards a lode of lost riches. I brought the carvers in to write on the walls three years later, Quon Lo's father among them. Guilt was eating at me. I had profited by looting the wealth of our fallen city. I wanted to give something back, if only by employing men who still practised our arts to create something beautiful, if hidden.' He thumped the bottle onto the bench beside him. 'I would not meet Uon Elia until a year after *that*, while my miners and I continued digging through the rubble, until we met the tunnels he and the other stonespeakers had been excavating for the last forty years.'

He blew air through his nose and smirked, then held his cup out to Koro Ha for a toast. 'In this way, we are alike. We became involved in this for our own reasons. Yours, ambition and perhaps to right some slighted pride at the empire's refusal to recognise your talents. Mine, pure spite and greed, gradually darkened by a sense of loss, until I found Uon Elia and realised what could be accomplished here.'

'To all that was lost, then,' Koro Ha said and tapped the rim of his cup against Orna Sin's. 'And all that we both, in our ways, have found.'

Orna Sin smiled and they both drank, neither imagining how swiftly it could all be lost again.

'Traveller-on-the-Narrow-Way was a commoner from birth.' Koro Ha slowly walked from one side of the pavilion to the other, his hands folded behind his back, his gaze sweeping over his students, meeting their eyes in random order to be as sure as he could that they were all attentive. Behind them, lurking on his stool, Mr

Mah watched silently, lips curved in his thin, empty smile. 'When he was not much older than you, the boy who would become Traveller-on-the-Narrow-Way chanced upon a starving official ousted from his position by one of many wars that gripped Sien in those days. The official begged the boy for food but, curious and compelled towards learning even in youth, Traveller-on-the-Narrow-Way demanded a trade. For, despite his poverty, the official carried a stack of books bound with cord.

'At first the official resisted, but in the end his stomach won out in the struggle against his mind and he traded a primer in logograms and copies of the Book of Laws and the Book of Sacred Poetry for a basket of rice. These texts were all that existed of the canon at that time, having been composed by the emperor himself.

'There was no system of imperial examinations at that time, and thus no way for a farmer's son to advance in the empire, but boundless curiosity would not be satisfied by the narrow horizons of a small village. When a travelling doctor passed through, Traveller-on-the-Narrow-Way convinced the old man to hire him as an assistant to carry his medicine chest and keep his records. Thus he hoped by travelling to learn all there was to learn, and perhaps—if fortune favoured him—someday reach Centre Fortress and the feet of the emperor who had composed such wondrous books.

'In his journeys, Traveller-on-the-Narrow-Way observed all manner of life in the empire. He saw how the failure of one member of a community in his duties, be that member the magistrate of a province or the mere son of a fisherman, could ripple outwards, disrupting the harmony and flourishing of all. He saw also how disruption in harmony led to vulnerability, both to dangers from without and within. These observations he recorded in his aphorisms, which he gradually compiled into the Classic of Streams and Valleys and the Classic of Living and Dying, two of the most important texts of Sienese doctrine.

'One day, long after he and the old doctor had parted ways, Traveller-on-the-Narrow-Way came upon a trio of hunters in a forest in the heartland of Sien. The hunters, while stalking elk, had been set upon by a pack of wolves. The leader of the group, a tall and elegant man who dressed in silks finer even than those of a magistrate, had been injured while driving the wolves away. Traveller-on-the-Narrow-Way offered his medical knowledge in service. The elegant man, impressed and grateful for his aid, revealed himself as the grand-nephew of the emperor himself. He offered Traveller-on-the-Narrow-Way riches, or land, or a wife from the imperial household, all of which Traveller-on-the-Narrow-Way rejected. He asked instead for the one thing he had longed for all his life: an audience.

'So it was that Traveller-on-the-Narrow-Way met the emperor of Sien and, after all the proper acts of obeisance had been made, presented the emperor with the books he had composed. Whether by luck or by fate, the emperor read them that very night and sat awake until dawn in contemplation. Come morning, he summoned Traveller-on-the-Narrow-Way and told him of the grand project upon which he had embarked, and which the very books Traveller-on-the-Narrow-Way had purchased from the ousted official were to begin—that of composing an underlying philosophy to unite not only the kingdoms of Sien but all the world. He invited Traveller-on-the-Narrow-Way to stay at the academy he was then building for that purpose, which is now the Eastern Academy Quarter, a section of Centre Fortress vaster than all of Sor Cala where scholars from throughout the empire work to refine the canon further with their own insights and observations of the natural world.

'Today,' Koro Ha went on, before pausing to retrieve a sheaf of papers from his table, 'you will read and copy one of Traveller-on-the-Narrow-Way's most famous and important aphorisms.'

A muted groan rose from the students, particularly Quon Lo, who still struggled with calligraphy despite his brilliance in other subjects.

'No complaints!' Koro Ha frowned with mock severity, followed by a gentle smile. 'This will help you not only to practise your handwriting but to better memorise the aphorism, which I assure you will be referenced dozens of times during your imperial examinations.'

He placed a sheet on each student's writing desk, then began his usual meander around the room while they set to work. The sounds of grinding ink and paper rustling beneath slate weights filled the pavilion. Each sheet featured the quote *When all things align according to their proper place, peace and harmony reign; when things fall out of their ordained position, all descends to chaos and disruption*, followed by six sets of guiding lines, each to be filled with a copy of the quote. The students began to write. Koro Ha praised skill and diligence where he saw it and corrected stray lines or sloppy brushwork where they appeared. Lon Sa, as usual, was the first to finish.

'Excellent work.' Koro Ha offered the boy a blank sheet of paper. 'While your classmates finish, you may practise any characters or aphorisms you wish.'

Lon Sa took the page and began to write while Koro Ha returned to his meander. He paused with Quon Lo to correct a misplaced article in the logogram for *harmony* before kneeling beside Kan In, who still struggled with many basic logograms. While he did so, Mr Mah eased himself out of his chair. With hands folded behind his back and face all gentle curiosity, the scribe began a slow lap of the pavilion. This was something he did from time to time, and thus something Koro Ha noticed—as he noticed all of Mr Mah's movements, down to the slightest shift in the angle of his gaze—but did not find troubling.

'Curious,' Mr Mah said, his voice just loud enough for Koro Ha to hear. 'Might I ask what you are drawing, Lon Sa?'

'It's not a drawing,' Lon Sa muttered.

'Oh?' Mr Mah knelt down beside the boy. 'Then what is it?'

Koro Ha fought the urge to bolt upright. He helped Kan In with one more logogram, praised his work, stood, and made his way as casually as he could towards Lon Sa and Mr Mah. The moment his gaze found Lon Sa's paper, his blood froze like water flung into the air on a winter's day.

Instead of the angular articles of Sienese logograms, Lon Sa's paper bore the rounded, looping knots of Toa Aloni scrollwork.

'It's all right, Lon Sa.' Koro Ha hoped Mr Mah would not notice the quaver in his voice.

'It's writing,' Lon Sa said, hesitantly.

'Is it now?' Mr Mah swung his gaze to Koro Ha, his small, soft smile widening.

'Lon Sa's father is a stone-carver,' Koro Ha said, which was a lie but the only excuse that came to mind. 'He still practises Toa Aloni scrollwork. The boy likely picked it up at home.'

'I see.' Mr Mah touched his chin and bobbed his head. He gestured to the page of copy-work Lon Sa had completed. 'Consider the sages, little

Lon Sa. Is this the ordained place for these scrawlings? It surprises me that your tutor indulges such deviance from imperial doctrine, which, if I must remind you, finds no place for the barbarian indulgences of conquered cultures, lest they erode the purity and clarity of thought.'

Wetness gathered in the corners of Lon Sa's eyes. 'But—'

'And now you talk back to me, when my relationship to you is that of the elder brother to the younger?' Mr Mah's sleeves fluttered as he jabbed a finger in Koro Ha's face. 'Did you tolerate such heterodox behaviour in your previous students, Koro Ha? Might this be the root of the tragedy at An-Zabat?'

The loom of Koro Ha's mind spun frantically, working to weave a response that might stifle Mr Mah's mounting anger rather than worsen it.

'You're wrong!' Quon Lo blurted, springing to his feet.

Mr Mah's heavy lids peeled back from his eyes. Slowly, he faced Quon Lo, who stood with balled fists and a quivering lip.

'Am I?' Mr Mah folded his hands across his belly in a posture that reminded Koro Ha of a serpent coiled to spring. 'About what, if you do not mind explaining?'

'Quon Lo is simply defending his teacher,' Koro Ha said. 'As is proper, as the sages—'

'I would like the boy to explain,' Mr Mah said. 'Go on, Quon Lo. What am I wrong about?'

Quon Lo breathed heavily, his nostrils flaring, his furious gaze flitting from Mr Mah to Koro Ha and back again.

'Scrollwork is beautiful,' Quon Lo said. 'Why shouldn't we use it to write?'

A storm of feeling washed through Koro Ha—pride, undercut by terror, all roiling beneath thunderheads of foreboding.

'It appears you have failed to teach at least one foundational point of doctrine.' Mr Mah's voice was cloying as poisoned syrup, his posture rigid with moral outrage. 'What a wondrous opportunity to correct your mistake. Go on, Koro Ha. Explain to the boy why he must never again dally with regressive writing systems.'

It would be an easy thing to parrot back the doctrine that Koro Ha himself had memorised in childhood, which had made him view his

father's pride in his craft as imbecilic and worthy of disdain—a doctrine
he had never really believed in, but accepted as an idea to be memorised,
repeated, and incorporated into his thinking without question because
it *had to be accepted* if he wished to advance his station in the world.

The tutor stared at him, questioning and cataloguing each moment
of delay. And in those eyes, Koro Ha saw that his observer had already
made up his mind to report that this school had at the very best failed
to educate its pupils properly, had at the very worst actively eroded
their morals, and in either case ought to be shut down immediately,
its tutor imprisoned indefinitely for corruption of the youth.

A quote from Traveller-on-the-Narrow-Way occurred to him: *Is it
not better to strive for the mountain top than to settle in the foothills?*

'Well, Koro Ha?' Mr Mah said. 'Correct your student.'

'Quon Lo was inelegant and disrespectful in his delivery, Mr Mah.'
Koro Ha hardly believed the words even as his mouth gave them
voice. 'But the boy has a valid point.'

Mr Mah tilted his head. 'Pardon me?'

'The Book of Sacred Poetry emphasises the value of Sienese logograms
over other writing systems in elegance, clarity, and depth of sophistica-
tion.' Koro Ha's heart raced, but not only in fear. For the first time since
his imperial examinations, he felt the old rush that came to him in the
moment of putting his mind to an intellectual challenge with his future
itself at stake. 'Insofar as one's focus is on discussing, weighing, recalling,
or otherwise interacting with ideas found within the Sienese canon, it
cannot be argued that any writing system but Sienese logograms is most
suited. This is evidenced by the difficulty one encounters in even the most
intensive effort to translate any of the classics into a second language.'

Mr Mah opened his mouth to speak, but Koro Ha continued as
though he had not noticed. He turned away and began to pace, attempting a posture of deliberate, sophisticated contemplation, though his legs
yearned to flee.

'However, one must therefore logically deduce that, just as Sienese writing aligns itself to the discourse of Sienese ideas, other writing systems
must align themselves to the discourse central to their cultures of origin.
Thus it seems likely that An-Zabati letters might capture subtleties of trade
and exchange, or of life in environs defined by wind, sand, and heat.'

He pressed on, knowing his arguments, no matter how brilliant, would fall on deaf ears. Fighting though it might be hopeless. 'Is it not the case, after all, that many horse breeders in the Sienese heartland have adopted the practice of braiding the lineage and qualities of steeds they wish to sell into the manes of those steeds in Girzan knot-script, as the Girzan horse lords do themselves? Might it then be that the Toa Aloni script is, as Lon Sa describes it, beautiful in some way not immediately translatable to the Sienese mode of thought? Might it be better suited to capturing some qualities of stone, or fine timber, or of our mountainous environs, which simply did not occur to our emperor, in all his wisdom, while he composed the hundred-thousand logograms in Centre Fortress? As the very quote these students have just finished copying explains, things in this world have their proper place and function. Could it not be—'

'We all know you were capable of passing the examinations, Koro Ha,' Mr Mah snapped. 'Simply because an argument can be constructed does not make that argument *true*. And you neglect one key facet of doctrine: the emperor's knowledge has never, for a single moment, been limited. Whether he composed the logograms here or in the middle of the sea, any nuance of meaning, any poetic subtlety worth considering, would have occurred to him. All worth knowing has been incorporated into the logogrammatic system.'

'If that is true, then why did the emperor summon Traveller-on-the-Narrow-Way upon reading his aphorisms?' Koro Ha set his jaw. 'Why would the Eastern Academy Quarter exist at all, if there is nothing left to be discovered and all is already contained within the emperor's mind?'

The smile returned to Mr Mah's lips. 'And now there is no question that you are unfit to teach.' He swept his gaze once more over the students and shook his head sadly. The moment of elation Koro Ha had felt collapsed into the pit of his stomach. 'I pity you, children. I pity your parents, who were duped into paying for this ludicrous education you have received. I promise that you will not be subjected to such mal-formation any longer.'

He bowed to them, as though he had done them a service, while the children stared up in confusion. Only Quon Lo and Lon Sa seemed to understand what was happening. Their eyes welled as Mr Mah walked away from the pavilion without another word.

'I'm sorry!' Lon Sa blurted. Tears ran down his cheeks in rivers. He grabbed the page of scrollwork he had written and made to tear it.

'No, no.' Koro Ha knelt beside the boy and eased his hands down to the desk, then away from the page. He stared at those looping lines that had sealed his fate, and Orna Sin's, and all they both had dreamed for Toa Alon. 'This is beautiful work. You have done nothing wrong.'

'But I got you in trouble,' Lon Sa sobbed.

'It is not your fault.' Koro Ha squeezed the boy's shoulder, wishing he could take away all the guilt and pain that Mr Mah had brought down on Lon Sa and Quon Lo. He looked to the other boy, whose face still quivered with rage. 'It's all right, Quon Lo.'

'No, it isn't.' Quon Lo's shoulders heaved as he swallowed a sob. 'The empire will hurt you now, just like they hurt all the stonespeakers. But it isn't right!'

The other children began to chatter at that, sharing worried glances and whispered questions.

'It *isn't* right—that is true,' Koro Ha said, 'but I will be fine, Quon Lo. I promise. You help Lon Sa get home, now. Class is over for the day.'

He said these things, though he did not believe them, and held down his surging terror long enough for the children to pack their things. They were old enough now to come and go without escorts, but he saw them to the gate nonetheless and bade them goodbye one final time.

Lon So wrapped him in a desperate embrace before he went, tears still trickling from the corners of his eyes, whispering *I'm sorry* over and over again. Eventually, the boy peeled himself away, tucked his head, and dashed through the gate, his sandals slapping the brick streets and the hem of his robe fluttering. Quon Lo lingered a moment longer.

'You're a good teacher,' Quon Lo said finally. He nodded once, an awkward, reluctant version of a Sienese bow. 'I won't ever believe otherwise.'

Koro Ha smiled and thanked him. The moment the boy disappeared behind the garden gate, Koro Ha let all his composure collapse into a spasm of panic. After a dozen long, gulping breaths, he found the strength to turn, and walk, and then run to find Orna Sin.

20

The Fox
and the Wolf
Foolish Cur

Awind sharp with the last of winter's chill whipped through the valley, snapping the hems of soldiers' coats. As we descended, the light dusting of snow faded from the pines until their bristly needles stood a muted green against the iron grey of the sky. I paused at the turn of a switchback with a view of Iron Town. It rested on a hilltop in the middle of the valley, like the gate of a tomb. Every step towards that garrison yard and those stained cobbles was a fingernail picking at an old scar. A heavy banner hung over the gate, rippling in the wind—a red wolf on a black field.

'You all right, boy?' Doctor Sho lingered behind me. Okara paused and turned back, his tongue lolling.

'Just resting.' I adjusted the straps of my pack—a portion of the luggage Clear-River had been condemned to carry. He was somewhere ahead with the mules. I had been unable to save him from that fate, though he carried a canon of witch-craft in the pocket of his robe. He could reach it and practise accessing the three powers I had carved and anchored to occupy his mind, at least, through the long, heavy-laden days.

Easier to think about him than about what had been carved out of me and left bleeding on the tiles of the town below and the struggle that lay ahead.

I resumed my steady pace, step after step, jostling open old agonies.

Something ghostly hung over the Army of the Fox while it arrayed itself, a haunting sense of lines in a poem repeating, only twisted, the logograms exchanged for near twins with different meanings. A fractal branch in the lightning stroke of the pattern of the world.

I had been here before. This physical place, yes, the stretch of flat, denuded ground before the walls of Iron Town, but also, insofar as our lives are narratives, I had already told this story. This was a second chance, perhaps, an opportunity for redemption, or at least to begin healing the wound that still wept for Oriole.

We had a single banner. It had flown from the lintel of the magistrate's hall in Burrow and now hung from beneath the tip of a spear that stood defiantly just beyond bow-shot from Iron Town's walls.

A crow flew up from the forest's edge. Six arrows darted out from the battlements to chase it, squawking in outrage, back to the shelter of the trees.

'What's your plan, then?' Doctor Sho asked.

Any common soldier, whether defending those battlements or laying camp in the shelter of the trees, might have marched beneath one banner or the other, their loyalty to the Army of the Fox or the Wolf only an accident of timing and geography.

'I'll get them to talk.'

'And if you can't?' Doctor Sho pressed.

My uncle strode out from his command tent to survey the palisade lines. But for the lack of a mount, he might have been me five years ago, given that same errand by Hand Usher.

'I'm composing this bloody mess of a poem one line at a time,' I muttered. 'We'll find the verse when we need it.'

* * *

But of course my uncle's fatalism had only hardened at the sight of Frothing Wolf's banner, as though proximity to his rival calcified his hatred.

A runner came jogging into the light of the small fire pit I had laid with Doctor Sho and Clear-River at the edge of the war camp, though Doctor Sho had since wandered off to lance blisters and bandage rolled ankles after our long march.

The runner saluted me. 'The Sun King requests your presence in his command tent.'

Words that worried me, even as they conjured hope. Harrow Fox had not spoken with me since I had challenged his authority at the last war council. Either he meant to heed my advice and parlay with Frothing Wolf—now that he could pretend the notion had been his idea, rather than mine—or he meant to take the measure of my contrition on the eve of battle, to test whether or not he could trust my promise to obey.

'Are you coming along?' I asked Clear-River.

'The summons was only for you, Foolish Cur,' the runner said, hasty to return, perhaps with some other errand or message to deliver.

Clear-River looked up from the pyramid of kindling he was building, baffled. 'I'm no better than a pack mule to your uncle now.'

'You have experience convincing people to look past their suspicions and co-operate,' I said. 'You'll be there not as his advisor but as mine.'

The runner huffed an exasperated sigh. I waved for him to go without me. He saluted again and darted off. Clear-River watched him go and shook his head. 'Anything I say they will hear as the voice of Sien.'

'You haven't a drop of Sienese blood,' I argued.

'Blood isn't the question. Prejudice is a matter of perception, not of anything real. And I am *certainly* perceived as Sienese. Let that be my advice, I suppose. If you want them to work together, you need to break down whatever false beliefs keep them apart.' His expression soured. 'Though, of course, they have certain perceptions of *you* that might make that impossible.'

'Your confidence in me is a tremendous support, thank you,' I muttered.

He shrugged and turned back to the fire pit. 'Just promise me you won't crush their minds as you did mine.'

I cocked my head. 'Sympathy for your enemies?'

'There are certain fates we shouldn't wish on anyone,' he said flatly, and I thought of Atar and her reaction to the contact I had forced between our minds. Using transmission as a means of compulsion, as I had so nearly wielded it against Clear-River, would be a brutal form of torture.

I had no desire to lead the rebellion and less desire to bend its leaders to my will by such violence. Yet more—far more—lay at stake than my own moral sentiment.

'I will do what I can,' I said. He nodded, hearing a promise. I wondered whether I meant it as such, or as an apology, or as pre-emptive self-forgiveness.

I left Clear-River there, felt a warmth on the back of my neck— the wake of his conjuring a tongue of fire to light his kindling—and sought my uncle's command tent, my body thrumming with nervous energy, my mind swimming.

On the way I caught sight of Running Doe leading her squad out on patrol. My stomach lurched and I realised that the course of her patrol would lead past the old mine shafts that had been the start of Oriole's undoing. They had been filled, their support beams blasted apart with chemical grenades—one of Hand Usher's first orders upon our taking of the town.

Running Doe spotted me. She raised her hand, touched the scrap of burnt wood at her lapel, then reached for the bone where she carried it in a loop on her belt. I need not be so afraid, I told myself. Running Doe was only leading a patrol, not embarking on a foolhardy, half-considered adventure in imitation of ancient, romantic heroes.

My uncle's command tent faced Iron Town's walls, only a dozen paces beyond the thin trench that marked the reach of a bow. His every coming and going was a challenge to Frothing Wolf, a dare to her archers on the wall. It was easy for me to imagine Oriole pointing out the strategic idiocy of this. A moment of carelessness on my uncle's part, or a lucky shot, and the slow-boiling conflict between the two armies of the Nayeni rebellion might come to a sudden end. Yet my uncle, for all his cleverness and instinct for waging an asymmetrical war, was not one to abandon a compelling symbol for the sake of safety.

I entered the tent and found, again, the map table bearing a sketch of Iron Town strewn with tokens. My uncle's cadre stood around him—Tawny Owl, and the man I thought of as the Vulture and whose name I had never bothered to learn—along with my grandmother, who frowned at my arrival.

'At last, we can begin.' My uncle gestured to an open space in the crowded tent near my grandmother. I did not move, only studied his map of Iron Town. A few unique tokens lay among the dozens marked with Frothing Wolf's sigil—tokens carved with an imitation of witch marks.

'You mean to attack, then?' I asked. 'Not even give her the chance to kneel?'

'She might come down from the walls and kneel whenever she wills.' My uncle's voice was harsh.

'Ought you not make some overture if you truly mean to entertain an alliance?'

'We have discussed this—'

'And I left that discussion unsatisfied.' I let my voice rise. Here was a line I had hoped not to cross. I had so little reason to trust myself—Oriole had died here, in this place, because of my ambition—but I would not bend my own sense of justice to further the goals of others. Not again.

My uncle's cadre closed around him. My grandmother tensed but made no move.

'Which of us rules here, Nephew?' my uncle said.

'Neither, truly, until Frothing Wolf and her army are joined to ours, whether by alliance or by force,' I said.

He planted his knuckles on the table and stood, rising to his full height and bulk. I felt a subtle warmth, smelled a waft of cinnamon.

'Very well,' I said. 'If you refuse to begin negotiations, I will.'

I saluted him and turned my back, ready to weave a shield of light, half expecting fire to lance out from his raised hand but not knowing what verse would follow in the wild poem I was writing.

The wake of his magic receded, but he did not call me back. I stepped out into the camp, stitched together the frayed edges of my soul, and veered.

This was not my fault. I was trying to save them, even if I had to drag them howling and spitting from the quicksand of their own foolishness.

I darted up and across the killing field. A horn blared a warning call from somewhere on the wall. Bows snapped. Nayeni arrows proved no more difficult than Sienese bolts to deflect with a whirl of wind.

Soldiers flinched and dropped their weapons as my shadow swept over them, then rose to their hands and knees, watching me in confusion when I conjured no fire. I circled the town, searching it with the sharp eyes of an eagle hawk. Frothing Wolf had long possessed the same shrewd caution as my uncle. To flee the Army of the Fox, or take shelter in the magistrate's hall, however, would be to abandon any claim she might make to the Sun Throne.

The Sienese invasion had taught the Nayeni a great deal. Not the least of its lessons was that no one has a *right* to rule, only the strength to defend their claim, whether it be from a conquering empire or a rival to a long-lost throne.

A cramping wake seized my flank. Two dark shapes darted towards me, first a raven, broad-winged and heavy, followed by a falcon with bright iron spurs glinting on outstretched talons. If I had known these witches well, I might have reached into their minds and convinced them that I had come to parlay. Wearing the shapes of beasts as we were, I could not so much as shout my reassurances.

Flames roiled from the raven's wings, then flashed towards me. I conjured a shield of light and rolled through the fire. The falcon turned faster than the raven, faster than my eagle hawk's wings could manage. It dived past me, and I screamed as its spur tore a strip of meat from my leg. I reached for lightning, felt its feverish wake, and held it close, but fought the urge to burn them both from the sky. My purpose was to *prevent* the slaughter of one Nayeni army by another, not to initiate it.

The raven wheeled to make its own attack, fire welling around its blazing eyes and down the arch of its wings. The falcon caught an updraft and repositioned itself above me, waiting for the moment when I would be engulfed in the flames and blinded, unable to manoeuvre away from its next assault.

We might have duelled thus above Iron Town for far longer, but I saw an opportunity.

The raven cried and hurled fire. I threw my wings wide and called the wind. The raven squawked in surprise as the wave of heat and light it had hurled at me blossomed like a forge stoked by bellows, then rolled back towards it, the heat caught and carried by the gust I had conjured. The falcon, above, dived for the flashing tongues of fire.

It took only another curl of wind to shape the trajectory of the falcon's brutal dive and pin its wings. Black, white, and brown feathers erupted as the falcon slammed into the raven and the two went tumbling towards the earth, not injured too badly to arrest their falls, I hoped, but stunned and distracted, giving me a chance to continue my search.

A lance of fire darted towards me, streaking bright against the iron-grey sky. I dived beneath it, then followed the wake of its conjuring, rolling and shielding myself with light as three more lances blazed to life. The first two carved the air around me. The third splashed against my shield.

There, upon the wall, arms sheathed in fire and face twisted into a snarl, stood Frothing Wolf. The scar that ran to the line of her jaw gleamed white in the light of her flames. Her grey hair, cropped to a jagged hem, fluttered wildly, and her mouth was a white-and-yellow smear of teeth.

I veered and landed a dozen paces from her. Shock flattened her expression for a moment, only for it to blaze anew with grief and fury.

'You!' she roared. 'What the *fuck* are you doing here?'

'Wait, Frothing Wolf,' I said, showing my hand and the stump of my wrist. 'I've come to parlay.'

She raised her arm, snarled, and hurled fire.

I caught her assault with a shield of light. Flames poured from her in pulsing waves. Their heat bled through my shield and I wondered, for the briefest moment, if her fury alone would be enough to shatter my defence.

'I don't want to fight you!' I shouted.

I heard a brittle laugh.

'Frigid Cub's death was a tragedy.' I stepped forwards, parting the flames before me. 'I was wrong, then, to serve the empire. Hate me—I deserve it. But we can only liberate Nayen together.'

'Keep her name out of your mouth.' Frothing Wolf's voice shifted with the scent of cinnamon. The fire vanished, and with it the pressure of its heat against my shield. I stumbled forwards just as Frothing Wolf darted towards me, wolf's jaws open wide.

I felt a spike of true, mortal fear—the first I had known since dragging my grandmother back from the brink of death. Frothing Wolf's teeth gleamed, dripping spittle, jutting out from the black depth of her maw.

I felt a heavy wake of transmission and a sudden cramp down my side.

With a sharp cry, a brown blur slammed into Frothing Wolf's flank, knocking her off balance. Her teeth snapped on empty air, gusting me with warm breath. She turned her head, snarling at the eagle hawk latched onto her back, tearing with its beak, drawing spurts of blood.

Frothing Wolf bit and snapped at the eagle hawk, then reached for fire. I felt the warmth of her magic, the precursor to the flames she would conjure to burn her assailant to ash.

'No!' I shouted, heart still thundering and head still fogged from fear, knowing only that either Clear-River or Running Doe's death would be on my head. My mind raced through the lower currents of the pattern, chasing the few but potent memories of Frothing Wolf I carried, memories weighty with mutual hatred and mirrored pain.

Quickly, desperately, I found her mind and filled it with walls—no message conveyed by transmission but barriers, cutting her off from her magic.

The wisps of fire around her muzzle became smoke. Contortions gripped her body, hurling her to her side. The eagle hawk clinging to her flank let go and fluttered to the balustrade, where in a burst of cinnamon it became Clear-River, on his hands and knees, gasping for breath. Frothing Wolf loosed a howl that collapsed into a cry of horror and pain while she writhed and shrank back to human form.

'You swore, Alder,' Clear-River said, trembling, eyes furious.

'All I've done is block her magic,' I said. 'It was that or kill her.'

Frothing Wolf stumbled to her feet, body heaving, blood dripping from where eagle hawk's claws had torn her side. She pulled one of her swords free of its scabbard. Clear-River scrambled away from her, shifting his grip on the canon of witchcraft to hold a handful of flame ready, but her gaze did not so much as flit in his direction.

'I'll carve you apart,' Frothing Wolf seethed. 'Leave you a bleeding mess like you left my daughter.'

'And she will still lie dead in the ground,' I said. 'What will vengeance accomplish, Frothing Wolf?'

'Not a fucking thing.' She brought the sword up and lunged. I slipped backwards a few steps, let the tip of her sword carve the familiar patterns of the Iron Dance, then conjured my own blade—one forged of wind, thinner and sharper than hers. My parry wrapped her sword in grasping winds. I twisted and she shouted in pain, but her hand opened before the bones of her wrist broke. Her sword clattered to the balustrade between us.

'If I must strip you of every weapon to make you hear me, I will,' I said.

She bared her teeth, flexed her hands, and balled them into fists.

'Alder!' Clear-River shouted, pointing over my shoulder.

I turned to find a storm of feathers barrelling towards me. An eagle hawk, this time, rather than the falcon and raven I had already cast down. My blade of wind became a whirling net that spun up and pinned the eagle hawk's wings. It shrieked, careened into the wall of the balustrade a few paces behind me, and collapsed, its wings cocked at broken angles.

A roar tore itself from Frothing Wolf and her knuckles cracked against the side of my head. I doubled over, my eyes full of sparks. She dropped her hips and rose with the second blow, bringing her fist up towards my face.

I was skilled enough now to wield more than one wisp of wind. Before she could shatter my nose, I wrapped her at ankles and elbows. She yelped and fell to her knees, then collapsed onto her stomach. She raised her eyes, still blazing with hatred, and spat a gobbet of blood at the hem of my robe.

'If only you put this fighting spirit to work against the empire,' I said, failing to mask my frustration.

'Fuck you,' she snarled.

The eagle hawk behind me screamed. Cinnamon scent swirled from it, carried by the wind that held her. It resolved into Burning Dog, spitting and thrashing to try and free herself from her bonds. She roared a half-coherent curse and veered again. Then, with a serpent's glinting fangs, she lunged for me, slipping through a gap in the net of winds I had woven. I backpedalled a moment too slow and sharp pain lanced up from my calf, followed by a blush of fiery venom.

'Ha!' Frothing Wolf snarled in triumph.

I answered her with a heavy sigh. Two heartbeats later, I had chased the last of Burning Dog's venom from my blood with healing magic. I glanced at Clear-River and felt a welling of regret, but reached through the pattern and bound Burning Dog's mind as I had bound her mother's. Her serpent's body thrashed, rolling away from me as it unfolded into human form. A horrified expression built on her face, then burst to fury. Before she could draw a sword and make another attempt on my life, I bound her arms and legs once more in ropes of wind.

'Will you listen to me?' I snapped, rounding on Frothing Wolf. 'Or will we go back and forth, clawing at each other's throats, I unwilling to kill you and you unable to kill me?' I steadied myself. This was not how I had hoped this conversation would progress. 'You want revenge against me, fine, but I cannot let you take it. Instead, I offer you a truer, more complete revenge: the death of the emperor and the destruction of Sien.'

'Hah!' Frothing Wolf shook her head. 'An empty promise you cannot hope to keep.'

'I intend to keep it,' I said, gesturing to Clear-River. 'Do you see the strip of bone he carries? It granted him the power to veer, and to conjure flame, and to wield magics from the far edges of the world. More than a match for any Hand of the emperor. And you have felt yourself the depths from which my own power now draws. But you are right. I cannot hope to keep that promise if you and my uncle waste Nayeni blood in your pathetic squabble for power.'

'Might want to cut the speech short, Alder,' Clear-River said, clambering to his feet. He pointed down the balustrade to where a dozen soldiers stood uneasily, swords and bows drawn, working up the courage to come to Frothing Wolf and Burning Dog's rescue. With a flick of my wrist I conjured a tongue of fire and threw it at them, leaving them to tumble and scream and drop their weapons in a blind panic.

Burning Dog sneered. 'You would claim the Sun Throne, then?'

A heavy silence held but for the whirling of the bonds of wind around my prisoners while I wrestled down the last of my hesitation.

I was not fit to rule, but neither was my uncle, and neither was Frothing Wolf. If the choice was between trusting their idiotic ambition and trusting in my own, the decision became obvious, yet I still flinched away. 'Any such claim, whether I make it or you do, or my uncle does, is empty and meaningless while Sienese legions still occupy Nayen.'

A cramping wake seized me. I looked across the killing field. A vulture, an owl, and a pair of eagle hawks darted up from my uncle's war camp and towards the wall.

'What say you, Frothing Wolf?' I said. 'Alliance and a chance at revenge, or whatever humiliation my uncle has in mind?'

'So you will kneel to him, then?' Frothing Wolf replied. 'He, who would sooner steal from a half-starved village than defend it. You have a knack for choosing the wrong side, Cur.'

'I am through with choosing sides other than my own,' I snapped. Clear-River cocked his head, and I wondered what he thought of this exchange. 'But you must give me a reason to stand him down rather than give him what he wants and use him as I must.'

'Cruelty remains a Sienese virtue,' Frothing Wolf sneered.

'And stubbornness a Nayeni one,' I countered.

She licked blood from the corner of her mouth and stared up at me in disgust. The cramping down my limbs grew deeper.

'Choose quickly,' I prodded. 'They are nearly here.'

'Fine, bleed you,' she said. 'We'll bow.'

'I'll let them tear me apart before I bow to either of the bastards,' Burning Dog rasped.

'Until the empire is scoured from these shores, we'll bow,' Frothing Wolf pressed on, half for my sake and half for her daughter's. 'And then you'd better kill me like you killed Frigid Cub or I'll cut your throat in the night.'

'You can try,' Clear-River muttered.

Frothing Wolf snarled at him just as an eagle hawk crested the battlement. I released the wind binding Frothing Wolf and Burning Dog
and retreated from their minds, though I held ready to subdue them
again if they so much as flinched. Frothing Wolf stood slowly, keeping
her hands visible, and motioned for her daughter to do likewise.

A waft of cinnamon scent turned the perching eagle hawk into
my grandmother.

'What is going on here, Cur?' she demanded.

Before I could answer, my uncle, Tawny Owl, and the Vulture
landed and veered, leaving me standing between them and Frothing Wolf. The Vulture fingered the knives at his belt and Tawny Owl
reached for her sword.

'There's no need for that,' I said. 'Frothing Wolf and I have come
to an agreement.'

Harrow Fox kept his face placid, but I could see the storm brewing
behind his eyes.

'Have you now?' he said. Something flickered beneath his mask.
He swallowed words. *I did not give you such authority*, perhaps, or *Will
you ally against me, then?* Some climax to his long suspicion of me,
born with his first glimpse of burnt wood pinned to a lapel.

For all my hand-wringing over my loyalty to him, my unfitness
to lead, and the horrors that had always followed in the wake of my
ambition, I felt not a whit of regret or remorse. Perhaps I was not the
right person to lead Nayen, but the path I would set it on was true and
good and righteous.

'To settle the question of who will sit the Sun Throne is a pointless
exercise so long as Eastern Fortress lies in imperial control,' I said.
'There will be an alliance between the armies of the Wolf and the Fox.
We will march together to free our homeland, and onwards to end
the empire.'

I offered Frothing Wolf my hand. She curled her lip, took it, and
heaved herself, growling, to her feet. I turned to my uncle and offered
him my hand in turn. 'We will fight together as equals,' I said. 'Or we
will be destroyed as rivals.'

Anger flickered in the corners of his eyes. My talk of equality, I
was sure, echoed meaninglessly in his ears. I had usurped him as he

had known I would. Yet my betrayal was only the product of his refusal to see past the threat I posed to his power. If he had accepted me as I had wanted him to, if he had used me for my mind and my advice as well as my magic, I might have stood by his side while we forged this alliance. Murder glinted in his eyes, but he clasped my hand.

'Will you open the gates to my soldiers?' Harrow Fox said to Frothing Wolf, his voice cold as steel. 'They have marched hard from Burrow and need rest and fodder.'

'There is little enough fodder to be had,' Frothing Wolf answered. 'The Sienese burned what they couldn't take when they emptied the town.'

'We will forage on the way,' I said. 'Our people will eat and drink what there is to be had tonight, together, and sleep well, but tomorrow we march for Eastern Fortress.'

In their first moment of unity, both my uncle and Frothing Wolf blinked back confusion.

'And leave Setting Sun Fortress at our backs?' Harrow Fox said.

'They will not expect it,' I said.

'Because Eastern Fortress is defended by a legion, three Hands, and a Voice.' Frothing Wolf narrowed her eyes, not put off as my uncle was, but curious.

'Your task will not be to take the city but to hold it once Hissing Cat, my cadre, and I have overcome its defences.' I felt braggadocious and absurd, but I had seen what transpired on the Girzan steppe, and Okara had shown me what to fear. Atar would do everything in her power to restrain the Girzan witch of the old sort, this Ral woman, but there was no telling when the emperor, now threatened from the west and from the east, might take the risk of tearing open the delicate peace between humanity and the gods.

The war in Nayen needed to end, and swiftly. Then, united with the An-Zabati, Atar, and their Girzan ally, we might stand a chance of bringing the emperor himself to heel.

'You both have seen what I can do,' I said. 'Do you doubt me?'

My uncle agreed with a grunt and Frothing Wolf with a sneer and a nod.

I had left them both little choice, only made them into weapons towards my ends: the salvation first of Nayen, and then of the world. Such ends I pursued perhaps too quickly, with too little thought. For all I had learned in my rise through the ranks of empire and my turning to rebellion, there was a great deal I had forgotten, and more still that had fallen upon my mind like rain upon a leaf, rolling away to leave nothing but a fading trail.

21

A Lure in
a River of Blood
Hand Pinion

At the head of his column, Pinion crested a hilltop. There, at last, was Setting Sun Fortress, sprawling through the valley beyond the circle of its ancient walls. Tension that had coiled in his shoulders unwound, leaving him feeling slack and fatigued, as when he had seen his name written in gold atop the list of successful examination candidates.

The white shroud of Hand Beneficence's coffin, still carried at the front of the column, gleamed bright in the sunlight of early spring. The soldiers who marched in formation around the fallen Hand wore scarves wound tightly around their faces, despite the warming weather, and thin streams of incense smoke trailed from burners mounted to either side of the cart. Pinion could not help but wrinkle his nose as it passed.

As the column came in sight of the town, a cheer went up from soldiers and common folk alike, putting a pause to the interminable Nayeni marching song. The promise of shelter, warm food, and more than a few snatched hours of sleep in the dead of night had united them all in a moment of shared relief.

Ought Pinion to have felt proud to have led them so far, enduring bandit attacks, holding the column together despite collapsing morale and his captain's thinly veiled threats to mutiny? Or ought he to laugh and throw himself from his horse to be trampled and crushed beneath the column's wheels, a madman who had murdered, who had left children, old folk, entire families behind to starve or be slaughtered simply because they could not match the wild man's pace he set?

Soon he would know. Either way, he would be able to rest, whether in chains until the day of his execution or riding behind Voice Age-of-Plenty while the column pressed on to Eastern Fortress, relieved of command and all its hateful burdens. And so he laughed and let the soldiers walking past him think what they may.

Smoke began to billow up from Setting Sun Fortress, a few thin columns at first, but they grew over the course of the day until a black, acrid cloud darkened the town. Flakes of ash drifted down, and with them a subtle smell not unlike that wafting from Hand Beneficence's coffin.

Voice Age-of-Plenty rode out to meet them at the head of his own winding column bristling with spears. Pinion's first thought was that they had ridden out to take him captive. Hand Beneficence had been right: the emperor did not, after all, speak to his Hands.

But then he thought of the smoke and the vastness of the column at Voice Age-of-Plenty's back. And beyond the column, a crowd of citizens, huddled among carts and wagons, oxen and mules laden down with furniture and all manner of belongings. At this distance it was difficult to tell for certain, but the crowd seemed far too small.

The smoke continued to roil, thick with the stench of burning corpses. Pinion's thoughts swam, horror and revulsion pushing at his breastbone. His breath came fast. A heat like lightning flickered up the length of his spine and made time stretch like a bow drawn to fire.

Two realisations struck at once. The first, a balm. The second, an arrow through his throat.

He spurred his horse forwards. Captain Huo and Commander Zhu of Iron Town rode to catch up with him, followed by their standard bearers. Again, Pinion dug with his spurs, rising in his saddle, urging his mount to greater speed. Huo shouted a curse and urged him to slow his pace. They ought to meet Voice Age-of-Plenty, their elder brother in the grand hierarchy of empire, with at least a semblance of dignity.

He was near enough now to make sense of the crowd, to see with just enough detail to be certain. A homogeneity of dark hair, of Sienese clothes. Not a curled red-brown lock among them. Not a woman moving as boldly and brazenly as her men. A miserable crowd, forced from their homes, but all wearing at least some wealth: jewelled hair-combs, turtle-shell pins—decorations that no Nayeni commoner would waste precious copper on but that even the lowliest Sienese merchant could afford.

'Hand Pinion!' Captain Huo reined in beside him, his mount breathing in protest of the sprint after a long, unyielding march. 'What are you doing?'

'What better way to rile the survivors into open war?' Pinion murmured, his voice scratching the back of his throat.

Half-formed thoughts, gleaned by the emperor's scrutiny of his mind, resurfaced. A plan to mirror the strategy of a Stones board, creating an opening. A false retreat, giving the rebels easy victory after easy victory, crafting an illusion of power and potency to lure those who fostered hatred for the empire to Harrow Fox and Frothing Wolf's banners. A swollen rebellion would retake their island, driving the empire back to Eastern Fortress, where at last Pinion would turn and resist their siege. All while a punitive army sailed, with the emperor himself at its head, mighty enough to crush the rebel armies against the walls.

To stamp out the latent embers of rebellion, the emperor would stoke them, to make them glow brightly enough to find and extinguish.

There had been questions such as this on the imperial examination. Thought experiments meant to chart those jagged edges where moral sentiment misaligned with doctrine and, if not smooth them, at least give each candidate the opportunity to demonstrate their willingness to suborn their personal feelings.

Justice, cruelty, good and evil—these were nebulous, unwieldy concepts. The will of the emperor alone could burn away all ambiguity. Duty alone, whether to family or empire, could motivate right action.

An essay might justify the slaughter of a town in the abstract, but could it justify the stink of ash and blood on the wind?

'This was necessary,' he whispered, to hear the words, as though they might become more true and less monstrous once pushed beyond the confines of his skull.

A great and terrible nightmare had been brought to life here in the streets of Setting Sun Fortress, all to the aim of fulfilling their plan—Pinion's plan. For it was his, as this violence was his. A slaughter like the world had not seen since the emperor's wrath fell upon Toa Alon. An outrage to stir up sedition in all but the most loyal—or fearful—of hearts.

And this was but a prelude to the brutality to come, Pinion was sure. At Eastern Fortress, and afterwards, the empire would reassert its power in Nayen, reclaiming the territory it had abandoned to bait the trap.

Voice Age-of-Plenty and his retinue approached, riding beneath a red banner bearing the imperial tetragram and the Voice's personal seal. The Voice himself was perhaps a decade older than Voice Usher had been, with lines of silver bright in the black sea of his hair. His mouth was sharp between gaunt cheeks, and his eyes seemed to pierce through Pinion like a pair of scalpels.

Captain Hou and Commander Zhu bowed, nearly touching their chests to their saddle horns. Voice Age-of-Plenty nodded in return, then cocked his head at Pinion, who realised with a start that he had yet to make obeisance. He bowed, hurriedly and too deeply, and felt his bile rise.

'Greetings, Voice Age-of-Plenty,' Pinion said.

'Is something troubling you, Hand Pinion?' The Voice eased his horse nearer. 'You seem ill.'

'Only fatigue, Your Eminence,' Pinion replied, trying to sit straighter, to flatten his face, to mask the horror that threatened to close his throat. 'It has been a long journey.'

'Indeed.' Voice Age-of-Plenty nodded knowingly. 'I have been tracking your progress since Iron Town through the structures that bind us all to the emperor. Your haste to carry out the emperor's command is commendable, though a slightly longer delay at

Iron Town might have given Hand Beneficence the opportunity to see reason.'

What was one more layer of guilt and shame piled atop all the rest? Pinion only dipped his head. There was relief in this, too, after a fashion. He had been following orders, but who could describe that moment of violence as anything but murder? 'Of course, Voice Age-of-Plenty. I will accept whatever punishment is warranted.'

'Punishment?' Captain Huo blurted. He kneed his mount forwards. 'What are you talking about?'

'Hand Beneficence died of a fit, brought on by advanced age,' Commander Zhu said softly. Pinion looked to him. The stately commander's face was twisted in confusion and disbelief. 'Did he not?'

'Have no fear, Hand Pinion. What, after all, would you be punished *for?*' Voice Age-of-Plenty said. Then, to Commander Zhu and Captain Huo: 'Hand Beneficence refused the will of the empire and attacked Hand Pinion, who defended himself. Tragically, the elder Hand died in the conflict. This was kept from you for the sake of expedience, as I am sure you can understand.'

Captain Huo's expression progressed from surprise to outrage to disgust. Commander Zhu stared blankly. Both men, Pinion imagined, would be waging the same battle within themselves, an impossible struggle to reconcile this revelation to imperial doctrine and, in the end, what the empire had asked them to do and accept. That same battle swirled within Pinion, too, its tripartite front shifting moment by moment, seeking an equilibrium that seemed less and less attainable.

'You brought the Nayeni with you, I see,' Voice Age-of-Plenty said. 'An interesting choice. It will be only a matter of time until they realise what we intend.'

Pinion blinked. Even after what had been done to the city, the brazen cruelty of the Voice's unspoken suggestion had the power to shock him. Voice Age-of-Plenty smiled knowingly and nodded to Captain Huo.

'You are furious. I can see it. At times the emperor's will seems inscrutable to our limited minds, but what anger you feel at Hand Beneficence's betrayal, and Hand Pinion's secretiveness, you now have the opportunity to expunge.'

Captain Huo's steed canted a few paces sideways, huffing, as its rider's hands went slack on the reins. 'I don't understand.'

'You do.' Voice Age-of-Plenty leaned towards Huo, as might a co-conspirator. 'Yet you do not *need* to. Accept only the word of the emperor, declaring that the Nayeni alone are to blame for the many tragedies of your long journey.'

Pinion saw the battle raging behind the captain's eyes, the lines shifting. Duty gaining strength while moral feeling collapsed beneath the onslaught.

'Your Excellency,' Commander Zhu cut in, his own struggle revealed only in subtle twitches below his eyes and above his ample beard. 'Your order is to exterminate the Nayeni contingent of our column. Is that correct?'

Voice Age-of-Plenty nodded slowly. 'It is, Commander. If you require a justification, here is one. You have been raided all along your march by rebel forces, have you not? Who suffered the cost and casualties of those raids? Not the Nayeni in your company, but only ever the Sienese. How did the rebels always know where to strike, where your defences were thinnest and where the prizes to be taken were of greatest value?'

By watching from the forest! Pinion wanted to shout. *And why would they bother to steal the clothes from an impoverished peasant's back when a merchant's wagon stood not a dozen paces away?*

'Spies among the column, Commander,' Voice Age-of-Plenty went on. 'They may live in our cities, pay our taxes, and make obeisance when required, but these barbarians—all of them—would sooner burn down civilisation than submit.'

Commander Zhu took a slow breath, then nodded, the battle behind his eyes resolving into grim acceptance—whether of defeat or of the cost paid in victory, Pinion could not say. The commander wheeled his horse around and began to ride back towards the column. 'Come, Captain,' he said flatly. 'There is work to be done.'

The tautness in Captain Huo's shoulders slackened. His hands tightened on his horse's reins, yet the hatred in his eyes still burned. He turned his mount to follow the commander, who gave quiet orders to the members of his retinue. They, in turn, rode ahead.

When had the balance between right and wrong tilted so far? When he had killed Hand Beneficence? When he had nearly butchered a man at Burrow for refusing the order to abandon his home and his family?

'You shouldn't do this,' Pinion said, his voice a breath of a whisper.

'What was that, Hand Pinion?' Age-of-Plenty sidled his mount closer as the column collapsed in on itself. Cries of alarm rose, howled in the Nayeni tongue. A sword fell and a bright arterial spray arced across the snow.

'This isn't war,' Pinion said, his voice finding its firmness. 'This is slaughter.'

The crowd of Nayeni refugees compressed as those at the front fled jabbing spears and flashing swords. Confused shouts sounded from further back from those too far away to see clearly the newborn horror. Commander Zhu led his cavalry into the forest, sweeping a long arc behind the column, penning them in.

'But Hand Pinion,' Voice Age-of-Plenty said softly, 'this was *your* idea.'

'You aren't just luring out the rebellion.' Pinion's eyes refused to leave the terrible scene, picking out portraits of violence. Here, a father shielded his children with bleeding arms even as a spear point punched through the base of his skull. There, a woman screamed and lunged towards the man who had cut off her hand, swinging a pair of shears in her good arm until a crossbow bolt burst her heart. His eyes flitted from brutality to brutality, lingering on screaming faces, a severed leg, a throat torn open and spraying blood. 'Who *wouldn't* take up arms after this? You're creating rebellion—not only stoking the embers but setting the flame!'

Pinion spoke as in a dream, not believing his words could affect the world yet speaking them anyway. They were true. They felt *right*, even while all he had done, all he had enabled, all he had *planned*—the world itself, as he had known it—twisted into wrongness.

They felt like words Oriole would have said, his face red with frustration, staring up into their father's cold face.

'Call them off,' he demanded as a family fleeing into the woods fell, their bones splintering beneath the hooves of the cavalry. 'Do it, or I'll ride out there and stop this myself.'

Pinion reached for his reins, only to find that one of Voice Age-of-Plenty's retinue already had them in hand.

'You are exhausted, Hand Pinion.' Age-of-Plenty's voice was muted, far away, echoing from across a vast gulf. 'Come. You should rest. There is a palanquin that will carry you, at least for a time, as we set out for Eastern Fortress.'

Pinion stared at him while the screams of horses and the dying filled the air behind him.

'Come, now.' Voice Age-of-Plenty's tone shifted until it held the force of threat. 'You would not wish to ride the rest of the way to Eastern Fortress bound, would you? What an embarrassment that would be for your father. Enough, I fear, that he may feel compelled to retire, especially after such a treasonous outburst from the mouth of his son. However tired you might be, those words will prove difficult to forgive.'

The man who held the reins of Pinion's horse began to lead it away, towards the main column of Voice Age-of-Plenty's army, and, shocked by the Voice's words, Pinion let him. He stared at the gentle rise and fall of his horse's neck and shoulders, listened to the thump of its hooves and the swish of the grass around its fetlocks. Imagined himself at home, riding in the practice yard with Oriole and Yul Pekora, their horsemanship instructor. A moment when his mind had been occupied by nothing but pure joy and the enlivening fear of tumbling from the saddle.

Would Oriole have let himself be led away, his back turned to such cruelty? Or would he have ridden with Captain Huo and Commander Zhu, sword in hand, to do the brutal butchery that was the price of empire, of luxury, of the simple pleasures Pinion wished never to have left? Or would he have thrown his body as a pitiful dam across the torrent of violence, as he had set himself against their father on behalf of his servant playmate?

The palanquin resolved out of the crowd of soldiers and citizens of Setting Sun Fortress, huddled together in a tent city made ready to flee the killing field that had been their home. A few watched the butchery on the hilltop disinterestedly. Others wore open masks of horror, but more nodded in grim satisfaction.

Far, far too complicated for any didactic tale or aphorism or examination essay to capture.

Pinion stepped down from his horse and up into the palanquin, collapsed into its seat, and closed the doors and shutters tight, muting the clang of steel and cries of pain. And as he sat there, in the quiet, with tears threatening his eyes, a painful clarity struck him, as though a scab had been peeled from his mind.

This was the point of it. All of it. The doctrine. The examinations. The profound weight of duty to family and nation. The canon of sorcery itself. All a means to channel a river of violence to the emperor's ends, and to build the banks high enough to obscure the horror of what had been wrought. *Does this feel right, Wen Alder?*

And he laughed bitterly, quietly, deep in his chest while long-suppressed thoughts swirled up from the silt at the bottom of his mind. *What does* right *even mean to a person like me?*

This had been his plan, though he had not been callous enough to fit this piece to the puzzle. If this horror did not rouse every half-patriotic Nayeni in the world to war, every Nayeni with a scrap of moral feeling and the strength to carry a spear into battle, nothing would. The emperor would crush them against the walls of Eastern Fortress and bathe their island in blood and fire. And in the midst of it all, Pinion would have his revenge.

He could hope for satisfaction, at least. If not for justice, then a sense that the pain he suffered had been meted out in turn to those responsible for Oriole's death.

At the very least, when they all lay dead he might find a warm corner of his room, and a book, a pipe, a pot of tea, and put it all— vengeance, memory, duty, guilt—from his mind.

Or perhaps, having glimpsed beyond the banks of the river, even for a moment, he would never know peace again.

22

Cadre
Foolish Cur

The garrison yard was not as I remembered it. There was no pounding rain or boot-churned mud. No prisoners bound to stakes. No stones cracked by fire and lightning while blood sluiced through the gaps, carrying me into a red desperation that blurred until I nearly lost myself, pounding against the canon's walls.

I took a sharp breath. Crisp morning air, scented with the first green of spring. Winter's last dusting of snow clung to the tiled yard, which was empty save for myself, Clear-River, Running Doe, and the ten soldiers who would become my cadre—five hand-selected by Harrow Fox, the other five by Frothing Wolf. Only one of their number wore the burnt-wood fetish. My uncle had chosen him either as a gesture of good faith or to distract me from some subtler machination, or the fetish was a poor disguise. Perhaps the second and third possibilities simultaneously.

His paranoia was infectious. I chased it to a shadowy corner of my mind and held up the ten canons of witchcraft I had finished making the night before.

'You have been chosen to wield a new sort of magic,' I declared, pacing in front of them, Clear-River and Running Doe at my back.

'I did not choose you, for, despite what Harrow Fox and Frothing Wolf believe, I am not interested in ruling this island or its people, only in liberating it and in crushing the empire. A goal we all share in common, yes?'

A few of them nodded grudgingly. One, a lanky sharp-faced man from the Army of the Wolf, crossed his arms and cocked his head in open disbelief—an adolescent sort of resistance, perhaps to my authority, perhaps to my subversion of Frothing Wolf's. I paused in my slow pacing.

'What is your name?' I asked him.

He shifted uncomfortably. 'Torn Leaf.'

I tossed one of the canons of witchcraft to him. He balked in surprise but managed to catch the strip of bone against his chest.

'Do you see the four markings in the bone?' I had added healing sorcery to my canon, anchored to a carving of the Sienese logogram for medicine, simplified in the same way that I had simplified veering. Rather than turning the magic outwards, as the emperor had done, I had turned it inwards to bolster the body's ability to heal itself—less precise, but useful without a year of studying anatomy.

Torn Leaf studied the canon, holding it like a shard of jagged glass.

'Touch the first mark,' I said.

With the benefit of instruction from Clear-River and Running Doe, by mid-morning all ten could conjure a candle flame. Perhaps drawn by the wakes of their magic, Tawny Owl appeared at the edge of the courtyard, her mouth twisted with open resentment. What had taken her years of study with my uncle to master, I had conveyed to my cadre in hours.

'You deserve a measure of credit for this,' I told her. 'Without your help, and the chance to study your witch marks, I could not have made my canons.'

'We are ruled by a sorcerer out of ancient myth who doles out magic as he sees fit.' She took a step towards me. Brave of her, considering her words. 'Tell me, Cur. Is there any point to this war if we must become like the empire to win it?'

'I *left* the empire to fight with you,' I snapped. 'You compare obvious similarities and ignore the deepest, most meaningful differences.'

'I compare what I can see.' Tawny Owl shrugged. 'Is it not common for Sienese sons to challenge the authority of their fathers?'

'No.' Her ignorance made it so easy to dismiss her accusations. 'It is not common. It goes against the most foundational virtues of Sienese doctrine, in fact.'

'And yet here you are,' she said, nodding towards my cadre. 'Doing this.'

What was I doing, arguing with her? What did it matter what one young witch thought? Yet my anger burned hot and the urge to defend myself prodded at my tongue.

I was spared the indignity of fruitless debate by a wake of veering and the appearance of Frothing Wolf's Raven, who landed on the balustrade above the garrison yard. His gaunt face bore a few bruises and a nasty cut below one eye as evidence of our brief duel.

'Frothing Wolf and Harrow Fox wait in the magistrate's hall,' he called down, his affect flat beneath his mottled bruises. 'They sent for the both of you.'

Tawny Owl waited for me to respond.

'Shall we?' I gestured for her to lead the way.

She scowled, but veered and took to the sky. I followed, darting over the empty streets of Iron Town to land in the courtyard of the meagre hall where Frothing Wolf and I had first met. The echoes of old lies met me in the vestibule and heralded my entry to the audience chamber.

The magistrate's velvet-padded seat stood empty upon the dais, framed by pale stains on the wall where banners had once hung. Frothing Wolf leaned against one of the cedar columns, gazing down with a clouded expression at a heavy table that ran the length of the room. Harrow Fox sat at the far end beside a young, gaunt-cheeked boy. At the sound of our arrival, the boy's head snapped up from the bowl of congee before him, eyes wide with terror.

'No cause for fear, child,' Harrow Fox said, his voice more gentle than I had ever known it—more, even, than my imagination would have warranted, had someone else described this scene to me.

The boy watched me a moment longer. Not afraid of Tawny Owl, then. At last he returned his attention to the bowl and spooned another mouthful of congee past his thin, blue lips.

'A child of Iron Town,' Frothing Wolf murmured from where she lurked upon the dais. 'Led away from this place by the Sienese Army. One of the only survivors of—'

'Wolf!' my uncle snapped.

The boy's hand hovered halfway between the bowl and his mouth, his spoon trembling, slopping congee onto the table. Harrow Fox called for a guard and one appeared from a recessed hallway.

'Stay with the child.' Harrow Fox let the guard take his place beside the boy, then nodded towards a door upon the dais. It led to a small dressing room with a pair of padded chairs, chests that stood empty but for scraps of fine fabric, and a wardrobe stripped bare.

My uncle positioned himself behind one of the chairs. He gripped the arch of its back, his knuckles white. 'By the boy's account, the Sienese led the people of Iron Town to the gates of Setting Sun Fortress only to slaughter them. The boy survived and managed to find his way home.'

'Or near enough,' Frothing Wolf said. 'A hunting party found him a half morning's walk away sprawled out in the roots of a tree.'

'Monsters,' Tawny Owl, standing behind me, spat.

I wished I could share her outrage. Instead, my mind was caught swirling in an eddy of confusion. I thought back to the boy sweeping Oriole's grave, his shoulders hunched beneath the weight of grief. In our shared pain and fear of the future, we had shared, too, a moment of rare honesty—one that had resonated, years later, when Pinion had led his men from Greyfrost Keep rather than put a sword through my spine while I dragged my grandmother back from death.

My belief in his goodness—or, at least, my hope for it—had been misplaced, it seemed.

'I have had word, too, from raiding parties we sent to harass the Sienese column.' Frothing Wolf began to pace. 'They tell of black smoke rising from Setting Sun Fortress. None ventured near enough to say for sure, but rumour holds that the Sienese massacred the Nayeni there and burned the city to the ground.'

Harrow Fox ground his teeth. 'This was always the ultimate end of their conquest,' he growled. 'First they offered wealth through trade, then they ruled at the edge of a sword. Now, perhaps because they have no more use for our kind, or because they have learned to fear us, they will slaughter us all.'

Frothing Wolf grunted her agreement.

'A good thing, then, that you are working together at last,' I mused. It was easier to spin a joke at their expense than dwell upon Pinion's sudden brutality.

Both would-be Sun Kings fixed me with pointed stares.

'But this changes nothing,' I went on. 'We will rally what forces we can and press on to Eastern Fortress.'

Harrow Fox worked his jaw but gave a heavy nod. 'A lesser people might be cowed by the empire's brutality, as we can be certain they intended. Not the Nayeni. Word will spread of this atrocity and the people will rise like embers scattered upon a dry and brittle field.'

Frothing Wolf rolled her eyes.

Harrow Fox scowled at her. 'What? Do you disagree?'

'Not at all,' she answered. 'I will have our scouts fly out and raise the villages.'

'Not yet,' Harrow Fox said. 'Let rumours ferment awhile, then gather our people in the garrison yard. Here is a chance to unite our forces, Frothing Wolf. Resentments will still fester between the ranks.'

She regarded him sceptically but shrugged her shoulders. Then, to my astonishment, both looked at me for confirmation.

I shook my head. 'I am no leader here.'

Harrow Fox took a deep breath and crossed his arms. 'As you say then, Nephew. It is good that we are all in agreement.'

We left the ransacked dressing room, Frothing Wolf to infect our forces with a rumour of Pinion's crimes, Harrow Fox to loom protectively over the boy while his mind worked behind his clouded face. For my part, I sought out Hissing Cat.

The empty husks of abandoned homes and empty tradesmen's shops leered at me as I made my way on foot towards the empty warehouse that had become her lair, sifting through feelings of horror at Pinion's betrayal of my trust. I should never have let him leave Greyfrost. A single graveside conversation—no matter how sharply I remembered it, no matter how it resonated with the last echo of my friendship with Oriole—could not counter-balance the weight of imperial doctrine.

I had let him live, trusted in the goodness I imagined within him, and thousands had died.

Yet one more mistake to carry. More deaths to hang on my over-burdened shoulders alongside those I had killed at Burrow, those who had died because of me at An-Zabat, and Oriole.

Frigid Cub, too, lest I forget my debt to her mother.

Like a thunderclap, a weight filled my mind.

<If you are here to tell me of Setting Sun Fortress, you were slower than a starving child,> I said.

<Not that,> Okara replied. <I've come to warn you. Tenet is on his way to Nayen.>

I tilted back my head and stared into the iron-grey sky. The sim-mering guilt, thickening to self-hatred, found here its proper object. Every horror, every mistake, was a product of the emperor's philos-ophy. He, with his doctrine and his empty promise of magic, had set me on this path. Any harm I had done in following it, or in my desperate struggle to *leave* it, was not my fault but his.

<Tenet's empire is in disarray,> Okara went on. <He will put it to rights, if he can, else harvest his crop of weapons early and hope they will be enough.>

His meaning was clear. Here was an opportunity to put an end to the empire and the threat it posed to peace between humanity and the gods.

<Your mother once said that all magics were permitted to me,> I said. <Tell her—tell them all—that I have no desire to start a war. I am no threat to them, or to the peace. Only to the empire.>

<Very well.> Some deep emotion stirred within his mind, unfamil-iar to me. Some feeling known only to the gods, perhaps. <What do you intend?>

<To go to Eastern Fortress.> A droplet of rain struck below my eye. <To put an end to Tenet's cruelty and his plans.> And, in doing so, avenge not only myself and Oriole and the An-Zabati but every other shattered life left in the wake of his conquest. Clear-River's. My mother's, my grandmother's, and my uncle's. Every soldier in the Armies of the Wolf and Fox who had suffered, as Tawny Owl had suffered, beneath the heel of an imperial boot. Even the lives that were

not but that might have been, such as the one Pinion might have lived had he not been twisted in service to Sien.

<Then I wish you luck,> Okara said and faded from my mind.

At the creak of the warehouse door, Hissing Cat looked up from the glowing coals she stirred with the tip of her needle.

'Conjure a flame,' I said.

She narrowed her eyes at me but did as I instructed. I made myself a sphere of jade, submerged in the pattern, and reached out towards the iron spike of her will. It would have been easier, I think, to lift a mountain with my little finger. I retreated from the pattern, panting, wiping beads of sweat from my brow with the back of my hand.

'What was the point of that, Cur?' Hissing Cat tilted her head, rattling the skulls that perched in the grey cloud of her hair. 'Did you think a few months of marching would make you a match for me?'

'The emperor sails to Eastern Fortress,' I said, 'or so Okara claims.'

She barked a laugh.

'There is more.' I told her of the boy, of the massacre at Setting Sun Fortress, and watched her mirth turn sour before curdling into open rage.

'You might have hidden away for a dozen lifetimes,' I said, 'but Nayen is still your country. You taught the first witches. Tenet means to destroy us in a prelude to his war against the gods.'

'I told you before that a war between the two of us would be little better than an apocalypse,' she snarled. 'More, that *I would lose*.'

'Perhaps,' I said, 'but we might stand a chance together. There is a weapon I might wield that both you and Tenet have been denied.'

A stillness settled over her. She regarded me with neither her usual detachment nor the open fury she had worn only heartbeats ago.

'I have spoken with Okara,' I said. 'The gods will not retaliate if I seal the pattern to stop the emperor.'

'Is that so?' Hissing Cat said quietly. 'Or is it only one promise layered atop another?'

'There must be trust at some point,' I argued. 'The gods have their agenda, and I have mine, but we both want Tenet dead and his empire broken. Like Frothing Wolf and Harrow Fox, we should unite in that purpose rather than let suspicion lead us to our doom.'

A ripple marred the placidity of her face. 'Perhaps. But you do not know them as well as I do. They are as cruel as Tenet, and less predictable.'

'But they do not sow chaos as they once did,' I said. 'Meanwhile, he destroys lives wherever the long arm of his empire reaches.'

I saw the struggle behind the mask she wore, deep in the shadows that wreathed her face. Old wounds and older terrors dredged to the surface, warring against what I had asked of her. Yet new horrors cried out for justice and needled her with guilt—not for damage done but for damage allowed while she hid away, unable to put her own fears and frustrations aside and stand against the growing tide of Tenet's cruelty.

'You are right, of course,' I said. 'I will not take the risk of sealing the pattern, regardless of what Okara says, unless I must. Help me defeat the emperor without doing so.'

Her eyes flitted to her needle and her pile of shoulder blades where they lay, waiting for oracle runes. 'I suppose it's this or wait for the war and do nothing,' she muttered. 'Fine, Cur. Let's break the bastard before he breaks the world.'

23

Flight

Koro Ha

'They know.' Koro Ha braced himself against the doorway to Orna Sin's office, his legs shaking and his lungs burning, though he could remember nothing of his run across the garden. He had been standing at the gate, bidding Quon Lo goodbye, and then he was here, sweat soaked and terrified.

Orna Sin removed his spectacles, looked up from the paperwork scattered across his desk, and inhaled a long, steadying breath. He gestured to the second chair in the room. 'Who knows what? Be specific.'

'Mr Mah.' Koro Ha collapsed into the chair, gripping the arm rests with quivering hands as though they might shatter if he squeezed them tightly enough. 'He saw Lon Sa writing scrollwork and Quon Lo stood up for him, and then I…' Koro Ha shut his eyes. 'I made the mistake of trying to defend the boys with Sienese doctrine.'

Orna Sin tapped his spectacles against his chin. 'So Mr Mah, and therefore Magistrate Tan, knows that one of your students was scribbling scrollwork in a moment of boredom, which he might have learned at home or from any number of decorations throughout this garden, let alone this city, and that you hold somewhat unorthodox views on certain points of doctrine.'

252 The Garden of Empire

'He said he would see to it that I never teach another lesson.' Koro Ha shook his head. 'There was such *hatred* in his voice, Orna Sin. We have to take this seriously.'

'Which means doing what?' Orna Sin leaned back in his chair. 'Do they know about Uon Elia and the buried city? What the children have been learning there?'

'No,' Koro Ha said, 'but they will begin to investigate. They may search this garden. What is to stop them from finding out?'

'They will probably interrogate you, at least,' Orna Sin conceded. 'They may do the same for me, as your employer. They may try to force me to sever ties with you.'

'They may do far worse than that.' How could Orna Sin be so calm? A lifetime of skirting the law had evidently left him far too accustomed to danger. 'They may go after the children. *You* might be able to sit through several hours of imperial questioning. I am not so sure about myself, and I doubt a nine-year-old student will have the fortitude to withstand that kind of pressure and keep the secrets that must be kept.'

Orna Sin pounded his fist on his desk, winced, and opened his hand, dropping the twisted remnants of his spectacles. He began picking bits of glass from his palm.

'We have to protect Uon Elia,' Koro Ha said. 'If the empire finds him, any hope of reviving Toa Alon will be lost.'

'How many thousands of hours of Mr Mah's time and thousands of taels spent on his salary did the empire waste?' Orna Sin wondered aloud. 'I thought they would give up long before now.'

'Not wasted, in the end.'

Orna Sin glared at him. 'You're right, of course. Uon Elia must be protected. I will bring in craftsmen to seal the tunnel. We can open it up again once this has all blown over.'

'It won't blow over,' Koro Ha insisted. 'A Hand has betrayed the empire. There can be no greater embarrassment. Wen Alder escaped them, and so they will punish his associates instead. "Fruit, sweet or sour, is a reflection upon the branch that bore it," to quote the sages. I am that branch, and now they can see that I, again, bear sour fruit in the form of children who hold heterodox ideas, talk back to their superiors, and have learned to write in barbarian script.'

Orna Sin's fingers hovered over the last few bits of glass in his hand. 'Then we put you on a ship. Get you somewhere the empire will not think to look for you. Somewhere safe.'

Koro Ha recalled the Black Maw, seen as a jagged silhouette on the horizon, and tried not to imagine himself situated on that backwater with only pirates and smugglers for company.

'A thought that makes you nauseous?' Orna Sin chuckled. 'You are one of the empire's enemies, now. You'll only find help among its *other* enemies.'

'It isn't that.' Koro Ha shook his head. 'You might smuggle me away and save my life, but it won't be enough.'

Orna Sin frowned, unconvinced.

'*Think*, Orna Sin.' Koro Ha felt his composure finally breaking. There had been a chance, for a brief, beautiful moment, that his life could have meant more than service to the young scions of imperial wealth. All lost, now, to a moment of idle distraction. 'How many people know of Uon Elia? You, me, the excavators who discovered him with you, and his five students and their parents. You and I might have kept the secret strict, but what are the chances that none of the children have told their classmates, or a beloved, trusted aunt, or a friend who lives down the street? They will question *everyone*. They will not stop until they find the weak place in the armour we built around this secret, and they will break it. If Uon Elia is to survive this, he must come with me. And he *must* survive.'

'He survived beneath their feet for seven decades!' Orna Sin protested, grasping at any scrap of hope.

'They weren't looking for him before,' Koro Ha pointed out gently.

Orna Sin's face contorted, betraying the storm that raged within him as reality, at last, took hold. 'How many more years does he have?' he asked. 'Will we be able to bring him back before what time remains runs out?'

'If he is captured, all is lost,' Koro Ha said.

'Perhaps we can send some of the students with you, Lon Sa or Quon Lo, to continue learning—'

'Do you think their parents will agree?' Koro Ha shook his head.

At last, Orna Sin heaved a sigh. 'Fine. Go and make what preparations you must. I will see about a ship and do what I can to convince Uon Elia. The old bastard will cling to the walls of his cave, I'm sure.'

'You convinced me to abandon an illustrious career in Sien,' Koro Ha said. 'He may be older and more stubborn than I, but he is not a fool. He will see the wisdom in this.'

Orna Sin grunted and drummed his fingers on his desk. 'Your former student has a great deal to answer for. If you ever find him out there in the world, punch him in the jaw for me.'

Koro Ha smiled. 'Very well, though I doubt I will get the chance.'

With that, they parted ways, each to their own preparations, Orna Sin to convince the most precious cargo of his career to let himself be smuggled out of the only home he had ever known, and Koro Ha to see his family.

'Koro Ha!' Eln Se exclaimed, shock gradually giving way to a smile. 'You must have been quite busy at that school of yours. It's been a while since we saw you. Come in, come in.'

She ushered him to the table in the courtyard, bustled off to the kitchen for some beverage she could offer him, then called up to their father, who she explained was taking a day to nap and recover after a month of difficult work on a carving for one of the up-and-coming merchants of Sor Cala.

'Your employer likely knows the man,' she said.

'Is Rea Ab home?' Koro Ha hoped to see his niece one more time. They had only begun to get to know each other and already they would be torn apart again. And, unlike his previous absences, this time he would likely never return to Sor Cala. He added, feeling a swell of guilt that he had not thought of her husband, 'And what of Yan Hra?'

'Rea Ab is at the market and Yan Hra is working.' She emerged from the kitchen with a plate of roasted nuts and a bottle of the rice beer their father liked, her expression grave. 'Is everything all right, Brother?'

'I would prefer to explain only once,' he said, his heart sinking, picking up the roasted flesh of a walnut and fiddling with it, too agitated to eat anything. During the ride from Orna Sin's garden, he

had tried to formulate some explanation to justify his sudden, permanent departure from Toa Alon. Now, his mind was blank as a fresh
sheet of paper. For years, the promise of one day returning to visit his
family, no matter how fraught that visit might be, had kept homesick-
ness at bay. Word of his mother's illness and his father's advancing age
had been enough to pierce that defence. Neither had filled him with
such longing as he now felt to linger a while longer, to be a part of this
family he had all but abandoned.

'Look who it is!' his father called, hobbling down the stairwell.
'Come to visit twice in a year. I suppose that's an improvement, at any
rate.' He lowered himself onto the chair across from Koro Ha, sighed,
and opened the bottle. 'What brings you around, Son?'

'I'm leaving Sor Cala,' Koro Ha said.

'Oh?' his father said, the bottle hovering at his lips. 'The school not
working out?'

Koro Ha ignored the jab. 'Something…happened with one of
my former students. An incident which has cast imperial suspicion
upon me.'

'Suspicion?' Eln Se hovered near the table, her hands clasped and
brow furrowed. 'Of what?'

'Treason,' Koro Ha said flatly. 'Or, at least, teaching in a way that
would have my students question doctrine, not simply accept it,
which is the same thing as far as they are concerned.'

His father set down the bottle, his expression growing severe.

'What happened?' Eln Se said breathlessly. 'Where will you go?'

'What happened is not important,' Koro Ha said. 'My employer
knows of a place where I can disappear. I will go there.'

'Disappear?' Eln Se said. 'What will you do? How will you survive?
Koro Ha, *what is going on?*'

'I'm trying to tell you.' He took a deep breath to calm himself. 'I have
savings. Some of those I will take with me, to keep me going until I
can find work. Scribes are needed everywhere, even in the most remote
of backwaters. What I cannot take with me I will ensure my employer
delivers here, to you. But you must hide it. The empire will come
looking for me. Sudden obvious wealth will draw their suspicion.'

'It's that bad, eh?' his father said.

Koro Ha met the man's gaze and saw fear and worry there, things he had not imagined his father, hard man that he was, ever feeling on his behalf.

'It is,' Koro Ha said. 'I'm sorry. I should have visited more often.'

His father grunted. 'You did what you could. Kept a roof over our head in hard times.'

'Even so…' Koro Ha choked, propriety and sentiment wrestling in his throat. 'I wish I could tell you all of what I have been doing, this last year. Of the things I was trying to build. The children of my school—not all of them, but some—have heard stories not told here in a generation. Toa Aloni stories. They learned knotwork as well as calligraphy, and…' And saw for themselves, he wanted to say, what remains of Sor Cala, the domes and the stone faces that survive buried beneath the city. And some of them, he was sure, would have one day inherited Uon Elia's greatest secret: magic. 'But the empire will question you, and the less you know, the safer you will be.'

'Koro Ha—' Eln Se began, then broke off, sobbing.

His father reached across the table, took his shoulder, and squeezed while his eyes lit with something that all Koro Ha's experience of the man told him could not possibly be pride but that surely seemed to be.

'They'll sooner crack the Pillars in half than pull any of your secrets out of me,' his father said. 'When do you leave?'

'As soon as the ship is ready,' Koro Ha said. 'I will try to find a way to write to you once we arrive, but…'

His father nodded. Eln Se sobbed again, then wrapped him in her arms, holding him tight. 'Wait at least for Rea Ab to return,' she said. 'Please. She should know her uncle.'

He patted her back but shook his head. Regrets swelled and swirled in him and held him to his chair until the moment was shattered into panicked fragments by a loud, insistent banging at the door.

Silence fell on the house for a heartbeat. Another flurry of banging sounded, then a voice called out in Sienese, muffled but commanding. Eln Se stood bolt upright, her gaze swinging to the door.

'You were followed?' Koro Ha's father whispered urgently.

Unless Mr Mah had sprinted all the way to the magistrate's hall—which Koro Ha very much doubted—barely enough time had passed for word of Koro Ha's misdeeds to reach the magistrate before he'd left Orna Sin's estate. Koro Ha shook his head, hardly daring to breathe.

'Help him hide,' their father said to Eln Se, then pushed them both towards the stairwell. 'I'll deal with these bastards.'

'Open up, in name of emperor!' the voice shouted, switching to broken Toa Aloni. 'Or we will be breaking down door!'

Eln Se spirited Koro Ha up the stairs to a window that led out onto the roof. 'Hide here.' She passed him a mat of rushes. 'Crouch down and cover yourself with this.'

No time for questions, nor even to think. He eased the shutters of the window open and took a careful step out onto the tiled roof. The tiles dug into his stomach and feet where he braced himself with the toes of his sandals. His heart thundered against his chest while Eln Se draped the mat over his head and shoulders.

He heard muffled shouting and heavy footsteps on the stairs, then in the upper room. Had Eln Se closed the shutters? The hairs on the back of his neck felt like needles, as though a thousand eyes had fixed upon him.

'You have had no contact with your son?' a muted voice asked in Sienese-accented Toa Aloni.

'Not in the past few months,' his father replied. 'What is this about? Has Koro Ha done something wrong?'

There was no immediate answer, only the banging of chests being thrown open, the clattering of baskets being strewn across the floor, the snap of some piece of fabric being tossed aside. A grunt, then a thump as the mattress was upended.

'What is going on?' Eln Se wailed, voice straining against terror.

'The tutor Koro Ha is wanted in connection with rebellious activities throughout the empire,' the Sienese voice said, growing louder. Koro Ha heard the heavy sound of boots on the wooden floor, drawing nearer and nearer, almost to the window. 'Any who harbour him will face severe punishment, equal to those who render aid to enemies of the emperor himself.'

'My son is a scholar!' his father snapped. 'He passed your damn test. Why should he turn coat against you now, after abandoning his own family to serve you?'

The footsteps stopped. Koro Ha held his breath. The sharp smack of a palm striking flesh erupted, followed by a pained groan. Koro Ha clenched his fingers tight to keep his hands from shaking and clattering against the roof tiles.

'If you have any word from your son, inform your district magistrate immediately,' the Sienese voice said. Footsteps sounded on the stairwell, then faded. The door slammed shut and a handful of muffled voices speaking Sienese rose from the street below.

At last, he heard the shutters bang open.

'Quickly!' Eln Se hissed. 'Get inside.'

He scrambled through the window and collapsed, his arms and legs seized with uncontrollable shivering.

'You need to go *now*,' Eln Se said, already stuffing clothes into a rucksack. She tossed him a simple pair of trousers, a faded green shirt, and a threadbare travelling cloak. 'Put those on. They'll recognise you in a second by those silks.'

Koro Ha pulled his robe over his head, feeling—somewhere deep below the churning panic—a twinge of embarrassment for his sister to see him in his underclothes. She paused in her packing only to take his robe and add it to the rucksack, not bothering to fold the silk.

'You can sell it,' she said, 'but don't wear it. Every well-dressed Toa Aloni at the docks will be detained.'

'Where's father?' Koro Ha asked, closing the last button of his shirt.

Eln Se shook her head. 'Downstairs, on his cot, with a piece of meat on his eye to keep it from swelling.'

A pit opened in Koro Ha's stomach. He ran down the stairs to find his father sprawled out, moaning softly, with a thin slab of goat steak slapped onto the side of his face.

'That bastard hit harder than I thought he would,' his father muttered. 'Easy to hide bulk under all those robes, I guess.'

'I'm sorry,' Koro Ha said, kneeling at his father's side. 'This is all my fault.'

His father smiled weakly. 'You're damn right. And about time you caused some trouble, I say.'

Eln Se appeared in the stairwell and thrust the rucksack at Koro Ha. 'I'll wrap some bread and dried fruit in a cloth,' she muttered. 'You'd better get on your feet, Brother. They could be back any minute.'

Koro Ha's father cupped his son's cheek, patted it once, and then pushed gently against his chest. 'Go.'

The urge to say something meaningful nearly paralysed Koro Ha. He stood at the side of the cot, his father seeming at once powerful and frail. How ought a relationship between father and son, often fraught and distant but loving, in the end, be brought to that end?

'Koro Ha!' Eln Se thumped his shoulder with a packet of food. 'Put this in your bag and *go*.'

He took the packet. Did as she said. Tried to think of words for *this* relationship, with his sister, with whom he shared so little in common.

'I'm sorry,' he said. 'I've put you in danger.'

She blew air through her nose. Tears threatened the corners of her eyes.

'Get out of here,' she said. 'Write to me, if you can.'

'I'll see you again,' he lied.

She only smiled, took him by the shoulders, and walked him to the doorway.

'Good luck!' his father called from his cot. 'And make the bastards bleed!'

Koro Ha almost laughed. Who was he to warrant such a battle cry? Only a tutor on the back slope of middle age who had taken a chance on a principle and made himself an enemy of those who ruled the world.

Eln Se poked her head out of the doorway, looked up and down the alley. 'The harbour is that way,' she said, pointing. 'Stoop a little, like sailors do, and trust that the bastards won't be able to tell you apart from every other poor dark-skinned soul in this city.'

She hugged him, held him at arm's length. 'I don't know what's going on,' she said, 'but I'm proud of you. And Mother would be too.'

He hugged her back, said goodbye, and walked away, his back bent and his body thrumming with the urge to run.

* * *

Even on an ordinary day, a man dressed in commoner's clothes would draw suspicion in the district of walled estates where Orna Sin lived, yet Koro Ha disobeyed Eln Se and made his way there. He kept to alleyways and the edge of the road, trying to walk with the aimless gait of those desperate out-of-work labourers he had so often seen in childhood.

He rounded the corner onto Orna Sin's street and hesitated, sweeping the area for any guards or imperial agents who might be lying in wait. Seeing none, he steeled himself to approach the gate.

A hand clamped down on his shoulder. It belonged to a stocky hooded figure who dragged him into an alleyway.

'I'll go with you! I'll go!' Koro Ha babbled, all his eloquence lost to panic. 'Don't hurt me!'

'Shut up.' Yin Ila, captain of the *Swiftness of the South Wind*, threw back her hood. 'There are a dozen Sienese guards lurking in the garden who will be just *giddy* that you decided to come back. Follow me, and keep your head down. We need to get to the harbour.'

'What about Orna Sin?' Koro Ha said while Yin Ila pulled up her hood and set off. 'And Uon Elia? We can't leave him.'

'If Uon Elia is that recalcitrant bastard we had to smuggle out the servants' gate in a merchant's cart while the empire dragged Orna Sin away, then he's already on the boat,' Yin Ila said. 'Now let's *go*.'

Koro Ha followed her, the streets blurring into a wash of white, brown, green, and grey, the sounds of the city buzzing in his ears. Orna Sin had been taken. Likely to be tortured for information and killed. What would happen to their students? The parents of those students, particularly the five who studied under Uon Elia?

Koro Ha might escape, but he would leave such a wake of suffering behind.

'We have to help him,' Koro Ha said, suddenly nauseous. 'You're smugglers, aren't you? Accustomed to daring escapes and flouting the law?'

Yin Ila snorted and shook her head. 'From a jail out in some backwater, maybe, but he's in the magistrate's garden. There's no getting in or out of there without being noticed. The best thing, the *only* thing we can do for him, is see you and Uon Elia to safety.'

Koro Ha wanted to argue, as though he could articulate his desperation in a way that might convince the salt-toughened woman half-dragging him through the streets to turn around and shatter every chain that held Orna Sin captive. But broken hearts and stirring words alone could not overcome the strength of the empire.

The *Swiftness of the South Wind* had already raised two of its three gangplanks and lay low in the water, heavy with cargo. The first mate alone remained on the dock, speaking to the harbourmaster while the crew made final preparations to ship out.

Yin Ila made a sharp whistling sound like the cry of a songbird. The first mate glanced in their direction, then positioned himself between them and the harbourmaster before jabbing his finger at the manifest. While they argued, Koro Ha and Yin Ila boarded the ship and slipped belowdecks. Yin Ila shouldered a barrel aside, then knelt and produced a small brass pin that fit snugly into a crack in one of the floorboards and turned with a click. A hatch swung upwards, revealing a space just deep enough for a grown man to sit hunched over. And there, peering out of the shadows, Uon Elia huddled in terror.

'It's all right,' Yin Ila said. 'I brought you some company.'

Uon Elia flinched backwards, blinking against the light. He took a deep, shuddering breath, his head shaking on his bony neck.

'No,' he muttered. 'Nothing has been all right for decades. And it seems, Master Koro Ha, that, for you and I, nothing ever will be again.'

24

Flowing Towards the Sea

Foolish Cur

The leaves of early spring cast the forests of Nayen in emerald. As I flew over the island, I watched snow melt rushing to the sea, filling the floodplains in the south of our island on their way. So, too, flowed rivers of men and women, dressed as well as they could for war, with sickles and hunting bows braced against their shoulders.

As word of the atrocity at Setting Sun Fortress spread, every township and village emptied itself, as though a thousand dams had been shattered, spilling righteous fury into the countryside, ready to drown the Sienese.

My own anger roiled alongside them as I followed those rivers back to Iron Town. Already the mustered forces of the rebellion overflowed the walls. Our seven hundred warriors—the greater half belonging to the Army of the Wolf—had swelled to at least three thousand and, if my survey of the island was any indication, would swell by at least three or four thousand more.

Nearly two full Sienese legions. Fewer than the imperial forces gathering at Eastern Fortress, and far too few to overcome the punitive army that the emperor led from Sien, but enough, I thought, to hold the city if we could take it.

I swept down to the modest courtyard of the magistrate's palace and veered. Cramps seized me, forcing me to pause, wincing, for a moment. A full day on the wing carried with it a substantial cost, but it had been worth it to see with my own eyes the island's vengeful rise. My heart ached for Setting Sun Fortress, as did the heart of every brave Nayeni, it seemed.

Yet we had a second disadvantage beyond numbers. I crossed to the far corner of the courtyard. Wakes of sympathetic cramping and wafts of cinnamon scent rippled out from behind a stand of bamboo, where Clear-River oversaw my cadre at their daily practice. Doctor Sho lingered at the edge of the grove, as I had asked him to. The clawing terror birthed by my own first memories of veering clung to me, reawakened by my cadre's first attempts. Terror that quieted only when I knew that he was standing by, ready to intervene.

Clear-River, Running Doe, and nine of the new recruits to my cadre stood in a circle on the far side of the grove. A hawk crouched in the centre, its wings held tight against its body. In a burst of cinnamon scent, the hawk resolved into Torn Leaf. He crouched for a moment, taking slow breaths and massaging his arms, then looked to Clear-River with a satisfied grin.

'How long was that?' he asked.

'A count of twenty,' Clear-River answered. 'Better, but not yet good enough to fly.'

Torn Leaf's grin flattened, but he still seemed satisfied as he stood and filled the empty space in the circle. Clear-River raised an eyebrow at Running Doe. With the stoic expression of an ill-prepared student called to answer a difficult question, she walked to the centre of the circle and gripped tight her canon of witchcraft. I offered her a wave of encouragement, which only turned her face bright red.

'How are they faring, Sho?' I asked quietly, sidling up beside the doctor.

He shrugged his rounded shoulders. 'Making progress. None have gotten stuck yet. That little trick with the strips of bone seems to be working well enough.' He rolled his gaze towards me. 'You've been out surveying the island.'

It felt oddly like an accusation. 'All of Nayen has risen up. It reminds me of a quote from the sages.'

Doctor Sho perked up at that. 'Which one?'

'Traveller-on-the-Narrow-Way, in the Classic of Streams and Valleys,' I said, and recited:

> *The empire, like a garden, must be watered.*
> *With aid to the people in their time of need.*
> *Without these things, the nation becomes dry and brittle,*
> *and the fire of rebellion, stoked from a single falling spark,*
> *will rise up and consume all that is good.*

Doctor Sho harrumphed. 'There was more to that passage. They must have edited it.'

'Really?' I scoffed, and then was surprised that I had done so. Was it so unexpected that Tenet would alter his doctrine and his classics, just as he added to the canon of sorcery? Both were tools built in service to his ends, no more unchangeable or inherent to the world than an early draft of a poem. 'What was removed?'

Sho scratched at his beard. Conversation that wandered close to his past always made him uncomfortable. I resigned myself to yet another dead end and turned my attention back to Running Doe. She had squeezed her eyes shut. In rhythm to her deep, slow breathing, the heavy wake of the canon of witchcraft rolled out from her, but I felt only the faintest stiffness and a gentle whiff of cinnamon. Whatever had blocked her previous attempts to veer persisted, despite the fact that every other member of my cadre had managed it.

'It's been a long time,' Doctor Sho muttered. 'This might not be the exact wording, but it was something like this:

> *As the varieties of plants and animals that enliven a garden*
> *make it a place of joy and comfort.*
> *So the myriad peoples will become the strength of the empire,*
> *so long as they are not neglected,*
> *left to grow brittle,*
> *and to burn.*

I pondered the words. 'That doesn't sound like Traveller-on-the-Narrow-Way. The sentiments, perhaps, but the cadence is wrong, and some of the word choice is strange.'

'Maybe the aphorisms *you* know have the wrong cadence,' he groused.

His bizarre response that left me open-mouthed and confused until a cramp pulsed out from my core, curling my fingers and toes with waves of sudden agony. The world filled with the harsh smell of burnt cinnamon. With yelps of pained surprise, Torn Leaf and three of the others went to their knees. At the centre of the circle crouched an eagle hawk, wings held wide and feathers splayed.

A moment later, the wake snapped back, like a bowstring held taught and then released. Running Doe crouched on her hands and knees, panting heavily, a wide grin heavy on her face.

'I did it!' she breathed.

'And it hurt like a bloody knife in the guts!' Torn Leaf struggled to his feet, clutching his belly.

'Which wasn't her fault.' I stepped into the circle. 'If anything, you should be in awe of the power she has just demonstrated.'

'But she didn't do anything special,' Torn Leaf went on, glaring at me, his face all hard, grimacing angles. His expression rankled the most Sienese part of me that wanted respect from my cadre, my students.

Clear-River, whether anticipating my anger or sensing it, cut in. 'He has a point, Alder. The spell and its source were the same. How can you explain the greater potency of its wake when Running Doe wielded it as opposed to when I did, or Torn Leaf, or any of the others?'

'One of my teachers once told me that things want to be what they truly are,' I said, forcing calm into my voice 'The magic of veering changes the nature of a thing, if only temporarily. The wake it leaves is the resistance to that change. We can surmise, then, that of all of you, Running Doe is the most herself.'

I offered her a hand. She took it and let me help her to her feet, then leaned close.

'I'm sorry, but…' She frowned. 'What the hell is that supposed to mean?'

I blinked, then barked a laugh. She glared at me and withdrew to her place in the circle, embarrassed.

'It is difficult to say,' I mused aloud and shuffled the question to the back of my mind, where my subconscious could mull over it. Perhaps I would present it to Hissing Cat as well, though she had grown even more reserved than usual since our last conversation. 'At any rate, we should congratulate Running Doe on her hard-won success.'

'That you should.' My grandmother walked into the courtyard. Heavy bags hung beneath her eyes as her gaze swept over my cadre. It lingered for a moment on the burnt scraps of wood that Running Doe and four of the others wore. 'The lot of you should be very proud. I've never before seen a new crop of witches made ready to harvest so quickly. Thanks to you, we might have a fighting chance against the emperor and his Hands.'

My cadre exchanged satisfied glances while my grandmother sidled a step closer to me.

'We should speak,' she whispered. 'Meet me in the forest tonight. I'll conjure a candle flame.'

I began to ask her why, but she pressed a finger to her lips and gave a subtle shake of her head. I felt an echo of her knocking at my window, of forest shadows and the warped floors of the Temple of the Flame, and nodded in agreement. We had shared dangerous secrets before, but when we had lived beneath my father's roof, her every lesson had been illicit. If she were to teach me, she had to do so in the forest, shrouded in night.

Whatever she wanted to discuss would be similarly dangerous. The fractures that threatened the Nayeni rebellion had not yet fully healed, it seemed.

'Running Doe, lead practice with windcalling,' I said and reached into my pocket. The previous night I had crafted an eleventh canon, the first I had completed with all five of the magics I intended to give to the witches of my cadre.

Running Doe nodded sharply, then told her students to pluck leaves from the stand of bamboo. Soon a series of overlapping chills swept down my spine as they began to make the leaves dance in the cups of their hands.

'Clear-River.' I gestured for him to join me in the far corner of the courtyard. He did so, a curious expression on his face. There was something else, a subtle hardness behind his eyes. He wore it always when we were alone now, ever since the short-lived siege of Iron Town and the unification of the armies of the Wolf and Fox. I took the strip of bone from my pocket and offered it to him.

He ran a hand through the wild tangle of his hair. 'You've finished it.'

'I have.'

'I thought the first would be for Running Doe.'

'Well, if you think it ought to be,' I said and stepped to the side, as though making ready to call her over.

'No, no,' he said quickly and took the bone from my hand. He traced the fifth mark—a circle within a circle, inspired by Hissing Cat's previous lesson—with his fingernail, careful not to touch it with the pad of his thumb.

'This magic was not part of any pact,' I said. 'It has had no formal name, until now. I have decided to call it severing.'

He cocked his head but waited for me to go on.

'It is the magic I used to escape Voice Usher's binding sorcery,' I said. 'Unlike the other four magics of our canon, it reaches through the pattern of the world into the pattern of a mind and does its work there.'

A sudden paleness made his freckles stick out like dark stars on a white sky. His thumb flinched away from the fifth mark. His thick curls swept across his face as he shook his head once, furiously. 'Alder, you invaded my mind. It was the most horrifying thing I have ever experienced. I don't care how useful this is or whether it's the key to our victory. I won't do the same to another person.'

A hot wave of embarrassment rushed through me. Koro Ha would have castigated me for lack of clarity. 'No, I'm sorry, you misunderstand. This is a shield, not a weapon. As I said, it is a way to escape binding sorcery. Without it, the moment a Hand of the emperor manages to wrap you in chains of light, you will lose the power to wield magic. It *protects* your mind from their interference. All you need do is press your thumb to the fifth mark and any outside power will be stricken from your mind.'

I should have apologised for what I had done to him, and for what I had done to Frothing Wolf and Burning Dog. But it had all been necessary, hadn't it? And I hadn't *forced* them to agree with me, only communicated with absolute clarity.

Yet the necessary can still be harmful. There was value in accepting fault for the flawed means required to pursue good ends. This is, perhaps, the greatest lesson of my life.

It would have been an easy thing, and would have saved us both so much heartache, if I had only found the words. My throat closed over them even as I found the will to speak them.

Strange. Not long ago, I had been so willing to shoulder guilt and blame. Now, I felt a premonition that this first apology would shatter some vital gear of a terrible machine within me and I would collapse, unable to go on doing what was necessary, if horrifying, to save the world.

Instead, I put a hand on his shoulder. 'It is a gift, Clear-River. To protect you from what you fear the most.'

Something flickered across his face, a feeling I did not recognise, or perhaps one I was unwilling to accept.

'Then I'll say thank you, Alder.' He tucked the bone into his pocket and turned back to the cadre. I watched him and Running Doe teach them a while longer, until the present began to resonate too strongly with memories of Voice Golden-Finch's garden, and Hand Usher, and poisoned days I had once thought beautiful.

Long after the stars were out in full and the myriad birds of evening had given way to the occasional call of an owl, I felt a subtle flush and smelled the barest hint of cinnamon. I took the form of a raven and followed that warmth and scent from the merchant's house where Doctor Sho and I had taken up residence, over the walls of Iron Town, and into the forest.

The night was clear and crisp, rich with the fresh scent of new growth and budding flowers. My grandmother sat amid the gnarled roots of a fir tree, a flame cupped in the palm of her good hand. She snuffed it out as I approached.

'Here we are again,' she said, breaking the silence.

Despite her power, which I had once thought so vast, age had caught up with her. She seemed to have grown frail since Greyfrost—a lingering cost, perhaps, of the battle between Voice Usher's magic and mine, which had left her arm withered and shrunken as the branch of a dying tree.

'Last time we met like this, you left me with magic and an injunction to keep our people's ways alive,' I said. 'I wandered for a time, but I am doing what I can now. Nayen is united in common cause. Soon, the empire will be defeated and our island restored.'

The fingers of her withered hand curled. 'Is that so?' She let the question hang in the air. I felt an urge to answer it, but I knew my grandmother well enough to feel the weight and meaning of her pause. It needled me with childish guilt.

She leaned back against the rough bark of the tree. 'Have a seat, Cur.'

I eased myself onto a fallen log and waited.

'What do you make of this massacre at Setting Sun Fortress?' she asked at last.

'A terrible thing,' I said. 'Though not surprising. The empire is cruel and capricious.'

'But not stupid.' She leaned forwards, eyes sharp. 'If their intention was to slaughter Nayeni, they could have done so long ago. Why do this now, when the rebellion has momentum enough to turn this violence into a tool for recruitment?'

I thought of the scene of brutality on the Girzan steppe that Okara had shown me and Atar had described—corpses scattered between a dozen tents, the elders of a culture slaughtered and butchered like animals. There were other examples, too—the violence that had ripped through An-Zabat only a single day after the empire at last added windcalling to its canon; the obliteration of Sor Cala, the jewel of Toa Alon.

'Perhaps we give them too much credit,' I said. 'They are human, just as we are. How long did Frothing Wolf and Harrow Fox let petty jealousy and ambition stand in the way of the unity required to fight the empire?'

'But that is exactly my point.' She jabbed a finger at me. 'Why give us something like this to unite behind? Why stoke the fires of rebellion?'

The next words nearly caught in my throat, but I forced them into the world, and in doing so forced myself to accept their likely truth. 'Hand Pinion may have succumbed to his own worst nature. I have read the Sienese classics of tactics and battle, and any commander would call him a coward. Perhaps he felt that dealing out violence would re-establish his strength.'

She grumbled in her throat and leaned her elbow on her knee. 'Perhaps. But I say again, the empire is not stupid. There was a Voice at Setting Sun Fortress. The emperor would not indulge a single Hand's whims. Not when doing so might tip the balance of a war.' Her withered hand scratched at the side of her neck. 'This is some kind of trap. I know it in my bones. Like the promises of wealth they wielded to worm their way onto our soil. You may be foolish, Cur, but you aren't stupid either. I am right in this.'

I considered her words, fighting down a simmering apprehension. It was easy enough to explain Setting Sun Fortress as nothing more than an expression of the empire's worst nature. Yet the emperor, at the very least, must have anticipated how the people of Nayen would react. I tried to conceive of the island as a Stones board, as Oriole—always my better in strategy—would have imagined it. Apprehension boiled into panic.

'If it is indeed a trap,' I said, forcing calm into my voice, 'I intend to reverse it. A punitive army sails to Nayen, led by the emperor himself.'

Her eyes went wide. 'How do you know this?'

'I flew far in my trip around the island. Their ships are still weeks away. Eastern Fortress will fall before they arrive.'

'And then they will besiege us before we can resupply and fortify the city.' She sprang to her feet. 'Have you told Frothing Wolf and your uncle about this?'

I shook my head.

'Why the bloody hell not?' she fumed.

'As I said, I intend to reverse the snare. The emperor must not know—must not even suspect—that we anticipate his coming. Eastern Fortress will fall, and while the emperor prepares to besiege it, Hissing Cat and I will catch him unaware and put an end to him.'

'And if you fail? You lead us all to certain death! Gods, Cur, I see it now. They *wanted* us united. More, they wanted every half-sympathetic

Nayeni able to hold a spear to join us. Who will take up the cause of Nayeni liberation after this? Who will dare to *whisper* of freedom?'

'There is more at stake than only Nayen,' I said, fighting the urge to stand and stare her down. 'The emperor must be destroyed, Grandmother. This is our best chance. Yes, the risk is great, but the risk of doing nothing is greater.'

'Oh, I would love to see the bastard's head on a spear,' she snarled. 'But when I left your father's house, I left you with the most important task: keeping our ways, our people, alive. Now you gamble it all like a handful of coppers. You are powerful, Cur, but you have always been overconfident.'

'I won't be alone. In truth, I will only be Hissing Cat's second.'

'Ah, good.' She gave an exaggerated nod. 'Not even gambling on yourself, but on some ancient stranger with a half-understood agenda of her own.'

'What would you have me do?' Despite my best efforts, I found myself on my feet, towering over her, reminded again of how frail she had become. 'The cost of failure will be high, but not higher than the cost of going back to hiding in the mountains, winning meaningless skirmishes, taking, losing, and re-taking the same dozen villages and unimportant towns again and again. We could learn from the Wind-callers of An-Zabat, who would sooner let their city starve than give in to the emperor.'

My voice had taken on a tinny whine, as though we were back in the Temple of the Flame and I was begging her to teach me to conjure fire. I took a deep breath to calm myself and spoke with all the authority I could muster. 'This war will come to a final end, Grandmother. We will succeed or we will fail, but either way it will be *over*.'

She stared at me. Then she nodded slowly, stood, and rolled back her shoulders. 'I hope so, Grandson,' she said, and strode past me, back towards Iron Town.

'Wait!' I called after her. She paused but did not look back. 'You must not share what I have told you. Not even with Harrow Fox.'

She scoffed. 'Perhaps you should not have told *me*.'

The stub of my severed hand itched. I could reach into her mind, build barriers around what I had told her, prevent her from so much as *remembering* it, let alone sharing it with Frothing Wolf and Harrow Fox, who might balk if they knew they were the bait in my trap. It would gall me, but I had done worse things for worse reasons.

'Please, Grandmother,' I urged. 'Promise me. It must remain a secret. There could be spies among us—'

'Such as that magistrate you adopted and made into a witch?' Now she did turn around, her expression inscrutable in the shadows. She sighed, leaned her head back, and gazed for a moment at the stars. 'I was never any good at this part,' she said quietly, then went on with a sneer, her voice hardening with every word. 'Fine, Cur. I'll keep your secret. You are right, I suppose. The emperor has to be destroyed for this to end. This might be our only chance. But at what cost? You are treating lives like tools. Worse, like pieces upon a game board, to be spent and risked and lost to achieve your aims. I wonder if this is the empire's influence on you. I hope so. Then, at least, this callousness would be but a product of the evil I already fight, rather than some evil all its own.' Her withered arm flexed. 'Would that you had let me die at Greyfrost, that I might not have witnessed this.'

I stepped towards her, my heart hammering, something dark and painful gripping my throat. 'I am sorry, Grandmother. What is necessary is not always good. But this *is* necessary. It is the only way for the war to end in victory.'

'Perhaps, boy. But I have lived through several endings.' She lowered her gaze, shook her head once, and continued on her way back to the walls. 'They are never as final as they seem.'

25
Shelter
Koro Ha

In the week after their flight from Sor Cala, Koro Ha used what
little he knew of astronomical navigation to track their journey,
squinting at the sun and stars and scribbling rough calculations on
scraps of paper. Uon Elia spent most of each day hiding in the hold,
shying from the width of the sky and the brightness of the sun, coming out only at night to brace himself on the gunwale and stare at the
horizon in silent awe. After his first fatalistic words upon their departure, Uon Elia had said nothing, despite Koro Ha's many attempts to
draw him into conversation.

On the eighth day out from Sor Cala, a coastline appeared on the
horizon—the dark, jagged shape of the Black Maw. A home to pirates
and smugglers, Yin Ila had called it on their previous visit. Safe, perhaps, from the empire, but dangerous in its own right and no place to
guard the last of the stonespeakers, let alone find students to whom
Uon Elia might pass down his art.

The next day, beneath a cloudy sky, with a brisk wind to churn the
waters, the *Swiftness of the South Wind* eased its way under the power
of its oars through a forest of jutting rocks that rose from the ocean
floor, which Yin Ila called the Teeth. Some broke the surface, but she

claimed that far more lurked just below, invisible to the eye but no less threatening to the hull. The pilot nudged the ship gently this way and that with the tiller, avoiding obstacles either by memory or by some method of discernment unimaginable to Koro Ha. The Black Maw itself loomed large, a jagged-edged cone of porous rock.

As they came around the back side of the island, the pilot cut inland. Beneath a harsh overhang, ships stood moored to makeshift wooden docks. Severe, narrow switchbacks led up to a small city built into the walls of a vast cove lit by hundreds of hanging lanterns. The walls of the cove sloped inward, forming a concave ceiling over the cove like the mouth of a colossal cave.

Koro Ha went below and, after a great deal of cajoling and badgering, managed to compel Uon Elia onto the deck. The stonespeaker gazed slack-jawed at the scale of the cavern before them.

'Not that different from home, is it?' Koro Ha said.

'Incredibly different,' Uon Elia replied, 'but wondrous in its own way.'

The old stonespeaker's voice sent a jolt of surprise through Koro Ha after so many days without speaking.

'I'm glad you think so,' Koro Ha said. 'Perhaps living here for a time will not be so bad.'

To his frustration, Uon Elia only grunted in response and returned to his sullen silence.

'Come,' Yin Ila said as the oarsmen brought the ship to a halt and a whoop of relief went up from the crew. Not everyone on board, it seemed, had been confident in the *Swiftness*'s pilot. 'Orna Sin keeps a room here. It's yours for now. I'll show you to it.'

Koro Ha shouldered his rucksack and helped Uon Elia down the steep gangplank. The dock proved no less treacherous, constructed as it was from the curved hulls and rotting decks of countless shipwrecks. Koro Ha supported Uon Elia as they picked their way across the precarious, many-angled walkway.

'Victims of the Teeth,' said Yin Ila, showing a pair of golden incisors in her broad grin, which added striking points of colour to her dark, handsome face. 'You see? You are well protected, here.'

The streets of the Black Maw, if they could be called such, were little more than staircases cut roughly into the rock. Uon Elia panted and puffed his way upwards, pausing every dozen steps to brace his elbows on his knees and cough until he'd caught his breath. Finally, they reached a wooden facade complete with broad double doors salvaged from some massive merchant ship.

'The *Wavebreaker.*' Yin Ila gestured towards the structure with her chin. 'One of the nicer hidey-holes on offer.'

The reassurance only added to Koro Ha's deepening misery.

A wash of cool air swept through the doors as they entered the *Wavebreaker*, dizzying Koro Ha after the heat that radiated from the dark rock of the island. To Koro Ha, accustomed as he was to an increasingly luxurious series of tutor's apartments, the narrow room Yin Ila led them to seemed little larger than a closet. Uon Elia collapsed onto one of the cots and lay staring at the wooden ceiling.

'Orna Sin owns this place, so no need to worry about payment,' Yin Ila said. 'You'll be safe here for as long as you need to stay.'

Koro Ha did not point out that neither of them could begin to estimate how long that might be. He only thanked Yin Ila, squeezed her hand, and asked her to send word of Orna Sin should she learn anything.

'I'll spread word that there's a scribe here looking to make what coin he can.' She smiled, a poor mask over her own uncertainty. 'People on the Black Maw aren't fond of records, but some of the larger operations haven't got any choice but to write a few things down. That should keep you in food and such for the time being.'

She left them then to fend for themselves in a strange place full of dangerous people, protected only by the wealth and reputation of a friend who very likely languished in a Sienese prison. If, of course, he was not already dead.

As she had promised, Yin Ila spread word of Koro Ha's skills, and every week or so a captain or quartermaster would call at the *Wavebreaker* in need of a scribe, usually to read recently acquired documents of unspecified origin. These often included the manifests of ships that their bearers—if they had any rightful claim to the documents in question—ought to have already known.

Between these short bursts of employment, Koro Ha was left with large stretches of empty time and no meaningful way of filling it. A month into his exile on the Black Maw, a ship put in bearing a small library. He traded his silk robe to buy up as many volumes as he could, many of which turned out to be dubious histories of the imperial provinces composed by a retired magistrate. After two months, Koro Ha had wrung the text dry of any meaning—as well as any amusing absurdities worthy of ridicule—and was again left despondent.

He took to walking the stairs cut into the face of the rock, an activity that at least devoured time and left him tired enough to sleep at the end of a long day. More than once he invited Uon Elia to join him, but the stonespeaker would not respond. He spent his days staring vacantly at the ceiling, the walls, or the sea through the lone porthole in their room. Only once in the first month did he speak, to ask Koro Ha if he had seen anything growing on the island in his wanderings. Koro Ha had not.

'This is a dead place,' Uon Elia muttered. 'Not fit for life.'

'You endured decades beneath the earth,' Koro Ha said. 'This, too, will end.'

Uon Elia grunted, turned back to the window, and returned to silence, giving no sign of when he would speak again.

Three months after their arrival, dark clouds gathered in the northeast. A storm, bearing down from the open sea, struck the Black Maw. Winds howled against the porous rock while rain and waves turned its paths slick and treacherous. Typhoon season, the owner of the *Wavebreaker* told Koro Ha. Those ships already in port would stay there till it ended, and no new ships would be arriving anytime soon.

Isolation and boredom clawed at him, caged as he was within the confines of this bizarre shipwreck-turned-inn. The curving wooden walls left him longing for the set of landscape paintings that had been his silent companions for so many years, now abandoned, boxed up somewhere on Orna Sin's estate. He found some solace in the *Wavebreaker*'s ample supply of cheap liquor and spent most of a month either drunk or hungover, writing morose poetry by night before tearing up the pages by day.

Ten years of study with Teacher Zhen. Sweat and tears. The examinations. Three decades of work as a tutor. A life spent trying to crack the wall separating the upper echelons of Sienese society from their provincial subjects. But then Wen Alder—that brilliant, idiot boy— had seen the right and wrong of the world and betrayed the empire, dragging Koro Ha and who knew how many other unfortunates down with him. Now it all would end in self-imposed exile on a scrap of jagged stone in the middle of the sea raked day and night by wind and waves, his mind left to decay and fester in a stew of sorghum wine.

Until one morning he woke to the sound of rattling breaths and vicious coughing. Uon Elia struggled in his bunk, pushing himself upright on shaking arms. Koro Ha, shocked awake into sober clarity, eased his hands beneath the stonespeaker's back and gently helped him up into a more comfortable position. Uon Elia took deep breaths, his lungs grating as though they were full of gravel.

'Thank you,' he gasped.

'We should get you a doctor.' Koro Ha's mind reeled. After seventy years of living beneath the earth, why would sickness take the old man now?

Uon Elia shook his head and squeezed Koro Ha's arm weakly. 'If I could be helped, I would do it myself. It has been growing for years and years, kept at bay by my magic.' Another fit of coughing nearly doubled him over. Koro Ha held him but could think of nothing else to do. Eln Se would have known. She had tended their mother during her slow decline while Koro Ha was away teaching in Sien.

'Stress and the weather here haven't helped,' Uon Elia said softly once the fit had passed. 'It came on faster than I'd hoped. But that is the way of such things.'

'There is nothing you can do?' Koro Ha said, an old, buried regret resurfacing. *The way of such things.* He'd left to return home the day after receiving word of his mother's sudden decline, only to set foot in Sor Cala weeks after her funeral.

'I can hold on a while longer,' Uon Elia said, then looked up at Koro Ha, his rheumy eyes searching. 'Long enough, at least, to pass on what I must.'

Koro Ha felt a strange, disquieting numbness. 'To me?'

'There is no one else,' Uon Elia said. 'Not unless these storms stop and the next ship brings us a bright Toa Aloni ten-year-old.'

Koro Ha laughed, in part because of the horrifying absurdity of what Uon Elia proposed. He, who had spent his life chasing a dream of success within the imperial system, now an outcast, to spend the rest of his days—and they might be long in number, if Uon Elia was any indication—stranded on a rock in the middle of the sea, the last vessel of Toa Aloni magic.

'My knowledge either dies with me or lives on in you,' Uon Elia said after a long, laboured breath. 'It is your choice.'

'It shouldn't be me,' Koro Ha said, swallowing regret and mania. 'I was happy—thrilled! ecstatic!—to help you, to guide those children, to help them rekindle what Toa Alon was before the empire destroyed it. One of them should learn this from you, should carry on the torch of our ways and our magic. Not me.'

'Nonsense,' retorted Uon Elia, his voice gathering strength.

'Do you know why they came for us? Not because of Orna Sin's crimes, nor your secrets, but because a former student of mine betrayed them to join his people in rebellion. He has cast aside everything I taught him and taken up the sword. And, much as the empire may be my enemy now...' He swallowed a lump and a wry chuckle slipped through his clenched teeth. 'I think I hate him for it, Uon Elia. It feels like he has betrayed me, as well as the empire. And you say I should carry Toa Alon's future, become the guardian of its magic—'

'I do.'

Koro Ha ran a hand through the tangled curls of his hair. 'I am Toa Aloni in flesh and blood, but my mind is Sienese.'

Uon Elia heaved himself up on his elbows. His body shook with effort, but he held Koro Ha's gaze and spoke firmly. 'You are Toa Aloni. I saw the light in your eyes while I taught those children. You believed in what we did. Your student hurt you, but you must not hate him. He resists, just as we stonespeakers resisted by surviving, as Orna Sin resisted by skirting imperial law, and as we will go on resisting, even in our banishment. Resistance is not a thing without cost. But if enough of us accept that cost, perhaps the world can change—and for the better, for once.'

He collapsed, taking a deep, rattling breath before going on. 'Yet you are right. It *ought* to be one of the children who carries on our magic. But it *will* be you, and not undeservedly. Not only because there is no one else.'

Koro Ha leaned his shoulder against the curved wall of their room, once the bulkhead of a ship, old hopes dying within him, but with them old regrets. The last finger clinging to the future he had hoped for at last gave way. In a life where he had made many poor choices, this, despite its incongruity with all that he had dreamed, was hardly a choice at all.

Once the storms had passed, Koro Ha helped Uon Elia to venture down to the docks, where smugglers and pirates sold and traded with each other and the island's few permanent inhabitants. The stonespeaker shut his eyes and leaned heavily on Koro Ha's arm while they walked the ad hoc marketplace.

'There's little chance we'll find material for the traditional pigments,' Uon Elia muttered, eyes pinched shut while they made their slow way down a boardwalk of broken hulls, slick with recent rain and swaying in the wind and unquiet waters. 'But if there's anything of use to be found, I will find it.'

'With your eyes closed?' Koro Ha said.

'With dowsing magic,' Uon Elia said. 'The simplest of our arts. The first you will learn.'

Koro Ha still struggled to accept the new future unfolding before him. His life had always been defined by text. The classics. Doctrine. Poetry. Perhaps his own writings, when he indulged them or was forced to sell his literacy for wages.

Magic was a thing bound in tragic history or locked behind the thickest walls of imperial secrecy, reserved for only the highest echelons of Sienese society. Wen Alder's marking with the tetragram had been the closest Koro Ha had ever come, and had assumed he *would* ever come, to magic. Perhaps, in a few years, Quon Lo or Lon Sa—or Tul Elna; the stonespeakers always counted women among their ranks, after all—might have begun to learn, and he might have borne witness, but he had never imagined *himself* as the student.

In the end, despite his dowsing, Uon Elia was unable to find the cobalt he required for the colour of his ink. He decided instead to do what he could with the verdigris that clung to every copper coin on the island.

'It is entirely safe and sterile,' Uon Elia insisted when Koro Ha eyed him scraping green flakes from a handful of coins into a small clay pot. 'Cobalt would yield a better colour, of course…'

Uon Elia mixed the verdigris with charcoal, a few drops of water, a pea-sized pearl of acacia gum, and a splash of sorghum alcohol filtered through a cheese cloth, all ground together with a wooden pestle until it became a paste, green and bright as leaves in early spring.

Koro Ha took a deep breath, trying desperately to settle his mind. He balked from the procedure—from the weight of it rather than merely the pain. New responsibilities would settle on his shoulders as the ink settled into his flesh. Responsibilities that seemed impossible to fulfil, stranded as he was on a tiny island, surrounded by no one but pirates and smugglers.

He should have been enduring Bo Spring-Happiness's blank stares and inattention, gritting his teeth, dragging the boy towards what little success he could manage and then easing into retirement. His own cottage. Decent wine and a pipe every night. Maybe a servant or two. The companionship of other scholars, if he was lucky.

'I can hold your lip with my fingers.' Uon Elia stoked the brazier and heated the tip of a contraption he had made from a sewing needle and a length of string. 'Or I can prop it open. There is a device I can make quickly, from strips of wood, that will—'

'Fingers, if you must,' Koro Ha said, trying to hide the wince in his voice.

Uon Elia pointed to the liquor bottle. 'Take a drink first to dull the pain a bit.'

Koro Ha swallowed a mouthful of sorghum liquor, hissing as it burned down his throat and warmed his chest.

'You'll need more than that,' Uon Elia said.

Koro Ha took three more swallows.

Uon Elia took the needle glowing from the coals, picked up his pot of ink, and crossed the room to the chair on which Koro Ha sat. 'Bite down on this,' he said, handing Koro Ha a scrap of wood wrapped in cloth. 'I don't want you biting me or cracking a tooth.'

The statement did little to ease Koro Ha's worry, but he bit down and waited while Uon Elia dipped the needle. Regardless of his misgivings and the winding road that had brought him to this moment, he *wanted* this. A purpose. Why else had he let Orna Sin lure him away from his intended path?

In the moment Uon Elia pushed his upper lip away from his teeth and jabbed the needle, he realised that his anxiety was in truth something more sublime, more profound. It was born of fear not of danger, nor of failure, but of having been cast into the centre of great forces, like the captain of a ship pulled into a raging storm, hoping he had the ability required to pass through to the other side.

An uncomfortable greatness was thrust upon him, accompanied by several minutes of agony as Uon Elia made the mark of his power, prodding from the back of his upper lip down. Koro Ha tasted blood and swallowed it.

And then it was over, the last injection made. As pain diffused and softened, something deeper and more frightening welled into him, taking its place.

A light flickered at the centre of his mind. A stream gently bubbled through his consciousness, like a stray thought or a half-remembered word, waiting for him to reach out and grasp it.

This was magic, he knew, yet dared not reach for it. Not yet. Not without guidance.

'There.' Uon Elia backed away, coughed into his cheeks, wiped blood from the tip of his needle, and smiled, showing the twin of the mark he had just made. 'I wish we had a mirror. It suits you, believe it or not. One might even call you dashing.'

Part Three
Hubris

Interlude

A Storm to Scour the World

Ral Ans Urrera is no longer a thinking thing.

Memory haunts her as she travels, day and night, the wind-skiff's kite full before her, the grass hissing against the hull, her leaden body held aloft by grief and rage.

She remembers the pulse of joy at the sight of the tents atop the mesa, the glacial cataracts filling the dry air with a gentle, frigid spray that cut sunlight into brilliant colours. Then the creeping dread. The emptiness where the whickering of horses, the shouts of children, the laughter of women at work should be.

She remembers the corpses with the clarity of a pool filled only by the rain. Their blood soaking the hide floors, the earth beneath. Bones and meat displayed as by a butcher. Shanks and legs. Tongues. Heads, their eyes still staring, their faces swollen and putrid and all but unrecognisable.

But they had been the tents of her people, painted with their patterns. And, in one of those bloated faces, she sees her father's eyes.

Then, as the stillness of stupefaction breaks into grief, the memories become unclear, stirred and rippling and muddied. She calls lightning. Fills the air with smoke and the stink of burning flesh. Screams her grief at the uncaring sky, begging for the Skyfather to hurl a spear to scour the world clean, to devour the empire, devour her, and leave loam and ash for a rebirth into something better, for there can be no more goodness in this life.

And a voice, as though in answer, speaking into the back of her mind: *I have thrown that spear.* A voice silenced by all too familiar light, blinding and binding her, and muting all but her agony.

Time blurs. She remembers choking on smoke and her own voice, calling again and again for her father and mother, for her sister, for the elders who brought her into her power. And it *fills* her, as it filled her then, lying in the smoke, Atar screaming her name.

She grasps, as she grasped in the belly of the ship, but wrapped in the storm of her agony and anger, in the memory of shattered flesh and bone, the pain that lances through her is but a biting fly.

The aurora bends, flickers, and breaks into a thousand dimming stars.

The Hand of the emperor stares at her, says something softly, his eyes slowly widening in disbelief.

His turn to break, to become no more than a smear of glistening ash.

Now she sits on one of the benches of Atar's wind-skiff, wrapped in a silver-threaded scarf against the chill that has settled in her bones. Atar sails back towards the Waste. Ral will become what the An-Zabati wanted: a weapon in their war.

'Turn around,' she says.

Jhin looks up from that little book of his, where he is always scribbling. Atar frowns back at her from her place at the front of the ship.

'Ral, there is nothing—'

'There is.' Ral sees an unfamiliar flicker in the dancer's eyes. Something like fear. 'You promised to take me home, Atar. My people's true home was never the steppe.'

Jhin tilts his head, curious. It is a weakness Atar shares.

'Where is your home, then?' she asks.

'Sail north and east,' Ral answers, finding no word for the Skyfather's Hall, nor its soaring, jagged walls, in the trading tongue. 'You will know it when you see it.'

Another moment of hesitation while Atar considers, and Ral feels the first stirring of a new anger until Atar calls a wind, sending a fresh chill down the length of Ral's spine, and begins to turn the skiff.

Ral wakes with the dawn, her body aching from a night sleeping on the sand, and not long after their cook fire is doused Atar begins to speak, spinning mad tales mangled by the imprecision of the trading tongue. Talk of gods, of war, of the voice of a great wielder of magic speaking into her mind from across the sea. Jhin watches it all, jotting in his little book, but says nothing. While Atar speaks, her eyes flit from side to side, though the dancer's voice is heavy with conviction.

'You do not truly believe these things,' Ral says.

Atar meets her gaze. 'I do not know them for a certainty, but they are a warning from one I trust well.'

'I understand your fear.' Ral smiles, hoping to soothe her. 'But this is not a wind you can turn aside.'

'He spoke to me from across the sea, wielding magic he was never granted by any mark,' Atar presses. 'That should be impossible, as your magic is impossible. It is not difficult, then, for me to accept his warning, even if it is difficult—'

'Will you take me home, as you promised?'

Slowly, Atar shakes her head. 'We should go back, Ral, even if Fire-caller is wrong. Gather my people. With your help, we might—'

'You saw me break the binding light?'

This time she nods.

'Then you know I do not fear them. Not anymore. No Hand or Voice can hold me.'

'But you can still be killed.'

Ral sighs and leans forwards, stuffing disappointment down below the churning anger with the rest of the things she cannot afford to feel.

'I am sorry, Atar,' she says, and reaches for magic.

She has seen it wielded twice now. Has explored its painful texture, learned it as intimately as her own power—a far simpler way to learn than nights lashed to the back of a horse, bathed in the roar of thunder.

Atar shouts and topples onto her side, wrapped in ropes of light. Ral feels them like a distant echo of the tormenting aurora, but extending from the back of her mind. No threat to her. She has conquered this magic, made it her own.

'What are you doing?' Atar demands.

Ral gathers up their supplies. She arches her brows at Jhin, who sits with his brush dripping ink onto his little book. He curls into himself and fails to meet her eyes. 'I will release the spell when I am on my way. If you are fortunate, herdsmen will find you.'

'And if they don't?' Atar twists against the bonds.

Ral shrugs, lifts the silver bowl from one of the rucksacks, and sets it beside Atar. 'At least you will not want for water.'

Atar goes on calling after her as Ral mounts the wind-skiff, but she pays the words no mind. Nor does she entertain the twinge of regret that threatens her.

She does not know Atar's magic as well, but she has spent weeks now in the company of the An-Zabati, upon their ships, feeling the chill of their power. The wind she calls echoes the storm within her, swift and furious. The grass hisses in terror at her passing. The earth trembles. Even the bones of the wind-skiff shake and threaten to shatter, but she does not care.

Let it all fall apart. Only let her have vengeance.

Clouds billow overhead. Fat raindrops patter on the splintered deck, slick Ral's hair to her skull, and threaten to batter the kite-sail back to earth. Cold, both brought by the storm and in answer to her magic, wraps her bones and fills her lungs. For three days now she has held a reckless wind, pausing only to eat handfuls of dried fruit and drink from the lone waterskin aboard—kept in case of emergency, for no An-Zabati windcaller ever feared want of water.

She cannot see the sun or stars, but it no longer matters. The Skyfather's Hall stands tall on the horizon, a jagged crescent of stone heaved up from below the earth. No larger than the tip of her finger at first, now tall as the palm of her hand and visible as a dark smear even through the haze.

The wind-skiff leaps over rolling hills, its pontoon arms shrugging in flight for a heartbeat before crashing and cracking back to earth. The maelstrom fills the sail as much as the wind Ral has called. Still she does not relent. She will either break against the walls of the Sky-father's Hall or break through them.

She is a storm. To let herself be slowed will spell her ending.

The wall draws ever closer till it dominates the horizon, and her awe draws up a memory, the founding myth of her people: the Skyfa-ther's fist falling from among the stars to shatter a tyrant king, casting up waves of stone in its wake.

The memory distracts her from the path ahead. One of the pontoons cracks against a buried boulder. The deck bucks beneath her, then leaps from the earth and rolls in the air, dumping her to the ground.

When the world stops spinning, she finds herself lying in the basin between two hills, pain pulsing from one shoulder and pounding at her ribs. She tries to stand. A lance of agony strips her muscles of their strength. She collapses, gasping.

The rain hammers her and the wind screams. Thunder rumbles through the haze. Lightning flashes.

She feels it all twice, once in her body and once in that strange second way honed on the back of a stallion. Her flesh might be broken, but her spirit, and her magic, are strong. Too strong to accept her own suffering.

A distant, bestial sound seeps from her throat, but she finds her feet, her good arm clutching the fragments of her ribs while the other hangs loose, the shoulder grinding in its socket.

Ral fixes her eyes on the Skyfather's Hall. Takes a step, bites her tongue to keep from blacking out, and takes another.

The gates of the Skyfather's Hall are polished oak, banded in iron, fixed to hinges as tall as she is. They do not match the walls of uncut stone rising from the earth in waves. She looks to the top of the walls, expecting drawn bows or grenadiers ready to hurl fire down upon her, but makes out only vague silhouettes through the mist and rain.

She breathes deeply, fills one lung and swallows bile that rises with the pain in the other, and places her good hand against the wood.

The cold of windcalling crackles into furious heat, surging up from her core through her fingers, fanning out into arcs of lightning, black-ening the boards, turning them to ash and flame. She hears nothing but the drumming of her own heart as she calls another wind, this one dense and solid as a fist, to pound the blackened gates to splinters. They buckle inwards and fall, carving through the rain. The earth leaps beneath her feet as they collapse. Sculpted stone horses rear in the four corners of the plaza beyond, their nostrils flaring and forelegs stirring the air. Carved generations ago, they are a presentiment of the fury visited here this day, she is certain as she strides through the plaza, dislocated arm swinging freely, shattered ribs forgotten.

She calls up a robe of sunlight, bright and shielding, and a wind to buoy her failing body, and lightning to roar in her hands, cold and heat warring within her as the world roars in answer to her magic. The Sienese come for her as she strides through the city, towards the long house at the heart of the Skyfather's Hall. Soldiers at first, with crossbows and grenades that they never have a chance to wield before she scours their lives from the record of the world.

The plaza pours into streets built wide enough for horse lords to ride three abreast, parading their herds in full regalia. People run from her, screaming, and cower behind the walls of their earthen houses—but not all. Some, who have not forgotten the stories of the elders, watch in awe. A few gather kitchen knives, hammers, hunting bows, and simple tools and follow behind her, recognising her for what she is and seizing liberation.

They are to her as raindrops to a river. She carries them in her current, towards the centre of the city. Another gate bars her way, smaller but flanked by towers where guards stand ready, among them a Hand of the emperor. Bolts dart from crossbows and find the bodies of her followers, who answer with stones and slings and arrows of their own. Ral feels the roiling weight of the aurora, sees the Hand raise his arm as the ropes of light wheel down.

The light touches her and burns away before her fury like grass in drought. She makes a gesture of her own, in mockery, though pain seizes her flank and shoulder. Twin bolts of lightning arc upwards. Thunder roars, and with it the towers and the gate they guard burst into charred wood and shattered bodies.

Dust settles on Ral's shoulders as she presses on. The Hand lies in the rubble. His eyes jitter in his head and a soothing magic rolls out from him. A shallow cut along his brow begins to close, as though sewn shut by some invisible needle. Ral pauses, watches as he rises up on his elbows, tries to lever himself off the broken rafter that skewers his gut.

She takes pity and burns away the last of his life.

The long house is in sight now, its ridge carved with galloping horses, manes whipping in the wind. A Girzan decoration flanked by Sienese corruptions—columns built to either side of the grand stair, wrapped in coiling lion serpents.

A gust of wind hurls the doors open. Shafts of light carve through the darkness from high in the bracketing of the ceiling. One falls upon a raised dais and the throne atop it, upon which sits a robust, thick-shouldered man. Hair like threads of ink-dark silk flows over his shoulders. Silver lines shimmer on his brow.

He rises, hands folded in his sleeves. Opens his mouth and begins to speak in the tongue of her people.

Lightning burns out from her, scores a furrow down the length of the chamber. The Voice raises a shield of light to mirror hers, deflecting her rage into the ceiling, the walls, until fires seethe and fill every corner with flickering light and shadow. The Voice lunges to the side. The wide backing of his throne explodes into a cloud of flaming splinters, but he rolls, finds his feet, and hurls his own bolt of lightning in answer.

Ral staggers backwards, feverish heat and pressure building where his attack hammers her shield. The pain in her ribs and shoulder surge, but she keeps her balance, finds her focus. She is a storm. She will not be—

Another lightning strike sends her to her knees. She gasps, clutches her ribs.

The Voice stands tall now and walks slowly, one hand behind his back, the other outstretched, hurling bolt after bolt of magic.

Ral's robe of light flickers. She can feel it fading from the world, the chill it draws down her spine lessening as her grip weakens and it sloughs away. A shadow pushes in at the edges of her vision, building with each throb of pain.

Even the storm within her begins to fade.

She sees her father, seated tall atop his saddle while they ride away from the Skyfather's Hall at the head of their herd, his mouth full of warnings, his eyes bright but worried. Then she sees those eyes again, lit by roaring flames, shouting for her to run, vanishing behind a stampede of horses while the Sienese destroy their camp, scatter her people, and—because she hesitated, because she could not bear to leave them all behind—seize her, wrap her in chains of light, and bury her in the bowels of their ship.

A face peers up at her from the blood-smeared depths of a tent, its eyes dead and empty, its flesh swollen around a broken skull. One of dozens, but she cannot draw her gaze from it, cannot shake the feeling that she knows those eyes, that she saw in them, not so long ago, a bright flash of pride and a flicker of worry.

Grief claws at her throat. She sags, the physical pain, the pressure of the Voice's lightning, the fading of her shield forgotten. There is only the swallowed agony, the sobs captured and forced into the hollow of her chest, left to fester and infect the marrow of her bones.

What are you doing, Daughter?

Words not her own, crackling and bright, echo in the aching cavern of her mind.

Is this the way a storm should end?

A sob roils up to fill her throat and she collapses to the floor.

The surging, feverish heat of the Voice's lightning ceases. She is left shivering, wrapped in the last fragments of her shield, ribs and shoulder grinding against the splintered floor. A shadow falls over her. It is too much effort to raise her head, to look her killer in the eye.

'Will you come quietly, now?' the Voice says in flawless Girzan. 'You are through, I hope, with running away?'

There is a spark of confusion somewhere deep in the cloud of her pain and grief.

The Voice grunts. 'No words in your own defence, eh? You cost us four Hands, a Voice, and a windship. I can only trust in the emperor that you will be worth such sacrifice. Hard to believe of a woman, but here we are.'

Her confusion flares into a burning question. She finds the strength to turn her head, to roll her eyes up towards the looming Voice, who sneers down at her in fury.

'What do you want with me?' she asks.

'To stop you from destroying this place and killing any more of its people.' The Voice smooths a lock of hair and shrugs. 'And then to take you to Centre Fortress and the emperor, where you should have been delivered weeks ago.'

An answer that is not an answer. 'To what end?'

The Voice glares down. 'The emperor has not deigned to share his designs for you.'

Her thoughts spin, filling with the bodies she has shattered in her wake. 'They didn't know?' It seems impossible. How could anyone commit such brutality, pour such hatred and terror into the world, without reason?

'It is not our place to know, only to obey.' The Voice opens his hand. 'You seem to have found a way to break binding sorcery, but there are other, more direct ways of controlling you. I have permission to drain you of blood to the point of death, kept alive only by healing sorcery, if you will not co-operate. What do you say, girl? Do you prefer the more painful road?'

She tries to move, but her muscles are cords of dead weight looped around her bones.

The Voice narrows his eyes at her. 'Gone silent, have you?' He reaches to his belt, draws a knife, kneels beside her. 'Make up your mind or I will make it for you, and I doubt you'll agree with my decision.'

She remembers the Hand, skewered, his life's blood pouring into the rubble of a guard tower, and remembers the strand of cool, calming magic he clung to. She paws for it with the last of her strength.

The Voice's eyes widen. He stands, steps back, but her good hand finds the hem of his robe and pulls. Not much, but enough to topple him and send the knife tumbling from his grip.

Darkness seeps in at the edges of her vision, but her rage burns hot. The knife is there, by her hand. Her fingers find the blade, then the polished wood of the handle. The Voice shouts, scrambles to his feet, reaching for magic. Then screams as she plunges the blade into his thigh. She pulls him to the ground beside her, scrapes the blade free, drives it into his stomach, his chest, his throat, again and again until the world falls silent and the numbing darkness drags her down.

Pain returns first, carving its way up and down the lines of her limbs. Then warmth, the gentle glow of dying embers. She opens her eyes. The Voice sprawls beneath her, robes crusted with blood. Bile rises in her. There is no more rage, no more storm to burn it away.

Around her, the long house is scarred but standing. She rolls off the Voice's corpse and finds her feet, shaking and breathing heavily. Sound filters in through the shattered places between the rafters. Shouts of battle. Clashing steel.

The storm may have died in her, but it still surges through the world. It will find her, sweep her up again, and carry her to her purpose before long. For now, she is too exhausted to think of anything but rest. She heaves herself up the stairs to the Voice's dais and slumps onto the charred remnant of his throne.

Time slips through her, leaving an impression of the setting sun, of seeping cold, of quiet in the aftermath of chaos, of footsteps and a voice that draws her out of stupor.

'Ral?' Careful steps, skirting the rubble, the corpse, the pooling blood. She opens her eyes. An impossible, familiar face peers up at her, wind burnt, lined with concern and fatigue. 'Are you all right?'

Ral smiles. Of course the dancer would find a way to follow and would come to understand. 'I am fine, Atar. I need to rest now that it is over.'

But of course—as the words within her, yet which are not her own, are quick to remind her, speaking from the well of her pain—the storm is only beginning.

26

A Plan

Foolish Cur

On the march from Iron Town, I attacked the education of my cadre with urgency. Eastern Fortress loomed ahead, and all twelve of them—Running Doe and Clear-River among them—would need at least the four magics I had granted with my canon. Yet the curious inconsistency evidenced by Running Doe's struggle to veer reappeared.

Torn Leaf, despite his skill with veering and flame, proved a poor hand with windcalling, never able to shape the air into anything more complex than a shield or a lance. I had him exchange strips of bone with Running Doe one night, theorising that defects in my carvings or the bones themselves explained these differences. Yet Running Doe remained unable to hold her veering for more than a handful of moments, and Torn Leaf proved unable to weave the complex shapes of wind I asked of him, though his face turned purple and the cold wake of his effort chilled us all to the bone.

Each of their minds interacted differently with the canon I had made, or perhaps with the pattern of the world itself. My canon was a seal, but they were all different sorts of paper with differing weaves and grains. Some drank the ink, leaving a vibrant but indistinct mark, while others, more densely woven, captured a sharper but less richly coloured image.

Did Hands and Voices of the emperor similarly differ in their ability with the channels of the canon? Or had the emperor, understanding the sorcery of transmission far more deeply than I, anticipated such differences and compensated for them?

As we descended into the lowlands of Nayen, the pines and firs of the mountain forests gave way to the leafy and vibrant lowlands, and a troubling realisation swam up from the churn of these thoughts. The canon and the pacts had defined what magic could be done, but when I reached into the pattern of the world, unhindered by pact or canon, I could do *anything*. I tended to wield the powers with which I was familiar—veering, windcalling, shielding sorcery, and so forth—but I might have found the roots of a mountain and hauled them up to spear an enemy upon spires of jagged stone.

Katiz and Atar led their people because of their talent with the magic Naphena had chosen, just as my uncle had made a claim to the Sun Throne backed by the heat of his flame and the strength of his veering. At the making of the pact, the witches of the old sort had negotiated for these powers, passing them on to their people. Hissing Cat claimed that she had chosen conjuring fire and veering for their utility, but I had known her long enough to see her fascination with flames and beasts. Had her choice been only an arbitrary inclination?

Who might have risen to power if the witches of the old sort had chosen different magic for their pacts? How much of history had been shaped by ancient choices cast upon the pattern of the world with hardly a thought for how their ripples might define the lives of those born hundreds, even thousands of years later?

How might the choices I was making even now shape the world to come?

Such heady thoughts troubled me as we descended towards Eastern Fortress and confrontation with the emperor.

* * *

'The key will be a swift and certain victory,' Harrow Fox said, seated at his map table, his heavy fingers laced together. 'We have no navy but a few fishing boats, and thus no way to prevent their escaping by sea or receiving reinforcements and resupply from the mainland.'

My gaze darted to my grandmother in the shadowy corner of the command tent. Her good hand tightened around the head of her cane as she met my gaze, but she kept my secret. For the time being, at least.

'They outnumber us.' Frothing Wolf, arms crossed tight, paced the length of the cramped tent. 'They have fortifications and better weapons. Better magic, too.' She glared at me. 'I'll admit your little bone sticks are clever, but they're untested in combat and your cadre is barely trained.'

Her misgivings rankled. 'I'll grant that we should not rely over-much on them, but I know their capacity and know as well that they are a match for most Hands of the emperor.'

'We have eighteen witches we can count on,' my uncle said, staring at the map and the wooden tokens he had been arranging, 'plus the twelve untested bonewielders Foolish Cur has made, against the combined Hands and Voices of Iron Town, Setting Sun Fortress, and Eastern Fortress. A dozen sorcerers, at least, I would suspect.'

'And Hissing Cat,' I added. 'And me.'

Harrow Fox frowned. 'Indeed. And do the two of you plan to bring the city to its knees on your own?'

'Of course not. Even a vast well of power can run dry.' And, I did not add, we would need to save ourselves for our duel with the emperor. 'I agree with Frothing Wolf's plan. Assuming she can make contact with her agents in the city.'

Frothing Wolf showed her teeth. 'Our people are ready and waiting for a signal.' She took four tokens marked with crude carvings of her sigil and placed them on the map, behind the walls of Eastern Fortress. 'There are at least four hundred loyalists in the city. Likely more. There may yet be witches living among them, though I cannot say. More than enough, at any rate, to raise a commotion, start some fires, slit a few important throats, and open the gates.'

'In the tumult, our armies will rush into the city, seizing the harbour, the garrison, and the governor's estate.' Harrow Fox placed his own tokens on the board.

'Hissing Cat and I will lead the strongest of my cadre against the imperial sorcerers,' I said. 'The moment they wield magic, we will trace their wakes and fall upon them like hawks upon field mice. The rest of our witches will provide support to your forces. If done well and quickly, we should be able to seize an advantage in magic. Once the sorcerers fall, the city will fall.'

It *would* fall, and when it had Hissing Cat and I would strike out across the waters and catch the emperor reeling and distracted by his defeat, as vulnerable as he would ever be. There was no need to tell my uncle and Frothing Wolf about the punitive army he led to Nayen. If we succeeded—and we *would* succeed—it would be destroyed before making landfall. In the unlikely event that we failed…well, neither Harrow Fox nor Frothing Wolf could hope to save Nayen from the brutality that would follow.

Harrow Fox surveyed the table with a solemn nod. 'For the first time in my life, I feel we might truly win our freedom.'

'Indeed,' my grandmother murmured from her corner. 'If only we had not wasted decades squabbling over a throne we'd yet to retake.'

Frothing Wolf barked a laugh and fixed me with a fiery glare. 'We'll have time enough to settle old scores when this is through.'

Pride stirred in me. For all the harm I had done, for all the lives shattered in my wake, at least my legacy would include this. Victory over the empire would be vengeance, yes, but also the tilling of a field and the planting of a new garden where a peaceful and prosperous future for Nayen might grow.

Of course, no moment of happiness could last long. This was a lesson taught time and time again throughout my short yet eventful life.

'If you yet consider the scales unbalanced between us after Eastern Fortress has fallen, we can settle them,' I said. 'But I have as much cause to hate you, Frothing Wolf, and I've no wish for blood.'

She shook her head once, sharply, as though shrugging off a blow. 'No, Cur, you don't.' Then, to my uncle: 'Burning Dog and I will leave word for our agents. Be sure the column is in position in three days' time.'

She brushed past me and left the tent. My uncle took a long breath and leaned back in his chair. 'We will need to deal with that eventually,' he said softly, 'but not until the war is won, Nephew.'

'Let's not loosen the already fragile bonds of our alliance by plotting betrayal,' I said. 'Once the war is won, I intend to vanish back into the wilds, where I can live in peace.' And where, under Okara and Hissing Cat's tutelage, I might finally drink deeply of all I had learned of magic. I knew enough to comprehend how little I truly understood, and still felt the longing that had gripped me since I first felt warmth in the wake of a conjured flame.

'Is that what you want, Nephew?' Harrow Fox drummed his fingers on the map, then showed his palms and shrugged. 'Very well. I hope you find your peace. But first, we've a war to win.'

'Indeed.' I turned to leave. 'And so I should see to my cadre.'

As our army had descended into the south of Nayen, the land had levelled and the forests had thinned. My uncle had pitched his command tent in the centre of a clearing, and all around the lights of campfires bled through the gaps in the trees and stands of bamboo. The cacophony of camp life, that of both the soldiers and the camp followers who had attached themselves as our army had grown, drowned out the natural choir of the forest.

As I approached my cadre's campfire, I felt a gentle swell of calm. They sat in a circle around our fire, each with a blade in one hand and the canon of witchcraft in the other, thumbs pressed tight to the mark for healing sorcery. Torn Leaf took a deep breath, braced himself, and nodded sharply. One of the others drew the edge of her dagger across the back of his arm. Blood welled and pain rippled across his face, until a soothing wake rolled out from him and the wound began to scab and close.

I watched in astonishment. It had taken me months of practice and study to heal the smallest of wounds. My cadre, in contrast, had learned to knit flesh in a matter of days. The canon of witchcraft might be as constraining as imperial sorcery but, whether due to its simplicity or to the absence of my direct influence, my cadre were far quicker to learn and master it—at least, when they did not encounter the sort of unexpected block that had prevented Running Doe from veering.

Clear-River glanced up at my approach and brushed clear a patch of earth with the back of his hand. Some of the leaves he swept away were stained with blood.

'Just ensuring they can shrug off a few arrows or a nasty cut without too much trouble,' he explained as I sat beside him. 'Things went well with the Wolf and Fox?'

'Well enough. I'm to divide us into three parties. One will provide support to our soldiers. The other two will accompany either Hissing Cat or myself on a hunt for Hands and Voices.'

Clear-River nodded thoughtfully. 'And who's to go where?'

I laid out my thinking. As I did so, his face became like a distant storm viewed through an oiled-paper wall.

'You're troubled,' I observed.

He blinked as though woken from a dream. 'No, I...' The storm broke through, creasing his brow and twisting his mouth. 'A few months ago, I tried to kill you. With good reason, I thought. And...' He laughed wryly. 'Well, perhaps I still do. But I understand now. You. The empire.' He gestured with his canon of witchcraft. 'All of it.'

'I think I had a similar moment in An-Zabat,' I said.

'Maybe.' He shook his head. 'Before you and Harrow Fox brought your little army to Burrow, Hand Pinion nearly executed my garrison commander. Married to a Nayeni woman. He wouldn't abandon his family on Hand Pinion's orders, so the Hand nearly had his head cut off right there in the garrison yard, in front of his men.'

'What happened to him?'

He turned the canon of witchcraft in his hand, examining the carvings in the bone. 'I managed to talk Pinion out of killing him. Then, about a week later, your uncle lit his head on fire.'

I remembered the man, with his striking horizontal scar. 'I'm sorry.'

Clear-River worked his jaw and shrugged. 'He was a good soldier. Maybe a good person. He kept the peace in Burrow, kept our people safe, and seemed to believe in what I was trying to build. But that's one of the things I've come to understand.' His fist closed, white knuckled, around the canon of witchcraft. 'The only thing that can keep good people alive is power. I didn't have it then. I thought I could build a sanctuary within the structures of the empire, as though I could borrow the empire's power and use it to my own ends.' He scoffed and his voice turned sour. 'I should have known better. Though maybe it would have worked better if I'd been a Hand.'

'I have good reason to doubt that,' I said. He looked up at me, eyes rimmed in red. I offered a shrug of my own. 'Our stories are far from the same, but we learned similar lessons.'

Slowly, carefully, as though approaching a strange beast that might leap for his throat if he startled it, he nodded in agreement. 'I've been feeling…strange, to say the least, about fighting alongside the rebellion. I sent patrols to hunt your uncle's people down not so long ago. And your people killed a lot of mine even more recently.'

'But you are Nayeni, in the end,' I said.

'I am, yes. But that's not why I'm here.' He adjusted his grip on the strip of bone. 'I want the world to be a better place, Alder. A safer place. That won't happen until this war is over.'

'And you think we have the better chance of winning it?'

Another laugh, this one short and brittle. 'What do I know? I'm here now, and you've given me power—something to build on, maybe—and the empire never gave me anything but a title and a salary.'

'Then I hope you get a chance to build with it,' I said. 'There was good in Burrow, Clear-River. I'm sorry to have broken the peace you built twice over.'

'Well, then, I'm sorry for trying to gut you.'

I smiled. 'Far from the worst thing anyone's done to me.'

He blinked, then burst out laughing—a clear, ringing note this time that reminded me of the single evening of our friendship, Voice Golden-Finch's banquet, and our adventure out into the night. Pleasant memories now, though they had at the time been swiftly tarnished by sudden violence, secrets, and the pitiful power games of children.

'All right, enough self-pity,' he said when the laughing fit had passed. He stood and dusted off the back of his robe. 'Shall we share the Wolf and the Fox's plan with your cadre?'

Soon we had gathered Running Doe, Torn Leaf, and the rest to us. I explained the plan I had been describing to Clear-River and began doling out assignments. Those most skilled in flight would accompany either me or Hissing Cat in our hunt for the imperial sorcerers. The rest would be assigned to different companies within the Army of the Wolf and Fox.

As I gave them their assignments, Running Doe crossed her arms and hunched her shoulders. When I had finished, I drew her aside.

'Is there something wrong with the plan?' I said.

She glared up at me. 'It's a fine plan, but you're using me wrong.'

I had placed her in a support role, considering her skill with wind and fire. 'How so?'

'The thick of the danger will be in fighting the Hands and Voices. That's where I should be.'

Her reaction surprised me. If anything, defending ordinary soldiers against chemical grenades and sorcery would be the more difficult task. I said as much and she scowled.

'I was the first of your cadre,' she said. 'I've been doing this longer than any of them.'

'You have,' I agreed, 'though you were last to learn to veer and still struggle to fly for lengths of time. When we hunt the sorcerers, we will do so on the wing.'

'I can do it.' She curled her hands into fists and stepped towards me. 'Give me a chance.'

She stood a hand's breadth from me, her dark eyes searching mine, full of determination. I thought of myself, desperate for my grandmother to teach me magic, and then for Hand Usher to stop wasting my time, and finally for Atar to open the way to the secrets of windcalling. And, in taking a deep breath to collect my thoughts, I became distinctly aware of the camp-smoke-and-sweat smell of her, and of the fact that she was nearer to me in age than I often considered. A sudden mental shift, like words in sand disturbed and rewritten by the wind.

My mind became a slurry of scents and memories and newly imagined possibilities. It was mad, wasn't it, to conjure such a thought mere days before battle? And so suddenly. Though…we had grown to know each other well, and since Burrow I had counted her among those I trusted most in the world. She had, after all, saved my life.

'Well?' she demanded. 'If I prove that I can veer long enough, will you let me fight with you?'

'Yes,' I said, the word bubbling out of me, poorly considered. I scrambled to say something else—anything else—as though speaking more might mask the alluring and uncomfortable notions swirling in my mind. 'But only if you can meet my challenge.'

She glared at me. 'What might that be?'

'Tomorrow you will not march but fly, if you can.'

Her eyes went wide, which made something below my sternum flop like a carp lunging for a waterskimmer. They were dark, but there was such a *richness* of colour there—

'Well, then,' she said, her dimpled smile twisting in a wry shadow of the thrill she had felt upon first conjuring fire. 'I'll just have to prove you wrong a third time, Foolish Cur.'

She turned on her heel, defiant and full of purpose, and returned to her place with the others. I watched her walk away, perhaps too long, desperate to take back the challenge, to mend the tear it had rent between us. Clear-River coughed. Loudly.

'For all your influence over Nayeni politics,' he said, the corners of his eyes glinting with mischief, 'you *still* don't understand its people.'

'What do you mean by that?' My embarrassment had flashed into muted anger.

'Nothing at all, Alder.' Clear-River followed Running Doe back to the circle. The cadre cleaned their knives and stowed them, then sorted themselves according to the assignments I had given, some to practice forming domes of wind to shield against chemical grenades, others the sudden shift between channels of my canon that would be needed in duelling with imperial sorcerers.

I went among them, feeling the cramp and warmth and chill of the wakes of their magic mingling and overlapping like light dappling a shadowed forest floor. Where I felt suggestions might be helpful, I offered them, though explaining techniques for wielding magic was a more nebulous and difficult form of instruction than the adjustments my grandmother had once made to the angles of my arms while I practised the Iron Dance. Running Doe occupied a corner of the small clearing by herself, where she sat with gritted teeth, veering and returning to human form over and over again, as though her capacity with that magic were a muscle that might be strengthened through continual use.

For all their effort and practice, my cadre had wielded magic for only a few short months. I could but hope that in the first true test of my canon it would prove a match to the emperor's, just as I could but hope that Hissing Cat and I could overcome the emperor himself.

That hope alone made it possible to lead these people into battle, as I had once led Oriole. Some of them would die, but their deaths would matter in a way that his had not—no mere victims to the ambitions of others but sacrifices for the sake of a better world.

Or so I told myself, though the telling did little to ease the growing tension in my chest.

Okara emerged from the forest licking the remnants of some creature from his teeth. I scratched his ears and wondered if Hissing Cat, Tenet, Naphena, and the other witches of the old sort had felt like this when they had begun their war against the gods. Every great and meaningful endeavour, I reasoned, must feel impossible to those who begin it. Yet I had no choice but to begin, or else to watch the pattern of the world either remade to suit the cruel vision of the emperor or submerged into the darkest depths of violence and chaos.

A sense of purpose offered reassurance but little comfort. Thankfully, I had the head of a snoozing dog draped across my lap. It was enough to buoy me, at least for another night.

27

A Challenge

Foolish Cur

Running Doe fixed me with a long, measured stare. Around her, the other members of my cadre packed up our camp. A belief had sprung up among them that the more a person brought with them into veering, the more difficult it was to hold the form. They distributed her belongings among themselves: weapons, armour, bedroll, rations, a few extra scraps of clothing. She wore only her tunic, trousers, and the burnt scrap of wood, and she carried only the canon of witchcraft.

'We made a deal,' she said firmly, 'and you'll hold to it.'

'Of course,' I agreed.

She nodded once, sharp and defiant, then took a deep breath and pressed her thumb to the canon of witchcraft. Cinnamon scent overwhelmed the crisp, dewy smells of the spring morning. Cramps seized my limbs as she took the shape of an eagle hawk, stretching her talons and flexing her wings. After a final pointed glare, she took to the skies.

I spent the day glancing upwards, worrying when she flew out of sight that her spell had collapsed and she lay somewhere, bones broken after falling from the sky. My heart leapt into my chest whenever I glimpsed her silhouette, sometimes a dark blur against the clouds, else resting and preening in the limbs of a roadside tree. Always the muscle-clenching wake of her magic, so unusually potent, gripped me.

We ate on the march, scraps of dried meat or sticks of fish paste preserved with pungent spices. Once, I saw Running Doe clinging to a branch, tearing bloody strips from a freshly killed rodent, though I had never taught her nor any of my cadre to hunt. Perhaps some latent instinct had taken hold, buried deep into the form of an eagle hawk, core to its nature within the pattern of the world—a curious thought that survived only until a second eagle hawk landed beside her with its own rabbit in its claws. It looked down at me, swallowed its prey whole, and leapt from the branch to the road. I flinched as it burst into a cloud of cinnamon scent and resolved into Hissing Cat, sitting on her heels and sneering at me.

'What's going on with the girl?' she asked.

I blinked, taken aback. 'If she holds her veering for the day, she'll have won the right to fly out and hunt Hands and Voices with us at Eastern Fortress.'

Hissing Cat cocked her head to the side, baffled. 'We're to arrive tomorrow, Cur. She'll be bone tired.'

Something I had failed to consider, fool that I was. I spat a curse.

'Worse, you don't seem to have thought through the fact that she's not exactly accustomed to feeding herself on the wing,' Hissing Cat went on. 'Lucky I noticed the poor thing—hard not to, what with her flying around leaving a wake like a boulder fallen in a pond. I decided to lend her a hand.'

'Thank you for that,' I muttered, my face warming with shame. I nearly pointed out that it had been Running Doe's idea before realising what a profoundly stupid excuse that would be. Instead, I walked to the tree where she still perched, tearing at her meal.

'That's enough, Running Doe,' I called up to the eagle hawk. 'You've proven me wrong. You'll fly out with me tomorrow. I should never have put you to this challenge to begin with.'

There was something disdainful in her eyes. She screamed, stretched out her wings, and leapt from the branch to vanish somewhere above the forest canopy.

We had made a deal and, idiotic though it might be, she was committed to making good on her end. Terrible possibilities swirled in my mind, each carried by a different image of her death—falling from exhaustion, or caught in a flash of battle sorcery, or pinioned with crossbow bolts.

'You look like you just swallowed a mouthful of rotten fish,' Hissing Cat observed.

If Running Doe died tomorrow, it would be my fault. I could not bear to voice the thought aloud, but it haunted me all the rest of the day while I watched the sky, attending to the cramps pulling to the north in the wake of her magic, praying to the wolf gods, the sages, and whatever other powers might hear me until at last, as the sun began to set, the Army of the Wolf and Fox began to make its camp.

I was too distracted to do much but lay my own bedroll, leaving Clear-River and Doctor Sho to gather firewood and prepare our simple meal. The sun hung just above the horizon and cast the clouds in red and purple. Running Doe should have re-joined our camp, ready to return to her human form and gloat before collapsing to her bedroll. Had exhaustion caught up with her? Did she lay in the roots of some tree, clinging to her eagle hawk form with her last gasps of strength in a desperate bid to win our bargain?

'Foolish Cur, you're wanted,' Tawny Owl said, nearly making me jump. 'That's thrice now.'

I had broken the emperor's canon, left Atar behind in the Batir Waste, and pulled my grandmother back from the precipice of death, yet turning away from the forest's edge with the wake of Running Doe's veering dragging at my muscles proved nearly impossible.

Tawny Owl's hand clamped down on my shoulder and spun me around. 'It's bad enough being sent to fetch you. Don't waste my time.' She looked past me, to where my eyes had been fixed, her frown sharp and confused. 'Who's flying around out there? Some scout or other? What are they looking for?'

'Just one of my cadre keeping an eye on our trail.' My own voice sounded like an echo up from some deep well. 'Wouldn't want to be caught in an imperial ambush the night before we attack Eastern Fortress, would we?'

She grunted, then led me through the camp. Harrow Fox and Frothing Wolf had gathered their cadres and officers outside the command tent. I was surprised to see perhaps a dozen of the forty-odd people gathered wearing the burnt-wood fetish, though whether it retained the connotation of special allegiance to me, I could not say.

Harrow Fox explained once more the strategy that would carry us to victory, but my mind ever wandered back to Running Doe and his words fell empty on my ears.

Dusk had turned the sky a dark purple and Harrow Fox finished his explanation by torchlight, yet still the wake of Running Doe's magic held me. The sun had set. She had won our bargain, surely. Harrow Fox and Frothing Wolf dismissed the gathering with short, triumphant speeches that drifted through the fearful mist of my thoughts and left nothing of any substance behind.

The wake grew stronger. She had returned to camp. Why, then, hadn't she returned to human form? I began to run, wincing at the seizing in my calves with every footfall.

She perched on the ground in the light of the fire. Hissing Cat crouched nearby, her face, hair, and skulls full of shadows. Doctor Sho, too, lingered at the edge of the circle of light, his medicine chest beside him. Running Doe cocked her eagle hawk's head at me, lancing me with new terror. Had something gone wrong in the canon, leaving her trapped in her veered form, unable to release the spell?

A breath of cinnamon washed that fear from me, and with it the cramps that had held my arms and legs all day.

Running Doe stood tall and met my eye. She took a single, shaking step, and collapsed.

I went to my knees to catch her. The curls of her hair swept across my face as her head came to rest on my shoulder. Her heavy breath warmed my cheek, rich with the dregs of her veering's scent. She blinked up at me, eyes still defiant.

'There,' she whispered. 'I did it.'

I wondered if the depths of my guilt and shame showed in my face as pride and exhaustion filled hers with inner light. 'There was no need.'

She shook her head, a hard smile dimpling her cheeks. 'I wanted you to see, Cur. I wanted you to see.'

Her eyes fluttered shut and her next breath carried her into a deep, bone-weary sleep. I looked to Doctor Sho. 'Make some tea. Or soup. I don't know. Something to rejuvenate her when she wakes. She can't go into battle if she's this tired.'

'And who's going to stop her?' Hissing Cat said wryly. Okara, curled at her feet, looked up, as though to lend her sentiment his support.

Doctor Sho kept a tent nearby where he often treated exhaustion in newly arrived recruits. Thankfully, it was empty that night. I carried Running Doe to one of the bedrolls in the shelter of the tent and laid her down.

'I'm sorry,' I whispered. I sat beside her, watching her breathe, studying the lines of fatigue on her face. At some point, Doctor Sho brought me a bowl of congee flavoured with herbs and bits of dried pork. He gave Running Doe a quick examination and pronounced her tired but hale.

'She'll recover,' he said. 'You should get some sleep yourself.'

'I wouldn't be able to,' I answered, and ate, and waited for the fear to subside.

I woke, my back aching from having slept against a tent pole. The sound of distant music drifted through the canvas, flutes and drums and Nayeni voices singing—strange, on the night before a battle.

Running Doe's breath came in the slow rhythm of sleep beside me. I set the back of my hand on her brow, feeling for fever. She scrunched up her eyes and murmured, and fear that I had woken her darted through me, but her breathing returned to its slow, even rhythm. Gently, I eased the stiffness from my knees and back and left the tent. Though the moon and stars were out in full, casting the forest in cold light, my cadre's bedrolls lay empty, along with Doctor Sho's. The music drifted from an orange glow through the gaps in the trees, where silhouettes like shadow puppets moved in rhythm.

'Foolish Cur?' Running Doe stood in the mouth of the tent, the blanket draped over her shoulders, rubbing at her eye.

I swallowed around the lump in my throat. 'I must have woken you. I'm sorry.'

'No, it's fine.' She cast about the campsite and frowned when her gaze settled on the freshly cleaned cook pot. 'I'm a bit hungry, though.'

'I'll find Doctor Sho. He can make you a soup, or—'

'Ah, no thank you.' She wrinkled her nose, then looked to the orange glow in the distance. 'I'm sure there'll be something decent to eat over there.' She cinched the blanket tight and set off through the undergrowth. After a few dozen paces she looked back and tilted her head. 'Are you coming?'

I followed a few steps behind her, uncertain of what to say. She sighed, grabbed my arm, and pulled me along. 'If you keep dragging your feet, I'll starve to death where I'm standing.'

A warmth spread up from her hand like a wake of magic. She held me by the right wrist, just above the stump where Voice Usher had cut my hand away, and I felt suddenly aware of how close her fingers were to that puckered scar.

'I'm sorry,' I said. 'I should never have put you up to that challenge. It was stupid of me.'

'You said that before,' she muttered. 'I didn't believe it then and I don't believe it now.'

'You don't believe that I'm sorry?'

'No, I'm *certain* of that. But it wasn't stupid, and it made sense. You needed to know that I was strong enough to fight alongside you.' She looked back at me. 'Now you know.'

'I suppose I do.' The words escaped me like a long-held breath. 'But I should not have made you prove it. I should have trusted you.'

Her hand tightened like a claw, then relaxed. She looked back to the path through the undergrowth and the orange glow ahead. 'It's all right. Some things have to be proven.'

We emerged into one of the wider clearings. A bonfire rose high at its heart. Around it, a few soldiers sat playing simple instruments while dozens more danced in a wild, spinning circle. Voices rose in song, both from the dancers and from those at the edges of the clearing, weaving through the keening pipes and throbbing drums. I recognised a few of the members of my cadre, Torn Leaf among them, their arms thrown over each other's shoulders, moving together in the dance. Doctor Sho traversed the circle, the white wisps jutting from his balding head catching the glow like tufted clouds at sunset, and crossed to us with a skewer in his hand.

'You're awake,' he said with a note of surprise. 'And on your feet!' He looked Running Doe up and down. 'How do you feel? Nauseous? Any stubborn cramps or lingering stiffness?'

'Just quite a lot of hunger,' Running Doe said, smiling.

Doctor Sho nodded, furrowing his brow. Running Doe's gaze drifted to the skewer in his hand. With a start, he offered it. 'I'm sorry. They've been passing a bottle around.'

Running Doe let go of my wrist to accept the skewer and I felt an odd mixture of relief and disappointment. She tore into the unidentifiable meat. Doctor Sho coughed.

'Well, ah, I'll go fetch a few more of those,' he said and set off back towards the fire.

'He's a very strange man,' Running Doe murmured around a mouthful.

The scene before us, in its entirety, was strange. In a day we would pitch battle against the mustered strength of the empire in Nayen, yet rather than take this last opportunity to rest, these soldiers drank and danced and sang, expending strength that might mean the difference between life and death.

'You look troubled,' Running Doe observed. 'More than usual, I mean.'

I sought a way to express my misgivings that would not sound too pessimistic. I settled on, 'Shouldn't we be preparing for battle rather than singing and dancing?'

She tilted her head. Her curls flickered red-gold in the firelight. 'For many of them, this will be their last night, their last chance to celebrate the lives we have lived together. Those who survive will remember those who die, not in their deaths but in this moment, fire-lit and happy. Isn't that how it should be?'

My last memories of Oriole were full of blood and agony, and before that the anxiety of a pointless rivalry that Usher had cultivated between us.

'Indeed,' I said softly. A part of me, schooled in the pragmatic military theory of Sien, conjured objections. An army fought best well fed and well rested. But another part considered the painful truth that any given member of that army might not see another night, no matter how well fed and rested. This seemed a more honest reaction to that truth. Perhaps not the most tactically sound, but centred in the humanity of these men and women who would fight and die side by side.

'Better to celebrate life at some risk of death than to cower in fear,' I mused.

She smiled and the warmth of the fire seeped into my chest. 'You're starting to sound Nayeni.'

'That's good, I suppose,' I said, grinning. 'Though I'm not sure what you mean.'

She stepped close, reached out, laced her fingers through mine.

'D-Did you, ah, want to dance?' I stammered, feeling profoundly foolish and profoundly alive.

Slowly, she shook her head. 'There are other ways of celebrating life, Foolish Cur.'

I could think of nothing to say, save, 'Are you certain of this?'

She barked a laugh. 'You spent years studying poetry, and now, when it might finally be of some use, that's your best line?'

'I'm...sorry?' I said, my mind all but empty.

She smiled again and answered by leading me from the circle of firelight, back to the solitude of the tent, where we began a slow, careful dance of our own, warm beneath blankets against the chill of the night. Simpler than the dances Atar had taught me, but just as profound and heart stirring.

Afterwards, Running Doe lay with her curls splayed across my chest. Her fingers traced over my shoulder, down the length of my arm, to the stump of my wrist, where they lingered.

'You could restore it, couldn't you?' she said sleepily, half thinking. 'Surely it would be simpler than veering.'

I held my arm up in the moonlight that bled through the walls of the tent. The pink scar was a slash of silver-white against the dark backdrop of my skin. 'I could,' I said, 'but I don't want to. Not yet.'

She looked up at me, her brow creased in confusion.

'I spent most of my life chasing ambition,' I went on. 'I left too much ruin in my wake not to carry some of the burden myself.'

'But you said *not yet*. When, if ever?'

'Perhaps never,' I said. 'Perhaps when I feel the good I've done in the world counterbalances the harm. Why? Does it bother you?'

She shook her head, tickling my cheek with her hair. 'No. Only that you are so powerful, yet it seems strange that you would spend so much to heal others without fully healing yourself.' She yawned. 'Then again, I spent the day as an eagle hawk and I've just finished exhausting what little energy I had left, so perhaps everything seems a little strange and dream-like.'

I stroked her back and kissed the top of her head. 'I can go somewhere else if it will help you sleep.'

'No, no,' she said and curled into me. 'Stay. This is nice.'

A few moments, or perhaps a pleasant eternity, passed in silence.

'What happened today...' she began, then frowned and changed tack. 'I left my home village with a friend. Bright Coral. We both had things we were running from and thought we might find something like safety, or at least a chance to strike back at the world in Harrow Fox's army. She died at Greyfrost.'

A different kind of silence held while I waited for her to continue.

'I wasn't with her when it happened,' she whispered. 'One minute she was next to me, then a grenade went off and a piece of the wall collapsed. We got separated. When I found her again, she was dead.' She touched the side of her neck. 'An arrow.'

'I'm sorry.'

She sidled closer, pressing her cheek tight against my shoulder. 'I probably couldn't have stopped it. But if I'd been there, at least I would know that for sure. I didn't want something like that to happen to you. You're important to me, Foolish Cur. Not in the same way you're important to everyone else. Or...well, I knew who you were, of course, but it wasn't until I saw you with Doctor Sho in his clinic, in Burrow. The most powerful witch in the world, and you spent your days tending the wounded. It was then that I started wanting this.'

'The most powerful witch in the world spends her days asking questions of old bones,' I said. Running Doe glared up at me. I smiled. 'I'm joking. Thank you. Do you know when I first noticed you?'

She shook her head.

'When you chased those two boys away from that cartwright's house,' I said. 'I was unsure of my uncle. I still am, in some ways. But after that, I had some faith in the people who followed him, at least.' She nuzzled against me. 'I'm glad,' she whispered.

Her breaths grew long and deep. I lay there, awake, lingering in the moment, feeling the weight and warmth of her, listening to the distant flutes and drums, treasuring life for those fleeting heartbeats in the dark.

28

The First, Most Vital Choice

Hand Pinion

Voice Age-of-Plenty gave no order that Pinion be confined, yet a pair of guards walked beside his palanquin, their shadows outlined upon the silk screens that covered the windows. They brought food on the rare occasions that he asked for it and routinely replaced his bottle of rice wine. Setting Sun Fortress had been abandoned, but its Sienese citizenry carried their belongings with them, including the stock of its cellars.

Pinion slept only when exhaustion and alcohol dragged him down into a churning, red-stained fog. Shadows like puppets, like the silhouettes of his guards, moved in the emptiness, arising suddenly into images of perfect clarity with a flash of steel, an explosion that shook his bones, a red mist, charred and broken bodies.

Oriole's grave, littered with brittle leaves, unkempt.

Wen Alder's face, twisting from the boy who had shared in Pinion's grief into the monster who had twice now shattered the world.

Dreams that left him reeling. He would wake, head pounding, disgusted with both the empire and himself, horrified at the pride he had felt in having his plans accepted by the emperor and the brutality those plans had visited upon Setting Sun Fortress, until sleep dragged him down again into a dream like a broiling pit of hatred—for Alder, for the Nayeni who resisted the empire and brought its wrath upon themselves. Hatred for himself, for doubting the emperor's wisdom, for his squeamishness in the face of what imperial doctrine deemed *necessary.*

Waking was better than sleeping. Not at first, when he arose from the fog with a pounding headache and a churning nausea, but after relieving himself and filling his belly with a bottle of wine he attained a state of placid, slippery emptiness. And so he was carried, swaying gently, mindlessly basking in the warmth of early spring sunlight or wrapped in furs against the pleasant chill of night. A serene, endurable existence until sleep took him again and he swam in terror, disgust, and rage.

So his days continued, until the morning when he woke to a sudden burst of sunlight and the rasp of the palanquin door. Pinion blinked and grimaced against the light while his heart found its normal rhythm, easing down from the excitement of some nightmare remembered only as the dregs of fear and a metallic taste in the back of his mouth.

Voice Age-of-Plenty stood over him, his face open and welcoming. 'Hand Pinion,' he said. 'We will arrive in Eastern Fortress today. You should make yourself presentable for your father, I think.'

His father, to whom he owed everything, deference most of all.

He wanted to spit in the old bastard's eye.

With a grunt, he rolled over and shut his eyes tight against the sun.

'It is your duty to stand and give an account of all that has happened,' Voice Age-of-Plenty said, growing stern like a tutor with a rebellious student. 'At the very least, to explain Voice Usher and Hand Cinder's deaths.'

'They picked a fight they couldn't win,' Pinion muttered. 'There's little more to say.'

Voice Age-of-Plenty sighed and turned his attention to the palanquin bearers and guards. 'Hand Pinion is not to be carried today. See that he drinks a pot of tea before we reach the city. I'll arrange for a quick bath at an inn before he goes to meet Voice Golden-Finch. He is not to touch alcohol, nor any food richer than plain rice. Is that understood?'

The guards made a slow, baffled salute.

Pinion sneered. 'Is this some sort of punishment?'

'No, Hand Pinion, it is for your own sake,' Voice Age-of-Plenty replied. 'Now get up. You have been drunk for three weeks. Get your blood moving. Stagnation has a way of making the mind fester.'

Which would be easier? his sluggish, pounding mind wondered. *To resist or comply?* Resistance would mean humiliation, certainly. Perhaps death, though he was the only surviving son of the governor of Nayen. It seemed unlikely that any executioner's sword would touch his flesh, regardless of what he had said at Setting Sun Fortress, short of his taking up arms against the empire.

No. The true difficulty would be the sudden loss of direction. There would be no easy future for him. No life of tea and books and companionable conversation. Either he would answer for all that had transpired since Greyfrost and return to his role as Hand of the emperor, or he would have to chart some unknown path of his own making through the world. Or he could remain a drunkard. A burden upon his family. A living gravestone to all he could have been.

Voice Age-of-Plenty leaned through the door of the palanquin. 'Do not force me to have these poor men dump you out of here.'

Pinion grumbled but steeled himself and made his choice.

Three weeks of sloth and stupor had stripped him of strength. Oriole had always been the athlete, spending his days riding or practising with sword and bow. Pinion had done what was required of him in those arenas and little more. Now he flagged at the back of the column, encircled by guards who wore annoyance plain on their unfamiliar faces. He might have asked for a horse, he realised, too late to do so without deepening his embarrassment. At least the sweat and the stoppered skin of lukewarm tea slung around his neck had sobered him up. If he must stand before his father, he would do so with a straight back and clear eyes.

Within the Sienese canon, there were hundreds of tales of cowardly wives who threw themselves into cisterns or hanged themselves with their silken sheets, overwhelmed by some sudden misfortune or despairing at the death of a beloved son. Others told of girls who, upon learning they were to be wed away sight-unseen to the magistrate of some distant land in service to their father's and family's interests, took their own lives in protest.

Pinion thought of those girls, of their unwanted marriages, and found it impossible to see cowardice in their actions. Such self-destruction was a way of throwing back the cruel indignities of the world, of refusing to follow the demeaning and terrible path forced upon you. Of taking control in one final, deliberate act.

If he was to destroy himself, he wanted his father, at the very least, to know *why*.

And he wanted at least a taste of justice, first, and to see the brutal plan he had devised succeed. For all the deaths he carried to have been for *something*.

He would live long enough to see Wen Alder's body torn apart and hung from hooks above the city gate. None of this horror would have happened, after all, if not for him.

And then, when Pinion had nothing left of value to live for, he would drink and let the stillness carry him away.

A warm bath and a dozen pots of ink-dark tea later, Pinion sat in the antechamber to his father's reception hall dressed in a robe of yellow silk embroidered with curling white feathers. Its softness agitated him, as did the distant music of some unseen flautist in the garden. His hair, after being vigorously combed free of knots by one of Voice Age-of-Plenty's servants, hung like black waterfalls down the slope of his chest. He held his hand in his lap and studied the glittering lines of his tetragram.

He had wondered if his anger would fade once he had sobered up, once the dust and ash of the road had been washed from him and he felt again the gentle touch of luxury. It still burned, but differently. Lower, but with more intensity.

He ought never to have been forced to watch heads split like cordwood, to hear the dying cries of children, to learn that every delicacy he had ever tasted, every scrap of silk he had worn, every comfort he had known was built upon butchery. For how else to explain how casually Voice Age-of-Plenty had given the order, or how quickly Commander Zhu and Captain Huo had carried it out?

A part of him had long known, he supposed, since well before he had passed the imperial examination, yet to witness such brutality conveyed a different sort of knowing. Text, no matter how brilliantly composed and thoroughly detailed, could not capture the rawness of reality.

The brass-banded double door groaned open just wide enough for a single body. The sharp sunlight of early spring cut through the lamp-lit gloom. Captain Huo strode through the gap. The freshly polished scales of his armour hung over the blue robe of his rank. He held his helmet in his hands, its peacock plume shimmering in the sunlight. He seemed a different person than the one Pinion had known and struggled with. Clean shaven. Dressed in finery.

Was it too late for Pinion to be so transformed?

Captain Huo had taken a seat across the wide antechamber and fixed his eyes upon the floor.

'Interesting,' Pinion said, settling his mind back into old patterns of thought designed to navigate the labyrinth of imperial politics. 'It appears the emperor has not seen fit to explain things thoroughly to my father. Or, at least, Father has enough questions to warrant two witnesses. I suppose it all happened under his authority, though he had little to do with it, and his subordinates and peers will have their questions. He'll want details for whatever official narrative he decides to promulgate.'

The captain furrowed his brow.

'If you're here, and I'm here,' Pinion went on, 'it means he's trying to put the story of what happened between Greyfrost and Setting Sun Fortress straight. So, what do you intend to say?'

That puzzled expression remained. 'You and I ought not to speak of this, Hand.'

Pinion shrugged his shoulders. 'We ought not to have done many things. I for one intend to paint you as something of a hero. You stood up to me when you thought you needed to, though I was in the right to follow the emperor's orders. You had no way of verifying that, of course, and I will fully grant that I seemed to be going mad. We nearly came to blows, but neither of us was in the wrong. A fine story, wouldn't you say?'

The story mapped onto reality as Pinion needed it to be. If life was but a vast and nigh-inscrutable question upon a grand imperial examination, then it had a definite, if difficult, answer—one he had answered correctly, though the answer seemed horrific. He clung to that hope lest he fall into the churning, hateful pit in his stomach, as he had in the palanquin.

Huo nodded slowly. 'A fine story, Hand Pinion.'

Pinion leaned forwards. 'Will you tell its like?'

The pause before the captain's reply was broken by the opening of the inner door. A young steward in the Voice's yellow livery stepped through and bowed low, then gestured for Pinion to follow him.

Oil lamps burned bright on the cedar columns, filling the centre of the hall with blazing light and its edges with clinging shadows. Some trick of architecture and geometry drew Pinion's eyes along the silver-threaded rug that sprawled the length of the tiled floor to his father's dais. Voice Golden-Finch sat framed by lacquer panels decorated with scenes to match the season: orchids in bloom beside streams of running water, where hummingbirds flitted between the flowers. His throne bore twin lion serpents twining down the arm rests. Above his head a single piece of red silk hung, marked with the imperial tetragram in gold.

Pinion made obeisance on the first and second red cords laid across the floor, then waited, his forehead to the rug, at the third.

'You have travelled a long way in a very short time, my son.' His father's voice boomed through the hall, empty save for the two of them now that the steward had vanished into some hidden room. 'And alone, thrust suddenly from apprenticeship into command. It must have been difficult.'

'Thank you for your sympathy, Father.' Pinion waited, wondering how he would respond when formality and distant kindness transformed into accusation. Which would win out? The part of his mind that would rather drink itself to death than face the horror of Setting Sun Fortress, or the new-born cynic who saw a chance to rationalise away all his guilt and self-loathing? He swallowed against the dryness in his mouth. 'I hope I have done my duty well.'

Rather than an answer, Pinion heard the rustle of silks and footsteps upon the marble stair. No shadow fell on him, but he felt his father's presence looming. This aligned with no courtly script he knew.

'Rise, Hand Pinion.'

He looked up, empty of expectation, a coin spinning on its edge soon to fall to one side or the other. His father stood over him holding a scroll case of black ironwood. It bore a seal of golden wax stamped with the emperor's tetragram.

'It is a message from the emperor himself,' Voice Golden-Finch said.

The light glinted off that seal. Pinion stared, uncomprehending. 'He...what? Why not...?' He swallowed, cleared his throat, and found the deference and vocabulary that propriety demanded. 'I am honoured, though I was unaware that the emperor communicated in such a fashion. He could simply convey his message to me through you, or through Voice Age-of-Plenty, could he not?'

'He could.' There was a strained note in his father's voice. Pinion tried to parse it—an attempt to mask contempt, or pride?—but the surreality of the moment left him off balance. 'Yet he has chosen not to. The contents of that message are meant only for you, my son.'

Pinion's hands trembled as he took the scroll and broke the seal. The paper crinkled as it unrolled. The message was a sparse dozen logograms, each perfectly formed in ink that was nearly black but had a tint of redness at the feathered edges.

> *Is it not better to strive for the mountain top*
> *than to settle in the foothills?*
> *Those who serve will be rewarded.*
> *We will speak again, Hand Pinion, face to face.*

Pinion read it again, and then a third time, trying to peel apart each logogram as though to find within it some hidden meaning. The quote from Traveller-on-the-Narrow-Way baffled him. Was it an admonishment? An encouragement? Did the emperor mean to imply that he had been striving, or that he had somehow settled? Since Grey-frost, he had only ever been trying to survive.

'That message was brought by a swift clipper sailing ahead of the fleet that crosses from the mainland even as we speak,' Voice Golden-Finch said. 'A member of the emperor's Fist put it in my hand. With it, he told me that the ship which bore him will bear you out to meet that fleet, and the emperor, who travels with it. You leave tomorrow.'

Tomorrow? But he had only just arrived. His journey was at an end, surely.

What could the emperor wish to discuss that could not be passed through Pinion's father?

'What do you think it means?' Pinion wondered aloud.

His father took a step back, his eyes averted from the emperor's message. 'The seal was unbroken, Pinion. You alone know the contents of that message.'

'You're my father,' Pinion said. He offered the sheet of paper.

Voice Golden-Finch recoiled. 'It is not my place to know. If it were, he would have told me.'

'What is there to know? Only an aphorism from the sages, a tautology of imperial doctrine, and an invitation! It's…' Pinion shook the thin sheet of paper, listening to it crackle. His father's eyes widened in horror. He tried to bring himself under control, but his breath refused to slow and the trembling in his arms went on till his hand curled tight, crushing the message and its fine calligraphy.

'No!' his father cried and lunged for the sheet of paper. 'A written message from the emperor himself is so precious a thing. It bears the rare gift of his calligraphy. You mustn't treat it so casually!'

A stone fell from his throat to the churning pit of his stomach.

'Where was this outrage at Setting Sun Fortress?' he blurted, speaking thoughts even as they occurred to him. His fist tightened till he felt the edges of the paper cut into his skin. 'You leap to the defence of a piece of paper, yet Voice Age-of-Plenty, with a casual word, condemned hundreds to die!'

'The latter was an act of the emperor's will.' Voice Golden-Finch straightened and ran a hand through the long wisps of his beard. 'The former desecrates the emperor's very word.'

'I understand hierarchy and the duty to obey,' Pinion said. 'You did not see his face, Father. He watched children torn apart! Mothers and fathers skewered! Innocent people slaughtered like animals, and he did not so much as *blink*.'

'They are a barbarous, rebellious people, Pinion. You were at Greyfrost. You should—'

'Those townsfolk were no rebels.' His words tore at his throat, rumbled through the hall, growing like a storm. No Voice of the emperor could forgive such insubordination, not even of his only surviving son, yet he went on. The coin had fallen and the upward face was full of rage. 'One or two might have sympathised with the enemy, or given them succour, or spied on our column and fed intelligence to the rebels who stalked the woods, but they were not all guilty, Father. They took up no swords against us. Conjured no fire. They were our people. Our subjects. Our younger brothers and sisters in the vast family of empire, no? The emperor's children! And Age-of-Plenty butchered them like swine!'

Voice Golden-Finch's face had darkened to a thunderhead. 'You will refer to a Voice by his title, Hand Pinion.'

Pinion gawked at him, dumbfounded. 'You cling to propriety and find fault in its violation while I confront you with *horror*.'

'There is no morality higher than the will of the emperor.'

There could have been no more potent fuel to throw upon Pinion's anger. 'There must be!' he roared, and, hardly thinking, conjured lightning. It burst to life in his hand, directionless, then spat itself into the floor. Tiles shattered and melted, forming a black, pungent scar. Shards of paper turned to ash and floated from his hand.

He thought of Hand Beneficence, his robe charred by just such an outburst. A man doing what he thought was his duty. It was unthinkable, according to doctrine, to say that the emperor *should* have done differently than he did…but he should have visited Beneficence in the night and explained what he had intended. Why hadn't he? Was it through callous indifference, simple laziness, or neglect?

Whatever his reason, or lack thereof, the emperor—as impossible as it should have been—had done wrong. And if in Hand Beneficence's case, why not at Setting Sun Fortress?

'There must be a higher morality,' he said again, his voice a whisper in the silence after thunder. 'Why else would Traveller-on-the-Narrow-Way write so much of the emperor's own duty to his people? Something must stand above him, else he could *have* no duty. And it is a duty he has violated here, Father. You did not see it. I have to believe that if you had, you would agree.'

Voice Golden-Finch folded his hands into his sleeves. 'Whatever violence was meted out at Setting Sun Fortress was in answer to what Wen Alder dealt at Greyfrost.'

'It was not the same,' Pinion snarled.

'And need I remind you that this was *your* plan. Or so the emperor led me to understand.'

'I only wanted to lure Alder here. His death is the only one that matters. Repayment for Oriole's. All these others...' Pinion shook his head and gestured wildly. His father flinched, which made a strange satisfaction blossom in his chest. The old man was *afraid*. 'They serve no purpose,' he went on. 'If you obliterate the Nayeni, a rebellion will rise somewhere else, like weeds sprouting in a garden. Alder must be destroyed, yes, because his power is an existential threat. Rival, perhaps, to the emperor's. But these townsfolk? Even the highland bandits? Are they worth descending into the gory mud and slathering ourselves in wickedness? Did not Traveller-on-the-Narrow-Way write that our duty to the people of the empire, not only in the heartland but in all the provinces, is to protect them and to guide them and to foster their well-being? Is it the proper place of a Hand of the emperor to slaughter his brothers and sisters?'

His father's face had long since hardened. Speaking to it was little better than shouting at the shattered tiles. Pinion swallowed the thousand more words he might have voiced—the quotations from the sages, the structured arguments, the very tools he had been trained with to serve the empire. There was no point. Voice Golden-Finch would never be convinced.

Yet perhaps there was a point to his outburst. In speaking the truth, the burning coal in his chest had lessened and a fragment of guilt had fallen away.

'I could kill you where you stand.' His father's voice seemed thin. 'First for threatening a Voice, and then for these treasonous words.'

It was one thing to hear such a threat from a Voice of the emperor. It was quite another to hear it from his father's mouth.

'I have an audience with the emperor tomorrow,' Pinion said. 'If he wanted me dead, he would surely tell you. Unless the emperor wills it, to kill me would be treason.'

For a moment he wondered if his father would reach out with the sorcery of transmission and request permission to burn him to ash, but no weight settled upon his shoulders. Only his father's heavy, hateful gaze.

'Will that be all, Your Eminence?' Pinion said.

His father nodded sharply, then turned away, mounted the dais, and sat stiffly upon his throne. Pinion bowed once more. He was not certain why. Force of habit, perhaps.

No. It was more than that. As he backed away from the dais, he understood. He followed the rituals. He did as he was supposed to, because he was right. If the world was but a grand question, an intellectual puzzle to be solved, and the imperial canon was the key to solving it, then he had done so. His father, and with him Voice Age-of-Plenty and the emperor himself, had come to the wrong conclusions. So he would claim the foundations of morality for his own.

The young steward led him from the audience hall back to the antechamber. Captain Huo sat up straight as the doors swung open. Pinion dipped his head.

'I'm sorry, Captain,' he said simply. 'The story fell apart in the telling.'

29

The Battle of Eastern Fortress

Foolish Cur

Eastern Fortress sprawled along the coast of Nayen. Behind it, the sea glittered with the first pre-dawn light. Hilly farmland rolled from below our clifftop vantage to the walls, which rose and fell like the arching back of a lion serpent coiled around a clutch of eggs. If I were to veer and look down on the city with eagle hawk's eyes, I might see the torches of sentries walking the inner walls that divided the city into quarters and encircled the governor's estate at its heart, where I had spent the last days of my naivety and youth.

I scanned the harbour for pennants and banners, evidence of the fleet and punitive army the emperor had led from Sien. The masts of a few ships stood against the lightening sky, anchored at the docks and further out to defend the bay, but no more than usually kept berths in Eastern Fortress. We had been quick enough. If we could conquer the city, the emperor would still be at sea when it fell, as vulnerable as he would ever be. Hissing Cat, my cadre, and I would have our chance to strike at him in the chaos and confusion of the city's fall and the loss of his Voices in Nayen.

Which led to a truth that I had been avoiding: at some point in the battle, I would have to confront Voice Golden-Finch, and Pinion with him. The thought brought an ache to my chest. They were Oriole's family. Doing battle with them felt a kind of betrayal. Though, after what Pinion had done at Setting Sun Fortress, the justice to be had in their deaths might outweigh my personal misgivings.

'Foolish Cur, always deep in thought,' Hissing Cat said, joining me at the edge of the cliff. 'Of course, it's not difficult to reach the depths of a shallow pit.'

I frowned at her. Though even I had exchanged my usual robe for simple leather armour, she still wore only her voluminous ragged furs. 'Be flippant if you must. We all deal with uncertainty and fear in our own ways, Hissing Cat.'

She barked a laugh. At her heel, Okara barked in answer, then pushed his head against my hand. I scratched his ears.

'I can't help but feel you've taken the finer fruits of the harvest,' she said. 'Clear-River and Running Doe are the strongest of the twelve and the most experienced. Though I suppose Torn Leaf's half-competence balances the scales somewhat.'

'Not long ago you were complaining that you had no need for an escort,' I said. 'Now your escort's not enough. Which is it?'

She shrugged, making the skulls in her hair seem to bob their heads for want of certainty.

'I have a bad feeling, Cur,' she said. 'The bones have never wanted me to help you. All along they've told me to go back to my cave. Last night...it was like they were screaming.'

I felt a chill. 'Which do you put more stake in? Cracks in old bones or your own sense of what has to be done?'

'Naphena asked a similar question once, not long before she got herself killed.'

'I'm not Naphena. The gods are on my side.'

Her eyes flitted to Okara, who tilted his head and blinked at her. 'You're sure of that?'

'We have the same enemy,' I answered. 'For now, that has to be enough.'

She curled her lip. 'Remember what you promised me, Cur. There is a line you shouldn't cross, no matter how confident you are in Okara's friendship. Not unless you've no other choice.'

'The empire has to end, Hissing Cat, if the rest of the world is to have any hope at all.'

Her only answer was a bitter harrumph.

'Without your help, I *will* have no other choice.'

'I know, burn you, and I'm here, aren't I? Just let me know when the bloody work begins.' She snarled and stalked off into the forest, brushing past Doctor Sho on her way.

'Living up to her name today, isn't she?' Doctor Sho remarked.

'I didn't think Hissing Cat would be nervous before battle.'

'I doubt she's afraid for herself.' He seemed to ponder for a moment, then shrugged. 'But who can say? For my part, I'm not looking forward to the busy days to come, regardless of how the battle turns out.'

'I'm sorry,' I said. 'I know how you feel about violence.'

He waved a hand dismissively. 'If I didn't think this was a worthy fight, I wouldn't be trailing behind an army. It's not like your uncle's been paying me.'

'Perhaps not yet.' I grinned. 'You won't mind having the triumphant Sun King in your debt, of course.'

'I've had powerful men in my debt before. Once they don't need you, they've no real reason to make good on what they owe.'

I scratched Okara behind his ear, then gave him a gentle push towards Doctor Sho. 'I for one owe you a great deal, and I fully intend to make good. Though I need to ask you for one more favour.' The dog looked up at me, confused for a moment, then padded over to sniff at Doctor Sho's hand. 'Keep an eye on him. I'm finding myself more and more attached, at least when he isn't possessed by a god.'

'You say that as if he isn't as much my dog as yours.' Doctor Sho knelt and rubbed Okara up and down his flanks. 'I'll keep him right at my heel. No need to worry.'

Okara yipped and licked Doctor Sho's cheek. At the very least, those two would be safe. If all our planning and power amounted to nothing and the rebellion shattered against the walls of Eastern Fortress— or if, as Hissing Cat seemed to fear, she and I failed to overcome the emperor—Doctor Sho would slip away, vanish to some far corner of the world, and go back to peddling his medicines with Okara in tow. He could find a way to outlive the world itself, I suspected.

Something good would endure, even in failure. The thought blunted my fear and bolstered my hope.

'I'll find you after the battle and help you with the wounded,' I said. 'Now, I should find my cadre and make ready.'

He nodded. I turned to go. As I did, he took a step towards me, then hesitated, as though some word of warning had caught in the back of his throat, only for him to reconsider and swallow it. He thumped Okara's flank once more, then led the dog back towards the main column, where he would organise his own brigade of village herbalists, wise women, and mothers—the best medics the rebellion could muster.

I watched him go, wondering what he had nearly said. Perhaps not a warning but some sentimental well-wishing, something hewing too near to a goodbye for his comfort. I understood the impulse. Oriole's death haunted me, and as I walked back to my cadre a fear I had suppressed since waking began to boil up again.

Running Doe had become important to me. Clear-River, too. Even Torn Leaf, for all his occasional imbecility, had become a meaningful part of my life in these last few months, and the rest of my cadre as well, each in their own way. One or all of them might lie dead by morning. If I had been racked with guilt for Oriole's death, how much worse would it be for one of these people—followers, friends, even a lover, if only for a single night—to die because of orders I had given?

Every choice reshapes the pattern of the world—a heavy enough burden when those choices stood only to reshape one's own life and the paths one might traverse. How could anyone endure a life so full of choices that shaped the paths of others? Why did someone like Harrow Fox or Frothing Wolf—or the emperor, who had reshaped, shattered, built, and defined generations of lives—seek that weight of responsibility?

All my life I had wanted freedom. Pursuit of it had entangled me in bureaucracy, which offered only different ways to be bent to the empire's uses. I had abandoned the freedom I had found with Hissing

Cat in an effort to make good on what I owed to Nayen, to my grand-mother, to those who fought against the empire I had helped, in my small, strange, significant way, to build. But when my debts were paid, I would follow Hissing Cat's example.

I wondered if there were other places like her cave, places where the first witches had left traces of their knowledge behind. Perhaps the deepest secrets I had always longed for could be found in some painting preserved in the depths of some mountain or carved in stone in some forgotten city, long overgrown.

When the war was over and the threat Tenet posed to the pattern of the world dealt with, I would go in search of those secrets, I decided. Perhaps I could convince Running Doe or Clear-River to accompany me. Or, if not, perhaps Hissing Cat. It would be a challenge, I knew, to unmire myself from the web of obligations that had always pulled at me. Yet I resolved to try to find peace in the life I longed for, a life in pursuit of knowledge for no sake but to salve my own curiosity.

It was a pleasant, hopeful plan, if one that lay on the other side of a vast chasm that could only be bridged by a battle and a duel, neither one a certain victory. A plan as naive as any I had ever made.

The orange glow of sunrise lit the clouds, though the dawn twi-light left deep shadows on the denuded field between the walls of Eastern Fortress and the forest's edge. The light of mirrored lan-terns mounted to the battlements swept back and forth across the field as they had all through the night, each one a searching, preda-tory eye cutting through the thin morning fog that rolled in from the sea. I huddled in the undergrowth with Clear-River, Running Doe, and Torn Leaf at my back, my eyes on the battlements, watching the slow parade of torches, waiting for a sign that Frothing Wolf's agents in the city had begun to stir their chaos. Torn Leaf's battle harness clattered and his scabbards stirred the underbrush while he adjusted various straps. He and Running Doe still wore their swords, though they would fight with magic—an old habit that comforted them, I supposed, though I doubted the usefulness of bringing such tools.

I imagined Oriole beside me, thrilling in the audacity of the plan, in the quiet tension before battle, anticipating the surge of adrenaline once it began. He should have been with me. But of course, if not for his death, my path would never have brought me here. We might have served together on the walls of Eastern Fortress instead, defending against the rebellion's last, desperate attack.

Movement atop the walls drew my attention. A few torches fell from the battlements, then vanished. One of the mirrored lanterns stopped in the middle of its slow, sweeping arc. Smoke billowed, catching the glow of a fire.

The silhouettes of soldiers from other squads slipped from the undergrowth, crouched low, wrapped in cloaks, blankets, scraps torn from their bedrolls, or whatever else they could scrounge from their belongings, and holding their weapons close. Among the usual smattering of animal bones and carved fetishes, they wore sticks, leaves, and tufts of grass—a poor disguise at close distance but hopefully enough to cause an eye peering from the battlements to slide away in the gloom. Soon the field ahead of us roiled with soldiers rushing towards the walls, racing the sunrise, curving around the unmoving circle of light cast by the abandoned mirrored lantern.

We held position at the forest's edge. Ours was not to join in the assault but to attend to the pattern of the world and attack any wake of sorcery. I waited, body tense, for that first flash of lightning, that first breath of thunder and charred flesh, as a dozen people died according to a plan that I had helped design.

Small magics might leave a feverish feeling, or a cramp, or a chill in the lungs. A great magic, like one to tear down an empire, would cast a wake far more devastating. *But for the good,* I told myself. Like the agony of a purgative, or the pain of surgery. Necessary suffering to make the world a better place.

Better for whom? I thought in a voice so like Atar's that I wondered if she had somehow reached me through transmission. *Not for those who suffer. Not for those who drown in the wake of change.* But the thought was my own, rising from the depths where I had buried it and its like after Burrow.

Rebel soldiers swarmed towards the walls and I held my breath, until the inevitable shouts of alarm. A focused volley of crossbow bolts could have cut down our soldiers in their hundreds, but in their shock and panic the Sienese fired in scattered, uncoordinated bursts. Still, screams of pain rose from the killing field and dozens of hunched forms collapsed. Heads snapped back as bolts punched through skulls. Other bodies curled around a collapsed lung or punctured bowel, gasping and howling in slow, painful death.

'Lightning next,' I murmured. 'Be ready to veer.'

I heard my companions shifting in the undergrowth, adjusting their grip on their canons of witchcraft. Running Doe reached out and touched my wrist, seeking and offering reassurance.

Thunder clapped, but rather than a bolt of lightning, a flower of burning chemicals bloomed. Shattered bodies cartwheeled in the afterglow of the explosion. I grimaced, wondering where the other witches of my cadre were among the soldiers. They knew how to defend against grenades but had practised only against stones and pine cones.

Another grenade burst. Its light cast the silhouettes of our soldiers in stark relief against the thinning fog. Only a few hundred paces remained between the front line of our forces and the main gate of Eastern Fortress, which yet stood closed. As the roar of the explosion faded, a repeated, agonised wailing rose in its place—some poor soul caught in the explosion but still alive.

I worked my jaw. 'We may need to open the gate,' I said. 'If I veer, follow me.'

'Won't that leave us exposed?' Torn Leaf said. 'I thought the point was—'

'The point is to win,' Running Doe answered. 'If the plan falters, we find a new...'

Her voice trailed off as an explosion hurled stone and smoke from one of the two towers that flanked the gate. Flames roared from its shattered remains. A moment later, the great oaken doors began to swing outwards.

Two of the mirrored lanterns wheeled to concentrate their light in front of the gates. The defenders on the wall converged their crossbow fire, hurling a rain of bolts down on the rebels trying cross the illuminated stretch of road. I braced myself to watch dozens of Nayeni cut down at once, only for a sudden chill to fill my lungs. The storm of bolts spun away at wild angles, caught and cast aside by a whirling dome of air.

'Yes!' Torn Leaf shouted, leaping to his feet.

Torn Leaf's celebration proved short lived. A flush swept through me and a bolt of lightning flashed down from the wall, blasting up a geyser of earth. I did not hesitate to see if the witch who had called the wind still stood.

'Follow!' I snapped, and veered, and took to the sky.

As the cramps in the wake of their veering pulled at me, I darted over the killing field, my will like a knife cutting into bone, carving the pattern with my own burst of battle sorcery. Thunder split the air. Lightning burned down, bright as the noon sun. The battlements exploded where the wake of enemy lightning had emanated, showering the city behind in dust, rubble, and charred bodies.

I circled over the wreckage. Clear-River, Torn Leaf, and Running Doe followed, taking positions above me. A flurry of arrows darted up. I spun them away, all the while searching for any sign that the sorcerer in the rubble still lived.

Instead, a chill wake of windcalling surged out from further down the wall. I threw up my own in answer. A whirlwind burst into being and faded as our conjured pressure fronts collided. Like a stone dropped in a pond sends ripples through the water, the impact stirred the currents in the air. I beat my wings to reorient myself, just in time to spot the sorcerer, his scorched and tattered robes fluttering in the embrasure. Lightning crackled out from his upraised hands. I built walls of light between us, hoping that Running Doe and the others were behind me.

Battle sorcery crackled against my shield, pulsing in waves, probing to crack and shatter it. A winged shadow dropped to the battlement behind the sorcerer, then resolved into a tall, wild-haired figure. I felt the heavy weight of transmission, the chill of windcalling. The sorcerer turned his head a heartbeat before a blade of wind caved in his chest and hurled him from the wall.

Clear-River stood at the edge of the battlement for a moment, looking down at the corpse he had made, turning over some unspoken thought, then veered again and re-joined us in the sky.

Other wakes clawed at me—witches on the wing, raking the battlements with conjured fire while rebel soldiers pushed through the gates and into the streets of Eastern Fortress. Chills of conjured wind, the feverish flush of lightning, and the oppressive weight of binding sorcery roiled out in answer. I held for a moment, feeling the texture of the battle in the clashing wakes of magic.

A will as weighty as a mountain tore through the pattern, falling like a meteor upon the source of one wake of battle sorcery—Hissing Cat, doing her part to hunt the Hands upon the walls. Yet elsewhere, the tide had turned against Nayen. Above the battle now spilling through the streets, the wake of a veered witch collided with a bolt of lightning and vanished.

I darted for the source of that lightning bolt in the centre of a market square. A sorcerer dressed in gilded armour stood amidst a legion with shields raised and spears levelled. The Hand hurled whips of lightning over their heads into an oncoming swarm of rebels. His face snapped towards me, sensing the wake of my flight. He pivoted, mouth open in a snarl, and hurled his fury at the sky. I danced around a fusillade of lightning, deflecting those bolts that burned too close.

Clear-River trailed above and behind me, but Running Doe and Torn Leaf broke off and dived towards the Hand. My heart lurched as he turned his attention, and his sorcery, towards them. Torn Leaf rolled in the air, dipping beneath an arc of lightning. Running Doe darted like a kingfisher. The Hand took a step back and swept his arm towards her, ready to burn her from the sky. In a burst of cinnamon scent, she returned to human form, not bothering to slow herself. One of her swords flashed as she drew it. The sparks at the Hand's fingertips flickered out as she smashed into him sword first, tackling him to the ground. His head cracked against the tiles, but she tore the sword from his chest and slashed his throat for good measure.

Torn Leaf landed beside her. The baffled legion turned to face them even as he conjured a wheel of flame and sent it whirling into their ranks. The nearest rows of Sienese soldiers shrieked and beat at the fire sprouting from their bodies. The rest dropped their weapons and shields and ran, most into the thirsty swords and spears of the rebels who had, moments ago, cowered from waves of lightning.

I dropped to the tiles, veered, and helped Running Doe back to her feet. She nursed her flank but grinned wildly.

'That was well done,' I said.

'Bloody damn hell, it sure was,' Torn Leaf added, breathless.

Clear-River landed beside us, already frowning at the slaughter as the rebels tore into the panicking Sienese. 'How many more are there, Alder? If I remember rightly, the city should house no more than a dozen Hands and only one Voice. But given Pinion's retreat, we're not only fighting the city but every Sienese soldier and sorcerer left in Nayen.'

I looked to the corpse at Running Doe's feet. 'If we hunt the Voices, the rest of the rebellion will be left without our support. Our witches are capable but stretched thin and forced to reckon with grenades and Sienese crossbows as well as sorcerers.'

'If we let this drag on, they'll decimate the rebellion and we'll lose,' Clear-River said flatly. 'No matter how powerful you and Hissing Cat are, I doubt you can occupy a city by yourselves, nor defend it.'

At least, not without becoming tyrants even more brutal than the empire, crushing every spark of unrest the moment it began to glow. 'Point taken,' I murmured and reached through the pattern towards my memories of Hissing Cat.

<What is it? I'm in the middle of something,> she answered. I felt a rush of adrenaline—not fear but excitement—then a searing wake. White-hot flame lit up a section of the wall to the south, turning a stretch of stone to bubbling slag.

<I have a new plan,> I said. <Hunt the Voices. If we cut off the canon, the city will fall.>

<A sound thought,> she said. <Though, need I remind you, the emperor himself is on his way and drawing nearer by the moment. You managed to reach that An-Zabati friend of yours across half the world. Tenet can do much the same, if he needs to.>

I muttered a curse. Still, it would at least give our witches an advantage for a time while the emperor realised what had happened and reached out directly to his Hands. <We hunt the Voices, then we deal with the emperor. That was part of the plan from the beginning.>

I felt her grudging agreement, then retreated back into the pattern. I traced the wakes of imperial sorcery back to their origins. Three points: one at the heart of the city, the other at the fortified garrison near the harbour, and a third at the gatehouse of the inner wall. There the Voices waited, likely with forces kept in reserve, maintaining the canon.

'All right,' I said. 'Stay close.'

Running Doe searched my eyes for a moment, a question furrowing her brow, but she only nodded, wiped her sword, and sheathed it. I veered, took to the air, and followed the heavy channel of transmission to the nearest Voice of the emperor.

A flickering ribbon of light, little more than a glimmer in the air, trailed from the tower overlooking the gate to the inner quarter of the city. My stomach lurched at the realisation that this might be Voice Golden-Finch, Oriole's father, who had treated me well as a guest in his home. From childhood, I had been inculcated with Sienese values, deepest among them filial piety, particularly respect for one's father. Oriole's relationship with Voice Golden-Finch had been tumultuous, but no Sienese son could forgive his father's murder.

In my moment of hesitation, a whirling wake, flashing with chills and fever, tore through the pattern. Lightning burned out from the tower. I carved a shield of light between us, trusting my cadre to fall into place behind it. But the lightning blinded me to a subtler, truer danger. Shielding sorcery, after all, protected well against lightning and fire, but not in the least against wind.

A gust like a hail of daggers ripped through me. Blood spurted from a dozen cuts. The strength went out of my wings as delicate tendons gave way. Too surprised even to shriek, I plummeted. The city spun beneath me, stars blurring into lanterns and the roaring flames of battle. Through the fog of pain and shock I reached for healing sorcery. At once, a soothing calm settled and my wounds began to knit. I called a wind to hurl myself back into the sky, back towards the tower, where one of my cadre—though I could not say whom—ducked and wove around bolts of lightning and gouts of flame.

I redoubled the wind that carried me, taking a cue from Running Doe, treating my body less as a vessel than as a missile. I wove a curtain of light, fire, lightning, and wind around myself as I flew, blinding myself, with only the weight of transmission to orient my flight.

Magic poured towards me, battering with every power at the Voice's command. I felt a chill down my spine as he conjured a shield in desperation. It shattered like glass, scraping away the flames that wreathed me for only a moment, granting me a glimpse of the Voice's gaunt face, contorted in terror, heartbeats before our collision.

His body did not so much break as shatter, becoming so much dust and ichor mingling with the obliterated rock and wood as I tore my way through the tower. I wheeled upwards to a chorus of groaning supports and grinding stone as the tower listed, a drunkard dealt one solid blow to the side of the head, now collapsing. First blocks, then entire sections of stone wall fell to the earth, pulverising the nearby homes of the rich and powerful. Soon nothing remained but a jagged, broken tooth jutting above the gate.

I circled over the wreckage. The witch who had been evading the Voice's attacks joined me. I reached out with transmission, first with memories of Running Doe, then Clear-River, then, my heart aching and thundering, Torn Leaf.

<What the hell is this?> he demanded.

<It's Foolish Cur,> I said. <What happened to the others?>

<Don't know,> Torn Leaf answered, readily accepting my presence in his mind in a way that no one else ever had. <I saw you get tossed away by that wind. After that, I didn't have much attention to spare for anything but keeping myself alive.>

I searched the streets below us for the huddled, broken forms of fallen eagle hawks—and then realised the absurdity of what I was doing. My eyes, even an eagle hawk's eyes, were far poorer tools than transmission.

Releasing Torn Leaf, I fixated on my most potent memories of Running Doe, made only the night before. There, a flickering presence, weaker than it ought to have been.

<Running Doe!>

I felt a rebounding of awareness but no words, yet I could trace my sense of her through the pattern. I found her at the end of a smeared trail of blood and broken tiles on a flat rooftop, lying curled on her

side. She clutched the canon of witchcraft tight and gave off a soothing wake, gradually knitting a plethora of wounds.

I veered and knelt beside her, afraid that embracing her as I longed
to would agitate some unseen broken bone or bruise. Her eyes fluttered open.

'Bit of rough flying there,' she murmured. 'Just need to figure out
how a few of these ribs fit back together.'

A nervous, relieved laugh burst from me. Then, collecting myself, I
asked, "Did you see what happened to Clear-River?'

She shook her head weakly. 'I saw him get tossed like a pile of rags,
but not where he landed.'

A gnawing sickness gripped me, watching her knit herself back
together, wondering if Clear-River lay doing likewise, or dead, somewhere in the streets below. I had intended for them to help me in my
duel with the emperor, if only to occupy the sorcerers he kept as his
personal guard, his Fist. Yet, if they fared this poorly against Voices,
bringing them face to face with the emperor would be a death sentence.

My canon had served its purpose. They wielded magic with more
certainty and strength than Hands with twice their training. But even
if my cadre learned more quickly, most Hands, Voices, and Fists had
far more than a single year to hone their power, and the emperor had
lived for millennia. Had the canon of witchcraft been a failed project
from the beginning, attempting to recreate and usurp in a matter of
months what the emperor had been building for lifetimes? If so, I had
doomed those who followed me—who placed their trust in me, who
fought for me.

Torn Leaf landed beside me and veered, rolling his shoulders but
grinning. 'I spotted him,' he said. 'Clear-River. He's on his feet. Managed to right himself before he hit the ground. Just catching his breath,
he says. Seems the two of you took the worst of it.'

A relief, but one that did little to defray my sense that this had all
been a mistake, that I ought never have brought them with me.

'Well then,' Running Doe asked, pulling herself to her feet, still
nursing one flank. 'What next?'

It was too late for regret. Too late to castigate myself for yet again
allowing my reach to exceed my grasp.

'We've another Voice to kill,' I said, knowing that it would be Golden-Finch, already numbing myself to the agony of betraying Oriole's memory. Yet another painful wake of the change I would carve into the world. 'Follow me.'

30
An Impossible Offer
Hand Pinion

From the stern of the double-rigged skiff *Seafoam*, Pinion watched smoke billow against the waning moon. He felt the wakes of the battle, faint and distant. The rebels had begun their attack and the punitive army he sailed to meet was still two days away.

And now, while Eastern Fortress fell, he would stand before the emperor, either to answer for treasonous words or to be rewarded for the impending success of his brutal, brilliant plan.

The massed fleet of the punitive army loomed ahead—vast transport ships, a city upon the waves, their ribbed sails wide enough to blot out the stars. The foremost ship bore no name upon its mast but the emperor's tetragram in gold, glimmering in the lantern light that rose from the deck below. The sailors aboard the *Seafoam* referred to it as the *Ocean Throne*. Like the other ships of the fleet, its sails billowed with a wind from nowhere that filled Pinion's lungs with a chilling wake and cut across the waves with a speed that belied its bulk.

Nevertheless, they would be too late to spare Eastern Fortress the horror of battle. Another burden on Pinion's soul.

Such thoughts passed through him, leaving only a bitter emptiness. He was no Su White-Knife. He had never been. Even if his plan had worked perfectly, he lacked the strength and callousness his station demanded.

The emperor and his punitive army might yet dislodge them from the city, but the chance to annihilate them, exposed upon the battle plain, had been lost. The fighting would be hard and costly now, unless the emperor decided that Nayen deserved a fate akin to Toa Alon. With his power, he might drown it and all its inhabitants—the rebels among them—in a tidal wave, or cast the city into the sea. After Setting Sun Fortress, Pinion wondered if there were any line the empire would not cross.

Yet the hatred that had burned so fiercely, that might have let him revel in such horror, had faded.

At Greyfrost, while he stood over his tortured grandmother, Wen Alder had said something that Pinion only half remembered. But his last words echoed in his mind like an aphorism of the sages.

Does this seem right?

Right would be a life of poetry, of art, and of some simple work that left him with just enough wealth to be generous with his friends. No flashing swords. No screaming children or howling mothers. No cities condemned by the failure of an ill-planned trap.

If he had only realised all of this long ago, standing at Oriole's grave with Wen Alder, when he might have diverted from the path intended for him. Better to be a disappointment, but self-satisfied, than to loathe oneself for the sake of others.

A wildly un-Sienese thought, he realised, and laughed.

Perhaps Wen Alder would win the day. Perhaps Nayen would be free.

'You find the sacking of a city funny?' Captain Huo emerged from the hatchway to the aft cabin. 'I do not remember you laughing at Setting Sun Fortress.'

'Not at all, Captain,' Pinion said and turned from the city, where once again brutality was returned for brutality—one massacre for another, if the rebels had their way. He knew nothing of the captain's conversation with Voice Golden-Finch, nor why the emperor had summoned him to the *Ocean Throne* along with Pinion. Presumably to be rewarded for his part in the plan, or to serve as a witness to

Pinion's many failings. 'I can either laugh or I can weep. I prefer not to meet the emperor bleary eyed.'

For though Pinion had been summoned, he came with his own agenda. The emperor would answer for the suffering Pinion had endured, for the agony of living a life according to the designs of others.

If Pinion could not have vengeance, he would at the very least understand the cause of all his pain.

The *Ocean Throne* slowed, its sails billowing backwards as the Hand aboard—or perhaps the emperor himself—called a wind to ease it to a halt long enough for the *Seafoam* to come alongside and lower a gangway. Pinion held his head high as he crossed, his hands folded into the sleeves of the black robe trimmed with silver that he had worn on the day he'd passed his imperial examinations. Huo followed behind, his armour polished and glinting in the lantern light.

A soldier in a simple uniform that Pinion did not immediately recognise greeted them. He brought his fist to his chest in salute. The tetragram glimmered on the back of his hand.

'Welcome aboard,' the Fist said. Behind him, on a platform before the sail, another figure in the same uniform called a wind to fill the sails anew. 'The emperor will receive you atop the forecastle.'

Captain Huo returned the salute. Pinion only nodded. As he understood the hierarchy of empire, he stood above these Fists, who were selected from the imperial military rather than from the pool of examination candidates. They were not bureaucrats, nor military commanders, but only the emperor's personal guard.

As he followed the Fist to the forecastle, Pinion saw dozens more wearing that same uniform. No fewer than fifty had accompanied the punitive army. At the staircase to the top of the forecastle, the Fist touched Captain Huo on the shoulder.

'He will see you one at a time,' the Fist said. 'The Hand first.'

Pinion had never been a minister, but he understood how his father had handled murky matters of the law. There were two witnesses of merit to all that had transpired at Greyfrost and Burrow. The emperor would hear their stories, it seemed, and parse and compare them in search of the truth.

The emperor stood at the bow, one hand cupped in the other at the small of his back. Rings of coral and jade glimmered on his fingers. A cape of golden silk lined in ermine fur and stitched with uncountable silver hands hung from his right shoulder, draping his side. Flickering lights streamed from him, like the limbs of his Thousand-Armed Throne, extending upwards and outwards towards Nayen, Toa Alon, the Batir Waste, the Sienese Heartland—to every Voice in the empire. Three cables, two red and one gold, divided the bow into thirds, transforming it into an open-air audience hall with the stars for its ceiling. Above it all, like a pillar rooted to the centre of the world and holding up the heavens, loomed a crushing weight of sorcery.

Fear clawed up from Pinion's gut towards his throat. He had been resigned to failure, even failure unto death, before setting foot upon the *Ocean Throne.* Yet no philosophical distance, no detachment from one's own fate, could protect against the overwhelming presence of a god.

'Hand Pinion.' The emperor turned towards him. The tines of his crown jutted from his brow like the antlers of a lion serpent. Glass beads dangled on silver threads, obscuring his eyes. He wore a dark, thin beard and the sharp angles of his face gave no sign of his age, nor of the burden of a thousand-year reign. His voice carried as much weight as his magic. 'You have come a long way in so short a time. A few more paces need not intimidate you.'

Only then did Pinion realise that he had been rooted to the deck, having failed even to begin the ritual of obeisance. He stepped forwards, bowed, and touched his forehead to the first cable.

The emperor waved a hand dismissively. 'All of that is pageantry, and here we have no audience. Come. Join me.'

Pinion balked. He tried to do as he was bid, to walk forwards to the emperor's side, yet the command tore through the fabric of propriety. Though he might be disillusioned enough to stand up to his father, violating the structures of empire at the feet of the emperor himself— even at the emperor's bidding!—felt impossible, as though the author of logic itself had committed some profound fallacy.

'You seem troubled, Hand Pinion,' the emperor said. 'Why?'

Though his eyes were obscured, Pinion felt their scrutiny. Moments passed, each tightening around his throat, until he managed to stammer, 'Y-you are owed obeisance, Your Majesty.'

A smile like a curl of mist touched the emperor's face. 'I am. But does a man, in the end, tally the debts of ants?' He gestured to the gunwale. 'Join me, Hand Pinion. Let us talk.'

The dream-like quality of the situation put Pinion off balance. Fear still surged within him, but he had no way to react to it. How to fight on the battlefield of manners when the foundations of propriety had been shattered?

'Why should a man care to speak with an ant?' Pinion wondered aloud, hardly realising he spoke.

The emperor's laugh sent a shiver of terror down Pinion's spine.

'Why indeed? Perhaps because a certain ant has behaved in an unprecedented way. Ants might be objects of curiosity. I myself found them an amusing fascination in my youth, before the notion of the empire had so much as been planted in my mind. Ants and wasps. Did you know, Hand Pinion, that you are the first Hand of the emperor to argue with me and win?'

Pinion could think of no response, and still stood rooted to the deck. The emperor, once more—and with a severe turn of his mouth—gestured to the gunwale. At last Pinion's legs obeyed him, yet his knees wanted to buckle and his spine shivered as he strode past the second and third cables without so much as a nod of his head.

'It is not a thing done, you understand,' the emperor went on. 'An appendage does not correct the mind that moves it. A mouth does not speak against its master. Yet you refused an order. Presented an alternate course, as though I had not thought of every possibility and discarded every alternative. And you were correct.' The wisp of a smile again. 'You proposed a course I had not considered. One that, though brutal, would solve a great many problems.'

Pinion felt the urge to apologise for the failure of that course, which had only brought suffering down upon Eastern Fortress, but suppressed it. He was far out in uncharted, dangerous waters.

'I felt something in that moment which I had not felt in...oh, hundreds of years,' the emperor went on. 'Not since the departure of a dear curmudgeon of an old friend. One who had been with me from the beginning of my grand project, and who I intended to keep with me through to the end, in defiance of time itself.' His expression turned sour. 'He too defied me, though to less productive ends than you did.' Then, with a sudden ferocity: 'Well? Have you nothing to say, Hand Pinion?'

Pinion swallowed. 'I am sorry to hear of your loss, Your Majesty.'

The emperor tilted his head. 'I did not think it a loss. Not until you, as he did, saw through to my humanity. One can become fixated, myopic, to the point of self-destruction. Traveller would have put it in some sort of poetic aphorism. Something about ships and captains and navigators, I suspect.

'Things have been going awry, Hand Pinion. You may not see this yet, for you are young and know little, but as the empire grows it has become brittle. The rebellion in Nayen you know well, and you have certainly heard of An-Zabat, but there are cracks elsewhere, some vast and some only hair thin, but all profound in their threat. But the empire must grow further if it is to fulfil its purpose. To bring things to fruition now would only destroy all that I mean to preserve.

'I find myself in need of help. Of more than appendages and mouths. I require eyes that see in ways that I cannot. I need another Traveller-on-the-Narrow-Way to protect my empire from my own blindness. No one mind, no matter how vast, can consider every possibility, after all.'

Pinion shook his head, disbelieving. He had not known what to expect from this conversation, but had never imagined this. He had never *wanted* this. It was the sort of thing Wen Alder—not the rebel leader but the ambitious youth who had lived in their home and befriended Oriole—would have longed for.

'I made the suggestion merely to save my own life and secure my vengeance.' It was the only thing that felt like an honest response.

The emperor chuckled, softly this time, as at the endearing antics of a puppy. 'Further evidence of all that I have said. You sought to use me as every man seeks to use his fellows. What is the empire but an attempt to do just the same, but on a grand scale, to ends of eternal and universal worth?'

'But I failed.' Pinion heard a note of desperation in his own voice. Desperate for what? For the emperor's condemnation? What else could he possibly expect? 'The rebels arrived too quickly. Eastern Fortress will fall.'

'No, Hand Pinion,' the emperor said. 'It will not. Oh, it will burn for a time, and many will suffer and die, but these are small things. And in return for them, we will both have our vengeance. This is how it always was with Traveller, as well. He saw the possibilities that I could not, and I saw the means to seize them, to turn them from an idea into tangible reality, how best to reshape the pattern. You gave me an idea, but I have transformed it to best suit my purposes, and thus the needs of the world. A relationship which I would like to see continue.'

Pinion put his hand against the gunwale, first to steady himself and then to give himself an anchor to reality. The grain of the wood, rough against his palm, told him that this was no dream, no hallucination born of sun fever while Voice Age-of-Plenty's soldiers bore him to Eastern Fortress in that oven of a palanquin.

What could he say? The emperor had cast aside the constraints of propriety, but they had only ever been symbols of the true foundation of the empire. Order depended upon each individual—each *thing*, in truth—aligning to its purpose according to the emperor's will. And now Pinion had a new purpose. He could accept it or be without a place, without value. Left adrift, again, unto death or destitution.

The emperor's attention snapped away. One of the ribbons of light that streamed to the east pulsed and surged. The slight smile beneath the veil of glass beads widened into a furious grin.

'Ah, here we are. The trap is sprung,' the emperor said. A new wake, cool and light, then gripping the base of Pinion's lungs, roiled out from him. Shimmering light unfurled from the emperor's back, stretching out to either side like wings forged of golden blades. Wind whipped in from nowhere and bore him upwards, where he hung for a moment, his robe and cape fluttering, and gazed down at Pinion. His eyes were visible for an instant, black and depthless, like the spaces between the stars. 'I will have your answer when I return.'

The wind surged again. A crash like thunder sounded, and he was gone, visible only as a blur of light against the dark of the sky streaking towards the smoke that roiled from Eastern Fortress.

Brutality answered with brutality, answered with brutality.

There was no escaping the cycle, it seemed. It had drawn Pinion further and further in, unto the right hand of the emperor. He wanted to laugh. To weep. Instead, he sagged against the gunwale and heaved the contents of his stomach into the sea.

31

Hunting Voices

Foolish Cur

Two wakes of transmission loomed over Eastern Fortress, like twin chains of iron anchored to the pattern of the world. One emanated from the western quarter, near the harbour, the other from the heart of the city. A mountainous wake that could only have been Hissing Cat tore towards the western Voice, leaving the other for me.

Stray lanterns cast pools of red and yellow light below, as though to herald the blood and flames that would soon stain these streets yet untouched by battle. The wake led deeper, beyond the final ring of fortifications that separated the governor's estate from the rest of Nayen, a Sienese garden—the empire in miniature—built atop the ruins of what had once been the Palace of the Sun King. A garden where I had spent the brightest days of my youth, before war and suffering opened the door to disillusionment. A garden where the wake of transmission had its root, where Voice Golden-Finch bound the emperor's canon to the city.

I reached out to Clear-River, Torn Leaf, and Running Doe.

<Stay close to me,> I told them and dived towards the garden. The wind of my descent stirred the plum tree that grew above Oriole's

grave, casting a gentle shower of white petals from its branches. The Voice's transmission emanated from the reception hall nearby. Clear-River positioned himself to guard my back, his canon of witchcraft held before him like the hilt of a sword. Running Doe took her place beside me, brows knitted and shoulders rolled forwards as though preparing for a brawl.

Torn Leaf gawked at the rich woods and gilt paint of the pavilions, the artificial hill, the porous stone jutting from the nearby pond, the various exotic plants imported from throughout the empire. The landmarks of my coming of age. Basalt columns, narrow streams, and groves arranged artfully in what now, after I had spent so long in the wilderness, seemed a hollow gesture towards nature rather than any sophisticated recreation. All of it stood unchanged after half a decade. There, glimpsed briefly through gaps in a stand of bamboo, was the pavilion where I had first met Hand Usher, heard the tale of the pollical cat, and, with a clever answer, sealed my future, and with it the fate of the world.

'Burning gods,' Torn Leaf murmured. 'Could've fed my town for a year with the cost of that landscaping, I'll bet.'

'Wait until you see inside,' Clear-River said drily. 'The wealth in the reception hall alone rivals that of the rest of the island. And that is only a child's scrawling in comparison to the fine calligraphy that decorates the emperor's palaces.'

Torn Leaf's eyes widened. 'Guess I can see how you thought it a good idea to work for these bastards.'

'Quiet,' I ordered. 'Keep your eyes open.'

I let my awareness descend partway into the pattern, like a sphere of jade half submerged in a pool of water. Enough to deepen my sensitivity to magic without sacrificing attention to the world around me. Golden-Finch's attack might not come in the form of a burst of magic but a bolt fired from some hidden vantage—enough to kill me if it took me by surprise and pierced some vital organ or carried some fast-acting poison.

We were isolated by distance and high walls from the screams of the dying and the clash of steel. A distant rumble, like muted thunder, spoke to a detonating grenade in some far corner of the city. I took the path down from the hilltop, passing by the arch of white stones that marked Oriole's grave. I let my gaze linger upon it for a moment and then pressed on, trying not to think of the fact that I had come here, to our home, to kill his father and younger brother.

But why should I kill them? I knew them well enough, I thought, to subdue them by other means. My will might not match Hissing Cat's or the emperor's, but I could surely overcome a Voice of the emperor with no power in the old magic.

If I could avoid adding to the weight of guilt I carried, I would. Frothing Wolf and Harrow Fox might balk at the thought of keeping a Voice and a Hand prisoner, but I could sever them from the canon. A few strokes of a knife could remove their tetragrams. A cruelty Oriole could more easily forgive than their deaths.

'Golden-Finch! Pinion!' I called out. Birds, hiding from the terror that had descended upon their city, burst from a nearby bush in a drumbeat of wings and a chattering chorus. 'Come out and surrender! You are cornered here. The city will fall. It is only a question of how many need die, and how brutally, before it is done. There is no need for us to shame Oriole's memory by fighting.'

'Shame Oriole's memory?' Golden-Finch's voice echoed out from the open windows of the reception hall. 'Every moment you live shames his memory!'

I ignored the flare of pain his words stirred in me. 'Pinion can testify to the storm of fire and lightning I called at Greyfrost. You need only come out. Else I will level this garden.'

'How long were you plotting this, Alder?' Golden-Finch shouted in answer. 'All the while you lived in my house? Did you secretly revel in my son's death even as you placed your brick upon his grave?'

I ground my teeth. I had never betrayed Oriole. Never, in my own mind, truly betrayed the things I loved about Sien: its appreciation for beauty, for grace in form. Part of me, suppressed these last months while I became an agent of violence I abhorred, longed for them. For afternoons spent sipping tea and reciting poetry, or refining the line of my calligraphy. Yet I could not look past the brutality at the foundations of the empire, nor the mad ambitions of its emperor.

'Come out,' I said. 'How can this dialogue lead anywhere conducted through a barred door?'

'Where would you have it lead?' Golden-Finch laughed. 'Pinion did, indeed, tell me what happened at Greyfrost, and I have felt the wakes of destruction wreaked here. There can be no negotiating from a position of such weakness.'

'Very well,' I said. 'There will be no negotiation. Only a trade. Your surrender, and your son's, in exchange for your lives.'

'Simply kill me and be done with it!' His voice took on a note of hysteria. 'Or are you unwilling to admit that your revolution is the same as our conquest, only reversing the victims and the victors?'

The part of me that once thrilled at the prospect of confronting such moral questions began composing an answer, even as I recognised his accusation for the bait it was.

'He is stalling you,' Clear-River muttered in Nayeni.

In the pattern, I felt for the mountain-heavy wake of Hissing Cat's magic. It was still near the harbour. How had a lone Voice of the emperor, even supported by an honour guard of Hands, stood against her for so long? Elsewhere, more and more wakes of veering and conjured fire flickered out, and it was impossible to say how many of the chills of windcalling originated in the canon of witchcraft rather than the canon of sorcery.

'Stay vigilant and shout at the first sign of trouble,' I told my cadre in their tongue, then shut my eyes and descended deep into the pattern. I sought Pinion first, for I knew him better, recalling memories of our conversation at Oriole's grave and our brief confrontation at Greyfrost, his eyes full of terror and wonder, and the sound of his footsteps fleeing.

As when I had reached out to Atar, a current pulled me to the west, out over the sea. Pinion was not in the garden. Curious—and a relief, in that it would be far easier to deal with Voice Golden-Finch alone— but not a puzzle that demanded immediate attention. I reached instead towards his father.

I did not know Golden-Finch well, yet my memories of him were rich enough with anticipation, hope, dread, and regret to come easily to mind. The weight of his presence, standing upon the dais, welcoming me and my fellow candidates to the examinations, and later announcing our successes. His frustration with me while I fatefully argued in favour of Oriole joining the campaign against Frothing Wolf's uprising.

Memories I followed through the undercurrents of the pattern and into his mind.

Clear-River's consciousness had been whirling rapids, churning in terror. Atar's had been far calmer, but still a storm of fear and anger. Golden-Finch was a placid pool. Mirror-bright, clear as glass. This, despite the frustration in his voice, the rising fear and anger I had heard in our conversation.

And it occurred to me—too late, in a moment of cold fear—that Voice Golden-Finch would never be alone in his own mind.

<Hello, Wen Alder,> said a voice, echoing in my head like a thunderclap. As fresh to me in memory as my own father's, though I had heard it only once before, while I lay prostrate, my forehead upon a golden thread.

And with it, a weight like a mountain fell upon my shoulders.

32

Arrogance
Foolish Cur

I tried to scream a warning, but my jaw seized as though gripped by a steel vice. Running Doe took a step towards me, her face shifting from concern into fear, as the door to Golden-Finch's hall slammed open.

The smell of a thunderstorm. A chill rushed down my spine.

Lightning burned out from the open door, struck Torn Leaf's shoulder, and spun him through the air. He crashed into a grove of bamboo, where he lay among splintered stalks, trailing wisps of smoke.

<I wondered if you would have the hubris to reach into the mind of a Voice,> the emperor said, his words like the roots of a mountain grinding against the foundations of the earth. <But no, I thought. Hand Alder was so clever. Had so *painfully* realised the breadth of my presence after An-Zabat. Still, it was a worthwhile trap to lay. I had trouble finding you through the pattern without your tetragram. You were significant enough to take note of, but we had met only the once, and you had changed a great deal by the time I felt the need to seek your mind again. Everything would be so much easier if you simply reached out to me yourself. And when you let Hand Pinion live, I realised you just might be foolish enough to do so.>

Torn Leaf groaned but lay unmoving. Running Doe threw herself to the path as another lightning bolt arced out, cut through the air above her, and shattered a column of basalt. She looked to me, terrified, but I could neither defend nor comfort her so long as the emperor held me. Clear-River crouched and began weaving a wall of wind between us and the reception hall, and I felt a twinge of regret that I had not given them shielding sorcery.

No time to dwell on failure. I shut my eyes and focused on the weight of the mind settling in the centre of my consciousness, not unlike the iron spar of Hissing Cat's will but heavier, carving not the pattern of the world but the pattern of my own thoughts. I threw myself against it, trying to sever the connection between us as I had severed the bond between the emperor and Usher at Greyfrost.

An effort as painful, and as fruitful, as bashing my head against bedrock.

<Too late, I fear. But worry not. I have no wish to kill you. I find you, in fact, entirely baffling. Not the first Hand of the emperor to betray me, but the first to do so for a reason beyond his own idiotic and short-sighted ambition. Tell me, what aspects of imperial doctrine did you find so distasteful that you cast aside your future and chose, instead, an impossible war?>

Voice Golden-Finch appeared in the doorway, satisfaction tightening his smile. I reached for battle sorcery, all thought of sparing his life obliterated by my need to destroy him before he could harm my cadre. Yet the emperor's will constrained me, binding my power as surely as a cord might bind my wrists.

Golden-Finch raised his hand and pointed to where Running Doe lay. She roared, threw herself to her feet, gripped her strip of bone with white knuckles and hurled fire. It splashed harmlessly from a shield of hardened light, which faded, and was followed by a bolt of battle sorcery.

I screamed inside my head, having no control of my own voice, as lightning speared her through.

She staggered forwards a step and collapsed. Clear-River veered and took to the sky. The emperor held my head, even denying my impulse to watch Clear-River's flight, wondering if he would mount some further attack or flee.

<Come now. You cannot have expected any other result, bringing them into such a battle with hardly any training.> Then, after what felt like laughter: <You need answer none of my questions, Alder. You are an open book to me, now, and a fascinating one. It is like looking into a mirror, refracted through aeons of time. I am to you as the gods were to me. But you are so tragically mistaken. Did you never once question the source of all you came to believe about me—about my intentions, about how I might react to the various threats sprouting up throughout my empire? Or was Okara's little disguise as a wounded puppy enough to blind you to all his manipulations? *Think*, Alder. What better way to deal with a nascent threat than to pit him against an ancient enemy?>

His words should have torn through me, but I felt only the shadow of the pain they promised as I hammered against his will. A low moan made me open my eyes. Running Doe still breathed, her face twisted in agony, her hands clutching her strip of bone. Her fingers sought the logogram that marked the magic of healing.

Even if she touched it, she could not hope to seal her own wounds. Too weak. Too poorly trained. Led headlong, at a rush, into a maelstrom without anything like the power she needed to survive it.

<What sort of man leads people into war when he is unwilling to watch them die?> the emperor mused. <For all the faults you project onto me, you carry so many of your own, and with so little self-awareness.>

She was still breathing. I could heal her. I could undo the damage my hubris had done.

Where was Hissing Cat? If anyone could force the emperor from my mind, it was her.

Which recalled to me her last lessons. Transmission and the power to seal the pattern. I could never hope to overwhelm the emperor's will as I had cut off Voice Usher from the canon, and later Frothing Wolf and Burning Dog from their witchcraft. But I could do as the Girzan witch of the old sort had done and sever *myself* from the pattern, if only for an instant.

I reached deep, not into the pattern of the world itself but into the structures of my own mind and built walls there, as Hissing Cat had done when she had first taught me the magic of transmission, like the walls I had built to forge my canon.

<What are you—?>

For the first time since my earliest childhood, a bone-deep silence descended. That sixth sense with which I had felt the pattern of the world—at first in ignorance—became blinded to all but the structures within my own mind. I gasped at the shock of it—the sudden lack of texture, the *simplicity* of my every sensation—while the phantom limb by which I worked all magic pawed at the barrier I had made, desperate to unmake those walls which were my only protection from the emperor's transmission. Walls that reduced the world around me to the simple geometry of a landscape painting, as long as I maintained them. It was such an overwhelming shift in perception that I nearly forgot my purpose, until I heard Running Doe's strangled, rasping cry as Voice Golden-Finch raised his hand.

Though it terrified me to let down my defences, I released the wall that shielded my mind from the pattern and felt the rushing in of familiar complexity, the interweaving, eternal flow of energies. The chill down my spine. The scent of cinnamon.

I hurled an arrow of wind.

Golden-Finch toppled backwards, sparks flitting impotently from his fingers. Blood gushed from his chest, filling the heavy silks he wore, and he collapsed bonelessly to the ground, slapping the earth like raw meat. He gurgled, clutched the ragged hole where his heart had been, and lay still.

I went to my knees at Running Doe's side. Her breath came as shallow as that of a bird fallen from its nest. The fabric of her shirt had blackened and become intertwined with her burned and melted flesh. A complex wound to heal, but no more difficult than extruding the vines of carrion crawler from my grandmother's mangled arm, and I was more skilled now. I would do better. I would not only save her life but smooth away the scarring, leave no sign of her injury—no evidence of my mistake.

As I reached for healing magic, I felt a familiar, terrifying weight descend.

He had lurked in Voice Golden-Finch's mind, waiting to trap me, dominating me before I'd had a chance to mount any resistance. Perhaps, before, he had not known my mind well enough to find it through the undercurrents of the pattern, but now he certainly did, and there was no reason he could not do just as I had done to Clear-River, Atar, and Voice Golden Finch.

I might have tried to wield the canon of witchcraft to heal Running Doe while walling myself off from the wider pattern—and the emperor's influence—but the barrier within my mind might well have interfered with the structures of the canon. Her life hung in the balance, and the emperor was on his way. I had no time to experiment.

'Running Doe.' I pressed the strip of bone into her hand, guiding her fingers. 'I can't fix you now. You must keep yourself alive. Do you understand?'

She searched my face, her expression twisted in pain, but she nodded and tightened her grip. The gentle, soothing wake of healing touched me for only a moment before I turned my attention to my own defence.

I severed myself from the pattern again before the emperor could flood the pool of my mind. Once more, the world became muted, alien to my senses, attuned as they were to layers of intertwining depth. But the weight of the emperor's presence, too, had vanished. I was safe from him, for now.

But for how long? The moment I stepped back into the pattern of the world to reach for magic, he would be upon me.

Thankfully, Running Doe's breathing began to ease.

'Don't try to heal the flesh,' I said. 'I will do it. Or Hissing Cat will, when she gets here.'

Flakes of ash drifted overhead, rising from the chaos of the battle that still tore through Eastern Fortress. No sign of her, or of Clear-River, who it seemed had fled. I cursed him under my breath and crossed the path to where Torn Leaf lay among the bamboo. A fractal written in red and black crawled beneath the shattered and melted scales of the armour on his left shoulder. He looked up at me, obviously in pain but breathing steadily enough.

I turned back to the sky. Where the *hell* was she? It was impossible to imagine that a Voice of the emperor had delayed her for so long.

'Where is your canon? You should be able to heal this without too much trouble.'

Torn Leaf shook his head, grimacing. 'Dropped it. Sorry about that. In fairness, I was cartwheeling through the air at the time.'

A gust stirred the billowing smoke and something broad-winged cut through the drifting ash, then swept down towards the courtyard to land not far from Oriole's grave.

'Hissing Cat,' I said, turning towards the descending figure, which hung in silhouette against the rising sun. 'What took you—'

Silks billowed in the breeze, which curved around great wings forged and feathered by hardened light. Glass beads dangled from the tines of a golden crown. They clinked together as the figure strode forwards, his hands in his sleeves, his wings of light and wind fading.

As when I had seen him before—only the once, and only at a distance, shrouded in a fog of incense—he struck me as far too young for his station, despite the weight of millennia in his hard gaze, peering through the swaying beads, dark with a cold, unbending fury.

'You continue to fascinate, Wen Alder,' he said, stepping forwards, making no move to kill me. In that moment, he could have done so with a thought and faced not a grain of resistance. 'I will admit to the cleverness of this defence, considering the tool I used to attack you, insofar as a mouse who scurries down a hole is clever when he feels the shadow of a hawk. But if I wished to kill you, I might have done so from the deck of my flagship, out there on the sea. Or from the air. Snuffed your life like a candle, giving you no warning, not even a moment to wallow in regret, or fear, or even confusion. Do you know why I didn't?'

If I was to remain cut off from the pattern, I would need a weapon. I reached towards the hilt of Torn Leaf's sword, still in his scabbard. Drawing it would call his eye and likely put an end to our conversation, and my life.

'Answer me,' he commanded, casting his voice in iron and lashing out with all the authority of one who stood atop a hierarchy reforged from the shattered remnants of all the world's kingdoms.

I could only shake my head. Fear had left me unable to do more than focus on maintaining my defence while I searched for any opportunity, however dismal, to strike.

'You have been misinformed,' he said. 'I can think of nothing more absurd than to place so much trust in a god *defined* by deception. I have no wish to plunge the world into chaos, Wen Alder. What have I ever done to indicate as much?'

'You're lying,' I managed. 'You already *have* caused chaos. Everywhere the empire goes, there is suffering.'

'Everywhere the empire goes, there is *order*,' the emperor corrected. 'Given time, of course. Like a young colt, chaos must be broken before it can be rebuilt. You know the doctrine of Sien—my doctrine—nearly as well as any mortal. You understand its structure, its layers, its hierarchies. I do not want war, Wen Alder. Everything I have done, I have done to *prevent* it.

'Before I forged my empire, Sien was a cacophony of petty kings all clamouring for power, hurling their peoples at one another, drowning the land in blood. The rest of the world is much the same. You have seen this yourself in Nayen, in recent days. Ambition is no special talent of the gods. We are all cursed with it.

'I strive to create a world in which ambition can be channelled, put to use, for the mutual benefit of all. With an eternal emperor with a never-changing name atop the hierarchy, and with positions and power assigned by merit, with all from the wealthiest aristocrat to the poorest sheep farmer's son granted the opportunity to rise simply by sitting for a test. Carefully designed. Incomplete, of course. All must be folded into the system, yet they resist, unable to let go of their sentimental notion that their cultures ought to survive. Only one of their many flawed, blinkered perceptions of the world.'

He may as well have been speaking the ancient language of Hissing Cat's oracle runes or some tongue carried from the distant west on windships across the Batir Waste.

'Why, when I have worked so hard to build such an ordered world, would I risk it all for so short-sighted a thing as *revenge*? With the pacts, we have already hobbled the gods. Left them little more than spectators, watching the world turn, leaving them behind as doctrine devours the folk religions that are the last vestige of their influence. They are *desperate* for their freedom. To that end, Alder, *you have been used*.'

'Then why build up the canon?' I argued, hoping he would glance away just long enough for me to reach Torn Leaf's sword. 'Why arm your Hands and Voices as though to challenge the gods?'

He stopped walking. Smiled. Almost gently. Like a parent explaining some complex truth to a child not yet old enough to understand it.

'Only a fool fails to arm himself against a known enemy,' he said. 'I want peace, Alder. I fought hard for it, have dedicated my life to expanding and preserving it. It is the gods who want war.'

'Then why didn't they take the chance when Naphena built her obelisks?'

'Because we would have fought back. They are vicious and petty, but they are careful. Naphena's *crime*, if it can be called that, was not so severe as to demand war. They made an example of her, and trusted that their brutality would cow the rest of us. A strategy I have found useful myself, though I am not so weak willed as to be cowed. Now, they would use you to collapse our defences before reasserting their power when we are weak.' Only a few paces remained between us. He studied me from behind his glittering veil. 'What good has it done you, this bounding from faction to faction? There is no need for you to suffer so.'

Why toy with me thus, rather than strike me down? Only to watch me squirm? Punishment for my betrayal by way of humiliation? It seemed impossible that he told some version of the truth. Yet what evidence did I truly have by which to judge? Only the testimony of Okara, Hissing Cat, and the emperor himself—three beings whose lives stretched backwards to a time that survived only in mythic history, whose perspectives and goals were as alien as mine would be to one of the carp that swam in Voice Golden-Finch's pond.

'Come back to Centre Fortress with me,' the emperor said. 'I will make a place for you in the Eastern Academy Quarter. You and I will stand guard against the—'

A chill filled my lungs. The hairs on the back of my neck stirred. A wake of windcalling. The emperor's gaze darted away from me, towards Running Doe. A burst of pressure erupted from where she lay, her arm outstretched.

The emperor gestured with a finger and raised a gale to shield himself. Winds clashed, and through their churning the emperor hurled a bolt of lightning as bright as the sun. I drew Torn Leaf's sword and stood, thrusting for the emperor's heart.

Running Doe screamed. A single, heart-tearing note, and then silence. The smell of burning flesh, of melting steel.

The emperor looked down at me, his expression flattened by disappointment. A feverish wake roiled out from him and heat like a furnace radiated from his upraised hand. The tip of my sword glowed white hot as it drove towards that hand, and then melted away, steel dribbling to the earth like runoff from melted snow.

'This is foolishness,' the emperor said. 'Put down the blade, Alder.'

Running Doe's scream echoed in my ears, and with it Oriole's last rattling breath, resonating with such pain that my heart threatened to shatter. I might be powerful enough to turn the tide of a war and unite the halves of a rebel army, but I was still too weak to save the lives that mattered most to me.

But my greatest strength had always been my cleverness.

Okara had promised—or nearly had—to forgive anything if it brought about an end to the emperor's plans. If Running Doe yet lived, and if I was to have a chance to save her—if I was to save the rebellion, Nayen itself—I could only put my trust in the good faith of the gods.

I released the barrier around my mind and drove my will into the pattern of the world, a carving knife cutting deep. This was no magic I had seen before, no magic I had been taught, but from Hissing Cat's warnings and reluctant explanation I understood it well enough. A canon, of sorts. Walls, reshaping not the flow of a mind but the pattern of the world itself.

I drew a circle no wider than the span of my arms, cutting away a fragment of the world where the emperor and I stood, making of it a microcosm. Within those walls, I gathered the flow of the pattern, simplified enough now to be held entirely within my mind, and held firm, unchangeable, unimpeachable in its completeness. Harder than any diamond. Impossible even for the emperor's mountainous will to pierce.

His eyes went wide. The light and heat in his hand winked out, like the sun vanishing behind the moon.

White-hot steel carved through the meat of his palm. I howled and threw myself at him, taking him to the ground and pinning his hand to his chest. Curls of smoke and a gout of blood poured from his wounds—the first true evidence of his humanity.

We lay there for a moment, the emperor's breath rasping in his chest, blood bubbling from the corners of his mouth. I twisted the blade until it ground against his ribs.

His will rose up like a lion serpent, hammered at the cage I had built around us, desperate to break back into the pattern of the world.

'You have been *used!*' he snarled, voice wet and rasping, flecking my face with gore.

I shut my eyes, shut out all distractions—thoughts of the battle, of Running Doe's injuries—and focused only on maintaining the walls in the world that separated us from the wider pattern. I would not let them fall until he died.

A hand dug into my shoulder, pulled me from the emperor, and threw me to the ground. I rolled, shouting, and scrambled to my feet, ready to face my attacker.

The skulls in her hair glared at me, the empty sockets of their eyes seeming to burn with outrage. I faltered, my grip on the seal I had worked into the pattern nearly fading.

'I'm sure you'll tell me you had no choice,' Hissing Cat snarled.

'It's all right.' I felt off balance, almost concussed. A consequence of the effort required to maintain my seal, I reasoned. 'Okara said—'

The emperor coughed on his own laughter. With weary resignation, he gestured upwards with his good hand.

The stars hung obscured by smoke. Between them, the dark expanses seemed to blur and waver, like heat rising from the sands of the Batir Waste.

Behind me, I heard Torn Leaf gasp in disbelief.

Hissing Cat threw her will behind the emperor's, and the seal I had built shattered like porcelain.

Terror seized me, and pain like every vein in my body had been set aflame, and with it a certainty that I was dying.

Yet my heart continued to beat, and I realised what it was that I felt. Not sudden sickness, nor an attack, but only the wake of a magic weightier even than the emperor's will radiating out from the Thousand-Armed-Throne—a magic that could only be the work of the gods—that now tore the world asunder, reaching me without the protection of the barrier I had made.

Choked laughter bubbled up from the emperor. 'I needed only a little more time,' he murmured, then looked to me with blazing eyes. 'But this one...so *fucking* gullible.'

'Lie still, Tenet,' Hissing Cat said and went to his side. Another wake, like a sip of soothing tea—so weak, compared to what spiralled down from the sky—poured from her as she gently eased the blade from the emperor's chest.

'What are you doing?' I demanded.

'We will need him, now,' she said, her voice a tangled snarl, and tilted her chin towards the sky.

From the wavering haze above, impossible figures emerged. Flowers of wings unfolded, layered like petals, sheathed in prismatic starlight descended from the blurring gaps between the stars.

'No,' I muttered. 'If we kill him, they will forgive me. All the conflict will be put to rest.'

'If you kill me,' the emperor said, his voice gaining strength as Hissing Cat knitted his wounds, 'as I'm sure they hoped you would, you will deprive us of the best chance we have against them.'

'Don't talk,' Hissing Cat snapped. 'I'm trying to knit your shredded lung back together.'

I cast my mind into the undercurrents of the pattern, which roiled like a steaming cauldron as though a thousand white-hot coals had been dropped at once into its flow. I hurled myself into memories of the dog I had found, beaten and battered by the road, and nursed back to health. Of Hissing Cat's cave. Anything I could think of that might lead me to Okara, desperate to explain myself before things spiralled too far out of hand and the end of the world began in earnest.

But I could not find him, no matter how I searched. His mind seemed to have vanished from the pattern. Or perhaps the fabric of the pattern had already been too badly frayed, leaving me lost in the labyrinth of its tatters.

If I killed the emperor, there would be no cause for his war. The gods would see that, surely. All could go back to the way it was. Those strange, diffracted doors in the sky would close. The gods and the terror they carried in their wake would vanish. I would have time to find Running Doe, to heal her, to begin to build a life worth living rather than one defined by betrayal, horror, and war. I reached for battle sorcery and turned to the emperor.

His eyes fixed on me and flashed with hatred. A wake of magic like nothing I had felt before twisted my stomach and left me stumbling, seized by vertigo. The emperor worked a wonder I could not explain, which fit none of the powers of his canon, unlike any magic granted by any pact I knew. He disappeared with a clap like thunder as air rushed in to fill the void he had left, hurling me to the ground beside Hissing Cat. She fell forwards onto her hands and knees, the skulls in her hair rolling and clattering.

'You *idiot!*' she roared. 'You just had to go and do the damn clever thing, didn't you?'

'It was the only way.' A pathetic defence, one that would have felt childish even without the sob in my voice.

'I warned you away from this, and yet here we are.' She settled back on her heels.

'I thought—'

'No you didn't. You reacted. You decided that killing him would solve all our problems, regardless of how you managed to do it.'

'And where were you?' I demanded, hiding my shame behind anger. 'Together, we could have overcome him.'

'I came as soon as I felt his magic. That other Voice proved a wily bastard, and those half-witches you sent with me little more than a liability. I saw two struck down. The other disappeared. Fled, I assume.'

Yet more members of my cadre slain, brought into a battle we had hardly prepared them for.

I crossed to Running Doe, who lay within a scar that cut across the path. Steam billowed from her blackened wounds. I went to my knees, my heart aching even through the terror of the gods' wake. Memories pierced through the fog. Her courage. Her kindness. Her blushing face.

I felt myself pulled through the pattern of the world, as though seeking a mind through transmission.

<...Help...me...>

My heart stuttered. Somehow—impossibly—she was still alive. I went to her side. There, clutched in the burnt ruin of her hand, was the canon of witchcraft. The faintest trickle of a calming wake seeped from her. Just enough healing sorcery to cling to life, despite the certain mortality of her wounds.

But I could save her, at least. I had not led her to her death.

Little counterweight to the end of the world, but something to cling to, to give me a few moments of purpose. I reached deep for healing sorcery and poured it into her, as I had my grandmother at Greyfrost. As her rib cage took shape, she took a deep, shuddering gasp, inflating her lungs, and exhaled a scream that split my ears and tore my heart.

'I'm here. It will be all right.'

'Don't lie to the girl, Foolish Cur,' Hissing Cat snarled. 'The old battle lines have been redrawn.'

'But Okara—'

'Even if the gods could forgive your breaking the pact, Tenet did it too,' she pressed on. 'Folded and unfolded the pattern like a sheet of paper and slipped across the narrowed gap. He's likely back in Centre Fortress now, having one of his Voices or Hands or Fists or what have you knit him back together.'

One of the gods—a distant, glimmering silhouette built of light and impossible angles—reached out one limb towards the western horizon. I felt a twisting in the pattern of the world. Lights burst behind my eyes. Pain seared up and down my spine, left me bent double, fighting back vomit. For a moment my healing sorcery stuttered, like a brush slipping sideways in the grip of a startled calligrapher. Running Doe moaned as the magic that soothed her receded. I rebuilt the spell as quickly as I could, even as violet fire rained upon the western sea. Smoke and steam in equal measure rose where it fell.

'At least you won't have to worry about that punitive army,' Hissing Cat said.

'Tenet said Okara used me,' I said. 'That the gods, and not the emperor, wanted war.'

Hissing Cat ignored me, instead crossing to where Torn Leaf still lay among shattered stalks of bamboo.

'Lie still,' she said, and I felt again the wake of her healing, like a calming melody set against the discordant orchestra of the waking gods. 'Whatever the dog's intentions were before, he would be foolish to side against his own kind now.'

All my effort, all my planning, had amounted to nothing. A new, crushing weight settled on my chest. The wake of some god, or the emperor's counter-attack, or only my own despair.

'Stabilise her, quickly,' Hissing Cat said. Her gaze was fixed on a point out over the sea that seemed to draw the smoke from the city, where it began to clot and roil, forming a dark mass like a second moon. Where it hung, the pattern seemed…loose, like the fibres of an old and fraying garment. 'When she's not about to die, you go and find your uncle and Frothing Wolf. They need to lead as many people as possible—Sienese, Nayeni, it doesn't matter—to the centre of the city.'

'The Sienese haven't surrendered,' I protested. 'Shouldn't we wait—?'

'Which one of us has lived through the end of the world before?' she snarled. 'Do what I say. I can protect everyone within the city walls, but not beyond them, and that protection won't be a certain thing around the edges. There are limits even to what I can do.'

'Protect them from what?'

'We are bound to the pattern, Foolish Cur,' she said. 'Our bodies, our minds, everything we are. What do you think happens to people when the pattern starts to unravel?'

'We die?' I suggested.

'If only,' she muttered.

I looked to Running Doe. The skin of her face and upper body was wet and glossy, like that of a newborn. With more time I could smooth it, shape it, make it as though I had never led her here, into pain and to the edge of death. Her breathing was steady and her pulse, though weak, had ceased to fade.

'She'll live,' Hissing Cat shouted. She had stood. Wind whipped around her, clattering the ravens' skulls. The spar of her will drove downwards into the depths of the pattern, carving a vast ellipse that traced the walls of Eastern Fortress. 'Now go. I won't wait a minute longer than I have to, and I suggest being inside my seal. I can promise you won't like what crawls out of the shadowed places in the world when the pattern frays.'

Never had I heard such urgency in her voice. It spurred me to my feet and into the air.

I made it a few hundred paces beyond the inner wall of Eastern Fortress before one of the gods wheeled towards me, one of its countless wing-like limbs reached out, and my world filled with violet flame.

33

The Unraveling of the World

Hand Pinion

A sickening absence gripped Pinion's core, as though some vandal had scrawled a black smear in the heart of an ancient masterwork. He stood at the bow of the ship where the emperor had left him, gripping the gunwale, staring towards the centre of that awful wake. It ought to have been visible, an ethereal darkness or some billowing shadow reaching from heaven to earth, but only his sense for the pattern of the world told him anything was wrong. That and the fact that, in the moment the wake had manifested, the canon of sorcery had vanished from his mind like a hole punched through the world's fabric.

The Fists of the emperor who made up the crew of the *Ocean Throne* darted about the deck, clinging to frayed scraps of discipline by way of shouted orders while they checked the ballistae mounted to the fore- and aftcastle. Pinion had thought the weapons redundant, considering the *Throne* was crewed by sorcerers, but he now understood them for the precaution that they were. Captain Huo watched the deliberate but agitated activity of the crew, his face furrowed. Aboard the *Throne*, he alone was unaware of the terrible wound that had been dealt to the world and the equally terrible possibility that it heralded the emperor's death. For why else would the canon of sorcery disappear— not from a single mind, as at Greyfrost, but from the world entire?

A possibility that left Pinion adrift in numbed terror. If the emperor was dead, so many of the troubles and potentialities that weighed on him—the emperor's bizarre offer, his own alienation from imperial service—would be lifted, yet the world as he knew it would plunge into chaos. His mind conjured visions of countless smouldering rebellions erupting into wildfires. The brutality at Setting Sun Fortress would pale in comparison to the death and destruction to follow.

Brutality without end, until some new set of tyrants emerged victorious to impose their vision on the world.

A strange flickering in the corner of his eye drew Pinion's attention. A terrible dread began to build where his skull met his spine. The dark between the stars blurred, then opened, and then resolved into a shape that his eyes at first refused to comprehend. Some great sea bird, or a flower hanging in the air. Both and neither. Pearlescent wings unfolded, and unfolded, and unfolded. Dozens of sets. Hundreds. Like the petals of a fractal rose, each pair of wings churning the air to its own maddening rhythm.

Everyone on the *Ocean Throne* staggered to a halt as every eye aboard turned to the sky. More of the bizarre shapes appeared, all identical in their impossibility.

As he stared, Pinion's dread gave way to a reverent awe—the sort an insect might feel were it capable of realising that it clung to the wall of the emperor's court. Yet, though he was nothing, one of the beings extended a wing towards him in a gesture of welcome. Flames roiled from those iridescent feathers and swept down like a tidal wave, brighter than the noonday sun.

Awe collapsed back into terror.

Reflexively, though the canon had abandoned him, Pinion reached for shielding sorcery. Steam roiled up from the sea. Wisps of smoke curled from the deck beneath his feet. Screams pierced the air, then became strangely muted, as though the air through which they travelled had thickened.

This, then, would be his death, delivered by a creature too strange for any dream or myth.

The *Ocean Throne* came apart, not bursting into flames but falling to pieces, as though it were a tapestry unravelled thread by thread. The wooden deck became first like sand, and then like smoke. He plunged through what had been a solid floor, now a cloud of dust and grit billowing around him, protected only by the flickering curtain of light he had managed—somehow—to weave.

Shielding sorcery may have saved him from the strange, unmaking magic that had claimed the ship, but it offered no protection against the sea, which surged and churned as though tossed by a winter storm. His robes billowed around him, filling with frigid water. He twisted his body and tore at the silks until they fell away, then kicked towards the frothing haze that must surely be the surface. Salt stung his eyes and forced itself up his nose, prying at his lips.

His face broke into the open air and he gulped to fill his burning lungs. Around him, great slopes of hull, like the remnants of a corpse carved apart, rode the waves in their last moments before sinking. The winged creature had not bothered to annihilate the entirety of the ship, only to cut out its centre.

A hand clamped down on Pinion's arm and began dragging him towards a mast trailing shreds of rigging, one end sliced clean through like a limb carved by a butcher's knife. Pinion managed to pull himself onto the mast, hugging it to his chest, and only then did he see the other flotsam in the tumult. Arms and legs. A quarter of a torso. Floating bloodlessly, similarly carved by the strange, unmaking flames.

'Can you swim?' A voice shouted over the crashing waves.

Captain Huo clung to the mast beside Pinion, leaning close. Pinion nodded, reeling. How had Huo survived when it seemed all others aboard had not? How had *Pinion* survived? He ought not to have been able to wield magic in the absence of the canon, and yet...

'We need to get clear of the wreck!' Huo shouted. 'Tie yourself to the mast and kick for one of the other ships!'

Huo had a length of rigging line, which he looped over one shoulder, then the other, weaving a harness that would hold him above water, so long as the mast continued to float. Pinion caught hold of a handful of sodden rope, one end still bound to the broken mast. If it sank, it would bear them down, but he would never manage to swim to shore on his own.

'Why are you helping me?' he shouted at the captain.

Huo frowned. 'We do not have time for this.'

'You hate me!' Pinion insisted, ignoring Huo's protest. 'Why not let me drown?'

'It does not matter how I feel,' Huo snarled. 'You are Hand of the emperor, and my doubt in you proved empty. The emperor himself favours you. It is my duty to keep you alive.'

Pinion laughed, then spluttered as a wave filled his mouth with salt. Huo spoke as though it was a certainty that the emperor yet lived. Something terrible had happened at Eastern Fortress, something that had silenced the canon of sorcery and welcomed nightmares into the world.

Pinion knew without a moment's hesitation that Wen Alder lay at the heart of it. For who else held such power? The will of the emperor had been broken—an impossibility, but one that Alder had achieved before, at Greyfrost.

If not for Pinion's own cleverness, for his fear, for his unwillingness to answer madness and brutality in kind, perhaps he might have done more to slow Alder's march towards Eastern Fortress, given the emperor more time to close his trap. He might have saved the world from the destruction Alder had unleashed.

Despair filled him, and with it the impulse to release the mast and let the waves carry him down—a fitting end to an absurd life. But he felt a stirring in his chest. A rage, burning too hot for the sea to swallow, at all that Alder had done—to Oriole first, and to Usher, and now to the world.

Behind the captain, bright against the sky, the nightmare creature unfurled another wing.

No more time for doubt. The rope and the mast were the nearest thing to a lifeline he had, and Pinion would cling to them, would do everything he could to survive. He *would* outlive Wen Alder and see him punished for all the damage he had done. Pinion tossed the frayed rope over one shoulder, found its end trailing in the water, pulled it under the opposite armpit, and tied it around himself as tightly as the sodden fibres would allow. Huo nodded sharply, not yet aware that death hovered above him, its feathers flickering with iridescent light.

'Now kick with me. One of the other ships will—'

Violet flames burned down, sweeping through the fleet that bore the emperor's army. Men screamed, and then were silent. The sea surged beneath them. Pinion shut his eyes and felt himself borne upwards and hurled into the sky.

34

Traveller-on-
the Narrow-Way
Foolish Cur

Sheets of pearlescent fire swept towards me, carrying a wake of deepening terror. I wheeled away on eagle hawk's wings and called walls of light to my defence. The flames splashed against my shield. It held for a hopeful moment before coming apart like wet paper.

The fire set every nerve alight with pain. I screamed, carving deep into the pattern of the world. Barriers of light appeared and burst around me. I reached for healing sorcery, knitting and reknitting my flesh as the flames sought to unravel me. Half thinking, I called the wind—less a gust than a typhoon that bore me up and hurled me away from the agony and hateful wakes of the gods.

I tumbled to a stop just beyond the walls of Eastern Fortress, not far from the edge of the forest. Wounded Nayeni lay in the shelter of the trees while Doctor Sho's assistants went among them with bandages and tinctures. I took human form and ran, my legs cramping as much from exhaustion as from the wake of my magic.

'Head for the city!' I cried, raw voiced.

An older woman looked up in confusion from the man she had been tending. 'Has Eastern Fortress fallen already, then?'

I shook my head, stumbling to a halt beside her. 'It is safer than here. Gather everyone you can and make for the shelter of the walls.'

Her frown deepened. She gestured to the man in her care. 'These people are injured and can little afford this interruption, let alone to be dragged to the city. Tell me what this is about, and on whose orders, now, or be off with you and let us work.'

She did not recognise me—and why should she? Since Greyfrost I had kept myself aloof, fixated on preparing my canon and my cadre, always camping away from the main body of the column. Few of the rank-and-file rebels knew me. I cast about the forest for Doctor Sho, hoping for a glimpse of his medicine chest or the flash of Okara's fur. These healers would follow his orders, and he would understand Hissing Cat's warning.

The strange, glimmering mirage that had appeared in the gaps between the stars just before the winged gods emerged had settled in patches over the forest, as though light itself quaked and shook. The sight filled me with a sudden, aching terror and a memory of sheets of shimmering fire. I blinked, afraid that my vision had not fully recovered from those injuries, yet no matter how I tilted my head or narrowed my gaze, where the strange glimmers held I struggled to distinguish the blade of a fern from the bark of a nearby tree, or a tangle of roots from a fallen branch.

Around such a fray in the world, a shadow moved.

At first, I felt a swell of hope that it was Okara, following at Doctor Sho's heel. But no, it seemed more like a fox, long legged with hunched shoulders and a pointed face, skulking through a gap between two trees. Until I counted a fifth leg, and then a sixth, and saw no sign of a tail as it emerged. The darkness followed with it, and when I tried to look at the creature straight on, it drifted to the edge of my vision, as though my gaze had been frightened away. I reached for battle sorcery.

'Run! Now!' I shouted and pushed the healing woman behind me.

The moment the carving knife of my will touched the pattern of the world, the creature lunged, its maw wide, showing uncountable hooked teeth. Lightning burned from my outstretched hand. The creature spun away, hissing and clattering. It spasmed where it fell, pouring smoke.

The healing woman shrieked and ducked, covering her head with her hands. I took a cautious step towards the creature. My eyes still shied away from it, and the terrible wake that had filled the world since the emergence of the gods deepened, dragging at my joints. Yet I forced myself, as I so often forced the world to bend to my will, and fixed my gaze on the monster. It might once have been a fox or a dog, but as I had once been twisted by my first failed attempt to veer, so its body had been broken and rebuilt into something else— something eyeless and earless, all rippling muscle and teeth and claws. How it sensed the world around it, I could not begin to guess, but even in its death throes it tensed and turned its snarling, empty face at my approach.

'Gather as many of the injured as possible,' I said sharply. 'And run.'

This time, the woman nodded. 'We will need time to build stretchers.'

'Do what you can as quickly as you can,' I said and called the wind, ready to sever the creature's head from its body, when another clattering hiss sounded behind me.

The forest erupted with twisted bodies, no two alike in shape. Monsters contorted from beasts and birds lunged for me, their bright claws flashing out from the shadows. I answered with a storm of wind, fire, and lightning, leaving creature after creature a burnt ruin, till flames roared around me.

'There's no time!' I shouted, even as I burned a lunging monster to ash. 'Run!'

Terrified screams rose from the injured and their caretakers, and then shouted orders. The woman with me grabbed the man she had been tending under the armpits and began to drag him across the barren field, foolishly, wondrously unwilling to abandon him even to save her own life. Similar scenes played out around me, half glimpsed through sheets of lightning, lunging beasts, and burning trees—men and women risking their lives to bring as many of the wounded as they could to safety. I wanted to shout at them, to harry them to speed before the monsters' attention shifted from me to easier prey.

Only it never did.

The monsters kept coming, more and more of them, in their dozens, and with each that appeared the bone-wrenching weight of the divine wake pulled all the stronger. Yet they never attacked the healers, or the injured. The magic I wrought, however, was not so discriminating. Boiled sap popped and trees crashed to the earth, and flames roared everywhere I turned, drowning out the terrible howls and hisses of the beasts and the shouts of alarm. Our battle would surely endanger the wounded, but I was the sole object of the creatures' attention and hunger, it seemed. A fact I could not explain, but one I could use to draw them away.

I veered and hurled myself upwards, darting through the canopy of trees, flying low. The creatures followed, howling and hissing, flitting between the shadows and the glimmering tears in the forest below, fleeter of foot than any beast born of nature. Above, glimpsed in the corner of my eye, another shadow darted down, all razor talons and tearing beak. It slammed into me, ripping into my flesh, scattering feathers. A burst of wind and flame dislodged it, and summoned more. Ropes of blood spattered the leaves below me. Dozens of bodies clung to me with iron-strong talons, dragging me back to earth.

We crashed and tumbled to the base of a tree, where I spun wheels of lightning to scatter them, gritting my teeth against my magic's feverish wake. Yet more circled overhead, and the world seemed to have frayed thinner here with countless rippling fractures scattered through the undergrowth, resisting my gaze, blurring the lines between root and bush, earth and trunk. I heard the howls and thundering feet of the twisted wolves. Before I could catch my breath and work the cramps from my arms, they surged from the forest around me while their hawk-like cousins swooped down from the sky above. Again I fought them, hurling fire, wind, and lightning until again the forest burned, only now my limbs were leaden, my body shaking with chills, my mind a morass, the limits of even my strength in magic pushed to the brink.

A snapping, elongated beak burst from the roiling smoke and tore into my shoulder. I cried out, raw voiced, and with a gust of razor-sharp wind cast it back into the inferno consuming the forest. A claw found my thigh, bringing me to my knees even as I burned the beast that had slashed me into a bubbling, tar-black pool. I let my mind fall deeper into the pattern, working half a dozen spells at once, striking back while I knitted my body together as blow after blow found me, tearing away flesh and blood.

I needed time to think, to breathe, to plan.

Hissing Cat had warned me of creatures twisted from the fabric of reality, monsters that had stalked the world during the war the witches of the old sort had waged against the gods. Creatures unable to cross the barrier made by sealing the pattern.

As when I had so foolishly struck at the emperor, I carved deep, putting up walls. The oppressive wake faded at once, leaving me numb in the absence of despair. Howls and screams and otherworldly voices rang out. The creatures dashed away, towards the edges of my circle. A few staggered to a halt before reaching the barrier, gurgling and twitching, belching acrid blood before collapsing into piles of meat, protruding bone, and black ichor. Strange stomach-churning smells like dust and rotting flesh swirled in the smoky air.

Those monsters that had escaped stalked the edge of the seal I had made, snapping their jaws, snuffling in the blurred undergrowth. A few possessed eyes that fixed on me with a murderous desperation. Within the circle, the world reknitted itself. Looking at the burnt remains of an elder tree no longer left me reeling and dizzy.

I hugged my knees to my chest, surrounded by death and the charred skeletons of trees, hounded by the beasts that stalked the edge of my shelter on impossible wings and limbs that defied physiology.

No matter how I shut my eyes, squeezing them till lights burst behind my lids, snapping them open, hoping to wake from this nightmare, the monsters remained.

I was needed elsewhere, but I was safe only so long as I could maintain my seal. If I collapsed from hunger, thirst, or exhaustion, the spell would fade. Yet I could not veer without releasing the seal, and the moments of weakness as my shape changed would be enough, I was sure, for the beasts to tear me apart.

One of the beasts looked up, as though at the sound of a snapping twig. It bared flat teeth like the blades of shovels and lowered its head. The others did likewise. The nightmarish birds circling above me cawed as though some predator threatened their nests, and then flew away. The rest vanished into the undergrowth.

I sat, dumbfounded. Terrified to lower my circle of protection even as I realised that this might be my opportunity to escape. Footsteps and the crackle of leaves drew my attention.

Vertigo seized me at the sight of Doctor Sho, medicine chest upon his back and Okara at his heel.

'On your feet,' he said gruffly. 'After all that magic you were tossing about, things here are dangerously unstable.'

'How did you find me?' I blurted. 'How are you *alive?*'

'You nearly started a forest fire,' he said. 'It was either Hissing Cat or you, I figured. Are you hurt? You look all right.'

'No, I'm fine,' I said. I took a deep, shuddering breath. His presence reassured me. Made things seem normal, despite his countless abnormalities. 'A few wounds, but nothing I couldn't heal.'

'Well, you'll want to hold off on that for a time. And on flying. On all of it, really.' He offered me a hand. I took it, let him help me to my feet. 'The unwoven are attracted to magic, like spiders lurking on the edges of their webs, ready to chase the vibrations of a struggling fly, though in this case those vibrations also rip the web apart.'

'The unwoven?' I wondered aloud.

He pointed to one of the grotesque corpses. 'You're familiar, by now. Come. We should get moving. Can you carry this seal with you while you walk?'

'I don't know,' I said.

He frowned and scratched his balding head. 'Things haven't gotten bad enough yet that you *need* to. But they will. For now, if we hurry, we should be safe enough.' He glared up at the sky. 'I didn't think Tenet would actually go through with it. Certainly not yet.'

I felt my legs would give way again. 'He didn't,' I croaked. 'I did.'

Disappointment radiated from Doctor Sho like heat from coals. He said nothing, but his eyes spoke of re-evaluation. A redrawing of some internal map of our relationship.

As though sensing my distress, Okara padded forwards and nuzzled at my hand. My anger flared, and once again I reached through the pattern, seeking the god's mind, to confront him with the emperor's accusations and his own lies. Yet his mind eluded me, as though the god I had known no longer existed. Perhaps, if his lies ran deep enough, he never truly had.

'You will have time to explain on the way.' Doctor Sho turned to the forest. 'Come. Drop your spell and follow. We've lingered here too long.'

'Not yet.' My anger, though meant for the god, found an object in the obstinate, elusive doctor. 'For over a year you've spoken in circles, laying claim to knowledge that no mere physician, no matter how widely travelled, should have. Hissing Cat knows you. Speaks to you like an old friend, when she can have no old friends who have not lived hundreds of years. Now you name the abominations that attacked me and claim to know what is safe and what is not while the pattern frays and the world as we knew it ends. Who are you, Doctor Sho? How do you know these things?'

'It doesn't matter,' Doctor Sho snapped. 'On your feet.'

I ground my teeth and glared at him. 'You blame me for my mistakes—you and Hissing Cat both—but you parcel out information like a miser parcels silver. How am I supposed to do the right thing when I hardly understand the world?'

Guilt lined his face. He looked away, adjusted the chest of drawers on his back, and shook his head. 'We don't have time—'

'Then speak quickly,' I said. 'I'll not move until you answer.'

'Fine then, damn you.' His voice was sharp and ruthless as a blade. He took a breath, glowering at me. 'A man as long lived and transient as me wears many names throughout his life. The one you know best is Traveller-on-the-Narrow-Way.'

A creature in the distance howled. Okara-the-dog flattened his ears, growling low in his chest. Doctor Sho took a deep, steadying breath.

I stared at him in disbelief.

'I was not only there when Tenet began to build his empire; I helped him build it,' he went on, the words at first trickling out of him, then spilling as the dam broke. 'I believed at the time that it would lead to the eternal peace he envisioned. I was wrong. You may have tipped the scales and brought about this apocalypse sooner, but it was inevitable, just as Okara said. I left the emperor when I realised this, and when he rejected the only solution that could truly put an end to the cycle of world-ending wars.'

A curl of wind—bitterly cold one moment, full of a scorching, stifling heat the next—stirred the air between us.

'The world has ended, but we have a chance to rebuild it,' he said. 'No easy task, but you have never shirked from difficulty or danger, have you? Come with me, Foolish Cur. Let's build something from these ashes. Something that will last.'

Without waiting for an answer, he strode into the forest. Okara-the-dog watched me a moment longer. It may have been a trick of the light, or the glow of the fire, or a shimmer of the fraying world, but something like an ember flickered through the lines of his scars.

To save a single life, I had broken what should have been an eternal peace. What choice did I have but to hurl myself into the effort to repair it? Doctor Sho—no, Traveller-on-the-Narrow-Way, whose aphorisms were the foundation of the empire and yet echoed in the chamber of my skull—promised such a chance at redemption.

Who but a fool would refuse it?

35
The Black Maw
Koro Ha

Typhoon season came to an end. As summer gave way to a muggy autumn, the cycle of ships coming and going from the Black Maw resumed, and with it a return of the need for literate work. Koro Ha made records or translated documents often enough to keep Uon Elia and himself fed and clothed, but no more. He had a greater purpose now, and little time to accomplish it.

All through the typhoons, Koro Ha had hoped that the sickness gripping Uon Elia would fade with the rains, but the cough only deepened till he could speak only a handful of words before pausing to rest and gather his strength.

Pressured by the wet rattle in his teacher's lungs, Koro Ha applied himself to the study of magic with the same desperation that had gripped him in the months before his imperial examinations. He found again the unbreakable focus he had long thought decayed by age, his mind so captivated by the task at hand that he sometimes forgot to eat and sleep. A focus, and a purpose, that stripped him of the malaise that had lingered in him for so many years. There was no time for envy, or bitterness, or self-loathing.

No room for it in a mind desperate to absorb new knowledge and cement new skills.

And these were *certainly* new skills.

A mind well suited to picking apart every argument was not, as it turned out, well suited to meditation. A stray thought could shatter his consciousness into a thousand lenses, all scrutinising that initial point of failure when his thoughts had wandered, trying to break it down to prevent it happening again.

He persisted, and with Uon Elia's guidance—between bouts of coughing—Koro Ha gradually found that kernel of self within. The strange limb, divorced from the body and from thought, with which he reached into the stream of magic.

As Uon Elia had promised, he learned dowsing first. At first his targets were easily found in the market on the boardwalk. Silk, or a common spice, or a feather plucked from a rare bird. He held each in his hand while he felt its texture in the pattern of the world, then went out to the market to seek its like. As he became more skilled, the targets grew stranger and more specific. A hair fallen from someone's scalp and retrieved from the floor of the Wavebreaker. A piece of coral from shallows in the cove. A bit of cobalt, ironically enough, after Uon Elia at last found some in the market months after their need for it had passed.

These exercises came to an end when Uon Elia's breath became too shallow for him to walk further than from his bed to the common room. The old stonespeaker did not seem particularly troubled by this, merely taking it as reason to move on to the next subject of Koro Ha's education. He cut a thin line in the tip of his finger, held it out, and bade Koro Ha to heal it, explaining as he did so the intricacies of working such magic.

Whereas dowsing was simple enough—reach for the magic, attend to the material in question, memorise its texture as a hound might memorise the scent of its prey, and then follow that texture—healing proved far more complex. It was not enough to reach for the magic. Koro Ha had to shape its use, not only comprehending the energies involved but manipulating them—something he struggled with, until an analogy occurred to him: teaching was, in a sense, reshaping the pattern of a mind.

The first time he healed the thin cut on Uon Elia's fingertip, he felt a fluttering in his chest like nothing he had experienced since childhood, when Teacher Zhen first moved him to the front of the classroom.

'Well done,' Uon Elia said, his voice like wind through a perforated screen. 'Now we move on…to the last of the three…to cultivation.'

'But I've barely begun to understand this!' Koro Ha protested. 'You kept yourself alive for decades with healing magic. I've heard tales of imperial sorcerers reattaching limbs. I have no idea how to approach anything like that.'

'It is all the…same principle,' Uon Elia said. 'Buy some…books on anatomy. And…medicine. You are a clever enough fellow.'

So they moved on to the third method of magic in as many months, and the last magic of Toa Alon. Uon Elia directed him to purchase a ceramic pot and fill it with earth. A difficult proposition on an island composed entirely of rock.

After scouring the island and finding nothing but a single sandbar in the cove—too full of salt for his purposes, according to Uon Elia—Koro Ha resorted to placing an order with one of the outgoing ships. The captain, for whom Koro Ha had worked as a scribe in the past, arched an eyebrow when asked to return from the mainland with a bag of dirt. In the end he agreed, in exchange for Koro Ha's promise of a lowered rate on any future literate work the captain might require.

On the same trip to the boardwalk, Koro Ha managed to track down a Sienese medical text, taken by pirates from a looted merchant vessel. He planned to spend his time developing his skill with healing magic, at least until the ship returned with his dirt.

Uon Elia's condition worsened rapidly as what passed for winter so far south brought dark, heavy clouds. The weather itself did not seem responsible, only time. Koro Ha fed the old stonespeaker broth—made from bone, when it could be had, and seaweed when not—and hoped against hope for him to hold on long enough to pass on the last of his secrets. The most vital, and most hidden, kept longest from the empire, for which all of Toa Alon had been punished with the destruction of Sor Cala.

As Koro Ha watched the old man slip away—his already thin frame growing thinner, his wheezing breath becoming a near constant cough—despair crept in and threatened to erode the glow of joy and success. He searched his medical text for information on wasting diseases or ailments of the lungs, but he was no physician and too much a neophyte to piece together how he might help beyond providing comfort, warmth, and food.

Early spring, and the anniversary of their flight from Sor Cala, brought little relief. The heavy clouds birthed thunderous storms, and Koro Ha fought a mounting dread, listening to Uon Elia's coughing through the night, afraid to shut his eyes lest he wake to find the old man had passed in the night.

On one such night, while lightning flashed through the shutters over their little window, Koro Ha lay awake, listening to Uon Elia's breaths, praying the ship he had commissioned for soil returned soon enough for him to learn *something* of cultivation. Thunder rumbled and shook the timbers of the *Wavebreaker*. Then again, without the accompanying flash of lightning.

'Koro Ha!' a voice shouted through the door. 'Uon Elia! Open up!'

It took him a moment, but he recognised the voice. He put on a robe and threw open the door to find Yin Ila, a fresh scar along her cheekbone, her eyes wide and frantic.

'We have to go.' She pushed past him into the room. 'Take only what can fit in a rowboat. The *Swiftness* is anchored a way out from the cove. Too dangerous to bring it through the Teeth in a storm.'

She paused over Uon Elia's bed and studied the old man with an expression like nausea. 'Is he dying?' she asked.

'What's going on?' Koro Ha demanded.

'We were on our way back to check up on you,' she said, still watching Uon Elia's slow, tortured breathing. 'Plus trying to offload some...Well, it doesn't matter now. An imperial clipper, somehow sailing against the wind, cut us off. Raked the deck with arrows and set a sail afire with lightning. If they were trying to sink us, we'd be sunk. They were hunting Uon Elia, we think, and you. We managed to lose them in the storm.'

'Then we're safe, aren't we?' Koro Ha said. 'They couldn't have followed you.'

Yin Ila shook her head slowly. 'They came after the *Swiftness*, and they knew our routes. There's only one way that happened.' Grief and rage radiated from her eyes. 'Orna Sin talked.'

Koro Ha's stomach turned. His mind conjured a memory of Orna Sin's yellowed smile and piercing eyes on the deck of the *Swiftness of the South Wind*, the broad horizon of the sea behind him, his beard tossed by the breeze on their way to Sor Cala. The man's sturdiness. His unflappable persistence in the face of imperial oppression, even as Mr Mah began to scrutinise Koro Ha's lessons. What tortures had broken him? How much suffering had he endured?

'Can he walk?' Yin Ila nodded at the stonespeaker.

'We will have to carry him,' Koro Ha said.

Yin Ila worked her jaw. 'How much longer does he have, do you think?'

Koro Ha swallowed outrage. 'We're taking him with us, Yin Ila. That is not a question.'

She took a breath. Nodded. 'Take his knees. I'll take his shoulders.'

As they pulled Uon Elia from his bed, the old stonespeaker started awake, squirmed, and looked at them with panicked eyes.

'It's all right,' Koro Ha said. 'It's Yin Ila and me. We're taking you to the *Swiftness*. It's time to leave the Black Maw.'

Uon Elia soon calmed. Koro Ha chose to believe that he understood the situation and accepted it, not that his effort to resist had collapsed beneath the fatigue of his illness. As they crossed the commons, carrying Uon Elia between them, the keeper of the *Wavebreaker* peered out from the back room, a lantern in hand.

'He's taken a turn,' Yin Ila said. 'There's a physician aboard one of the ships.'

Koro Ha felt a pang of guilt at the lie. If the empire knew of the Black Maw, no one on the island—all criminals, in the empire's eyes, or at least the accomplices thereof—would be safe. He felt some inkling of a duty to save as many lives as possible. A moral spark that struggled against the dousing force of pragmatism. The passage through the Teeth was simply too narrow for everyone to escape at once, and there was a storm brewing.

Before he could make up his mind, the innkeeper shut her door, the moment passed, and Yin Ila led him out into the night.

Lightning lit their way down the narrow, rain-slick stairs. The force of the wind broke before it entered the cove, thankfully, but its howling planted Koro Ha's heart firmly in his throat all the while they descended towards the boardwalk. The warm, heavy rain filled his clothes, weighing him down with a greater burden than Uon Elia's body. The stonespeaker was little more than skin and bones, but Koro Ha had never been an athletic man and he was grateful when they at last reached and crossed the wreckwood planks to Yin Ila's rowboat. In the distance, shrouded by rain, Koro Ha could see the familiar silhouette of the *Swiftness*.

Yin Ila grunted with every pull of the oars as she fought the storm, dragging them over cresting swells towards the safety of their ship. As they left the cove, Koro Ha looked up from Uon Elia, nestled in the bottom of the boat, breathing quickly, agitated by all the excitement, and glanced back at the Black Maw. An angular shape emerged from behind the island. Little more at this stage than a shadow beneath red sails that billowed against the wind.

Yin Ila swore. The muscles of her bare forearms bulged as she pulled hard at the oars. Koro Ha felt a strange chill up and down his spine, as though something had rolled out from the Sienese ship and washed through him. A wind from nowhere filled its sails and with a burst of speed it darted into the driving rain, smashing through oncoming waves.

'Aren't you some kind of sorcerer, old man?' Yin Ila shouted above the slap of waves and creak of oars. 'Do something!'

Koro Ha braced himself against the gunwale to keep from being bounced out of the ship. Uon Elia blinked up at him, groaned, and screwed his eyes shut again. Despair stabbed at Koro Ha. They were on their own.

A thought shattered as Koro Ha felt the gentle tremor in his limbs in the wake of dowsing magic.

'Well?' Yin Ila shouted.

'Keep rowing!' Koro Ha shouted back. He turned to watch the Sienese ship as the wake of Uon Elia's magic changed texture. No longer a tremor but a sudden, vibrant energy, like nothing Koro Ha had experienced. Yet it reminded him of the first heady lust of adolescence; of poetry written to glorify war, full of muscle and vitality without mention of blood or breaking bone; of late nights studying the classics by candlelight with a dozen pots of tea coursing through him.

Something long and writhing, like the tentacle of some great nautical beast, burst up from the waters of the cove and wrapped itself around the Sienese ship. Then another, gripping its mast. And another, dozens of them, green arms reaching up from the deep. Some snapped as the ship ploughed forwards under the power of its phantom wind, but many held, bleeding away the ship's speed until it came to a straining halt. More tendrils reached up, lashed the ship, and bound it in place. Koro Ha looked to the waters, thinking to see the beak of whatever creature had caught the ship gaping wide to devour its prey.

Uon Elia chuckled, then fell into a fit of coughing.

'The seaweed growing in the cove,' he muttered through his rattling throat. 'There, Koro Ha. Now…you've seen cultivation.'

Before Koro Ha could answer, a bolt of lightning lanced down from the deck of the ship, slicing through several of the tendrils. The ship lurched forwards as another bolt cut away half a dozen more of its bonds.

'Keep rowing!' Koro Ha shouted. They were halfway to the *Swiftness of the South Wind*. He squeezed Uon Elia's hand. 'Please. We just need a little more time.'

The old stonespeaker took a deep breath and held it. Koro Ha felt the wake of his magic, but it faded quickly. No fresh tendrils sprang forth to replace those cut away.

'I haven't…' Uon Elia muttered. 'I'm sorry.'

'Then tell me how to do it,' Koro Ha begged.

The old man opened his mouth to answer but lost himself to a fit of racking coughs that left him doubled over, his hands clenched like claws and his feet kicking with every spasm of his lungs.

Another bolt of lightning. The ship surged free. It darted towards them, moving at a speed that seemed impossible, smashing through waves that should have cast it down to rot with the hundreds of wrecks that littered the waters around the Black Maw.

As though he had been struggling to comprehend some obscure poem, only for poetics and meaning to click into place like pieces on a Stones board, Koro Ha was struck with inspiration.

He reached for magic, gestured vaguely to the waters that still separated their little boat and the *Swiftness*, and dowsed. He moved his hand until his fingers began to quiver.

'There!' he shouted. 'Turn! Row there!'

Yin Ila stared at him like he was mad.

'Just do what I say!'

She drew her mouth into a hard line, set her jaw, and threw her back into the oars. The Sienese ship flew towards them, straight and quick as an arrow. Koro Ha watched the point in the water he was aiming for, desperately urging the rowboat to speed, praying to any gods that might listen for the waves to quiet, only for a moment, and let them place that point between themselves and their enemies.

The ship loomed, its moonlit shadow falling over them. Koro Ha waited for battle-sorcery to strike and shatter their little boat, but none did. Instead, archers appeared at the gunwale, firing arrows tipped with heavy barbs and trailing ropes. The first three arrows splashed harmlessly into the water. The fourth bit the wood of the boat's stern, just above the waterline, mere heartbeats before they passed over that fateful point in the water.

Wood crunched against stone. Water geysered up from beneath the hull of the Sienese warship. Lines snapped as it lurched to a halt, impaled on one of the Black Maw's Teeth. The archers on the bow screamed, lost their balance, and careened into the water as the ship's momentum bore it forwards to list heavily to one side.

'The arrow!' Yin Ila shouted.

It took Koro Ha a moment to grasp her meaning. He went to his knees, reached over the gunwale for the arrow that had bitten into their hull, and snapped it moments before the rope it trailed went taut.

The crew of the Sienese ship—those not leaping into the water—were frantically lowering their own boats. The front of the ship shifted suddenly to one side as water rushed through the rent in its hull. It twisted in the water, its boards popping and then bursting in an

ear-splitting crack. Koro Ha watched with mingled horror and satisfaction, until strange lights began to flicker above the surface of the
sea, drawing his eye, like waves of heat rising from black stone.

'Was that him too?' Yin Ila asked, her pace slowing as the Sienese
warship sank.

'No,' Koro Ha answered, his attention drawn back from the odd
mirage in the sky. A swell of pride filled his chest, rival to what he had
felt upon passing the imperial examinations. 'That was me. One of the
Teeth. I guessed we would be shallow drafted enough to glide over it,
and I was right.'

With the immediate danger past, Koro Ha knelt beside Uon Elia.
The old stonespeaker's forehead was clammy and his eyes rolled loose
beneath their lids.

Koro Ha extended his hand and reached for healing magic. Nausea
pulled at his stomach. Apprehension. No. This did not feel like anything born of his own mind and body but like the wakes of Uon Elia's
power, a thing imposed from outside.

He whipped his gaze towards the sinking ship. The strange shimmer in the air persisted, crowding the sky, the horizon, and the surface of the sea in the periphery of his vision. And there, in the wreck,
he saw the Hand, blood streaming from a wound on his forehead,
clinging to a mast with one arm, the other outstretched and bright
with lightning.

'Row faster!' he shouted.

Yin Ila answered only with a grunt and a muttered curse as the
Hand of the emperor hurled battle sorcery. Sparks lanced out, flickered, and fell impotent to the water.

The Hand's expression shifted, visible even at such a distance, lit
only by the moon and veiled in blood. His face filled first with confusion, then with terror. Another wake, weak and flailing, radiated out
from him as he tried desperately to wield his magic.

'Huh,' Yin Ila observed. 'We're not dead.'

And then something deeper shook the world, radiating out from
the heart of the Black Maw. The crack of splitting and grinding rock
echoed from deep within the cove. Water roiled and churned as stone
began to move.

Despite his recent experience with magic, Koro Ha's first thought was that he must have been dreaming. The sheltering overhang—that vast fingernail-shaped ceiling of stone that stood over the smuggler's town—began to descend, and then to list to one side, as though collapsing. Buildings slid from the walls of the cove and splashed into the sea.

The island was not falling but *turning*.

The realisation transformed the Black Maw in Koro Ha's eye, shifting it in an instant from mere geology to something bestial. Not a fingernail but the lower jaw of some vast hound or monstrous bird. A perception reinforced as the rest of that cyclopean head emerged from the sea.

Yin Ila shouted, the muscles of her arms corded like a ship's main lines as she pulled and pulled against the surge of water rushing towards the emerging monstrosity.

The sinking Sienese ship groaned and then burst apart as the tooth—truly named—twisted itself free of the wooden hull.

Koro Ha could only stare in awe. Limbs appeared—thin, seemingly composed of stone vertebrae—and arced through the air as the creature rolled over, then plunged back into the sea, casting up waves that rolled out in all directions. One of these caught their boat and tossed it like a child might toss a ball. Yin Ila grabbed the back of Koro Ha's gown and pulled him roughly down into the belly of the boat with Uon Elia. His stomach lurched into his throat. They hung, as though untouched by gravity, and then fell with a thunderous splash back to the sea. The boat's clinker-built joints groaned and threatened to snap, but held.

Despite bruises and rattled bones, Koro Ha scrambled to his knees and leaned against the gunwale. Fear had become an abstract thing. It gnawed at him but could not hope to overcome his desperation to witness whatever horror or miracle had visited the world.

The sea vomited up debris—the shattered homes of the Black Maw, themselves built of broken hulls. Bodies, some screaming, thrashing in the water. The Hand of the emperor, whose magic had failed him, was nowhere to be found. Above it all hung the vast, harshly angled head of stone that had once offered shelter to the empire's enemies, now looming over the waters like a second moon carved into the shape of a serpent's skull.

Lights burned in the hollow sockets of its eyes, vast and distant, so that their scale became impossible to comprehend. Yet Koro Ha could not help but feel that one of those eyes, were it lowered to the surface of the sea, would stand tall enough for any ship to sail through.

'What the *fuck* is that thing?' Yin Ila cried, still crouching in the belly of the boat.

With another chorus of grinding stone, the stone head turned away from them, shifting its gaze to the north and west, beyond the Pillars of the Gods, towards the heart of Sien. On six long, snaking limbs it carried itself, each step leaving a whirlpool behind, casting up waves that stirred the wreckage and detritus.

'I have read Sienese accounts of the age of legends,' Koro Ha murmured. 'Writings of terrible beasts spawned by primitive magic. Overcome by the emperor as he established his empire.'

A cry echoed over the waters. Koro Ha pulled his gaze away from the stone beast to find that the wave had deposited them not far from the *Swiftness of the South Wind*. Sailors waved and shouted, and Koro Ha heard more than one threat of abandonment if they delayed too long.

An island had awoken, stood up, and revealed itself to be a monster. The *Swiftness*—as anyone with any sense of self-preservation—would not be lingering to see what other secrets might emerge. Yin Ila again set to the oars. She pulled them alongside the ship, where a rope ladder already dangled in the water, then knelt beside Uon Elia, grabbed a coil of rope, and began wrapping it around his legs.

'Quit gawking and help me with him,' Yin Ila snarled. 'Unless you'd rather leave him behind.'

Yet as Koro Ha knelt beside her, the old stonespeaker's eyes flitted open. 'Koro Ha,' he said, his voice a breath of a whisper. 'Listen to me.'

'We're almost aboard the *Swiftness*,' Koro Ha said. 'It will only be a moment—'

Uon Elia's hand darted out to grip Koro Ha's wrist. Yin Ila paused in her work, as surprised as Koro Ha to see the old stonespeaker move so suddenly when they had both thought him days, if not hours, from the grave.

'There is deep lore,' he murmured. 'Old secrets lie buried beneath the Pillars of the Gods. Passed down…generation unto generation…

from the first stonespeaker. Had I time, I could have recited it to you, but...I am slipping away.'

'Tell me when we're aboard,' Koro Ha said, his voice cracking.

Uon Elia shook his head firmly. He stared up at Koro Ha with milky eyes, already gazing into some middle distance between death and life. A fit of coughing seized him, left him shaking, the moment of strength having fled and left him weaker than before. 'Find...them...' he wheezed. 'Among the windcallers...or the witches of Nayen...or the Stormriders, if any yet live.'

'How?' Koro Ha said. 'How can I find such people?'

'They will make...havens...' Uon Elia's fingers fell from Koro Ha's arm and collapsed bonelessly to the deck. 'Holes...in the pattern...'

A rattling breath escaped him, and he lay still.

'Uon Elia.' Desperation tightened Koro Ha's chest. 'What do you mean? Uon Elia!'

Yin Ila put her fingers to his wrist. Her expression darkened and she stood.

'He's dead,' she said. 'Come on.'

'What?' Koro Ha watched her mount the rope ladder in disbelief. 'And leave him here?'

'There is no earth for us to bury him,' she said, 'and no time to sew a canvas and roll him into the sea. Our ship is sailing, Koro Ha. We have to go.'

She began to climb, leaving Koro Ha to kneel beside Uon Elia's body. The old stonespeaker's eyes were still open, gazing sightlessly at the sky, where more strange mirages flickered between the stars.

Koro Ha reached out and closed them, and stood, and followed Yin Ila. The last stonespeaker, incompletely formed. He carried with him the hope of his culture. The strongest tie to what Toa Alon had been, before the empire. He would find the deep lore Uon Elia had spoken of, and he would survive.

No simple ambition, he knew, as he stood on the deck of the *Swiftness of the South Wind*, sails billowing overhead, watching the now-distant silhouette of the stone creature continue its long march across the sea.

About the Author

J.T. Greathouse has been writing fantasy and science fiction since he was eleven years old. He holds a BA in history and philosophy with a minor in Asian studies as well as a Master's in Teaching from Whitworth University, and spent four months of intensive study in Chinese language and culture at Minzu University of China in Beijing. His short fiction has appeared, often as Jeremy A. TeGrotenhuis, in *Beneath Ceaseless Skies*, *Writers of the Future 34*, *Deep Magic*, Orson Scott Card's *Intergalactic Medicine Show*, and elsewhere. In addition to writing, he has worked as an ESL teacher in Taipei, as a bookseller at Auntie's Bookstore in Spokane, and as a high school teacher. He currently lives in Spokane, Washington with his wife Hannah and several overflowing bookshelves.